T0362989

INTRIGUE

Seek thrills. Solve crimes. Justice served.

Cold Case Identity
Nicole Helm

Helicopter Rescue
Danica Winters

MILLS & BOON

COLD CASE IDENTITY
© 2024 by Nicole Helm
Philippine Copyright 2024
Australian Copyright 2024
New Zealand Copyright 2024

First Published 2024
First Australian Paperback Edition 2024
ISBN 978 1 867 29959 2

HELICOPTER RESCUE
© 2024 by Danica Winters
Philippine Copyright 2024
Australian Copyright 2024
New Zealand Copyright 2024

First Published 2024
First Australian Paperback Edition 2024
ISBN 978 1 867 29959 2

MIX
Paper | Supporting
responsible forestry
FSC® C001695

Published by
Harlequin Mills & Boon
An imprint of Harlequin Enterprises (Australia) Pty Limited
(ABN 47 001 180 918), a subsidiary of HarperCollins
Publishers Australia Pty Limited
(ABN 36 009 913 517)
Level 19, 201 Elizabeth Street
SYDNEY NSW 2000 AUSTRALIA

Cover art used by arrangement with Harlequin Books S.A.. All rights reserved.

Printed and bound in Australia by McPherson's Printing Group

Cold Case Identity
Nicole Helm

MILLS & BOON

Nicole Helm grew up with her nose in a book and the dream of one day becoming a writer. Luckily, after a few failed career choices, she gets to follow that dream—writing down-to-earth contemporary romance and romantic suspense. From farmers to cowboys, Midwest to *the* West, Nicole writes stories about people finding themselves and finding love in the process. She lives in Missouri with her husband and two sons, and dreams of someday owning a barn.

DEDICATION

For the "bad boy/good man" heroes.

CAST OF CHARACTERS

Palmer Hudson—Part-time rancher and part-time investigator for Hudson Sibling Solutions, a cold case investigation business run from the family's ranch. Used to be in the rodeo. Currently helping his little sister's best friend look into a family mystery.

Louisa O'Brien—Helps run her family orchard and has recently discovered that she may have been stolen as a baby. Wants Palmer to help her find the truth without anyone finding out. Has been in love with Palmer since she was a teenager.

Kyla Brown—The woman who messaged Louisa about the possibility she might be the baby who was stolen years ago. She is the stolen baby's sister.

Anna Hudson—Palmer's youngest sister and Louisa's best friend since they were kids.

Jack, Cash, Mary and Grant Hudson—Palmer's siblings, who also help run the ranch and Hudson Sibling Solutions.

Izzy Hudson—Palmer's niece.

Dahlia Easton—Grant's girlfriend, a librarian in town.

The O'Brien family—Tim and Minnie, Louisa's parents; Greg, Louisa's grandfather. All live on and help run the family orchard.

Hawk Steele—The fire investigator who gets involved in the case through a fire at the O'Brien orchard.

Chapter One

Palmer Hudson liked to have fun. He'd learned at an early age that life was going to punch you in the nose as often as it could, so you might as well enjoy the ride between blows.

That didn't mean he was irresponsible. Maybe, on occasion, he hit the bottle a little harder than he should, and definitely, on occasion, he was a little careless with women, but always, no matter what, Palmer showed up and did what he was tasked with doing.

Some days, it was ranch chores at the sprawling Hudson Ranch, which had been part of his family for five generations. And sometimes it was stepping in as investigator on one of the cold cases his family investigated as part of Hudson Sibling Solutions—his oldest brother's brainchild after the disappearance of their parents when Palmer had been twelve.

One day they'd been there...and then they'd been gone.

No one had ever figured out what had happened to them. But Jack had stepped up and taken care of the five minor Hudson kids. Jack had been eighteen and had taken on the weight of *everything*.

Had it turned him into an uptight tool most days? In Palmer's estimation, yes. He could hardly hold it against Jack when Jack had kept them together. Driven him to football practices, signed off on his joining the rodeo early, made sure there was food in the fridge and money in the bank.

Jack had been the glue so much so that, even though they'd each tried their hand at off-ranch things—Grant had joined the marines for a time, Cash had gotten married and had a kid, Mary had gone to college and Anna had tried her own brief stint at the rodeo—all these years later, they were all back home. At the Hudson Ranch. Running Hudson Sibling Solutions and living just outside the Sunrise town limits.

Family.

Nearing thirty, Palmer didn't consider his wild days behind him, but he supposed he was starting to understand the adult art of *balance*.

Mostly, he thought darkly when he recognized the raven-haired woman sauntering toward him. He'd been heading for the main house, but now he was seriously considering turning on a heel and beating a hasty retreat.

Louisa O'Brien was the one person, maybe in the whole world, who made Palmer Hudson *uncomfortable*.

Since she was his kid sister's best friend, he'd once enjoyed annoying and torturing Anna and Louisa whenever given the opportunity. It's what big brothers were for.

But ever since Louisa had come home from some fancy college out east a couple of years back, Palmer had done his level best to steer clear.

Because Louisa O'Brien had grown up into a flat-out knockout. Wavy black hair that she almost always hung loose around her shoulders, dark green eyes the color of deep summer and an almost-constant smirk that promised she knew a lot more than you did. Not to mention the way she wore her jeans—which he absolutely refused to notice ever since that *one* time he had very much *not* realized it was Louisa he'd been ogling at the local bar.

He might not have a lot of boundaries when it came to women, but Louisa was one.

"Hey, Palmer," she greeted, coming to a stop in front of him.

He hadn't run away, so he supposed he just had to deal. Much as it pained him. "Afternoon, Louisa. Anna's out of town."

"Yeah, I know. I actually came by to see you."

"What the hell for?" That was another thing about adult Louisa. He was forever saying the wrong thing around her when he'd never had trouble charming a woman in his entire life. From the *cradle*, he'd been able to wrap the female population around his...finger.

Of course, he didn't want to charm Louisa. He wanted to stay the hell away from her at any and all costs.

She grinned at him, green eyes wreaking real havoc

with his system—a system that should absolutely know better.

"I need a favor," she said, and though she tried to keep the grin stretched wide, he saw the shift in her eyes. Something serious lurked behind that attempt at amusement.

"Why don't you ask literally anyone else?"

"Why so grumpy?" she asked, reaching out to poke his chest.

He sidestepped her. He had learned that *nothing* good came from pretending like she didn't affect him. So, he just straight up *avoided*.

"Got things to do, Louisa."

"And people, I assume," she returned with a smirk. A smirk with *just* enough flirtation that he had to very firmly take his imagination to task. No picturing Louisa O'Brien in absolute any kind of state of undress. Ever.

"I need shady help," she said, as if she didn't know how she affected him when he had the sneaking suspicion she knew and used it against him. Routinely. "And you're the shady one."

"Anna's shady."

"No, Anna's vengeful," she corrected. "There's a difference."

It was true, but Palmer didn't have to like it.

"It's a bit delicate. I'd ask Cash, but he's not taking cases right now. At least, that's what Mary said. And as much as I trust Anna with anything... Well, I need a delicate hand."

It irritated him that she'd want to go to Cash over

him, which wasn't a fair assessment since he didn't want her coming to him. But still. Emotions and facts didn't always line up neatly. So, his response was a little gruffer than it should have been. "Since when is that my department?"

She blew a breath, frowning out over the distant mountains. Something twisted in his stomach. He very much wanted to fix whatever was worrying her. But he could not take that risk.

When she returned her gaze to him, he was sunk. "This is serious, and I need someone I can trust. I'd go to Grant or Jack, but they're just too…straight and narrow. I need someone who's not afraid to bend the law a little. I need answers at literally *any* cost."

"*Any* cost is a dangerous proposition, Louisa. You might want to rethink what you're offering." Because every now and again, the best defense was an obnoxious offense.

She frowned. "No one's paying you to be a jerk."

"Nope, I do it for free since I love it so much."

She laughed. That was another problem with Louisa. Sure, like everyone else, she didn't take him too seriously, but she didn't get bent out of shape. She took things as they came, and since that was his entire life motto, he couldn't help but respect it.

Her laugh died quickly though, and any attempt at humor too. She clasped her hands together, looking up at him imploringly.

Hell and damn.

"I found something that changes my entire life,

Palmer. I need answers. I need help. I don't know who else to go to."

"Like what?"

"Like…I don't think my parents are who they say they are. I don't think I'm theirs. And I don't think any of it was ever legal."

LOUISA WOULDN'T CRY in front of Palmer Hudson for a million dollars. She had pride. Some people had told her she had too much.

She didn't mind. Pride got a person places, and it kept them protected from people taking advantage. It protected soft hearts that didn't want to be soft.

So, she had her pride and she forced back every last *drop* of moisture in her eyes that threatened. Even though it was hard.

She'd never said the words she'd just uttered out loud to Palmer or *anyone*. She still didn't want to believe it. But the past six months had her feeling hollowed out and empty. Sad and scared. She couldn't live in denial any longer. She needed answers.

She hoped to *God* she got answers that were comfortable. With every passing month, it felt less and less likely.

"I don't follow," Palmer said, studying her in that careful way of his. Palmer played into his fun-loving, heavy-drinking, serial-dating reputation. He made sure everyone thought there wasn't much substance under that black cowboy hat.

But Louisa knew his family saw the substance underneath, and she knew that under all those bad boy ways he'd learned to cope with his parents' disappearance was a man who was careful with the things that mattered.

She wasn't ashamed to admit, in the privacy of her own mind, that she'd been in love with Palmer Hudson since she was thirteen years old. Who would have been able to resist? He'd been impressive at seventeen. Homecoming king. Football quarterback. Off to the rodeo, always smiling and laughing despite the tragedy that had befallen his family.

She'd believed—hoped—for years she'd grow out of those feelings for him. She knew he'd never, *ever* reciprocate those feelings. But hers stubbornly and religiously stayed, even after her four-year stint in New England for college.

Even if she sometimes entertained the fantasy he might reciprocate *other* things if not feelings.

Regardless, she loved him. And she'd bite her own tongue off before she admitted it to anyone.

That little wrinkle had kept her from asking for his help for months now. She'd tried to think of a way to bring it up to Anna that wouldn't send Anna flying off the handle. She'd considered, over and over again, consulting one of the other Hudsons. *Any* other Hudson.

But if everything she suspected was true, *she* was a cold case. And she needed help. Careful help. Determined help.

Palmer fit the bill. Unfortunately, more than anyone else. He wouldn't want revenge. He wouldn't tell anyone. He wouldn't follow every law to the letter.

He'd find her answers.

Maybe he'd tempt her in the process. Because, damn, the man was enticing. If that was the price she had to pay, then so be it.

"So, this woman found me on Facebook," she said, since starting at the very beginning seemed safer somehow.

"No reasonable story starts with those words, Lou." He looked down at her, so condescending, she almost turned and left right then and there. She didn't need his disdain. She didn't need *him*.

But she did need answers.

"She was a freshman at my alma matter," Louisa continued, trying to keep the snap out of her tone. "And she'd seen my softball team photo in the athletic complex from when we won our championship."

"Still proud of that one, huh?"

"I assume you're still proud of all your buckles?"

He didn't respond to that.

"So, she contacts you and says what?"

"That we're identical. And isn't that so weird? She sent me her softball picture."

"You opened an attachment from an unknown source?"

"Yeah, I did, Palmer. So buy me some antivirus software. The point is, she was right. She looked almost exactly the same as I did at eighteen. We decided to try to trace our family trees to see if we…connected somehow. Like long-lost identical cousins."

"And you didn't?"

"No. But then she suggested we do one of those ancestry DNA tests. You know? The ones that tell you where your family came from, and you can connect to other people with the same DNA or whatever."

"Sure."

"I was kind of excited. I thought it would be something cool. Like my great-great-grandma had an affair with some outlaw. I thought it would be fun, maybe funny. I entertained the possibility we weren't related at all and we're just freak doppelgangers too, but dreaming up how we might connect felt... I don't know. It was just *fun*. So I told my parents. I thought we should all do it."

He must have read something in her tone because his frown deepened. "They didn't go for it?"

"They forbid me."

Palmer's eyebrows drew together. "Forbid you? I didn't think your parents forbid you *anything*."

"Well, I wouldn't go *that* far, but no. They've always been lenient. Bent over backward to make me happy. I know that." She wrapped her arms around herself. It was silly. A silly thing to still be upset about, but it was *jarring* when parents got really militantly angry for the first time when you were *twenty-four*.

Even when they'd caught her with a beer after graduation, she'd gotten gentle talking-tos, despite every don't-drink-before-you're-legal lecture known to man. They just...didn't get mad. They were overprotective, but they were careful.

Now she wanted to know why. Why for twenty-four years they'd been so accommodating when all her friends had had more rules, more lectures, angry fights with their parents as they'd experimented with teenage rebellion.

But Louisa had never been able to rebel, even when she'd tried, because her parents did not forbid.

Until, as an adult, she'd asked to do a fun little DNA test. "They threw a whole fit. Said it was dangerous to give your DNA to those places and there was no way any of *our* DNA was going to be sent off to some shady business."

"It's not a bad point, Louisa."

She didn't groan, though she badly wanted to. "No, it wasn't. Still, I wouldn't have thought anything of it. If they'd been rational. If this woman hadn't told me…"

"Told you what?" Palmer asked.

This was the hard part. The part that didn't make any sense. The part that, for months, she had convinced herself wasn't true. Until Kyla Brown from Lakely, Ohio, had sent her picture after picture of family members who looked like Louisa herself.

When she'd never once been told she took after her parents. Never *once*.

"Her older sister was stolen as a baby. Kidnapped. They never found her—not a baby or a body. And they never figured out who did it."

"Louisa. You can't be serious." He didn't sound condescending this time. No, he sounded like he *pitied* her.

That was worse.

"I know it sounds out there. I want it to be a lie. A joke." She had to pause to swallow the emotion that threatened to envelope her whole. She'd been trying to deny it for so long, but she simply couldn't any longer. "I so desperately want it to be a bizarre coincidence. That's why I need help. Someone who can be… impartial. Who can find the answers at *any* cost. And who can keep a secret while I try to find answers."

Palmer didn't say anything at first. Louisa hugged herself tighter. The air had gotten colder, the wind picking up, likely blowing in a storm.

Palmer frowned then shrugged off his coat and settled it on her shoulders over her jacket, which wasn't doing its job.

"Storm blowing in," he muttered. "Come on inside for dinner. We'll sort it out from there."

That was not a no.

But it was the first step into finding out if she was really…who she thought she was. If her parents were good, honest people. Or liars and kidnappers.

Louisa let out a shaky breath as she followed him to the Hudsons' sprawling house, the warmth of his coat trying valiantly to chase the chill from her bones.

It was no use. None of this felt good or right, but having Palmer agree to help was a step.

They'd find the truth. Then she'd figure out how to deal with it.

Chapter Two

"You can't tell anyone," Louisa said before he pulled open the front door to the house he'd spent most of his life in. "I need this to be a secret."

He looked down at her. She only came to about his chin. The Hudson boys had been blessed with their father's height and, as their mother had liked to say, *his* father's hard head.

God, he missed his mother at the oddest times. Like walking into Hudson house with little Louisa O'Brien at his side needing help.

"We'll eat and then we'll talk," Palmer replied. He didn't need to lead Louisa to the dining room. She'd attended quite a few dinners here growing up. He remembered one memorable one, before his parents had gone missing, where Anna and Louisa had insisted on acting like dogs for the whole of the meal.

The only thing that had kept Palmer from partaking had been the potential teasing he would have gotten from his older brothers for joining in with the *babies*.

He missed having those sorts of problems now too. Those were simple problems.

But what had been simple since that fateful day when he'd been twelve?

Booze. Bulls. Women.

He sighed inwardly. But *not* Louisa.

The dining room was already full. Cash and his daughter, Izzy, were giving their menagerie of dogs orders. Jack was seated at the head of the table reading on his phone and Mary was putting the finishing touches on dinner with Dahlia's help. Dahlia was the one new addition to the house, ever since she'd had the bad taste to fall for Grant when they'd taken on her case last month.

When Mary looked up and saw them, she smiled. Ever the hostess. "Oh, Louisa. Anna isn't here. She got held up out of town. But come on in. You can eat her portion."

"Thanks, Mary."

"Just *where* has Anna been held up?" Jack asked darkly, putting his phone down on the table—screen up. Sometimes he looked so much like their father, it felt like Palmer had been shoved into a strange dream where his father was alive and well and right there.

But Jack wasn't their father, so no one really answered him about Anna's mysterious whereabouts. Anna had gone out and gotten her private investigator's license a few years ago and sometimes took on jobs outside Hudson Sibling Solutions. Mostly to make Jack angry.

It had worked.

"How's the orchard business?" Cash asked Louisa after the silence stretched out too long.

"Oh, same old, same old. Trying to convince Mom and Dad to take a vacation to somewhere warm while it's the slow season." Louisa took Anna's normal seat—which happened to be right next to Palmer's.

Grant entered the kitchen after a few moments, dropping a kiss on his girlfriend's cheek before taking his seat at the table. It wasn't really all that strange to see Dahlia at their table now. She seemed to fit right in with the flow of things, and Grant had certainly been less sour and uptight since Dahlia had come around.

Who could blame him? Dahlia was a looker, and a sweetheart to boot. She'd taken a job at the local library and seemed to fit right in there too.

It was a normal dinner. The kind they'd had a million times before. Louisa could be part of the family for as many meals as she'd eaten with them over the years. Of course, usually Anna was there, but Louisa was friends with everyone.

She might have a smart mouth, but that just made for a good fit at the Hudson table. She also knew how to make people laugh, particularly Cash's eleven-year-old. It was hard to imagine her at the O'Brien orchard with just her parents, who were considerably older than she was.

Considerably older. She was an only child. Could it really be possible she was some kidnapped baby? The O'Briens were…kind, quiet people. Oh, Tim O'Brien could talk your ear off about apple varieties and grafting, and Minnie was a member of every county quilting, baking and charity group that appeared at the whiff of tragedy, but they were just…normal.

Surely this was just… Well, he couldn't believe Louisa had been taken in by a scam. She was whip-smart and almost as cynical as his sister. But underneath that sardonic shell, she had a softer heart than Anna. Maybe she was simply entertaining this whole thing because she felt badly for the girl who'd lost her sister.

He studied her, trying to work out the angles of the story she'd told him outside. She was just missing something. He'd help her figure it out tonight and then that would be it.

Twenty-four hours tops.

Her gaze shifted to his and almost immediately darted away—until she realized he'd been staring at her. Then she turned her head and gave him a questioning look.

It really wasn't fair. If she'd been any random woman in any random bar, that green gaze would lead to a fun night or two and that would be it. It wouldn't tangle inside him, all barbs and strange feelings.

Because she was mixed up with his family in deep, thorny ways that couldn't be dug out of, she felt different. It wasn't *her*. It was the situation.

So, he'd fix the situation and get her on her way.

They ate, they chatted. Mary brought out dessert while Cash and Jack argued over whose turn it was to do dishes. Palmer didn't bother to add to the argument, though it was a grand tradition that dated back to childhood.

Mary kept the schedule, knew who did what and when, and never failed to swoop in and tell them what was what. It was why she always handled the meals. Her ultraorganized brain couldn't stand the rest of them messing up her very careful processes.

Jack's phone buzzed as they all lingered over dessert. Since he was the sheriff of Sunrise, he—and he alone—was allowed to keep his phone at the table during the family meal.

Not that Palmer didn't *occasionally* check his or make his evening plans under the table when no one was looking.

"Storm blew in a bit sooner than we anticipated," Jack said, reading his text. "Deputy Brink says roads are already a mess." Jack looked up at those who didn't live at the main Hudson house. "Everyone might want to think about bunking here tonight."

Izzy let out a little whoop of celebration, causing Cash to frown and the dogs to begin barking and yipping themselves. Dahlia and Grant just made moony eyes over each other. And…well, Palmer didn't dare look at Louisa.

As Jack began to clear the table—because it *was* his turn—Cash ushered Izzy out of the room with threats of homework and a bath, and Mary disappeared so as not to nitpick the cleaning-up process. Dahlia and Grant offered some lame excuse about going to *read*, and before Palmer could make a quip like, "So, that's what the kids are calling it these days," Louisa leaned over.

"Don't worry," she whispered, patting his arm. "I'll sneak into your room later."

Palmer sat stock-still.

Well. Now he *was* worried.

LOUISA HAD BEEN spending nights at the Hudson house since she was a little girl. She'd always stayed in Anna's room, whether they'd been kids or grown women. It felt natural to take Anna's room now, even with her not there.

The Hudsons had always made her feel welcome— before and after their parents' disappearance. She'd never once felt uncomfortable in this house. Even now, as she crept down the hall to Palmer's room, dressed in Anna's pajamas that she'd borrowed, *comfortable*.

Well, until Mary popped up on the stairs, causing Louisa to jump a foot and let out a little shriek of surprise.

Mary laughed. "Oh, I'm sorry. I didn't mean to startle you."

"It's not your fault," Louisa replied, laughing too, because, honestly… "I just thought everyone was asleep."

Mary looked from where Louisa had come to where she was *clearly* going. She blinked. Once. "You're not…" Mary trailed off. She was only two years older than Louisa and Anna, but far more…introverted and contained. Still, she had played with them as girls and sometimes hung out with them now as women—as long as they weren't going to bars or staying out late.

She also, more often than not, assumed the role of designated driver.

As much as Louisa considered Mary a friend, she wasn't her *best* friend, and she'd definitely never confided in Mary about her crush on Palmer.

"It's a prank," Louisa offered with a grin, lowering her voice into almost a whisper. "Promise."

Mary's relief seemed a bit *extreme* to Louisa's way of thinking. Would it really be *so* crazy if she was sneaking down the hall to twist the sheets with Palmer?

Do not let your imagination go down that lane of thought right now.

"Well, I am going to bed now, but if you need anything, just let me know."

"I know where everything is, Mary. Don't worry about me." She smiled at her friend and waited right where she was until Mary disappeared down the hall and into her own room.

Even after the door closed, Louisa waited a good two minutes before moving forward again. She wanted her wits about her when she dealt with Palmer. In his room. Late at night.

About helping you with your very serious issue, remember?

Right. Serious. Possible kidnapping and her parents were secretly evil somehow, when they'd always been loving and wonderful and *there*. And, okay, overindulgent to an extent, but Louisa thought she'd turned out fine despite it. Maybe she didn't *love* taking no for an answer, but who did? Maybe she *preferred* getting what she wanted, when she wanted it, but didn't everyone?

She wasn't afraid of hard work or patience or doing the hard things.

That was why she needed to stop procrastinating

and go into Palmer's room to discuss her potential life-altering secrets.

She didn't bother to knock. If she secretly hoped she might catch a glimpse of Palmer partially disrobed… Well, no one needed to know that but her.

He was not, of course. He stood—fully clothed—staring out the window in his bedroom at the dark, howling night. When she slid inside the room, he looked at her with a scowl.

"Not even a knock?"

Louisa didn't bother to acknowledge that comment. She studied the room around her. She'd been in his room before. Usually for the kind of pranks two little girls liked to play on an older brother. Palmer had always been Anna's favorite target, probably because instead of getting mad or trying to pull older-brother rank in a house without parents, Palmer just retaliated.

Things *had* changed since then. He no longer had posters of scantily clad women and bull riders and cars all over his room. Football gear and ranch wear wasn't littered over every surface. This was no longer a boy's room. At some point, it had turned into a man's.

Sure, a little messy—some dirty clothes littered here and there, way too many cowboy hats on way too many surfaces and a decidedly unmade bed—but it was mostly solid colors and sparse decorations.

It was oddly sad in a way. That he'd gone from decorating his rooms with all his interests to hiding it all behind…whatever this was.

And since she was sad and didn't want to dwell on it when her own life made her sad enough at the moment, she set out to irritate him.

"Mary thought I was off to drum up a booty call, I think." She plopped onto his bed, testing the bounce.

He stood—completely and utterly frozen—as far from the bed as he could get. She grinned at him, waiting for him to stop looking at her in horror.

Again, the *over*reaction irked—she wasn't exactly a child or a hideous beast—but she didn't let that show. She pulled her phone out of the pocket of the sweatpants she'd borrowed from Anna's closet.

"Let me show you a few things my maybe-sister sent me." She patted the spot next to her on the bed.

Palmer didn't move. She looked up at him, doing her level best to appear innocently confused. "What's the problem?"

"No problem," he said gruffly when he was almost never gruff. Stiffly, he moved over to the bed. Very carefully, he perched himself on the very edge of the mattress. Like he was afraid someone might burst in and accuse them of that booty call.

Heaven forbid.

She shook off her irritation—this wasn't the time or place. She'd tuck it away for later.

"First up is the picture of her." She held out her phone.

"There's a resemblance," Palmer said after a while.

"We're practically twins."

"That happens. I don't think it's a reason to believe your parents might be monsters. Even your parents' overreaction to the DNA test thing is understandable. Those companies have your DNA. There's a lot of questionable practices. You're working with a lot of circumstantial evidence and making a *giant* leap."

As if she didn't know that? Hadn't struggled with it for *months*? "Okay, so how can we work with facts that prove something? Do you think I *want* to be some poor kidnapped baby?"

"Well, no. But—"

"No buts. I hate this. I don't want it. There are just too many questions for me to ignore. And I...I don't know what to do next." It was hard to admit that to anyone, let alone Palmer. She didn't deal in uncertainty. She and Anna had that in common. They charged ahead, damn the consequences. These consequences were just too big. "I don't know how to... move forward."

"I suppose asking them is out of the question."

She sent him a scathing glare. She could just imagine the look on her mother's face. The utter hurt and devastation. The way it would change their family *forever*. Because her parents would always know she'd doubted them when they'd never given her reason to.

And if this whole insane story were true? "I need proof, Palmer."

He sighed and raked a hand through his hair. "Okay. Give me the family's names. I'll see what I can dig up."

Chapter Three

Louisa threw her arms around Palmer's neck. Right there on his bed.

"Thank you," she said, squeezing him to her. "I knew you wouldn't let me down."

It shouldn't have surprised him. Louisa was very… physical. Where Anna liked to kick and punch her way out of a situation, her best friend had always been about big hugs and linking arms and bumping hips and giving impromptu squeezes.

But, you know, never on his *bed*.

Palmer closed his eyes and thought of taxes. Calculators. The noise the dogs made when they ate too fast.

Anything but the way she felt with her arms around him. On his *bed*—

He pulled her arms off him. He didn't *jump* from the bed, because Louisa was too smart and too mean not to give him a hard time for that. But he eased off the mattress and frowned down at her.

"The names, Louisa?"

"Right." She looked down at the phone in her hand. "I'll text them to you." She tapped on her phone screen a few times and his phone on the nightstand chimed a few seconds later.

"I really do appreciate your help and..." She chewed on her bottom lip as she stood. A distracting habit he knew better than to focus on. Or had known better, before she'd entered his room. "I know you... It's just..."

"Spit it out, Lou."

She sighed, not reacting to the snap in his tone. "Please don't tell anyone. Not Anna, not your brothers. No one. I have to proceed with this believing it's a fool's errand. If anyone but you knew about me even looking into it, I would be too embarrassed to show my face anywhere."

"I'm not going to tell anyone," he muttered. Didn't that go without saying?

She didn't hug him this time, but she did reach out and squeeze his arm. Her green eyes were uncharacteristically soft. "Thank you, Palmer."

He only grunted—which reminded him way too much of his eldest brother. Palmer might have all the love and respect for Jack in the world, but he'd made every choice *ever* not to follow in his brother's uptight, stuck-in-the-mud, martyred footsteps.

Louisa slipped out of his room and he took his first full breath of the evening, but it still smelled too much like her. Vanilla and the hint of earth that seemed ever a part of her, like growing up on that orchard had made her one with the trees.

He shook *that* fanciful thought out of his head and eyed his bed. No. Bad idea.

So even though it was late, he did not go to sleep.

He was terrified of what might visit him in dreams if he did. He went down to the room they'd converted into a kind of security office, where he kept his computers. He looked at his phone and the names Louisa had texted him and got to it.

Like most computer work, he started with the easy. The surface stuff. Basic records anyone could see, news articles about the baby's disappearance. Then, once he'd exhausted that, he started to dig deeper. Past where your average Joe would know to or how to look.

Everything appeared normal. Louisa O'Brien existed in a completely separate life from Kyla Brown and her family in Lakely, Ohio. There was no connection, no overlap between the Browns and the O'Briens. Palmer couldn't find evidence the Browns had ever been to Wyoming or that the O'Briens had ever been to Ohio. There wasn't even any visible and plausible reason the Browns would want to trick Louisa into believing this scheme. They'd divorced almost fifteen years ago, and both their separate finances seemed to be in decent order. Mr. Brown had a little bit of a rap sheet for battery, and Palmer would keep digging into that, but he couldn't see how that would connect to the daughter reaching out to Louisa.

All of what he found should have proved exactly what Louisa wanted: the idea she was the missing baby was absurd and impossible.

But…

A little hack into hospital records did not yield the results Palmer had hoped for. He couldn't track down

Mrs. O'Brien's hospital records for Louisa's birth, though he could find other hospital records for all the O'Briens at different points in their lives.

It wasn't proof of anything, one way or another. But it raised a question—when he'd wanted irrefutable evidence that raised *no* questions and would get Louisa as far out of his hair as his baby sister's best friend could get.

A little while later when his alarm went off, he hadn't slept a wink, and didn't have any clear-cut way to prove to Louisa she should let this go. So, when he stepped out into the wild white of the Hudson Ranch the night after a blizzard, his usual jovial attitude was nowhere to be found.

It was good though, to trudge through the snow. To have to physically exert himself enough his brain wasn't full of Louisa. He made it to the barn and found that Cash was already there. Palmer moved forward and helped his brother dig the barn door out of the snow enough to get it open.

"Quite a storm," Cash commented by way of greeting. "We're going to need to do perimeter checks. Jack and Grant already dug out the shed and got those snowmobiles. They're driving down to pick up the ranch hands," Cash explained, referring to the small ranch staff they kept on year-round. They bunked down on the south side of the ranch. "They'll split up and handle the back portion. Mary's on Izzy duty, so it's just you and me up here. Best go in pairs."

Palmer nodded as he followed Cash deeper into the barn toward the remainder of the snowmobiles they kept always ready to go during the winter. The horses puffed in greeting. Mary and Izzy would come out and feed and water them once it got a little warmer, because even in blizzards the Hudsons all had roles and knew them.

"Hey, guys," a feminine voice greeted. Both he and Cash turned to Louisa standing in the entrance to the barn. She was wearing Anna's ranch gear, but there was no mistaking her for Anna.

"What are you doing?" Palmer demanded as she approached.

"It's a lot of work digging out of this," Louisa said, looking fresher than anyone had a right to in the midst of all this blinding white. "I'm here to help."

"We could use it," Cash said before Palmer had the chance to tell her to turn right back around and leave him the hell alone.

That would have been an overreaction, all things considered, but he still wanted to indulge.

"Palmer and I will get the snowmobiles out. Can you go let Marsh out of his pen?" Cash said, referring to one of the dogs that spent its nights in the dog pens in the barn with the horses. There weren't a lot of places on the ranch that didn't bunk Cash's huge canine menagerie overnight. "I'll take him with me, then you and Palmer can go together. Split our section. We'll get everything done quicker."

"Sure," Louisa agreed cheerfully, then turned and disappeared into the far section of the barn.

Palmer didn't realize he was glaring after her until Cash nudged him.

"Even you're not foolish enough to go there," Cash said on a half whisper.

Palmer didn't let himself immediately react. If he had anything going for him, even with his temper on boil, it was that he was not a man prone to behaving rashly. When he made bad decisions, he liked to spend some time relishing them.

He turned his head to look at his brother slowly. Maybe not calmly, but not reactively. There was a teasing glint in Cash's eyes, but there was something in the expression that spoke of *actual* worry. Nothing could have set Palmer's teeth on edge more.

"Go where?" Palmer said, letting the edge in his voice ring loud and clear.

Cash rolled his eyes. "You're practically drooling. Over *Louisa*. And I get it, but I'm reminding you to think with your brain instead of your favorite appendage." He got on his snowmobile and Palmer executed the same movement in unison on his.

"I… What do you mean? You *get* it?"

Cash gestured toward where Louisa had disappeared. "She's pretty. But she practically grew up here and is Anna's best friend. Growing up pretty isn't an excuse for you to be yourself. You hear me?"

"What I hear is you trying to play daddy—and I'm not sure if it's to me or to Louisa, but neither of us need it."

"What *I* hear is you very much not denying things you should be denying."

Palmer shot Cash a look. He knew he should smile

and laugh it off, but that his brother thought so little of him rankled. "Because you're my judge and jury?"

"No, but Jack will be, and Anna will run right home to play executioner." Cash turned on his snowmobile and idled it outside. Palmer had no choice but to follow. When they were both stopped outside, Palmer killed his engine and leaned toward his brother.

"Maybe it's none of y'all's business, Cash."

Cash laughed. Actually laughed. "Since when did that matter around here?" He sobered quickly. "You cannot mess around with Louisa O'Brien. It shouldn't even need to be said."

Palmer knew what his response should be. He knew how to handle this. Maybe he'd blame it on the lack of sleep, or the fact that he was actually helping Louisa, that he did none of the things he *should*.

He grinned at his brother, hunching deeper into the warmth of his coat. "Guess we'll see." Then he marched back into the barn. Marsh came bounding around the corner and Palmer paused to crouch and give the dog a good pet. "Do me a favor, Marsh," he muttered to the dog, "bite him. Right in the ass."

Marsh bounded outside to Cash like he was going to obey the order, but Palmer knew he wouldn't, considering Cash did all the dog training around here.

Palmer straightened as Louisa walked around the corner. The heavy winter clothes hid her figure, her hair, everything that made her *her*.

Except her eyes and her mouth and the freckles on her nose and—damn it all to hell. "Come on," he muttered, taking her elbow and all but dragging her outside.

Cash took off, Marsh sitting happily in the little snowmobile addition Cash had jerry-rigged for the dogs. Palmer hesitated as they approached his. In a storm like this, it was best to go in pairs on one machine. Check the fences and the cattle. Make sure no one got lost or hurt or too cold.

But he didn't want her pressed up against him in *any* capacity. He should convince her to go back inside. He kept walking toward his machine and all he could think of was what Cash had said. What Louisa said Mary had thought last night.

"What is it with my siblings thinking I'm out to seduce you?" he demanded.

She shrugged, though he couldn't help but notice a small hitch in her stride when he'd said *seduce*. "You seduce everything."

"Not *you*," he gritted out. Gritted because he was working very hard not to picture *that*.

They stopped at the snowmobile and she turned to face him. "If you haven't noticed, Palmer, I look good. Everyone in Sunrise knows you like things that look good."

It was true and yet, when *she* said it, it did nothing but tick him off. And create something wholly twisted and unwelcome deep in his gut. "I know what people think of me. Hell, I know what *I* think of me. But there are rules even *I* have always followed. No married women. No messing around with my sister's *friends*."

"Wasn't Mary friends with Freya? You messed around with her. And what about your brothers' female friends. Are *they* okay to 'mess around' with?"

He opened his mouth to argue with her but found no words.

"The whole thing is kind of archaic, don't you think?"

He pressed his gloved fingers to his temples. "I think I don't know how we got on this topic of conversation."

She opened her mouth, but he shook his head.

"That was *not* an invitation to explain how." He sighed heavily then straddled the snowmobile. He needed cold air and hard work and none of *this* conversation. When she didn't immediately climb on behind him, he glared over at her. "Are you getting on?"

She blinked as she looked from the seat to his face. "Yeah. *Duh.*" But there was something…strange about how she held herself. For someone who'd hugged him with absolutely no tension *in his bed* last night, she climbed on gingerly, like she'd never ridden a snowmobile in her life.

When she'd once created an incredibly dangerous course with Anna, and he'd watched her do ill-advised jumps into the air with one.

Jack had read them all the riot act.

It had been worth it.

This time around, they were adults, and she slid onto the seat behind him. They were separated by layers and layers of clothes meant to keep the cold Wyoming winter at bay. Even her arms wrapped around his middle as he took off into the snowy pastures were heavily padded.

This was nothing. They weren't really pressed together at all. He thought about the tuna casserole his grandma used to make that he hated, dive bar bathrooms, that time his friend's tobacco spit cup had upended all over his truck.

They puttered along the fence line, looking for damaged fencing or cattle that might look to be in distress. Palmer stopped at one place where the barbed wire drooped. Without him having to say a word, Louisa grabbed the tool bag from the compartment on the side of the snowmobile.

They worked in complete silence, using pliers and wire cutters to repair the fence. The sun had come out and Palmer gave half a thought to ditching his outermost layer, but he'd no doubt regret it on the ride back.

Back home. Where they'd be surrounded by people. So, he might as well discuss what little he'd found. "I did some digging last night," he said. "Not one overlap between your family and the Browns."

"Last night? What did you do? Stay up all night?"

Palmer shrugged. "You want this over, don't you?"

"Yes, I do. But I don't want you to... I need your help, but if I'd wanted someone to martyr themselves to my cause, I would have gone to Jack."

Another truth that rankled, deep and sharp. "Why don't you?"

She was quiet as they finished tying off the wire. He handed her the tools and she put them away as he gave the wire a testing pull. "Good," he muttered.

He moved for the snowmobile, but she stepped in his way, putting her hand on his chest.

Gloved hand. Many layers of clothes on his chest. And yet…

Hell, he needed to find those hospital records so this could be over.

"You don't have to help me if you don't want to, Palmer," she said. Her voice, so firm and devoid of any blame, reminded him of an elementary school teacher.

Putting him firmly in his place.

"I want to help. I just don't want my methods questioned."

"Fair enough," she said in that same obnoxious tone. "Did you find anything that proves I *am* my parents' child?"

He wanted to lie to her, but he couldn't. It wouldn't be right and…he just couldn't. "Not yet. I'm trying to find hospital records of your birth."

"Trying?"

"Yeah." He could see the wheels in her head turning. "But not everything is computerized, even for someone as young as you. So, it's not proof of anything. Okay?"

Louisa did not panic. Well, internally she was panicking, but she didn't let it come out. She just stood very still and kept her gaze on Palmer.

He was steady. A Hudson rock. The brothers might be different, but they looked mostly alike. Like their father before them. Tall and broad, dark-haired and charming smiles—though Palmer was the freest with his.

Louisa had spent far too much time as a teenager looking at *Palmer's* dark eyes when he smiled, determining what each different angle and width of smile really meant.

He wasn't smiling now, and she had no idea what anything meant. He said it wasn't proof.

"There should obviously be a hospital record," she managed to say, focusing on the darker ring of brown along the edges of his irises.

"Sure, but there's a lot of reasons why they might not be where I looked. Or maybe your mom gave birth somewhere else. Maybe she had a home birth?"

Louisa shook her head. "I mean, I know I don't remember since I was all of a day old, but they always talk about bringing me home from the hospital."

"Okay. Maybe once the roads clear up and you go home, you can find a way to ask. Or even poke around files or something. It isn't proof until we can prove there's *no* record."

"But…"

"Lou." He said her shortened named gently, and he took her arm and gave it a squeeze. "Don't jump to conclusions. Not yet."

She swallowed and nodded. "Of course not." The sensible thing was to focus on all the plausible reasons he couldn't find a hospital record for her. Too bad her heart felt like it was being twisted in a vise. She'd poked through her parents' files. She didn't recall seeing any kind of hospital record, just her birth certificate.

She hadn't been looking for that, had she? She

hadn't really known *what* she'd been looking for. And she'd been so afraid...

She cleared her throat and tried to focus on the task at hand. "We should finish our section."

He didn't move. He didn't let go of her arm. And the expression on his face was somehow...not pity. Why should it be? His parents had disappeared without a trace and no one had figured out what happened to them.

Even if she hated what she learned, it would be clear. It would be...terrible, yes, but not as traumatizing as losing your parents at twelve and never knowing *why*.

She was rooted to the spot, to his eyes, to the knowledge there was no hospital record of her birth.

"Louisa, we'll get answers. I promise you that. Even if they're not the ones you want, you're going to be okay."

She nodded, but she did not move. He muttered a curse then pulled her to him. She tried to think of it as a sort of big-brother gesture. She knew that's what he thought of her. Anna's friend. Another little pest.

Even if he *had* said the word *seduce* in her presence and it had made her desperately want to know what that was like.

To Palmer Hudson, she would always be a little girl.

He gave her a nice hug and patted her back and said reassuring words about getting to the bottom of things.

"I promise," he even murmured in her ear.

That, he couldn't actually *promise*. He didn't know there were answers to find. Sometimes, you didn't find out anything—as he well knew.

But she felt comforted anyway.

Chapter Four

The more time Palmer spent digging into Louisa's actual birth records, the more frustrated he became. Computers had always been a natural thing for him. He liked to tinker. He liked to laser focus into one problem and had no trouble failing time and time again without getting frustrated.

It was a bit like climbing on the back of a bull or a bucking bronc. If you just kept trying, eventually things worked out. And with computers, you were less likely to break your skull.

More likely to get arrested though, if you hacked into the wrong program.

They had to find you first. So he'd searched and hacked and searched some more, and there was still no authentic record of Louisa's actual birth. Checkups ever since, but no birth hospital record.

There could be a very reasonable explanation for that. Everything about the O'Briens was normal. Run-of-the-mill. There weren't even any major financial transactions—either way—in the period around Louisa's birth. No trips. Nothing odd.

Yet this one thing didn't add up. The fact that it didn't dug under Palmer's skin like a burr, making him uncharacteristically grumpy and short, to the point *Jack* of all people pointed it out.

"What crawled up your butt and died?"

Palmer studied his older brother, all decked out in his sheriff's uniform—which was just jeans and a button-up and that damn star badge he was so proud of—over the breakfast table. They had both already been out in the howling cold this morning and were now lingering at the breakfast table over coffee.

"Maybe whatever crawled up yours found a new home," Palmer returned, flashing a grin at his brother.

Before Jack could respond, Palmer's phone vibrated in his pocket and he pulled it out rather than deal with Jack.

It was a text from Louisa.

Can you come to the orchard sometime this afternoon? Mom and Dad are going to be gone from 1-3, and I want some help snooping.

He frowned at his phone.

Why can't you do it yourself?

She sent him an eye roll emoji, followed by a block of text that made him roll his actual eyes.

What do you think I've been doing for the past few days? I need fresh eyes and maybe someone who's

sneakier about hiding things like you used to hide
your beer in the hayloft behind the loose board in
the northwest corner.

He smiled a little at that. He'd always known someone had found his stash. He'd always suspected Cash
and his high school girlfriend—now ex-wife—but
Anna and Louisa made just about as much sense.

I always knew you two were thieving—

"Who are you texting?"

Palmer jumped about a foot. Not because the question startled him so much as *who* was asking. He
glared up at Anna. "Hell in a handbasket. When did
you decide to grace us with your presence?"

"Once the job was done," she returned, still trying
to see who he was texting even though he'd moved
his phone completely under the table. "Who are you
texting?" she asked again. "With that dopey grin on
your face."

"You always think my face looks dopey."

"This was *especially* dopey."

Without taking his gaze from Anna, he held down
the button so his phone shut off. "Just planning on
meeting someone at the Lariat tonight."

"Someone special?"

Jack snorted from the other end of the table. "Special? He probably doesn't even know her name."

Palmer forced himself to grin, though in his mind's
eye he was punching Jack square in the nose. "If

love can be blind, love can be nameless," he drawled, pushing back from the table.

As he'd known she would, Anna swiped the phone out of his hand when he tried to move past her. Hence why he'd turned it off.

She scowled at the blank screen then lifted her gaze to glare at him. "I know your passcode."

"No, you don't."

She huffed, a clear sign she was bluffing. "I could figure it out."

"Not before I got it back, you couldn't. Now, do you mind? I got things to do."

"What things?" Jack demanded, still sitting and drinking his coffee at the head of the table. Palmer always thought Jack resembled their father—more with every passing year—but it was in the mornings, with the Christmas lights twinkling and him sitting in Dad's chair, that it struck through Palmer like a pain.

"I'll send you an itinerary, drill sergeant," he said gruffly. Then, since Anna was distracted by looking at Jack, Palmer plucked his phone back and headed out of the dining room. He turned his phone back on and inwardly groaned at the *ten* text messages.

No doubt all from Louisa.

He took a quick glance behind him to see if Anna had followed him to the front of the house. She hadn't. Yet.

He grabbed his cowboy hat, settled it on his head and shrugged into his coat. It was still a cold, windy mess out there, but the roads had been cleared. So that the ranch looked like a Christmas postcard.

Palmer braced himself against the chill and headed for his truck. He kept expecting Anna to jump out at him and hurl more demanding questions, but she didn't.

And that, in and of itself, was suspicious.

Once safely in his truck, he looked at the texts Louisa had sent. Mostly chastising about his lack of response.

I'm saving you from Anna getting involved. You're welcome.

Are you coming or not?

On my way.

He tossed the cell into the passenger seat then started driving for the O'Brien apple orchard. He didn't have any compunction about snooping around the O'Brien house. That wasn't the cause of the churning weight in his gut. The way he saw it, he was doing them a favor.

If they *hadn't* stolen Louisa, and hell it was hard to believe they *had*, then he was saving them the emotional turmoil of *all that*. If they had? Well. They deserved what they got.

What concerned him was being in a house all alone with Louisa. *Not* because anything was going to happen, just because the woman was...

Okay, he could admit it in the privacy of his own head. She was terrifying. Stubborn and funny and comfortable in her own skin. And, worst of all, emotionally vulnerable. He didn't want to touch *that* with a million-foot pole.

Still, he took the turn to the orchard that would fork eventually and lead him to the house. He supposed it didn't matter if people saw him driving to the O'Briens'. He was friendly with all of them, and he could make up any number of reasons for his truck to be seen driving down the gravel drive.

But he had a bad feeling he and Louisa needed to be careful so the town gossips didn't start *wondering*.

They wouldn't know what they were *really* doing, but the potential of what they *could* be doing would spread through town like wildfire. Get to his brothers and, worse, Anna, in record time.

And what would he say? He couldn't very well tell anyone the truth any more than he could play along with potential gossip that he and Louisa were… involved.

No, no one would say *involved*. They would think, given it was him, it had to be a hookup. Sunrise residents might very well throw him in a cattle car and hope he ended up in the Nebraska prairie like the history lore said his ancestors did when a dangerous element tried to take over the town.

The house came into view. It was already decorated for Christmas—it was daylight, so no lights shone, but he could see the bright colors of the bulbs anyway. Wooden Santas and snowmen he knew Tim had made himself and Minnie had painted.

Louisa was waiting for him on the porch. Her nose was red, so she'd been outside for a little bit. He ignored the kick in his gut by getting out of the truck with a lecture on his lips.

"What are you doing? Trying to catch your death of cold?"

"What are you doing?" she retorted. "Trying to do an imitation of my mother?"

He frowned at her as he climbed the stairs of the porch, stomping the snow off his boots.

She looked up at him, and even though she'd had a snarky response, he could see all the worry, guilt and anxiety in her eyes. "Dad's at a doctor's appointment, and he always ends up chatting with Dr. Phillips then heading over to the Coffee Klatsch to gossip with whoever else is up there. Mom's at a church meeting until three, but she'll likely stay after checking on the Christmas poinsettias and who knows what else." She wrung her hands together, squinted at the drive toward the highway, then shot a guilty glance at the house. "Let's get this over with."

"You really don't have to—"

She held up a hand and waved it as she opened the front door. "Don't tell me I don't have to because I *do* have to. I need answers. And you haven't been able to prove to me that I should stop looking."

No, he hadn't. Since that ate at him, he didn't say anything as she led him through the house. He hadn't been in here much. The O'Briens hosted town events sometimes at the orchard, so he'd spent plenty of summer afternoons and evenings out among the apple trees, but he'd only stepped foot inside the actual house once or twice.

It was a lot like Hudson Ranch, except everything was on a smaller scale and seemed a little…older. Where he was certain, at home, Mary didn't let a single board or windowsill dare splinter, wilt or warp.

"All the paperwork for us, for the orchard, Dad keeps in his office. I've searched everything in there and found nothing. I've poked through their room a little, but no luck. And before you say, *Maybe there's nothing to be found*, let's skip the argument. Look around a bit, and if you can't find anything in an hour, we'll give it up."

Since she seemed *this* close to breaking, he didn't offer any advice or alternatives. He just nodded once. "Okay. Show me the files."

Louisa wasn't sure which annoyed her more—when Palmer argued with her or when he *didn't*. Because when he didn't, she knew he felt sorry for her. She *hated* that.

Of course, she hated all of this, and she just knew… there had to be something. Something here.

Palmer took a seat at her father's desk and meticulously pulled every drawer open. He looked through files and every single paper. He was thorough.

Just when she was sure he was going to look up at her and tell her there was nothing to be found, that she should give up and leave him alone, he pointed to the little corner cubby of the desk.

"Do you have the key to this?"

"Key to what?"

Palmer pointed again, but she didn't see a keyhole.

It was just a little decorative cubby. At least, that's what she'd always thought. Until Palmer reached out and pulled back a section of the wood—almost like a door, although she couldn't make out a hinge. And there in the exposed wood *was* a keyhole.

Louisa's vision threatened to gray, but she took a breath. It was just a small compartment in the corner of the desk. Sure, it was a secret compartment, but it was an old desk. Maybe there was nothing in there. She cleared her throat before she trusted herself to speak. "I don't know where a key that small would be."

Palmer shrugged. "No worries." He took his wallet from his back pocket and opened it on the desk surface. There was a little collection of bills, a condom, which she desperately tried not to think about, and a little bobby pin, which he pulled out.

"Have a lot of hair emergencies?" she asked acidly, because it looked like a memento and something about the sentimentality of it was worse than the practicality of a condom in his wallet.

He just grinned at her then pushed the bobby pin into the small keyhole. He fiddled with it for a while, until the door popped open. When she didn't move, didn't say anything, he looked at her.

Really looked at her. In that way he had that no one else did. Everyone thought they knew her. Parents. Teachers. Friends. Even Anna thought she knew everything there was to know about Louisa.

No one had predicted she'd want to go to Massachusetts for college though. No one had expected her to throw herself into a collegiate softball career then quit. Wholesale. And when she did things like that, everyone just thought it was a one off.

But Palmer had always looked. Tried to make sense of it. Because he was the same. Everyone thought they knew him, the carefree football star and rodeo cowboy who hadn't been as marked by his parents' disappearance as his siblings.

When he had been. Of course he had been.

"Lou?"

She swallowed, trying to shake herself out of her reverie. Better to think of Palmer and all he was than what might be hidden in that compartment.

Because he was staring at her, trying to see who she was in this moment, she told him the truth. "I don't think I can look at whatever is in there."

Something in his expression softened and she wasn't sure she wanted anything to do with Palmer's softness, but fear of what was inside that compartment overrode everything else.

"We're here because you want answers. If you wanted easy, or to do things without being afraid, we wouldn't be here. So, you might not want to look, but you're certainly capable of looking."

She knew she was capable. The point was she didn't *want* to be. She didn't want to face something that could potentially change her life forever. Why else would her father have a secret desk compartment?

"I'm right here," Palmer said, standing. He put his hand on her shoulder, both reassurance and a gentle nudge to take a seat in the desk chair. "No matter what

you find. You know you've got friends, Lou. We'll get
you through."

She sucked in a breath.

"Go on now."

Usually people telling her what to do was an irritation. Usually Palmer telling her what to do was more
challenge than anything else. But in this moment, it
helped. She reached forward and—

From nowhere, Palmer's hand flew out and stopped
her forward movement. Without a word, he shut the
little compartment's door and eased the wood slat
that covered it back into place.

By then, Louisa heard why. Footsteps. She sucked
in a breath and held it. How was she going to explain…?

A man appeared in the doorway. Not either of her
parents. Louisa jumped out of her chair and she might
have toppled over if Palmer hadn't been there to gently
keep her upright.

"Grandpa," she squeaked in greeting. "What are
you doing here?"

Chapter Five

Palmer had often been caught red-handed. Usually it involved dark rooms and fewer clothes. He didn't embarrass easily, because if he was doing something, he'd already decided not to be ashamed of it.

This was, of course, different. Still, Palmer didn't really react. That was usually the best defense. Louisa was all fifty shades of red, stuttering over her words with uncharacteristic fidgeting.

"Am I not allowed to visit my son's house? On the orchard my grandfather built from the ground up?" Greg O'Brien said, eyeing Palmer. Not Louisa.

That, Palmer figured, was a good thing in the short term. If Greg was suspicious of Palmer's motives, he wouldn't be wondering why they were poking around Tim's desk.

Louisa laughed. It sounded deranged at best. "I'm just surprised to see you."

Greg's hard gaze never left Palmer. "Clearly."

"Uh." Louisa blinked up at him like she was surprised to still find him there. "Palmer was just…"

Palmer decided there was only one way out of this.

He didn't like it. Hated it in fact. But it kept suspicion at bay, and he knew that's what Louisa wanted more than anything. So he grinned at Greg. "Lou here needed a lightbulb changed."

Greg's expression went thunderous, and poor Louisa—who wasn't all that naive but clearly new to subterfuge—just looked confused at what a poor excuse that was.

"That so," Greg said between gritted teeth.

"Yes, sir," Palmer replied, not letting his smile dim in the least. "But it's all changed now, so I can be on my way. I'll see you later, Lou." He grabbed his hat and slid it on his head, making sure it looked to Greg like he was giving Louisa a long *lingering* look when what he was really doing was making sure the secret compartment was all covered up.

Palmer didn't wait for Louisa to respond. He sauntered on past her grandfather and into the living room. He took his sweet time—no hurrying. He knew how to look like a man who'd just enjoyed himself.

Thoroughly.

Lord, he hoped Greg O'Brien wasn't half the gossip his wife was. Of course, one stray word to Louisa's grandmother and Palmer would find himself with Anna holding a knife to his throat by dinner.

Metaphorically.

Probably.

Palmer took the stairs. Usually the orchard was a pretty sight, but something about looking out at all those bare trees in the snow had a creeping sensation crawling up his spine. Like someone was out there. Watching.

That was absurd because there was nowhere to hide with leafless branches and only the slight rolling hills that separated one apple variety from another.

He glanced back at the house, all cheerful-Christmas decorated, but it didn't settle that odd *off* feeling inside him. He'd learned long ago that those feelings didn't really matter. Everything felt wrong when your parents disappeared without a trace. Everything felt wrong when you threw yourself into getting hit as hard as possible—by football opponents, by charging bulls, by angry men in seedy bars.

Wrong became normal. Accepting it, one of those life lessons. Still, he couldn't quite make himself move and leave Louisa alone.

She isn't alone. She's with her grandfather.

Who, speak of the devil, stepped out onto the porch before Palmer'd had the good sense to leave.

Greg O'Brien didn't look to be leaving, but he did look to be handing out lectures. Palmer sighed and waited.

"My granddaughter isn't one of your bar floozies," the man said. Low and clear. There were no threats, but he didn't need to offer one. The commentary was enough.

Palmer didn't respond right away. He also didn't back down from Greg O'Brien's angry gaze. He held it. Cool. Though his own temper stirred, he didn't let it out. He took his sweet time sliding his hands into his pockets and pretending to consider Greg's words.

"I appreciate the concern, Mr. O'Brien, but I don't consider anyone a *floozy*. It's an outdated term, don't you think? After all, how a woman chooses to spend her time—and who with—is kind of her business, isn't it?"

"Now, listen here—"

Palmer had no patience to *listen*. Or to be lectured for something he hadn't even done. He lectured himself plenty just for *thinking* about it.

"I'm sure Louisa can decide who she wants to spend her time with all on her own," Palmer continued with as little inflection on any of those words as possible. Then he calmly turned around and crunched through the snow back to his truck.

All the while, Greg sputtered.

When Palmer got in his pickup and drove down the lane, that uneasy feeling followed. He tried to ignore it, push it away, but it was persistent. When he looked in the rearview mirror at the O'Brien house... all he could think about was all those *what-ifs* he'd trained himself not to think about when it came to *literally* everyone else.

Apparently, when it came to Louisa, he was sunk.

LOUISA DIDN'T KNOW quite how to handle her grandfather. He was angry, and he did, on occasion, lose his temper, unlike his son, her father. But he was angry about all the wrong things, so she didn't know how to deal.

"Why don't I make you your afternoon coffee?" she offered. A distraction, hopefully. And they could get out of her father's office. Maybe he wouldn't think to mention it to her father.

Grandpa grunted then turned on a heel and left the room. She gave one last look around the office, making sure it was as it was when she and Palmer had come in, then scurried after him.

He wasn't in the kitchen. He was standing outside on the porch, and she could see through the kitchen window that Palmer was standing there at the foot of the stairs, listening to whatever her grandfather had to say.

Palmer's jaw was tight and, when he spoke, she could see the frustration in his eyes. But whatever he said was delivered with a calmness she did not feel. Then he turned and strode to his truck.

When the front door slammed open, she wrenched her gaze from the window to her grandfather entering the kitchen.

She was not afraid of her grandfather, but he wasn't a warm man. Not like her father. There was a steely iron will to Greg O'Brien, and she'd never felt comfortable enough to butt heads with him.

Did it mean something?

"What are you staring at?" Grandpa demanded. "And what on earth are you doing with Palmer Hudson?"

She didn't want to answer either question, but she could hardly just stand in the kitchen gaping at him. "Palmer and I...are just friends," she said weakly.

He grunted. "I've never seen him sniffing around here before."

It had taken a few minutes, but she finally had an explanation. "We're planning a surprise for Anna."

Grandpa only narrowed his eyes. "That boy is nothing but trouble."

She knew there was no reason to defend Palmer to her grandfather. People thought what they wanted to about Palmer, and it certainly wasn't up to her to stick up for him. Particularly when anyone she defended Palmer to would only consider her another hapless victim to his charms. "He's not a boy, and if he's getting into trouble, I suppose that's his choice."

Her grandfather's expression got all thunderous again.

"Is there something you came over for, Grandpa?" Louisa hurried on. "Dad and Mom are both in town. I was just about to organize some files for Dad when Palmer came over to deal with some things for Anna's surprise. Where's Grandma?"

"She's at that church meeting with your mother," he grumbled. He crossed over to her, doing something very out of character. He put his hand on her shoulder. "Louisa Jane. You're a good girl. You've got spirit and a good head on those shoulders, even if you did try to addle your brain out east. Trust me when I say Palmer Hudson is only going to lead to trouble."

It was hard to look past all these warnings and lectures. She wasn't used to them from anyone. *She* didn't get lectures. Not really. Maybe some hopeful reminders, but not *lectures*.

Maybe that's why she could see beyond the irritation of this one to what was behind this whole strange thing.

Her grandfather was worried about her. And considering that small speech included the most compliments he'd ever leveled at her in her life, or maybe even *anyone* aside from John Wayne, she thought maybe it came from a good place. Even if he was wrong about Palmer and why Palmer had even been there.

So, she forced herself to smile. "Okay, Grandpa. Do you want that coffee?"

He agreed, and finally let the whole Palmer thing go.

When her parents got home, they didn't seem surprised to find him there with her. He stayed for dinner, which was kind of odd since he usually ate dinner with Grandma and, if the church meeting was over, she was likely at their house alone.

And he'd never explained why he'd come over.

Later, when she was washing dishes shoulder to shoulder with her mother while Dad was out with Grandpa puttering in the greenhouse, Louisa wasn't really paying attention to her mother. She wasn't studying her in all the ways she had been these past few months, desperate to find similarities that were, in fact, skin deep.

She was thinking about the cubby in Dad's desk and if she hadn't been such a chicken they'd know what was in it. *Or you'd have been caught fully red-handed.*

Either way, how was she going to open it again?

She didn't know how to pick locks like Palmer did, and she had some doubts about ever getting Palmer to come back out here after her grandfather's lecture.

She didn't think Palmer cared about lectures, per se, but she knew he hated the idea of anyone thinking he could possibly be in the least bit interested in her.

Which was really insulting. It wasn't that she needed him to be interested—obviously he wasn't and never would be. But he didn't have to be so *appalled* at the idea. He could admit that even if *he* didn't find her all that attractive, even if *he* always saw her as a child, she wasn't one. And didn't look like one.

"Louisa?"

Louisa blinked over at her mother, realizing by Mom's concerned stare that she really had been tuned out. "Sorry." She smiled. "Daydreaming. What did you say?"

Mom sighed but didn't press the issue because she was used to Louisa's flights of fancy, which, yes, far too often involved Palmer Hudson. "Did your grandfather say why he came out?" Mom asked.

"Oh. No." Did Mom think it was weird? *Was* it weird?

Mom got a thoughtful look on her face. "Huh."

"What?"

"It's just, your father and I both saw him in town. I mentioned your plans to go over to the Hudsons' this afternoon. So he knew the house was empty. It seems strange he'd come out here alone."

Louisa stared at her mother, her hands deep in the

hot soapy water. "Why…would he do that?" she asked, trying not to sound as rattled as she felt.

"I suppose you were back in time to entertain him."

Which didn't actually answer Louisa's question.

And that was odd enough that it left Louisa feeling even more suspicious of the whole situation.

Chapter Six

"I think my grandfather knows something."

Palmer took a minute to just *breathe*. The last thing he needed was Louisa popping up at the Lariat in front of a bunch of people who would stoke whatever gossip fires were already started. But she was here, sliding in between him and the blonde on the next stool over he'd been trying to work up the interest to flirt with.

He had to look up at Louisa instead. Her green eyes were all painted up smoky and mysterious. She had bright red lipstick on and, God help him, a shirt that dipped dangerously low. Was that *glitter* all over that exposed skin?

He couldn't look. He couldn't close his eyes. She smelled like wildflowers and honey in the midst of a cold, townie bar whose Christmas decorations were all "Mele Kalikimaka"–themed here in the middle of rural Wyoming, like that made sense.

He thought about bull drool after a hard ride. The smell of the high school locker room after a rainy football game. That time he'd cut his hand on a rusty nail in a fence and needed stitches.

Anything, *anything* but all the things he noticed about Louisa. He took a long swig of his beer. "What are you doing here?"

"I'm meeting Anna. Mostly because I figured you'd be here." She gave the beer in front of him a long, considering look. "Skipping out on the hard stuff?"

He flashed a grin at her. "Just to start, sweetheart."

She didn't roll her eyes like he'd anticipated, and maybe hoped for. Instead, she frowned a little. Almost like she was *concerned*.

"What do you want from me, Louisa?" he muttered, looking back down at his beer and wishing he had ordered that whiskey he'd been pondering.

But it had felt *wrong* to sit here and flirt and get drunk and do his *usual* when Louisa had a secret compartment and an angry grandfather.

Now she was here.

She lowered her voice, leaning in close, and he did *not* look at her. He kept his gaze on the beer. "Look into my grandfather," she said. "Something isn't right there. He acted weird. My mom acted weird about him acting weird. Maybe…"

"Maybe *what*?"

When she didn't speak, he felt compelled to glance at her and hated that she looked hurt by the snap in his tone.

"I don't know *maybe what*," she said, her voice cool and quiet. "That's the whole problem. *I* don't know how to pick a lock, but I get the feeling you won't be coming to help me with that anytime soon."

He tightened his grip on the bottle. "I said I'd help you."

"Yes, but you're making it increasingly clear you don't *want* to help." He could tell she was trying to sound…snippy or strong or whatever, but it wasn't working. She was struggling under the weight of too many what-ifs to kick his ass. So, her voice wobbled.

He felt two inches tall. "It's not about *not* wanting to help. It's about not wanting to be around you, Louisa." And damn, did that come out *all* wrong.

She looked like he'd reached out and slapped her. Her face even went a little white, which made all that glitter somehow shine brighter. "Well, fine," she muttered, whirling away from him as if she was about to storm off.

He knew how it looked. He knew how not to over-react. But he simply couldn't let her stalk off and apologize later. He couldn't let that hurt settle inside her for a second longer. So he reached for her arm before she could move away and gently pulled her back to face him.

"Don't be mad at me. Think about why that might be. *Really* think."

"What the hell are you two doing?" Anna's voice demanded from behind him.

Palmer wondered if he'd actually died a few days back and been sent to hell. He didn't immediately drop Louisa's arm. That would look like he was guilty.

He didn't have a damn thing to be guilty about, which was half the frustration. He gently released

Louisa and turned to his angry sister. She was dressed just about as inappropriately as Louisa.

Okay, inappropriate wasn't *fair*. They were grown woman who could wear what they wanted. He just didn't know why he had to be in the vicinity of any of it. Particularly when half the guys in the bar were watching his *sister* with *that* look in their eyes.

"Your friend is annoying the hell out of me, so I was returning the favor," Palmer said. He didn't look to see Louisa's reaction. Couldn't let himself. "Now you're here to double-team me."

"Actually..." Anna replied, her anger already replaced by something else. Something that had Palmer frowning. "Karma must have stepped in and done it for me."

"Huh?"

"I saw your truck in the lot. All lopsided. Tire's flat."

Palmer swore under his breath, but it suited his mood and his luck of late. It was a good enough excuse to leave the bar and not witness whatever Louisa and Anna had up their sleeves.

Anna started dragging Louisa over to a booth and Palmer made a concentrated effort not to look at her, even though he could feel her gaze on his back. He paid his tab, a piddly one beer, and tried not to feel the stares of everyone in the bar who knew him and wondered why Palmer Hudson might come by for only *one* beer and leave long before ten.

Particularly after a slightly too heated conversation with Louisa O'Brien.

He really needed to get himself out of this mess. He pushed outside into the frigid December air—which had him thinking about Louisa's outfit all over again. What did she want to do? Catch her death of cold?

Not your problem.

If only that voice in his head was half as firm and determined as it should be. He trudged over to his truck in the gravel parking lot, then stopped a few feet away. Because from the faint glow of the bar he could see what Anna hadn't been able to.

A tire on his pickup wasn't flat. All four tires had been slashed. Cut to ribbons, really.

Palmer looked around the dark parking lot. It'd be easy to do something like this without anyone seeing. But who would do it? And why?

He looked right next to his pickup where Louisa's truck was parked. The O'Briens' Orchards logo right there on the side.

He couldn't picture Greg O'Brien out here slashing his tires, but he didn't know what else this purposeful, pointed outburst of anger could be about. *Particularly* with Louisa's truck parked right here.

Palmer let out a long sigh and then pulled his phone out of his pocket. Much as he wanted to deal with this himself, he was enough of a sheriff's brother to know he needed to call the police.

Great.

"WHAT IS *WITH* YOU?"

Louisa blinked across the booth at her friend, realizing she'd been staring at the door wondering how

Palmer was going to deal with his flat tire. Wondering a few too many things about Palmer instead of listening to Anna recount her latest PI case.

"I know you can get a little gooey-eyed about Palmer, but this is taking it a step too far."

"I am not gooey-eyed about Palmer," Louisa replied, more knee-jerk than anything. It wasn't about her usual Palmer flights of fancy.

Well, mostly.

Think about why that might be. Really think.

He hadn't made it sound like he didn't want to be around her because she was annoying or he hated her. He'd made it sound…

She had to push the thought away. She was sitting here with her best friend, and that was where her concentration had to be.

"What were you guys talking about all serious then? I can't remember the last time I've seen him in such a foul mood." Her eyes narrowed. "Were you two texting this morning?"

Louisa hesitated. Because she *had* been texting with Palmer, but she didn't know why that would be of any importance to Anna.

"If you are hooking up with my brother, at least have the decency to tell me."

"I'm not hooking up with anyone." At least that was the truth. She didn't want to lie to Anna. She didn't even want to keep this secret from Anna. She just knew… Anna would sweep in. She'd demand answers and justice. There would be no careful computer searches or snooping through her father's office. Anna ran on emotion, and in just about every aspect of her life, Louisa admired that about her best friend.

But she just couldn't let Anna's impulsiveness into this one. Not until she knew for sure. One way or another. "Anna. I need you to do me a huge favor."

Anna's brow furrowed. "What?"

"I need you not to worry about or ask about anything to do with Palmer for the next few weeks. Okay? I promise, after that, I'll explain everything."

Anna opened her mouth to no doubt promise, but Louisa knew her friend.

"Don't snoop around trying to figure this out. I promise I'll tell you everything. I just need time."

"You know I hate a cryptic mystery, Louisa."

"Yeah, I do know that. I'm asking you, as my best friend in the whole world, to suck it up and deal."

Anna snorted a laugh at that as she slumped back into the booth. "You don't play fair."

"That's why we're such good friends."

Anna laughed again. "All right. I promise. For two weeks. *Tops*."

Louisa smiled thinly. Great. Now she had a time limit. Palmer would *love* that. Before she could say anything else, or change the subject to a safer one, she saw the telltale flash of red and blue lights out the bar's window.

"What do you think that's about?" she wondered aloud.

Anna twisted in the booth to look out the window and frowned. "I don't know, but look... There's Palmer."

There he was. Standing under the light outside by the

entrance, little swirls of snow around him as he spoke to Chloe Brink, one of Sunrise's deputies. His arms were crossed over his chest, and he looked…furious.

Louisa hadn't realized she'd slid out of the booth to stand until Anna did the same.

"Come on," Anna said. "Let's go see what the big oaf has gotten himself into."

Louisa trailed after Anna, knowing it was none of her business. It was freezing outside, and she'd left her coat in her truck.

Yes, on the off chance Palmer might *look*.

Think about why that might be. Really think.

When they stepped outside, both Palmer and Deputy Brink turned to study them.

"Tires were slashed," he said, jerking his chin toward his pickup. There was another deputy with a flashlight inspecting the damage, so Louisa could see it wasn't just a flat tire as Anna had thought, and not even simply slashed like Palmer had said.

They were cut to ribbons. A kind of violently angry display that didn't make sense. Not in Sunrise, even at a sometimes-rowdy townie bar.

"Finally ticked off the wrong woman, huh?" Anna said. It was an attempt at humor, but Louisa saw the firm, angry disapproval on her friend's face. Anna might like to mess with Palmer, but that didn't mean she liked anyone else messing with him.

"Something like that." When Louisa looked back at his expression, and it was serious and focused on *her*, Louisa realized… He thought it connected to what was going on with *her*.

"Is that what you think happened?" Deputy Brink asked. "Pissed someone off lately?" She held a pen poised over a notebook.

"I don't know what happened, Deputy," Palmer drawled. "Because I wasn't out here. And no one came and announced their intentions or motivations to me."

Louisa wanted to chastise him for being snippy with Chloe when the woman was only doing her job, but she saw a barely leashed fury under Palmer's composed expression that she was… Not afraid of, exactly. But wary of.

"We'll take pictures. Ask a few questions. If you think of anyone who might have something against you, we can look into it…"

"But you won't find anything and mostly it'll all disappear. No answers found."

Deputy Brink stiffened, her expression bland as she flipped her notebook shut. "Your brother is the sheriff, Palmer. I'm betting it won't just disappear."

That didn't seem to change his mind on the matter. "I wouldn't bet anything serious on it," he muttered. "Thanks for coming out anyway."

Deputy Brink nodded stiffly then walked over to Palmer's truck to discuss something with the other deputy.

He turned to Anna. "Guess you're going to have to cut your night on the town short and drive me home. Unless you want to drag Mary out to pick me up."

"Why can't you just sit in the bar and get drunk like you usually do?" Anna replied.

"Because I don't really feel like having *fun* after my tires have been slashed, thanks."

Anna heaved a sigh. "Fine," she grumbled. Anna turned to Louisa. "You mind taking care of my tab?"

"Yeah, no worries. You two go. We'll figure out another night to go out." She gave Anna a quick hug then glanced at Palmer. His gaze was still dark, angry, and she didn't know...*anything* about what was going on in that brain of his, but she was happy to scurry inside and get away from the way it made her nervous. When her feelings for him rarely made her *nervous.* Embarrassed? Sure. Uncomfortable? Sometimes. Angry? Most of the time.

Nervous? It did not make *any* sense.

At the bar, she settled her and Anna's tab and while she waited to get her credit card back, her phone chimed. She looked down at the text.

From Palmer.

Figure out a way to come to the ranch tonight.

Her heart should not *flutter* about that. This was serious. Tire slashings and hidden desk compartments and her grandfather's odd behavior. None of it was about her and Palmer.

None of it would *ever* be about her and Palmer.

This was actually far more important. So she pocketed her credit card and hurried outside. Anna and Palmer were getting into Anna's car, but Anna hadn't shut her door yet. "Anna! Wait!"

Anna paused and Louisa jogged over. "Hey, I was

just thinking. I could follow you to the ranch. We can still hang out. Have a girls' night in." Louisa expressly did not look at Palmer, because she knew she would… well, reveal *something*. And Anna would see it.

"Oh, well, that's a great idea," Anna agreed. "Sure, come on out."

"Why doesn't she ride with us?" Palmer said. "Maybe this was all random and someone did something to her tires too. Her truck is right next to mine. No point in getting out in the dark and cold and making sure."

Anna frowned, but when she looked over at Louisa, it wasn't with any kind of accusation. "Much as I hate to admit it, he's right. We don't know exactly what's going on. Hop in, Lou. We'll get it sorted in the morning."

Louisa wished she could believe that.

Chapter Seven

Palmer left Anna and Louisa in the living room trying to talk Mary into making and drinking margari-
tas with them.

He wanted to talk to Louisa privately, but more, he'd
wanted to make sure she was safe. He couldn't think
of a single person who'd slash his tires like that. Sure,
he'd made a few women angry in his day as Anna had
suggested, but he hadn't done anything to anyone that
would prompt such a response. In fact, it had been
a while since he'd done much more than needle his
brothers and drink at home. The only thing he'd done
to ruffle any feathers of late was to be caught with
Louisa at the O'Briens'.

He still didn't think her grandfather was behind
this. A missing birth record, a hidden desk cubby, a
suspicious-acting grandfather...

Well, it added up to *something*. He hoped, for Louisa's sake, it wasn't what she thought it was. But it
was *something*, so he just couldn't...let her get in that
truck and drive home alone. He'd had to make sure
she was safe.

So, while Louisa and his sisters did their thing. He went to his computer room and set about doing some research on Greg O'Brien. Even if he'd had nothing to do with the truck, his behavior was strange, and Louisa had asked him to look into her own grandfather.

This didn't go any better than his initial investigation. He got more and more frustrated that he couldn't find anything *remotely* shady. Not even a speeding ticket. The O'Briens weren't baby-stealing criminals. Why was he beating his head against this ridiculous brick wall when she could just ask her damn parents why there was no hospital birth record?

He pushed away from the desk, determined to head up to his room and just forget this whole thing until morning. He was running on next-to-no sleep and nothing but irritation. And he still would have to deal with whatever Jack's reaction to the slashed tires was going to be.

Instead, when he walked into the hallway, Louisa was standing there. Just *standing*.

She was still wearing that getup from the bar. All skintight jeans and low-cut top and makeup meant to make a man think of things he should not be thinking about with Louisa O'Brien.

"I didn't find anything on your grandfather," he said. Because that's all this was about. Not how she glittered like some kind of mirage that was real enough to touch. For someone else. Never him.

She held his gaze and nodded solemnly. "I guess I figured you wouldn't." She tried to smile. Her mouth curved, but it didn't reach her eyes. "I guess I should

just…ask or leave it. We're not getting anywhere."
She was trying valiantly to act like it didn't matter.

He could see through all those attempts, the cracks
in her armor. Because so often he was trying that hard
too.

"Maybe we should check out that hidden cubby
before we ask or give up," he suggested gruffly, even
though he'd just been considering giving up entirely.
He just couldn't stand that look of defeat on her face.

She looked so surprised, and hopeful, he wanted…
to make it all right for her. Somehow.

He moved closer so they weren't speaking across
the space of a hallway, and she moved closer too.
Bringing the smell of honey and alcohol with her.

Her cheeks were a little flushed when she looked
up at him. "You drunk?" he asked suspiciously.

"No." He eyed her, but she didn't waver or say anything goofy. She rolled her eyes at his careful study.
"One margarita is hardly going to put me flat on my
face. Especially the way Mary makes them."

"You're a lightweight though."

"How would you know?"

"I know far too many things about you." You'd
think he was the one drinking, saying senseless things
like that. Like what he'd said at the bar. When he'd
never even finished his beer.

She just stood there, but her eyes studied him. Like,
if she stared enough, she could read every thought in
his head. He had the uncomfortable sensation she
might be able to do just that.

Still he just stood there. Looking right back because… She was beautiful. And strong and smart and he *wanted* her. Even if he didn't *want* to want her.

"Palmer. Back at the bar you said—"

He wasn't sure he could stand to hear his own words used against him. "I say a lot of things."

She nodded slowly. "I suppose you don't always say what you mean. But I think you meant what you said, but *I* don't understand what it meant. Because as far as I can tell, as far as you always treat me, you think I'm still just a pesky little kid."

"You're pesky all right." But she was determined. He could see it in the glint in her eyes. In the way she stood there, clearly deciding not to back down. To poke at this…and then what? What good could come from it?

"When you're with me, when you're around me, do you think of me as a kid? Or not?" she asked.

A kid. When she was dressed like that. When her casual touch made his body tight, and her laugh made him feel like he'd won every event in the rodeo. He'd wanted to touch her for too long now, a desperation that only seemed to grow. He couldn't stem the tide. He couldn't avoid her enough lately to avoid thinking about her.

"I've had just about everyone in a fifty-mile radius warn me off you this week," he said even though it didn't answer her question. Because it was a reminder. Of who they were, and how his wants did not matter.

No one wanted wild, irresponsible Palmer Hudson messing with sweet, upstanding Louisa O'Brien.

"Since when do you listen to anyone?" she replied.

It wasn't just a challenge. It was a statement of fact. He didn't listen to anyone. He did what he pleased, much as he could. He shouldn't, when it came to Louisa, except she seemed to have a few of her own wants.

He…could fulfill them. She was right there. Standing within reach. Why was he trying so hard to be… noble or good or right, when literally *no one* expected anything like that of him. If he touched her, if he kissed her… It didn't have to mean…

They both jolted at the sound of a phone jangling. He watched her hands shake as she pulled her phone out of her pocket—which gratified him even when it shouldn't. She frowned.

"It's my mom. She should be in bed." She turned away from him, drawing the phone to her ear. "Mom? It's late. Is everything o—" The noise she made instead of finishing the question was one of pure anguish. "I'll be right there," she managed to say in a choked rush, already moving past Palmer.

"Lou—"

"I have to go. The house is on fire."

PALMER HAD DRIVEN HER. Louisa had been too shaken up and everyone had insisted someone else drive. Anna had sat in the back of the car, holding her hand and whispering assurances.

Everything that happened in that hallway had fallen by the wayside because her mother had been crying. *Crying.* Her mother who'd saw off her own limbs before she cried in front of Louisa—or anyone.

Louisa could see the flashing emergency lights

from the highway as Palmer pulled onto the drive that would wind around to the house. Her heart was in her throat, and everything was just…wrong.

Because the closer they got to the house, the more she could see. The house. Engulfed in big, huge flames that didn't make any sense.

She heard Anna swear next to her, but she was in a kind of fog. Everything felt cottony even as she stared at the sight before her as Palmer pulled to a stop.

The home she'd grown up in. Her father and grandfather had grown up in. Flames and black soot and a firetruck working to arc a big blast of water at the blaze while the stars and moon glittered above.

The water was too late. She could see that even not knowing anything about fire. It had taken over everything.

It was all too late.

Palmer opened the back door. When she didn't move, he held out a hand. "Come on, Lou. Let's go find your parents."

It was the word *parents* that got her moving. And Palmer's hand. It was an actionable part of this whole thing. Take Palmer's hand. Find her parents. Step by step through…whatever nightmare this was.

His hand was larger than hers and firm. He didn't let her balk at what she saw. He led her right to her parents.

Mom was still crying. Dad was pale as the moonlight. When they registered that she was there, they both moved toward her and enveloped her in a hug.

She lost Palmer's hand somewhere along the way, but her parents were holding her. Crying.

So she cried too.

"Thank God for those darn dogs," Dad said, his voice scratchy—from smoke or emotion or both. "They kept up a racket until we got out of bed to see what was the matter."

Louisa's heart felt as though it stopped for a full minute. Her parents had been asleep and a fire had started and... She hugged them tighter.

"What happened?" she managed to ask after a while, still holding them close, one arm around each parent.

"We don't know," Dad said. "We just got out and called 9-1-1."

They all surveyed the many emergency services and personnel around them. Firefighters and cops and an ambulance. Thank God no one had needed the latter.

Still, it was clear there would be nothing left of the house. Nothing left...

"We can stay at your grandparents'," Mom was saying. "We'll...rebuild." She struggled with the word, and Louisa struggled to believe in *rebuilding* in the midst of all this destruction. But the orchard itself seemed safe. It was only the house that had been affected, hopefully. It had been an unfortunate accident and her parents and their dogs had survived.

That was all that mattered.

She looked around and didn't realize she was looking for Palmer until she'd found him in the crowd. Both he and Anna stood with one of the officers, talking.

It all felt a bit like a nightmare and there was the distant hope she'd just...wake up. And it would all go away. But the firefighters continued to contain the blaze. Friends came as news spread through town and the sun began to rise. There were offers of places to stay, clothes to wear. Food.

Everyone in Sunrise would rally around them and everything would be fine. A house was just a house. Things were replaceable.

She didn't let herself think about the strange secret cubby in her father's desk, because none of that mattered anymore. She wouldn't let it. Kyla Brown and missing sisters were someone else's problem.

Her parents were her parents. Her grandfather had been acting strangely because Palmer had been with her—and as Palmer had said, people were warning him off her right and left. Palmer, who was a genius with computers, hadn't found anything. The *singular* missing hospital record was a mistake. A fluke.

This was over. She needed to call Palmer to tell him so. No doubt he and Anna had gone home at some point.

Before she could take out her phone, she saw both of them. Still there. Plus Jack and Mary. Jack and Anna were talking to some of the firefighters. Mary was talking to a small group of neighbors, and Louisa could tell even from all the way over here that she was organizing things.

Louisa wanted to simply sink into the ground and cry some more, but she knew her parents would worry.

She needed to be strong for them. And she needed to tell Palmer this was all over.

She searched the rest of the yard then saw him a ways off, filling the dogs' water dishes. Louisa swallowed at the lump in her throat. Those dogs had saved her parents' lives.

Mom and Dad were deep in a conversation with Reverend Plumber that Louisa had only been half listening to.

"I'll be right back," Louisa whispered to Mom, giving her arm a squeeze before heading toward Palmer.

He watched her approach, and she realized he'd brought food and treats for the dogs. It wasn't just that he'd been giving them water, he was taking care of them.

She was going to cry all over again.

"We'll take these guys back to the ranch for a bit until you guys get settled somewhere. Mary's organizing everything. Clothes, food, you name it. You've got the whole town behind you and your folks."

Louisa nodded. It echoed all her thoughts and, what's more, proved her point. She had a good life. Great parents. An amazing community that would rally around tragedy. Why had she been about tearing that at the foundations?

"I just wanted to let you know that I'm done," she managed to grit out, every word a fight through her tightened throat.

His expression went to confused. "What?"

"I don't want to look into the whole dumb Brown family missing sister anymore. My parents are my parents and that's that. It was foolish, and I'm done. Thank you for helping me and keeping it a secret. Really. But I was wrong."

He reached out. He put his hand on her shoulder and gave it a squeeze. "Lou, it's been a day. Let's not jump to—"

"No. I'm done. I'm *done*. It's over. The end."

He blinked and she could *feel* all the ways he didn't approve, which didn't make sense. It made her angry. Which was better than all this terrible dismay. Still, he didn't argue with her. She kind of wanted him to. She wanted to have a fight.

His hand slid down her back. Then he gave it a rub up and down. Like he was trying to calm someone hysterical.

She wasn't though. She was *done*.

"Ed's heading over to your parents. Let's go hear what he has to say, okay?"

She wanted to argue with him. Shove his hand away from her. Or she thought she should want that, but she just…let him steer her back to her parents. His hand on her back like some kind of guiding force.

Ed Connolly, the fire chief, was standing in front of her parents, and as she approached, he nodded to her and Palmer.

"I'm real sorry this happened, and that we couldn't do more to save the structure," he offered. He wasn't covered in soot, like some of his men, but his face was red like he'd done some hard physical work.

"It's all right, Ed. We know you did the best you

could," Dad said, still sounding raspy. But the EMTs had checked her parents out and said they were fine.

Louisa held on to that like a talisman.

"I appreciate that, Tim. Unfortunately, I've got a little more bad news. We're going to have to bring in a fire investigator. We don't have one in Sunrise. So we'll have to reach out to the county and go from there."

"What?" Mom and Dad said in unison.

"Why?" Louisa and Palmer asked together.

"I'm sorry, folks. But everything we saw in there makes it look like someone set this. Deliberately."

Chapter Eight

Palmer hadn't been surprised by Ed's conclusion, though he could tell Louisa and her parents were. It was just too big a fire. Too out of control too fast in the middle of all this cold and snow.

Then there was the timing. Everything had started going bad once he and Louisa had found that hidden compartment. It didn't make any sense yet, but he'd make sense of it one way or another. Whether Louisa liked it or not.

She was in danger until they got to the bottom of whatever was going on.

Unfortunately, the whole past twenty-four hours made Louisa's grandfather look guilty as sin since he'd been the one who'd caught them in the office. And, according to Louisa, had never explained why he'd been there when he'd thought the house would be empty.

Now, the night after the fire, Louisa was staying under her grandfather's roof. Palmer had tried to carefully influence Anna to convince Louisa to stay at the Hudson Ranch, but Anna had insisted Louisa should be with her family and then started questioning why he was so invested. She hadn't been exactly wrong on the family point. Louisa *should* be with her parents, no doubt. He wasn't about to touch Anna's questioning about *motive* with a million-foot pole.

So he'd tried a more direct approach—*tried* being the operative word because Louisa refused to answer his calls or respond to his texts. He understood it, to an extent. She was in the midst of emotional upheaval and didn't want any more. And since the only thing she'd wanted him for was to help her solve a mystery, she didn't need to talk to him.

Maybe that bothered him, if he thought too deeply about it, but he wasn't one for thinking deeply. He was one for *acting*. So he had to take some things into his own hands.

He wasn't delusional enough to think Louisa would ever thank him, but he knew it needed to be done. It was the right thing to do. If she wouldn't look out for herself, he would.

He did another search on both of her parents in between some research for Grant's current case. Then spent a late evening poring over Greg O'Brien's life.

When that didn't yield anything to go on, he went back to Louisa's hospital records he *could* find. Then he dug around in his own family files until he found Anna's birth and hospital records. Louisa and Anna had been born in the same year, if not the same month. Maybe comparing what information Anna's records had and Louisa's didn't would yield some kind of lightbulb moment.

At first, there was nothing really. Just his sister's

birth information. His parents' information. But tucked
into the formal records of Anna's first days was a notebook piece of paper labeled "Thank Yous." There were
about thirty names—all divided into sections—in his
mother's perfect, precise handwriting. There were tiny
checkmarks next to each name, presumably after his
mother had written and sent the thank-you letters off.

It took his breath away for a minute. Not unusual.
It didn't matter how much time had passed, there were
always sneaky and unexpected things that slipped
under all his defenses and turned him for a moment in
time back to that twelve-year-old who couldn't com-
prehend his mother wasn't coming back.

He held very still, and breathed very carefully,
waiting for the wave of pain and grief to wash through
and leave a kind of emptiness in its wake. That was
how this went. Because Mom had been gone more
than she'd been in his life, and there was nothing he
could do about it.

He read every category of names, out loud in a whisper to anchor himself to the here and now.

Family. Friends. Ranch. Doctors & Nurses.

Doctors & Nurses. They would have all worked
at the hospital, and if they'd been around for Anna's
birth, likely most had been around at the time of Louisa's too. Maybe one of them remembered something.
An explanation of why the paperwork was missing.

For good or for ill. It was a small town; even Har-
vey, where the hospital was, wasn't a thriving metrop-
olis. Maybe someone there would remember.

And if this somehow tied to slashed tires and fires…

He heard the doorknob turn and quickly slid the list of names back into the file. He didn't try to shove the file back in its place. That would look too obviously like he was trying to hide something. So he turned and tried very hard not to scowl at Jack standing there.

"What's up?" Palmer asked, doing his best to sound casual. He even tried to smile, but doubted it landed.

"Grant said you'd found everything he asked for. I was just wondering why you're still holed up in here when it's dinnertime."

Palmer shrugged. "Lost track of time, I guess."

Jack drifted closer, frowning at the closed folder on the desk. And where the filing cabinet was open to.

"Why are you looking at family stuff?"

"I was looking for something of mine, but I got distracted." He opened Anna's file, pointed at the painful and wonderful memory of his mother. "Anytime I think Mary's as meticulous as they come, I remember she got it all from Mom."

Jack's expression didn't change, but he didn't say anything for long ticking moments as he looked at the list in Mom's handwriting. Maybe his face didn't outwardly show any emotion, but Palmer had a sneaking suspicion when his brother did that very still, silent thing, he was pushing down whatever complicated emotions he *did* feel.

Jack finally looked up from the list and met Palmer's eyes. "I know you're hiding something. I don't appreciate secrets, Palmer."

Palmer struggled with a flash of temper. Maybe

it was what felt like his mother's ghost that kept him from lashing out at his brother. Maybe it was something closer to maturity. He didn't know and didn't want to examine it to find out.

Besides, this wasn't about him. It was about Louisa. He wouldn't let Jack in on that when she was so dead set against it. Particularly *now* when she didn't even want him to keep looking into this whole thing. "Let's just say, I'm not keeping my own secrets. Okay?"

He didn't expect Jack's acceptance of that. Jack wasn't known for understanding or respecting his siblings' boundaries. Jack was a demanding bulldozer.

"I suppose that's fair."

"You do?"

Jack scowled. "Dinner is ready. Come eat. You can deal with whatever this is later."

Palmer was very reluctant to leave it be. He wanted to press on, but his older brother's goodwill would only extend so far. So he left the file where it was and followed Jack to the dining room. Grant was helping Mary put food on the table while Dahlia and Anna chatted in low tones. He could hear Cash and Izzy coming in through the back, stomping off snow, the dogs yipping in excitement behind them.

They all gathered around the table, just like they would have done when they were kids. When Dad sat where Jack took his seat. When Mom was the one serving dinner. Before Grant had gone to war or Izzy had been born. A lifetime ago, and Palmer missed it. He did.

But in this strange moment, looking back in time

for Louisa, knowing she'd just lost every material thing, he was grateful. So grateful his family had somehow weathered the storms and could come to eat dinner together. Night after night.

He was lucky, in a lot of ways.

So he ate dinner with his family, and he enjoyed it. He let himself be present. Laugh and eat. Clean up afterward with Cash and Izzy. Tease and enjoy his niece who would be a teenager the next time he damn well blinked.

He'd been thinking about getting older lately, but this solidified something inside him. Not just that he wasn't precisely *young* anymore, but that he really needed to figure out what was next. What he wanted out of his life. Coasting could only get a man so far, and he'd coasted long enough.

He sat in his office later that night, setting about to track down all the doctors and nurses who might know something about Louisa's birth. Determined to find answers for her.

And figure out some answers when it came to Louisa O'Brien for himself.

Louisa spent the days after the fire running herself ragged to help her parents in whatever way she could. She struggled to sleep in her grandparents' little house in town. She struggled to force herself to eat. So she kept herself busy. She kept herself focused.

When Mary and Anna encouraged her to take a break, she refused. When Palmer called and texted... she ignored it.

She just...didn't want to deal with him. She could fall apart in front of Anna or Mary without feeling embarrassed. Without feeling raw. They were her friends. They'd been through everything together.

Palmer was just...the man she'd trusted with a really personal secret. She could not for the life of her face him until she felt less like a dandelion that had been blown to hell.

She drove up to her grandparents' house after running to the pharmacy for her dad. It had been an emotional gauntlet of everyone she passed or interacted with wanting to wish her and her family well. To tell her how terrible it was, but how resilient they'd be and rebuild.

She knew that. She didn't need anyone to tell her. She *knew* everyone was just trying to be nice, to help and offer words of encouragement, but she wanted to cover her ears and run away.

Instead she'd smiled and issued thank-yous and somehow collected her father's blood pressure medication and then driven back to her grandparents' house. When she parked her car, she just sat there for a moment. There was a pickup with the fire department logo on it—Ed the fire chief's. Next to it, a slick sedan that she didn't recognize.

She sat there. Still gripping the steering wheel even though her truck was in Park. She forced herself to breathe slowly, in and out. She'd handle whatever this was. She had to.

For her family.

So, she got out and headed in, her father's prescription in her purse. When she stepped inside, she heard voices in the living room and turned toward them.

Arranged in her grandparents' cramped gathering room was her parents, both Grandma and Grandpa, Ed and a man she didn't know, no doubt the owner of that car outside. The man wore a suit and looked…cruel. She didn't know why that descriptor popped into her head, but the perception of him made her pause in the entrance to the living room.

Dad waved her in, and Mom pointed to her. "This is our daughter. She also lives in the house."

The man's cold gaze turned to her and he offered her a nod. "Ma'am. I'm Investigator Steele. I have a few questions for you and your family."

"Of course," Louisa acknowledged. There was no-where left to sit, so she stood where she was in the entry.

"Is there any reason you have to believe someone might wish your family harm?" the investigator asked of no one in particular. Like he was testing to see who would answer.

She thought of Palmer. Grandpa's strange behavior. The Facebook messages from Kyla Brown.

All. Your. Fault.

"I can't think of a single person who'd want to hurt us," Mom said firmly.

"Maybe business competition?" Mr. Steele offered.

"We don't really have much competition around here," Dad returned, looking pale and white and *un-well*. "We're all too spread out."

The investigator made a little note on his pad. He

looked up at her. Louisa felt like there was a big red word stamped across her face: *guilty*.

"I can't think of a single person," she managed to croak. "The town has rallied around us. Helped in every way they can. Mom and Dad are involved in the community and are always helping people. We hold community events at the orchard, and we've never had problems bigger than a teenage tussle or someone sneaking off with someone they shouldn't and getting caught—which never had anything to do with *us*. If someone set that fire on purpose, it must have been some kind of misunderstanding."

"That's quite a speech," the investigator said. The remark *felt* sarcastic, but there was really no inflection to how he said the words.

"Louisa? Is that Palmer's truck?" Mom pointed out the window where Palmer's pickup was indeed pulling into the driveway.

"I think so."

"Must have gotten his tires fixed then," Dad commented. "Why don't you go out and tell him we're a bit busy with Mr. Steele here."

Louisa nodded even though she didn't want to deal with Palmer. She also didn't want to deal with the way the investigator was staring at her. She turned and went back outside.

She hesitated on the porch. There had to be some way to get rid of him without having to have a private conversation. If she stayed this close to the porch, maybe she could just say they were busy.

He got out of his truck. He had his cowboy hat on,

and his expression was grim. Apparently, he hadn't taken her ignoring his calls or texts too well. Still, he looked handsome and capable in the afternoon sun, and there was some small part of her that wanted to run to him and lay it all on his shoulders.

The door behind her opened and the investigator stepped out, reminding her of all the ways that wasn't an option.

"Boyfriend?"

She looked up at the investigator, eyebrows drawn together. It didn't sound in the least bit flirtatious, but how exactly would that relate to an investigation? "Just a friend. Why?"

Mr. Steele shrugged. "You never know who might take thwarted feelings out on somebody."

Louisa felt her cheeks heat. "There are no…thwarted feelings." She thought about what Palmer had said at the bar, that moment in the Hudson hallway before everything had fallen apart. Where she'd thought… maybe he didn't look at her and see a little kid at *all*.

That didn't matter now. The investigator was jotting something down on his notebook page as Palmer crossed the yard. When Mr. Steele finished writing, he looked at her and he smiled. He didn't seem *quite* so cruel when he smiled, but she still had an incredibly *off* feeling about this man.

Still, politeness was so deeply ingrained in her, she smiled back. "Thank you for everything you're doing to get to the bottom of this, Mr. Steele. My family appreciates it."

He nodded then handed her a business card he

pulled from the back of his notebook. "If you think of anything or anyone who might have something to prove, just give me a call. Either way, I'll be getting to the bottom of things."

His delivery was so dry, so devoid of anything resembling inflection, she didn't know if that was some kind of attempt at comfort or a threat.

He walked away. Down the porch stairs and toward his car. He didn't say anything to Palmer as they crossed paths. Just nodded. Palmer nodded back with a puzzled expression on his face.

When he reached her, he didn't crest the stairs. He stood at the bottom and looked up at her. "Who was that?"

Chapter Nine

Palmer did not recognize the hot, angry ball of emotion sitting in his chest. It had popped up when the fancy suit had smiled down at Louisa.

And she'd smiled back.

Now it sat there, an uncomfortable burning sensation that he didn't know what to do with, but knew he needed to keep it to himself.

"The fire investigator," Louisa finally said, her eyes on the man as he got in his car and then reversed out of the driveway.

Palmer tried very hard not to scowl, because he had a very sinking feeling the emotion assailing him was *jealousy*. When he'd never been jealous a day in his life and had no reason to start now. He'd just promised himself to behave maturely, not get all caveman over a woman who wasn't even involved with him.

Much as you'd like to change that.

He scowled at the voice in his head. So, maybe he would. Didn't mean now was the time. Or that Louisa wanted anything to do with him. Oh, sure, she'd made it clear in that hallway and a few times over the past year she was *attracted*.

Attracted didn't mean much when a man had the reputation he did. Didn't matter what had come over him in the past few days, maturity or some kind of head injury, if he was even considering something with Louisa, it would not be the same kind of one-night stand he was used to.

Not only because he was pretty sure eighty-five percent of the town would conspire to murder him.

"Should an investigator be hitting on one of the victims?" Okay, that was not a mature or reasonable way to conduct himself. Maybe he was a lost cause.

"He wasn't hitting on me," she replied. Then her eyebrows drew together and her nose kind of scrunched up. "I don't think."

"You don't *think*?"

"Well, he asked me if you were my boyfriend. Then said something about thwarted feelings could cause people to set fires or something, which makes sense. It was just the way he asked was…weird."

Weird. Palmer looked darkly back at where the man had been…in his nice suit and fancy car. Now both gone. He turned to Louisa, arms crossed over his chest, trying so very hard to keep his voice even. "What did you say?"

"About what?"

"About me being your boyfriend?"

"That you're just a friend. You know, since you're *not* my boyfriend," she replied sharply even as her cheeks darkened toward pink.

Palmer shrugged. "I just meant because your grandpa caught us together at the house and I don't think he was buying either of our stories."

"No, but…" She blew out a breath. "He'll…figure it out. Whatever this is. Regardless of us. I know we didn't start any fires." As if it reminded her, she looked up at him. "Your tires are fixed. Any leads on that?"

He shook his head and thought about telling her to tell the investigator about it, and how he thought they might connect somehow. But he was an investigator in his own right and so was his brother. This arson guy didn't need to know everything until Palmer knew he was trustworthy enough to do the right thing with any information.

"What's the guy's name?"

She rolled her eyes. "Palmer, this is none of your business. I don't know why you're here but——"

"I'll get it out of somebody. You might as well tell me."

She huffed a breath but handed him the business card. He studied the print: Hawk Steele. Fire & Arson Investigator. Bent County, Wyoming. Palmer looked at Louisa. "That's not his real name."

"Ed seems to know him. I don't think he's a fake, Palmer. I certainly don't know why he'd have reason to lie about any of it." She held her hand out for the card, so he returned it.

He'd be looking into *Hawk Steele*, that was for sure.

For right now, it was just him and Louisa—her on the porch, him still at the staircase landing. She didn't look directly at him, instead scowling into the distance.

She didn't tell him to go or ask him why he was here. She just stood there, so he went ahead and took the stairs he hadn't stepped up when he'd arrived. She looked at him and there was a flash of something— something soft and vulnerable—before she blinked it all away.

He reached out and touched her face. Because she was building up those walls, brick by brick. Keeping everyone out while she fell apart on the inside. He knew all the signs. He'd been doing it most of his life. Her cheek was soft, and she jolted when he dragged his thumb across her cheekbone. "You're looking rough, Lou."

She jerked her face away. "Gee, thanks," she said, slapping at his hand.

"Don't be vain, now. You've been through the wringer and you're not giving yourself a break. Why don't you let someone take care of you?"

Why did he want it to be him?

"The whole town is taking care of us." She took a step away and crossed her arms over her chest like she was warding him off.

"I said *you*," Palmer replied. "You're taking care of your parents, holding it together for them, and you're not letting yourself fall apart."

She looked up at him, and her expression was all defiance, but tears glittered in those mesmerizing green eyes. "I have, in fact, cried on both your sisters' shoulders, thank you."

"Well, good." And it didn't matter that he wanted it to be *his* shoulder. That wasn't what this was about. Or not only.

"The fact of the matter is this investigator complicates things. Maybe this fire and my tires don't connect. Maybe none of it has to do with those messages from Kyla Brown about her missing sister. But even if they don't, he's bound to stumble across them. Poke at them and see if they do."

"Are you trying to make all this worse?" she asked. So frustrated. So close to her breaking point, but it was only because she was trying so hard to compartmentalize. To keep all these little pieces separate and within her control.

He knew. He understood. As much as he'd like to be able to let her do that, he knew it didn't help anyone. He *knew* her. Whether either of them liked it or not. She needed answers, no matter how she tried to tell herself she didn't.

"No, I don't want to make anything worse for you, Lou. I'm trying to tell you we need to figure it out first. I know you… No matter what the truth is, you love your parents. You want to protect them. So let's get to the bottom of this so we can figure out *how*."

LOUISA HAD BEEN certain she was done. She was leaving questions of her parentage behind. Maybe it had been the trauma of the fire talking, but she'd promised herself. Because her parents had survived and not been *burned alive*, and nothing else mattered.

Nothing.

Now Palmer was putting a different perspective on the whole thing. That finding answers might be required to protect her parents.

She didn't want to cry in front of him. She didn't want to cry. There'd been enough of that. She wanted to bury her head in the sand, take care of her parents and forget literally everything else, including the fire.

"I can't…"

He shook his head and didn't let her finish. "We can. We will."

We. Because she'd asked him for his help. She'd known…there wasn't a Hudson who'd give up. Who'd let her handle this on her own. In all their own ways, they would have helped because it was who they were.

But she'd only been able to really fathom asking Palmer for help, and even now she didn't know exactly why that was. It was more than some crush she'd had since she was thirteen. It was all those feelings that had twisted and dug deep and grown roots over the course of the past few years, and these past few months especially.

He'd touched her face. He'd told her he knew too many things about her, and maybe he'd never come out and said specifically he didn't think of her as a kid, she knew he didn't.

Something had changed.

She didn't know what he was doing *here.* Touching *her* and being all nice. This wasn't his usual thing. Sweetness and out-of-his-way help. Palmer wasn't selfish, exactly, but he didn't extend an effort for anyone unless he really wanted to.

Sure, he had obligation drilled into him because he was a Hudson. But Palmer was just…different. A little bit more willing to buck the trend. Not a fan of martyring himself like his brothers were.

He'd said it himself at the bar, that he didn't like to be around her. Even if that had to do with…other things, *attraction* things if she had to name it, he was going against what he liked…for her.

"Go tell your parents I'm taking you for a drive so you can clear your head. I've got some potential leads we can talk about."

She didn't even bristle at him telling her what to do. That's how tired and brittle she felt. "You take me for a drive, they're going to think things."

He didn't even flinch. Just held her gaze, his dark eyes steady on her. "Yeah, I know."

She tried to ignore the fluttering of her heart, because… Well, a lot of becauses. "I seem to recall that bothering you. Deeply."

He didn't say anything. He in fact let the silence stretch out, which had always been Palmer's greatest strength. He didn't need to fill a silence.

She desperately *wanted* to. So much, she was doing everything she could not to fidget, down to biting her tongue. She'd spoken last. It was *his* turn.

"I can go in and tell them, if you want," he said after that long, long silence.

She scowled at him. "I don't appreciate your high-handedness, Palmer," she said as haughtily as she could manage. Bickering with him was making her feel a *little* steadier though. Almost as if he'd planned it.

His mouth curved, ever so slightly. "I'm not so sure about that, Lou."

Unfortunately, neither was she. So she whirled around and marched herself inside. Her parents were still talking with Ed, so she decided to just tell her grandmother. It'd be easier anyway.

She hoped.

"With Palmer," Grandma said, frowning after Louisa had told her. "A drive?"

"Just to kind of clear my head." She tried to smile at her grandmother, but it faltered.

Grandma's frown turned into a full-on, narrowed-eyes scowl. "Do you think I was born yesterday, young lady?"

"Wh…what?"

"You don't think I ever went for a *drive* with your grandfather." She put the word *drive* in air quotes and Louisa's face immediately heated. For *so many* reasons.

"Please don't say that."

"What? You think your father was delivered by stork?"

"Oh, my *God*, Grandma. Please don't."

"All I'm saying is any young woman getting in a car with Palmer Hudson to *clear their head* better know how to protect themselves."

"'Bye, Grandma." Louisa turned away. Good Lord. She was twenty-four years old and, as aware as she was that parents and grandparents…did things, it didn't mean she ever wanted to discuss it with them.

Ever.

She launched herself outside, causing Palmer's placid expression to go questioning. "You okay?"

She nodded. Too hard, as she started for his truck. Then she shook her head because it was ridiculous. Her reaction. The whole thing. "I think my grandma just gave me *the talk.*"

Palmer, appropriately, shuddered as he came to walk beside her. "Please don't give me flashbacks."

"But…" She didn't want to come out and say all the grandparents in his life had died young, and before his parents had disappeared. He knew all that.

"Every elderly woman decided to be our honorary grandmother after Mom and Dad disappeared. The one thing people seem to remember when you don't have parents is to make sure to awkwardly lecture you about safe sex. Jack. Cash, since he considered himself a great expert, having gotten Chessa pregnant. Mrs. Riley. Mrs. Sanders. Coach Albright."

"No."

"Oh, yes. There's probably more that I've blocked out."

He opened the passenger's-side door of the pickup for her, and she'd give him, or maybe her grandmother, credit. She'd forgotten about everything to do with the fire and her parentage for the past five minutes.

But now it all came crashing back. Because the tires to this pickup had been slashed. And the only reason she was in a truck with Palmer was that she had asked him for help. And him not backing off when she'd asked him to.

Louisa wanted to be mad about it, but she just…

couldn't be as he climbed into the driver's seat. Palmer cared. Maybe it wasn't clear, to either of them, just *what* he cared about, but he cared.

And, as much as she hated to admit it, having Palmer drive her away from her grandparents' house was like taking a full breath for the first time since her mother had called her. She was being crushed from the inside out trying to keep it all together for her parents and...

Palmer reached across the center console and wrapped his fingers around hers. He squeezed her hand, his eyes still on the road. She looked down at his hand covering hers. His was big, rough. Very scarred—no doubt from ranch work and the rodeo. Maybe even those reckless football years. That was the thing about Palmer, he'd always been reckless. Flinging himself into just about anything.

Maybe that was why she'd fallen in love with him when she'd been still a girl. Why she couldn't get rid of the feelings now that she was an adult. She knew it wasn't exactly courage that had sent him punishing his body in different ways over the years. It was probably a lot of unresolved trauma, in fact.

But he wasn't *afraid*. And she had been. She'd always had the nice parents. The parents everyone wished they'd had. Wanting different for herself than they'd wanted for her had been hard. Going to college out east had been a leap into the unknown.

Because Palmer had showed her that you could, and that you could learn something from it, and the people who loved you didn't stop, even when you did something outside of the box.

She curled her own fingers around his. So that they were holding hands. A unit against whatever was out there slashing tires and setting fires. He was helping her, no matter what the truth about where she'd come from was.

Not too long ago, she'd sworn she'd rather cut off her own tongue than ever confess her feelings toward him. Not attraction, but the actual *feelings*. In this moment, she wondered if it would really be such a tragedy to tell him. "Palmer…"

Before she could find the words, something in him hardened. "Looks like we're being followed."

Chapter Ten

At first, when Palmer had noticed the nondescript sedan keeping pace on the highway, he'd wondered if it was a coincidence, or if someone was looking out for Louisa. If her grandmother had thought this was some kind of event that had necessitated a sex talk, maybe other people would too. It was a small town and people were nosy.

So, he'd taken a few strange turns. Back roads and scenic byways that no one would be following *accidentally*. Only purposefully.

And the sedan was still there. It was a Wyoming plate, but he didn't recognize the car and, no matter how he slowed, the car wouldn't get close enough for him to get a good view of the driver.

"Can you read that plate?" he asked Louisa. He dropped her hand so he could take a quick turn. At first, he'd had no destination in mind, but now he was starting to formulate a plan.

Louisa twisted in her seat and looked behind them. "No, it's too far away."

"Okay, text this to Anna." He waited for her to get

her phone out of her pocket. "Got a tail. Gray Toyota Camry. Maybe a 2010 model or around there. One driver, can't make out plate except it's Wyoming. Going to lead them to Dead Man's Bluff."

Louisa quickly typed that into her phone then looked over at him. "You know, weirdly, I don't want to lead anyone anywhere near *Dead Man's* Bluff. It was fun and thrilling when I was fifteen, but these days *dead man* just feels like a threat."

"If the person following isn't local, it'll give us the advantage. We know the parking, the trailheads, the terrain. They won't," Palmer replied, turning off for the dirt patch locals considered a parking lot for the difficult hike. And that was in the summer when it wasn't packed with snow.

"And if they *are* local?" Louisa demanded as he pulled to a stop.

Palmer shrugged. "I don't recognize the car. Seems far less likely."

"So the plan is to what? Park here?"

She was sounding close to panic, so he kept himself very calm and utilized his usual careless demeanor— even if he'd never be careless with Louisa. "No, we'll get out." He turned off the ignition, studied her clothes. She was dressed for winter, and while neither of them was prepared for a long hike in the freezing temperatures, they'd be all right for a while.

"We'll hike over to the lookout. Pretend we're…" He watched her wait for whatever word was next, and the more he waited, the redder her cheeks got.

Now was really not the time to find any sort of enjoyment out of that, but he was certainly not a saint, even if he had decided to step into maturity. "Talking," he eventually finished.

She narrowed her eyes at him but did not speak.

"We'll see what they do. Chances are, they'll drive on by. But they'll have to turn around once they get to the dead end." Palmer checked his watch. "It'll hopefully give Anna enough time to drive out this way, maybe spot the sedan and get a plate. Jack'll run it, then we'll know what's up."

"And if they don't drive right on by but stop?"

Palmer shrugged. "We'll play it by ear."

"Isn't that dangerous?"

He reached over and unlocked the glove compartment. He pulled out his holstered gun. He didn't always keep it there, but ever since his tires had been slashed, he'd figured it was smart. "Not as dangerous as you'd think." With that, he got out of the truck and into the cold.

The temperatures were likely hovering near zero all the way up here. He hooked the holster to his belt and then pulled his coat back down over it so whoever was following them might not be able to tell he was carrying.

He skirted the bed of the pickup and went over to Louisa's side. She'd opened the door but hadn't stepped down yet. "I'm pretty sure that's a sheet of pure ice," she said, pointing to the ground below.

"Here." He moved close as he could without sliding on the patch of ice himself. He held out his arms. "Jump."

"You're out of your mind," Louisa replied.

"I'll catch you, and then you won't slip and bust your head open."

"You'll drop me and we'll likely *both* bust our heads open."

"Ye of little faith." He held out his hands again. "I used to stay on my feet with three-hundred-pound linebackers running into me."

"Yeah, that was ten years ago. You're old now."

"Louisa, I swear to God."

"Fine," she muttered. She didn't look certain, but she perched herself on the truck's running board, then reached out. Instead of jumping, she crouched and reached out until her hands were on his shoulders.

Then she kind of leaned herself into him, and he caught her weight as she wrapped arms and legs around him—clearly desperately afraid he'd drop her or topple over. He had no problem keeping his balance though.

Absolutely *no* problem having her wrapped around him like this.

It wasn't the time. Maybe never was the time. But he'd like to keep holding her just like this. Right here. Just the two of them.

He heard the faint sound of an engine. Whoever was following them was getting close. So he sighed, moved back a few steps, then let her down on safer, less slick ground.

She didn't pull her arms from around his shoulders, and he didn't take his hands off her hips. In the bright winter afternoon, they stood there and looked at each other. Much like they had in that hallway just a few nights ago.

Palmer was well aware he should say something. Confess *any* of the feelings he had, yet his throat felt dry. He usually knew how to throw himself headfirst into just about anything, but this?

"They're pulling in," she said softly the second before her gaze left his and went to some point behind him.

Palmer turned slowly, sliding his arm around Louisa's waist. He'd keep playing the role of two lovers who'd gone on a drive for a little privacy. Even if it didn't feel so much like *playing* right now.

As he turned, he sighed heavily as he recognized the man behind the wheel.

"It's the fire investigator," Louisa said.

So Palmer went ahead and swore.

LOUISA DIDN'T KNOW why the sight of Hawk Steele made her more nervous than some nameless stranger, but her stomach tied itself in knots. Why on earth had he followed them? And he'd changed cars.

None of it felt good or right. Surely this wasn't procedure. Louisa was just enough worried about this man that when Palmer angled his body in front of hers, like he was protecting her from Mr. Steele, she let him.

"Mr. Hudson," the fire investigator said. "I just need to ask you a few questions."

"So you *followed us here*? In a different car than you had before?"

Mr. Steele took his sweet time to look from Palmer

over to her, still almost hidden behind Palmer's tall, broad frame. "Yes."

"Why on earth do you need him to answer any questions?" Louisa demanded before Palmer said anything. Because this was ludicrous. Palmer didn't have anything to do with this.

The man's blue fathomless gaze held hers. "Matter of course," he said without inflection.

Louisa stepped forward, ready to push Palmer out of the way and face this man herself. He made her *that* furious. Palmer's hand that had stayed on her held her firm.

"It's all right, Lou," Palmer said. He tucked his hands into his coat pockets and he rocked back on his heels with that devil-may-care grin he usually only trotted out when he was trying to piss off Jack. "Ask away, bud."

There was the flicker of something in the man's expression. No doubt irritation. No doubt what Palmer was going for. Because Palmer would always rather poke a bear than find a rational, reasonable way to deal with it.

Louisa wasn't going to let that happen right now. Not when this investigator had absolutely no earthly reason to question *Palmer* over a fire he had nothing to do with.

"We're not doing this here," Louisa said firmly to Mr. Steele. "It's no place for questions, and it was highly unethical for you to follow us here."

"Lou," Palmer said under his breath, but she turned on him.

"No, it's ridiculous. It's freezing and we're in the middle of nowhere." She glared at the investigator. "If you want to ask him questions, we'll meet you back at Hudson Ranch."

"'We'?" the investigator repeated. As a question.

Louisa wasn't sure if anything could have angered her more. She fixed him with her best death stare. "Yeah. *We*." She whirled around and marched for Palmer's truck.

She didn't look to see if Palmer followed. Wasn't sure she'd be able to face either of them if she'd stormed off alone like a child throwing a tantrum.

But she heard the crunch of boots on snow. Palmer following her, no doubt.

Mr. Steele called out after her, "Don't worry. I'll be right behind you."

She climbed into the pickup, probably looking ridiculous avoiding the ice, and trying desperately not to think of the way Palmer had held her as he'd helped her out earlier. Because she couldn't do it *all*. Protect Palmer, and want Palmer, and hate that investigator all while her mind reeled with why any of this was happening.

She settled herself into her seat as the driver's-side door opened and Palmer hopped in, easy and graceful and with none of the scrambling she'd done.

"Should have let me help you up, Lou," he said, and it was meant to be provocative. A memory.

But she was too mad at him. "Why did you have to put on the lazy, ne'er-do-well cowboy act?" she demanded as he started his truck. "Can't you think something through for once?"

"I think plenty of things through when it comes to you, Louisa," he said, holding her angry gaze.

She couldn't tell *how* that comment was pointed, only that it was. It made her feel that obnoxious embarrassing warmth in her cheeks.

"There's no reason he should question you."

Palmer shook his head and turned his attention to pulling out of the parking lot. "He considers me a suspect."

Louisa slumped back in her seat, crossing her arms over her chest. "That's ridiculous."

"Ridiculous or not, it's what he thinks. I would have preferred answering his insulting questions on top of a mountain."

"Why? So you two could end up grappling and see who could throw the other one off the mountain?"

He shot her a quick grin. "Fantasizing about it?"

She could honestly reach over and strangle him. "I do not understand how you can be so casual or cavalier when that man suspects you of setting a fire."

"I didn't set it. If I didn't sct it, he can't find evidence to prove I did. So what's there to worry about? Why not ruffle his feathers…or grapple in a snowbank?"

She *supposed* he had a point, even if she didn't like it. She glanced in the rearview mirror as the small car followed them down the twisty roads back toward Sunrise and the Hudson Ranch. Nothing about this felt right.

"Why did he switch cars, Palmer?" she asked,

leaning her forehead against the cold window. Outside, everything was white. Christmas was barreling up on them and everything was just *wrong*.

"I don't know," he said, and finally he sounded like he was taking this seriously. "Can't say as I like it, but there's this great thing about being an investigator myself. I can look into Hawk Steele, which I'm willing to bet a hundred dollars isn't his real name."

Louisa considered. She thought there was something fishy about the man, but he did seem to know Ed and have an official Bent County business card.

"I'll take that bet."

He shrugged. "Your loss, Lou." He pulled off the highway and onto the long drive that lead up to the Hudson residence. The humor and ease that was so *Palmer* tightened into something else there on his face. He didn't look at her as he pulled to a stop in front of the house. "Maybe Anna should drive you home."

"Why on earth would I go home?"

"Why would you stay?" Now he did turn to look at her, to pin her with that dark, serious gaze that made her heart flutter. Because this was new. He never used to look at her this way. In fact, she was pretty sure he *used* to make every effort not to.

"This man is investigating a fire that happened at *my* house. I was *with you* when I got the call it happened. When your tires were slashed. If he thinks you have anything to do with it, clearly, I'm the person to prove you don't. Besides, I need to be here to make sure that you don't do your *Palmer* thing and try to make things worse for yourself."

"Is that what I do?"

"Yes, Palmer. That is what you do. Believe it or not, I get it. But *now* is not the time."

"You get it, huh?"

I get you. "Come on," she said, and she pushed her door open, hopping out onto the gravel that had been cleared of snow. Mr. Steele was already out of his car, squinting against the bright sun as he surveyed the ranch around them.

When Palmer came to meet him, Mr. Steele gave a short nod. "Some spread," he offered, eyeing the ranch with cool detachment.

"That's Wyoming for you." Palmer sighed. "Well, you both might as well come on inside. I'm sure Mary's got some coffee or hot cocoa at the ready."

Chapter Eleven

Palmer didn't often believe in being hospitable, though it was a trait his mother had held in high esteem—which again made him think of Mary, who seemed to be doing everything in her power to become a carbon copy of Mom.

So much so that if Palmer had any time to worry about someone besides Louisa, he might worry a little bit about her.

Fires came first. And Hawk Steele was part of that.

Palmer held the door open for him then stepped inside himself, putting a buffer between the man and Louisa. She seemed to think he was green enough to run his mouth to incite the investigator, and maybe he was. But he wasn't going to do anything to hurt Louisa.

Palmer pointed down the hallway and into the big living room that they often held client meetings in. "We can take a seat in here."

Palmer let the investigator lead the way then followed so he could keep that buffer up between Mr. Steele and Louisa. Mr. Steele stopped at the entrance to the room and studied it.

"Make yourself comfortable," Palmer offered, pointing at the couch.

Mr. Steele glanced at the couch, but he didn't immediately sit. He seemed to be waiting for them to.

Palmer could play all the little power games. He was an investigator too.

Of things a lot more complex than arson.

Anna swept in, yelling at someone behind her, presumably Mary. The unreadable fire investigator stopped dead when he saw Anna. He looked at her like she was some kind of a ghost. When Palmer turned to look at his sister, her expression in return was nothing quite so shell-shocked. It was more of a smirk.

No one spoke, but there was *clearly* some kind of unsaid conversation going on between Anna and Mr. Steele.

"Do you two know each other?" Louisa asked, sounding skeptical and surprised.

Anna looked at Mr. Steele. Then at Palmer. The smirk didn't change. "You could say that."

Palmer did not groan, mostly because he knew that's what Anna expected him to do. Because it was clear, Anna had slept with the man who currently wanted to pin him for a fire he'd had nothing to do with.

Mr. Steele finally recovered, no longer looking at Anna but instead surveying the room. "Is there somewhere I can ask you questions in private, Mr. Hudson?"

"It doesn't need to be private, Mr. Steele," Louisa said firmly.

"You're not in charge of this investigation, *Miss* O'Brien."

"We can talk here," Palmer said before Louisa engaged in any more arguing with Mr. Steele. "Louisa, you should let your parents know you're here. Anna, she hasn't eaten all day."

"You don't know—"

He merely raised an eyebrow and her protest turned into a scowl. Because it didn't take being there or being particularly perceptive to know she wasn't taking care of herself.

"Oh, hell, Louisa," Anna muttered. "Come on."

"I'm fine," Louisa countered, but she let Anna lead her away with only one dirty look over her shoulder at Palmer.

He waited until he knew they were fully out of earshot and noted Mr. Steele did the same.

"Not sure we needed privacy when all you're going to do is ask me my whereabouts, probably ask about the police report the same night of the fire and, hmm, the nature of my relationship with Louisa and the O'Briens."

Steele didn't give away any reaction. He stood perfectly still, inspecting Palmer with that cool gaze.

"We can start there," he said after a long stretch of silence.

Palmer grinned, because he knew. He *knew* exactly what would be asked of him. And how little it mattered. "I was at the Lariat starting around eight the night of the fire. Then Louisa and Anna happened to come in around eight thirty or nine, I don't recall exactly. My sister, the one you seem to know, noticed my tires were low, so she mentioned it. She hadn't seen they were slashed, but I went out to leave and, once I did, and saw what had happened, I called the police."

"Your brother."

"No, I called the Sunrise Police Department non-emergency line," Palmer returned. He could try to be as cool as the man in front of him, but he'd never been any good at pretending anything except to be an exaggerated version of himself. It wasn't cool or terse or like Jack or Grant. It was smiles, charm and a total disregard for what anyone thought.

Luckily, he truly didn't care what anyone thought—so long as Steele got to work investigating the right thing. The longer this took, the longer Steele wasn't looking at the right person.

So he went through the rest of the night with the investigator. The officers who responded. Making Anna giving him a ride back and Louisa coming with them. The phone call that led him to drive her and Anna out to the O'Brien orchard.

The man took notes. When Palmer tried to get a glimpse at them, he saw they were written in some kind of precise shorthand. He couldn't explain why that irritated him, except everything about this man did.

And since he did, he decided to see if he could get under the man's frosty demeanor. "You make it a habit of sleeping with young women you don't have any business touching?"

Steele didn't so much as flinch, but the harsh line

of his mouth hardened. Still, his tone was as even as it ever was as he put a careful period at the end of the incomprehensible sentence he'd just written. He raised his gaze to Palmer's. "Do you?"

"Right. The third line of questioning." Palmer tapped his temple like he was on to Steele's line of questioning, because he was. Maybe Steele was good at his job, but so was Palmer. He'd been investigating things since he'd been twelve years old. "Louisa and I have always been friends. She was practically a member of the family when her and Anna were kids. We've always been friendly, but not romantic. I suppose we've had our disagreements over the years, but nothing serious. There's yet to be any more to that story."

"Yet?"

"That's what I said. I had nothing to do with the fire, Steele, and there's no evidence to even begin to believe I did. So why don't you stop trying to wriggle me into this little problem and focus on the real problem, which is the O'Brien fire."

"I know what *all* the real problems are, thanks."

"Do they involve Anna?"

There was a flash of reaction, but it was so quickly schooled away, Palmer wondered if he'd imagined it. "What happened between me and your sister is none of your business."

"Yeah, funny. That doesn't fly for me, bud."

"I don't really care if it does."

"You don't have sisters. Do you?"

"I don't have anyone. I can tell you this. I have no doubt your sister can take care of herself *just* fine.

Now, if you'll excuse me, now that I've followed this line of questioning, which was a necessary and an important part of my official, *legal* investigation, I have all those problems you mentioned to solve."

There was a slight hesitation, the briefest flicker of a glance back to where Anna and Louisa had disappeared and then almost an imperceptible shake of his head. "I'll be in touch," he muttered before stalking out of the room.

Louisa sat at the Hudson dining room table, her two oldest friends watching her as she ate a sandwich Mary had insisted on making. Louisa didn't want to eat it, but she did because they were watching to make sure she chewed and swallowed every bite.

"So," Louisa said, hoping that maybe if she got them distracted, half of the sandwich would be enough to satisfy them. "Exactly how did you end up sleeping with Bent County's fire investigator?"

Mary's eyes widened and she turned to Anna, who shrugged lazily. "Well. I was over in Bent following a lead on one of my private investigation cases, stopped in at Rightful Claim for a drink. He hit on me. One thing led to another." She gave a little shrug.

"You didn't mention any hookups to me."

Anna shrugged again. "Maybe it didn't bear mentioning."

But Louisa knew her friend well enough to know just about *everything* bore mentioning. Unless something about it had bothered her.

"He seemed pretty shocked to see you here, and

that's about the only emotion I've seen on his face," Louisa said, watching Anna's carefully blanked expression.

Mary leaned over and pushed the plate closer to Louisa. On a sigh, Louisa took another bite.

"Well, we didn't exactly exchange last names, Louisa. Or details."

Mary wrinkled her nose. "Anna. Anonymous hookups. Really?"

Anna only grinned. "Have you *seen* him?"

Mary shook her head in despair, and Louisa rolled her eyes. "*You* didn't seem surprised to see *him*," Louisa pointed out.

"I'm a private investigator. Just because we didn't exchange information doesn't mean I didn't *have* information. Besides, with a name like *Hawk,* it was pretty easy to find some details." Anna grinned at her sister. *"After."*

"Heaven help me," Mary muttered. "Let's put… *that* aside. Why is he asking Palmer, of all people, questions?"

"I don't know," Louisa returned. "Palmer came over while he was talking to my parents. Mr. Steele asked if he was my boyfriend. I said no, but I think he was banking on the fire being some kind of relationship quarrel."

"I guess it makes sense," Anna said. "If he has absolutely no leads, he's got to poke into everything. Palmer's been hanging around."

As if speaking his name conjured him, Palmer walked into the dining room. Without the investigator.

"Well?" Louisa demanded.

"Well. He asked his questions. I answered them. He left." Palmer shrugged negligently. "I didn't do anything, so it hardly matters."

"But why would he even think you did?" Anna demanded.

Palmer seemed to mull this over. "I'm not sure he did. I think he's just trying to get a clear picture of all the players."

"Since when are you a player in a fire?"

"It's the tire slashing and the police report, where you and Louisa were both there, right before the fire. If he's any good, and I hope like hell he is, he's trying to find a connection."

Louisa's stomach tied into a hard knot. A *connection* between those two things could only be what she and Palmer had been investigating, and if that were true…

Louisa stood abruptly. "I should go back to my grandparents' house."

"I'll—"

"I'll take her back," Palmer interjected over Anna's offer. "I was the one who brought her here."

"Yeah, what was that about?"

"I didn't want Agent Rabbit Rusty Iron there upsetting her family any more than he already had."

"Why were you together in the first place?"

"Because we were," Palmer said, because apparently he wanted to make this a *deal*. Likely as some sort of brotherly payback for having to know she'd slept with the fire investigator.

"You have a client coming in fifteen minutes, Anna," Mary said quietly. "You wouldn't be able to drive her anyway. And I want to go over the discrepancies in the books before you meet with him."

"Fine," Anna muttered, but she eyed Palmer then leaned forward and whispered something to him before she looked past Palmer to her. "I'm calling you later for the full story."

Louisa nodded numbly. There wasn't really a *full* story, other than the whole secret she still didn't want to let Anna in on. Especially now with so much going on. So much possibly…

It couldn't connect. *How* on earth would it connect?

With both Mary and Anna gone to deal with HSS business, Palmer turned to her. His expression was serious but unreadable.

"What did she whisper to you?" Louisa asked.

"That she was going to gut me while I slept and decorate the Christmas tree with my insides."

It surprised a laugh out of her. "Anna always is creative in her violence."

"That she is. Come on. Let's go for a walk before I drive you home."

She hesitated. Surely he just wanted to discuss the fire. Her grandfather. Hawk Steele maybe. There was nothing more to this wanting to take a walk than privacy to discuss what she didn't want anyone to overhear.

But there was *something* about the way he looked at her that was different. New. Not that it hadn't been there before, lurking in his expression at the oddest moments, but that he didn't attempt to guard it.

And how much that scared her.

"Or I can just drive you home right away, if you'd rather," he offered, like he could read her disjointed thoughts. Sense all the trepidation she had building inside her. And yet, none of that fear or concern or disquiet could outweigh what had always drawn her to him.

"No, let's walk."

She got to her feet and they walked back to the front of the house where they'd hung their coats. They bundled up and stepped outside. The sun was shining, so the afternoon held *some* miniscule warmth even in the midst of all this snow.

He led her away from the house, from all the ranch buildings. Along the fence line where evergreens were decorated with lights and natural garland no doubt Mary had made, probably with Izzy.

It was the kind of thing Louisa would have done with her mother if she'd been a little younger. If she could think of Christmas instead of all the problems around them.

"I know you don't want to upset anyone," Palmer said after they'd walked a while in silence. "I know you love your parents, but I think you need to take one of those DNA tests. And tomorrow morning, when I go talk to a few of the nurses who worked at the hospital when you were born, I think you should come with."

"If they're local…"

"I know," Palmer said gently. "Gossip is inevitable. Even if it's not, talking to people is something that could get back to your parents. I know you want to avoid that. I want to avoid it for you, Lou. But this… fires and investigators. It's dangerous. What's more important? Sparing their feelings? Or keeping you all safe?"

Both. Both were important. Both felt imperative, even though she knew safety was more important than feelings.

"Order the test," he urged. "Come with me tomorrow to talk to the nurses. I'll use my considerable charm to convince them to keep it quiet." He even grinned and winked at her, but she knew there was none of his usual ease behind it. He was trying to make her smile, and she couldn't.

"We'll have an idea once we talk to them, and if we think they can't keep quiet, we'll warn your parents ahead of time. But you have to know that's a possibility you might have to face going forward."

It sounded terrible. Except one part. "'We'?"

"You dragged me into this, Lou. You aren't kicking me back out."

Duty. That Hudson code of honor. *That's* why he was here. Not for any other reason. Except… "People are going to start talking. If they haven't already. About us spending all this time together. Particularly without Anna."

His expression didn't change, but something in his demeanor seemed to coil tight. "Yeah, they are," he agreed. With no inflection or any of his usual recklessness. This…was serious. She swallowed as he stopped their forward progress.

Louisa had been all over the Hudson property. She'd in fact spent many a summer afternoon hiding in this thatch of evergreen trees with Anna. Giggling over all the different things they'd found amusement in over the years.

There was nothing very funny about being here with Palmer. When her heart was heavy and her nerves were shot and he was so…good to her.

He took her hand. He studied her very carefully as he took a measured but deep breath. Then he pulled her closer.

And closer.

Her heart was clamoring in her chest now, and for all the different ways for over a decade she'd dreamed of Palmer Hudson pulling her close, she could not fathom how to behave in this moment. She wasn't inexperienced. She wasn't a teenager any longer. But in this moment, she felt like both—painfully unaware of *everything*.

"What are you doing?" she asked, her voice little more than a squeak when he'd pulled her close enough that their coats touched. She could feel the heat of him, and she couldn't control her breathing. She couldn't control *anything* when he looked at her with all the heat and intensity he never *once* had, even when he'd been telling her things like he didn't want to be around her.

"What I've been promising myself I wouldn't do since you came home from college."

Then his mouth was on hers. After all her years of dreaming and pining, and hating herself a little bit for the latter, Palmer Hudson was kissing her. And it was brighter, hotter and sweeter than anything she could have imagined.

Chapter Twelve

Louisa O'Brien tasted like she smelled. Of honey and summer. Her hair was silk against his cold fingertips, and their winter clothes were too bulky to really feel her body pressed against his, but it didn't matter.

She kissed like a dream he'd never allowed himself to have. Encouraging him not to bound forward in his usual reckless manner, but to slow down. To enjoy every second. Because this wasn't about chasing a feeling or finding a destination. It was just them.

She didn't touch him. And that had him pulling his mouth away, even if he still held her in place right there tucked against him. "You can tell me to stop."

Her eyes blinked open, green and magic. "Why on earth would I do that?" she asked, seeming truly confused.

It made him smile, even while something dark and a little painful twined with all this *want*. "You're a million ways too good for me, Lou."

Her eyebrows drew together. "That isn't true."

He wished he could believe that, but he knew what Sunrise thought of him. What his own siblings thought of him. Hell, what he thought of himself. Because in all his years of enjoying women, he'd never once let one matter.

Not like Louisa did.

"Everyone will think it. And be very, *very* vocal about it."

"I don't think it." She shook her head. "I don't," she repeated, reaching up to cup his face, her hands warm against his cold cheeks. Then she lifted to her tiptoes and kissed him. Like she could absolve him of all his sins by simple belief alone.

He wanted to believe she could.

There were so many things he wanted in this moment, and there were so many reasons why he couldn't have it. He sank into the kiss anyway. Louisa and the warmth two bodies could make together even in the middle of a December afternoon in the cold Wyoming landscape.

"I want you," he murmured. There was no other part of her exposed to the elements, so he had to satisfy himself by pressing kisses along her jaw.

"I guess here would be out of the question," she said on a dreamy sigh.

He laughed, though it was pained. "Yeah, it would be. Besides, your parents will worry. Maybe we shouldn't be giving Investigator Raccoon more ammunition." He eased back and smoothed his hands up and down her arms over her heavy coat. Trying to convince himself to let her go.

She studied him for a long while. He supposed he couldn't read her mind, because the stare didn't seem like regret. She *should* regret kissing him. She *should* want something better for herself.

Maybe instead of trying to tell her that, he could just try to be the kind of man who deserved her.

"This isn't just…a distraction. Is it?" she asked after a long while.

The word simply didn't make sense. "A distraction?"

"Like you feel some kind of sorry for me and thought that if you pulled out the Palmer charm—"

He was already shaking his head before she could even finish. "Do you remember one of the first nights you were home from college and you and Anna went to the Lariat?"

She seemed confused by the change of conversation, but she shrugged. "I think so. You were there. I hadn't seen you in a while."

"I was. And all I saw was this drop-dead gorgeous brunette and I wanted nothing more than to talk her into my bed—or the back of my truck, as the case may be."

Her mouth dropped open a little at that, but she didn't say anything. So he kept going, because she should know. She should be absolutely certain how this had come about.

"Then you turned around and it took my brain a few seconds to register it was you."

Her expression changed. Shuttered. "And then you didn't want to. Because I don't recall you being particularly charming that night."

"No, that was the terrible part. I still wanted to. I just knew I couldn't. So I was a jerk instead."

"I like to believe myself a great mystery," she returned, still sounding irritated. As she had been that night when he'd been so blinded by *her* that he couldn't do anything but behave badly. "But I think you know you *could* have."

"Could have talked you into bed? Sure. I think even in the deep denial I was in back then, I knew it wouldn't be that simple and easy, and that was all I was after. The ties and tangles of it all were something I thought I'd always want to avoid. I'm not the same man I was that night." It was strange to realize how true it was. How the world had changed on him, and slowly, so slowly he hadn't fully realized it was happening, he'd changed with it.

"No." She looked up at him, *into* him maybe. "Something changed. Didn't it?"

"I don't know exactly what it was. Cash settling into the single-dad thing and Izzy becoming this... girl with thoughts and opinions. Grant coming home from war. Anna getting her private investigator's license and not *just* to make Jack mad. Mary turning into Mom before my very eyes. All these adult things going on around me because we aren't kids anymore. I guess I'd been thinking if I kept being irresponsible enough, my parents would somehow come back and knock some sense into me. But they're gone. The rest of us aren't. The rest of them figured it out before I could."

Her eyes looked watery, and he wanted to believe it was the cold and not his words that had produced that reaction. But she wrapped her arms around him and simply hugged him, and they stood there like that for he didn't know how long.

It felt strangely like saying goodbye to that old version of himself. Since he didn't want to sit in that feeling, he gave her one last squeeze then eased away. "Come on. We should get you back to your grandparents' before your parents worry."

She nodded and they trudged back through their footsteps in the snow toward Palmer's truck parked in front of the house. She held his hand, and Palmer knew if one of his siblings came across that easy show of affection he'd be hearing *all* about it.

He supposed that was inevitable now. Because he'd kissed her. Because he'd accepted he could try to be good enough for her. So there was no going back.

"You know, I was thinking…" Louisa mused. "About Mr. Steele."

"That's insulting."

She laughed. "Not *then*. Before. Because if Anna likes him, maybe he's not all bad."

"You don't know how much it pains me to say this, but I think you know as well as I do that just because she slept with him doesn't mean she *likes* him."

Louisa wrinkled her nose, but she didn't mount an argument. They got into his truck and began the drive toward her grandparents' house in Sunrise. They didn't speak much during the drive. She'd clearly already moved back to thinking about the problem at hand if she was mentioning the fire investigator. As she should. This was her life burned to the ground.

His brain was still somewhere deep inside that kiss, and everything it changed for him.

When he pulled up to the house, she didn't immediately get out. She stared at the structure with a pained expression on her face. He couldn't begin to figure out what she was thinking, so he tried to take a page out of her book and focus on the matter at hand.

"Two of the nurses live over in Hardy. I'll come by in the morning and pick you up around eight. We'll go out to breakfast. Somewhere in Hardy, make sure we're not being followed, then go talk to each of them."

She slowly turned to look at him. Whatever she was thinking was hidden very well behind direct green eyes. "Breakfast?"

"Sure. We've got to make sure we're not being followed. By Fire Investigator Blackbird or anyone else."

"Palmer..."

"I know. I know. People will talk. I'm okay with that." For the first time, it occurred to him that she didn't keep asking for *his* sake. He cleared his throat. "If you are."

"What about your family?"

He felt a stab of pain born of a lot of things. Frustration. The annoyance of dealing with Jack. But mostly, the strangely strong coil of fear that she didn't want anyone to know. "I'll handle my siblings."

"I need to talk to Anna myself. I need to..." She shook her head. "You kissed me," she said, and it wasn't an accusation, but he didn't know what the hell it was.

"Yeah. If you had a problem with it, you probably shouldn't have kissed me back."

She shook her head again. "It's not a problem. It's just…"

He wanted to tell her to forget the whole damn thing, but she kept talking.

"My life is a mess. The biggest mess it's ever been. I hate all of this. Everything since Kyla Brown messaged me. But…" She chewed on her lip and he was almost distracted enough by that to forget the but.

But. "But?"

"You've been what I've wanted and told myself I'd never have for a very long time." She met his gaze and he saw the flicker of embarrassment there.

"Well, join the club, Lou."

She smiled a little. "I'm actually a founding member of the club going on a decade. You're relatively new in comparison."

He reached over and touched her cheek. "Long as we became members at the same time eventually, right?"

Her smile widened. "Yeah, I guess that works out."

He leaned across the console and pressed his mouth to hers. He wanted to linger, but they were in front of her grandparents' house. People might have to get used to the fact that he was planning on kissing Louisa O'Brien whenever and however he liked, but that didn't mean he had to give anyone a show.

"I'll be back in the morning," he said.

She nodded and opened the door. "I'll be ready." She hopped out and he watched her walk up to the house before he pulled away.

He didn't feel in the least bit *ready* for anything, but that didn't matter anymore.

LOUISA FELT BATTERED by conflicting emotions. Because her life had been burned down, and Palmer had kissed her.

She'd always told herself nothing would happen with Palmer, but truth be told, she'd always wondered if they could at least have a night together. Palmer wasn't exactly picky, and like she'd told him what now felt like years ago, she knew she wasn't an ogre or anything. A night was sort of the most she'd ever hoped for.

But Palmer hadn't just kissed her. He'd told her that story about the bar when she'd come home from college. That wasn't just a talk-a-woman-into-bed situation.

She'd love nothing more to ruminate on that, *obsess* over that, but she couldn't. Because there was so much to deal with when her family had lost everything except themselves and the orchard. There were insurance questions and a million things she'd never even considered in losing everything inside her home.

She kept trying to take some of the responsibilities from her parents, but now that they'd pushed on from their shock, they seemed determined to keep her out of it. Protect her from the hard stuff.

She'd never been more frustrated by that than at this moment. She wasn't a child to be protected. She was an adult, a partner in the orchard business, and a resident of the home that had burned down.

But they shut her out—as a team—and she'd had no choice but to go to her room and try to sleep. She, of course, hadn't. She'd thought of how to get through to them. She'd thought of Palmer kissing her on a cold winter afternoon. She thought of what happened if she wasn't her parents' child, about who could have slashed Palmer's tires and set her house on fire.

She wasn't sure when her thoughts stopped whirling enough to sleep, but she didn't sleep long or well. Still, when she opened her eyes and there was a faint light coming from the curtains in the little craft room she was sleeping in, she got up, took a shower and dressed.

She considered her reflection, but there was nothing to be done. Even if she could cover up the dark circles or try to make herself look a little extra pretty for her breakfast with Palmer, pretending that it wouldn't lead to talking to nurses who'd worked at the hospital when she'd been born, all her makeup had been ruined in the fire.

Because that thought seemed especially overwhelming, she pushed out of the bathroom and headed for the usual morning sounds of her grandmother and mother in the kitchen.

She stepped into the kitchen to the smell of cinnamon rolls and her grandmother in her very normal spot at the stove. Mom was not there, which was a little odd. Hopefully she was sleeping. "Good morning, Grandma."

"Morning, cupcake." Grandma looked over her

shoulder at her, then narrowed her eyes in stern consideration. "You need to eat."

Louisa pressed a hand to her stomach. Because now, on top of all the roiling stress, was the fluttering nerves of how she was going to face Palmer. Her entire future from top to bottom was a very inconvenient question mark.

Grandma tutted. "This inability to eat during tragedy must have come from your mother's side. I'm a firm believer that butter is the greatest comfort when everything falls apart. I haven't seen your mother this frail since before you were born."

Louisa frowned at her grandmother. She had a hard time imagining her mother being *frail*. "What happened before I was born?"

"All those miscarriages," Grandma said with the wave of her frosting knife. "She really had a rough go of it."

Louisa gaped at her grandmother. She had never once heard her mother even hint that she'd had a miscarriage or any sort of fertility issues. Maybe if she'd ever thought deeply about it, she'd wondered if there was something medical that had kept her mother from having a child until later in life, but she simply hadn't known enough to jump to that conclusion. "I didn't know that. Why didn't I know that?"

"Oh, I suppose your mother never was comfortable talking about it. It was a dark couple of years there. I'm not even sure I know how many babies she lost, poor thing." Grandma beamed at her. "And then there was you."

Louisa wished it could comfort her. It explained a lot about why her mother and father were so lenient with her, and she liked to think she'd been a good daughter to them. That even if they'd struggled, they'd ended up with someone who cared and was dedicated to the family and the orchard.

But in the midst of everything going on, it only seemed to point toward this meaning… She *wasn't* her mother's. That there was a very clear reason she wasn't.

"I won't force you to eat much, but I'm going to have to insist you have at least one roll," Grandma said when Louisa mechanically reached for the coffeepot.

"I'm actually going to breakfast with Palmer," Louisa said, trying to sound casual and not like her mother's sad fertility history made her want to run away. Luckily, losing everything gave her some reprieve for not acting like herself.

"Palmer Hudson," Grandma said. Her lips pursed and Louisa waited for a lecture. She almost welcomed it. It would feel normal amid all this other stuff that decidedly did not. "The Hudsons are a good family."

"They are," Louisa agreed, surprised that's where her grandma had decided to begin. She waited for a *but*.

None came.

"Handsome too. Especially the sheriff, but Palmer isn't hard on the eyes either." Grandma sent her a conspiratorially wink, shocking Louisa enough to laugh.

And, oh, she needed that laugh.

"No, he isn't."

"Still, you shouldn't drink that coffee on an empty stomach. Sit down and eat at least a half."

Louisa knew better than to argue with Grandma, so she sat and ate half a cinnamon roll, trying to listen to Grandma chatter on about church things. After a while, Louisa got the feeling Grandma was keeping her in the kitchen on purpose.

"I should probably go check on Mom and Dad. See if they need anything from town while I'm gone," she said, watching her grandmother's face carefully.

She saw nothing change there, but Grandma unerringly pointed out the window even though her gaze was in the sink washing her mixing bowl. Still, headlights and Palmer's truck were indeed on the rise in the moody winter morning. "There's Palmer now. You go on and enjoy your breakfast and I'll have them text you if they need anything."

Louisa didn't know how to argue with her grandmother, but it didn't feel right. It felt like everyone in her life was keeping a million secrets and she was the Ping-Pong ball being knocked around by them.

But she had never learned how to have conflict. It wasn't the O'Brien way, and worse, she just…hated upsetting her family. There was so much more upset to come—because no matter what was going on, someone had burned their house down on purpose.

Louisa said goodbye to her grandmother and then walked out into the frigid morning. The sun had begun to rise, but the sky was still in that winter-dawn blue stage.

She climbed into Palmer's pickup, not sure how to navigate *any* of this.

"Hi," he greeted with a smile.

He was just so handsome. It didn't change anything, or take away her bad feelings, but it soothed some of the edges enough she could smile back.

"Hi."

He immediately narrowed his eyes, studying her. "You okay?"

She'd known this about him, but she'd never had it so focused on her—that he watched people. Understood them. Often tricked them into thinking he didn't so he could make them feel better without them ever knowing he'd done it.

But he had. And on purpose.

So she ended up telling him. She went through what her grandmother had said about her mother. Explained it had always been a secret, as far as she knew.

"Well, I didn't find anything about previous health issues in my research, but I suppose I was looking at things from your birth on. I'll check into it. Maybe it'll give us some insight one way or another. But if it was really a *secret* secret, I don't think your grandmother would have mentioned it."

Louisa knew he was right and still…it sat on her heart. The knowledge. The way it connected to everything she'd started wondering. "They wouldn't have needed to steal me from *Ohio*. There would have been options," she said, not because she thought he needed to be told but because she needed to say it out loud. To reassure herself.

Palmer spared her a glance as he drove. "If there's something out of the ordinary, the medical staff would know or remember. So, we'll ask."

She was quiet the rest of the drive to Hardy. He turned on the radio and hummed to the songs that played. He didn't press for conversation or try to cheer her up, which allowed her to unwind and relax some.

He pulled into the parking lot of a diner she'd been to with Anna more times than she could count. Because they had excellent waffles, and they were her favorite breakfast food. She eyed Palmer. "Why'd you choose this place?"

He didn't look at her as he pulled into a parking place and turned off his truck. "They've got great waffles."

And she knew, the oh so *casual* way he said it, while carefully not looking at her, meant he knew. He'd brought her here because he knew she liked it.

She leaned over the center console and kissed him. Because in all this *terrible*, he'd made something good out of it.

He pulled back from her, but he was grinning. "You're going to get me into trouble, Louisa. Shocking."

She laughed and they got out of the truck and went inside the diner. They found a booth, and he surprised her by sliding in next to her rather than across. But they didn't discuss it. They ordered their breakfasts. Palmer kept conversation light. Nothing about the fire or her parents. He talked about Mary's Christmas preparations, the annoying present he'd gotten

Izzy with the express purpose of annoying the hell out of Cash, and the puppies one of Cash's dog had surprised them with.

It almost felt normal. If she swept aside everything actually happening in her life. If she somehow accepted this *thing* with Palmer was happening.

As they ate, they both glanced at the door when the little bell rang, and watched Mrs. Peabody walk in.

Louisa hadn't expected to see anyone she knew, though it was hardly a surprise. Hardy was only a twenty-minute drive from Sunrise and boasted more stores and had restaurants. Mrs. Peabody was in just about every church group with her mother, and the biggest gossip out of all of them.

And that was saying something.

The older woman immediately spotted them but didn't come over even as they finished their breakfast and asked for the check. But when the waitress came over and handed Palmer the bill, Mrs. Peabody was suddenly *there*.

"Palmer. Louisa. Good morning."

"Morning," they repeated in unison.

"How are you doing, Mrs. P.?" Palmer asked casually. His arm was resting over Louisa's shoulders, and he didn't make a move to pull it away or to put space between them like Louisa half wanted to.

"Just fine. Just fine. Good breakfast here. I won't keep you, of course, just wanted to stop by and say— she leaned forward conspiratorially "—you two make a real cute couple."

Palmer just grinned at her. "Thanks, Mrs. P."

She walked back to her booth and Louisa watched Palmer. His gaze was carefully neutral, but he quickly glanced at her to see what her reaction was.

It was kind of sweet. So she leaned her head on his shoulder for a minute. He kissed the crown of her head.

"Come on, let's get this over with."

Chapter Thirteen

Palmer drove the truck to the address he'd found for the nurse who had been on Anna's records. The plan was to start there and ask her about what staff she remembered from that year. See if there were any out-of-the-ordinary stories she remembered.

He'd considered calling the woman ahead of time, or even calling with his questions, but it was all too delicate. If there was something fishy going on, it was best to talk to someone involved in person, and without warning. That was something he'd learned working on cold cases.

Still, Mrs. Janice Menard might not be home when they got there. She might be a little leery about talking to two strangers about her job twenty-four years ago. He'd questioned a lot of people over the years, and some people *loved* to talk. While some people had watched too many cop shows and insisted on getting a lawyer first.

You never knew what kind of person you were going to get. For Louisa's sake, Palmer hoped Janice Menard was easy.

Luckily, they hadn't suddenly developed a tail. Hopefully that meant Hawk Steele was off looking for the actual arsonist this morning. Palmer didn't trust the man, but everything he'd dug up on him pointed to a brilliant investigator who went above and beyond. If there were secrets in Hawk's past, or an identity with a normal name, Palmer had yet to find it.

So he hoped that it was all true. Hawk Steele was a great investigator who would find the perpetrator so Louisa's family could have some closure.

And stayed the hell away from Anna while he did it.

Palmer drove into a nice little subdivision not far from the hospital. According to his research, Janice Menard had retired two years ago. He hadn't been able to find any information on her husband, but he'd been more focused on getting the information on the nurses as individuals. Then, if anything popped out, he'd dig more into their families.

He pulled to a stop in front of the address. The house was nice and well kept. Christmas lights wound up around the pillars in front of the door, and snowmen grinned from the windows. There was a large Christmas-themed wreath on the front door and little toy soldiers lining the walk up to it.

Palmer turned to study Louisa. He liked to think breakfast had distracted her for a bit. He knew it wouldn't last forever, but his heart twisted at the sight of her pale and studying the house like it had all the answers she wanted. And didn't.

She wanted the truth, and didn't, and if there was a complicated emotion he understood above all else—it was that. Because sure, he wished he knew what had happened to his parents, but at the same time...those details couldn't be pleasant or comforting, particularly all these years later.

So, he understood what she was going through. Better than most.

"We'll just ask her a few questions then go from there. Let me do most of the talking, but if you think of something you want to ask, go on and ask it."

Louisa didn't look at him, but she nodded as a sign she was listening.

"Lou..."

She finally looked at him and he reached over and fitted his palm to her cheek. "I know it all sucks. No one's expecting you to feel good about this, but I promise you, we're going to do everything we can to get to the bottom of it. Not just the truth, but the fire too. We'll get you answers."

"Thanks," she said. She didn't look any more comforted.

It ate away at him, but he also knew there were some situations a person just couldn't find comfort in.

He got out of the truck and took her hand when he came around to her side. They walked up to the front door together. Palmer dropped her hand when he knocked on the door, because he wanted to create a professional image when he talked to the former nurse.

A woman who appeared to be in her sixties, fitting the description of Janice Menard, answered after a few seconds and looked at both of them with a polite smile, but eyes full of wariness. "Hello. Can I help you?"

"Hi, my name's Palmer Hudson. I'm a cold case investigator with Hudson Sibling Solutions." He held out one of his business cards that Mary had made for them all to add "legitimacy" to questioning people. He almost never used them but figured this was one of those situations it might ease some of that wariness.

The woman took the card with wide eyes. She studied it then looked back up at him. "What's this about?"

"I'm investigating a cold case. We're talking to nurses who worked at St. Mary's Hospital here in Hardy in the late 90s and early 2000s. That's how we came across you."

"Oh, well. I'm not sure how I could have been involved in a cold case. I was a labor and delivery nurse." She pocketed Palmer's card.

"We just want to ask some questions. If you don't remember, you don't remember. But we're looking into a situation that might have been a little out of the ordinary. Like a newborn being placed with a family that wasn't theirs. Biologically."

Janice's forehead creased and she seemed to give this some thought. "That seems like something I'd remember, doesn't it? I was a nurse for over thirty years, and lots of things just blur together," she laughed. "But I think I'd remember a situation like that."

Palmer nodded kindly. "We just had to ask. Do you remember anyone you worked with maybe discussing a situation like that? Maybe not even specifically. Just something that felt off."

Again, Janice seemed to consider this. "Well," she said, eyeing Palmer then Louisa. "Now that you mention it… I'm not sure this is what you're looking for, but I do remember a little hubbub about…" She wrinkled her nose. "I don't remember the details, or maybe I never poked around for them. But definitely something hush-hush about a newborn, and it wasn't that I heard specifics, more hints of gossip. It was supposed to be a secret, but one of my good friends was the nurse. She didn't tell me anything except… Well, there had been a very odd situation, and if I'm remembering it right, it's right in your time frame."

Palmer glanced at Louisa, who'd somehow gone even paler. "Do you remember the name of the nurse?" he asked, reaching out and taking Louisa's hand.

Janice definitely studied the move, but Palmer found he didn't care when it looked like Louisa had been stabbed.

"Oh, sure. Birdie. Birdie Williams. We were the best of friends. We still keep in touch. Would it help if I gave you her address?"

"It would, Mrs. Menard. It sure would."

"I'll be right on back." She turned and disappeared back into the house, though she left the door open a crack.

Palmer gave Louisa's hand a little squeeze. "It doesn't mean anything just yet. Something to look into."

Louisa nodded but didn't say anything. He could

see her mind had zoomed into a million different possibilities, but he'd investigated enough cold cases to
know it was just as likely a dead end as anything else.

Janice returned with a little piece of paper. "Off
Rural Route 2." She smiled and handed it to him. "I
hope this helps you get the answers you're looking
for."

"Thank you, Mrs. Menard. We sure do appreciate
it. And if you think of anything else, call my cell. It's
on the business card."

"Of course." She moved to close the door but Palmer
held up a hand.

"I just have one more question, if you don't mind?"

"Oh, of course not." Her smile stayed in place but
she still held the door half closed. Hard to blame her
when they were strangers, he supposed. But still…
There was something that didn't sit right, and he
didn't know what it was just yet.

"What brought you to Hardy? You're one of the
few nurses I found on the roster who wasn't from
Wyoming."

She smiled even wider. "Family."

Louisa followed Palmer back to his truck feeling
numb, and it had nothing to do with the cold. This felt
like a lead and she…didn't want a lead. She wanted
to go home and bury her head in the sand.

Except her home had burned down, and something
worse might happen if she didn't figure out why.

They got into the pickup and Palmer began driving again, but instead of two hands on the wheel, he

put one over hers. "We just have to take it one step at a time."

She swallowed at the lump sitting in her throat. "Yeah, I know."

He drove and he kept his hand on hers, but she noticed that he wasn't exactly the same as he'd been after the diner. He seemed more alert. He was constantly looking in the rearview mirror, like he was waiting for someone to pop up out of the woodwork.

"What's bothering you?" she asked when he frowned even deeper as the GPS instructed him to turn onto a gravel road.

"I did a basic profile of Janice Menard. I don't recall seeing any family in the area. That's why I asked why she moved here."

"Maybe she meant extended family?"

"Could be. Or even her husband's family. This just feels… Can you look on your phone and see if you can find any pictures of this house she's sending us to?"

"Do you think she was lying?" Louisa asked, sitting straighter in her seat, her heart rate starting to pick up.

"I don't know. Just got a bad feeling about something."

She scrambled to get her phone out and typed in the address on the piece of paper while Palmer took another turn, this time onto a dirt road. She began to feel some concern too. This was way outside of Hardy. Deserted.

It did not feel right.

But she found a couple listings, with pictures of the house associated with the address.

"It looks like your typical old ranch house," she explained. "Maybe a little run-down, but this says it was built in 1920, so that makes sense. Especially if an older couple lives there."

"Birdie Williams is on my list of people to talk to, so it's not like Janice made her up. I'll look at my notes before we head in there, but if I'm remembering correctly, she retired five-ish years ago when her husband passed away. So, she's likely living there alone, unless there's family with her."

Louisa studied him for a minute. "You don't need to look at your notes, do you?"

"Huh?"

"You remember it all. Exactly as you said. You don't need to look at your notes. You're just trying to look like… I don't know. I don't understand why you go through such lengths to let people think the worst of you, Palmer." And she didn't know why she was bringing it up *now*, but it was just so incongruous.

He was helping her. He was practically the only thing keeping her together the past few days. Yet he still had to downplay what he was capable of. It didn't make any sense.

She loved him—and not even in that same way she'd thought she'd loved him at thirteen. This was deeper. More meaningful. *This* was an adult feeling, because she was an adult and she understood so much about him now.

But she didn't understand this.

"You don't understand because you don't have older siblings," Palmer replied. He wasn't trying to make a joke of it exactly. He was more making light of it. "Especially ones who are saintly sheriffs and war heroes."

She frowned. "So instead of, say, being proud of them, and confident in your own abilities and choices, you have to pretend to be the family clown and act like you don't care about anything?" Honestly, men really were the most infuriating creatures.

"You'd have to have siblings to understand," he repeated. He glanced at her with a kind of rueful smile before looking back at the road. This one was no longer plowed, so Palmer had to slow the truck to be able to determine where the road was and drive it safely.

"But I get your meaning, and you're right," he said. "I am proud of them, and I don't have regrets about the choices I've made, so there's no real reason to feel like I have to act down to less. It's a hard habit to break because that's how we work. The Hudsons and HSS are a well-oiled machine, and we all have our roles."

"I don't think you being who you are is going to somehow mess up how your family or business works, Palmer."

This time when he looked at her, he really smiled. "As I hear tell, I don't need any help with my ego, Lou."

"Yes, well, I think it depends on what ego we're talking about." She wanted to say something else, but she didn't know what. Just that she appreciated all that he'd done, and she wanted him to get the credit he deserved for it.

Palmer let out a low whistle as he slowed to a stop at the directive of the GPS. "Either the GPS is wrong or Mrs. Menard is." He inched forward in the snow, closer to the dilapidated house, squinting as he studied it.

"I think it's the same house in the pictures," Louisa said, looking at her phone then back up again. "I just think these pictures might be ten years old." The house wasn't just run-down now, it was clearly abandoned. She *hoped* it was abandoned. The ceiling was caving in, windows were broken, gutters hung off the roof. There was a barn next to it in even worse shape.

"It might appear abandoned, but look." He pointed out past the house. She squinted at the blinding white and didn't see anything.

"Tracks," he explained. "Some footprints, some snowmobile. Even if it *looks* abandoned, someone's been out here." He scanned the scene in front of them, and Louisa did the same.

She wanted answers to her life, but… "Palmer, I don't like this."

"Yeah, me either. Let's go. I'll do some research on Birdie Williams and we'll go from there."

Louisa nodded. She still looked around the house and the barn, trying to discern why it felt so disquieting. There were plenty of abandoned and falling-apart ranch buildings in this area, but this one felt…wrong.

"Can't go any farther forward or I'll get stuck in that bank," Palmer said. "Have to reverse and try to turn around." But before he could back out, she saw the flash of movement in the house.

Just as Palmer jerked her down and something around them exploded.

Chapter Fourteen

There was only one gunshot. It had shattered his windshield, which was far too close for anyone's comfort. Palmer covered Louisa's body with his the best he could in the cramped front of the pickup.

They were sitting ducks, even with the protection of the truck. "Stay down. I'm going to try to drive us out of here."

"But—"

"Louisa. Keep your damn head down and don't *move*."

She didn't pose an argument this time and Palmer moved, keeping his own head and body down as best he could, but putting himself in a position that allowed him to gauge things a little better.

"Call the police. Text my family. Whatever you can do on your phone without moving."

He jerked the truck into Reverse, angling his body so he could see out the side-view mirror. If he wasn't careful, he'd just reverse them into being stuck in the snow.

"I don't have any service," Louisa said.

"Of course not," he muttered. He carefully eased his foot onto the gas, pulling away from the house, still waiting for another shot to go off. It didn't, but he could hardly be grateful when he couldn't see beyond what he could make out from the side-view mirror.

He was so focused on reversing that it took him a minute or two to realize something was wrong. Even more wrong than just the situation.

He smelled…gas.

He shoved the truck into Park. "Out!" He reached over and undid her seat belt for her, then practically dragged her across the console. He didn't even think about gunshots at this point because he knew that if that first bullet had done the wrong kind of damage, the truck could very well explode. Regardless of whether they were in it or not.

Louisa didn't mount an argument or struggle against him as he pulled her from the pickup, or if she did, he was too focused on getting her to safety to notice it.

"Run," he said once they were both free of the truck and on their own two feet. He kept her hand in his as he started running. He pulled her in a kind of zigzag pattern just in case whoever had fired was waiting.

The sound of the truck exploding echoed through the quiet winter morning. He pulled Louisa down behind a snowdrift. The snow wasn't any kind of protection from whoever was out there with a gun, but it kept them out of sight from anyone in that house or barn.

He peeked over the snowbank at his truck. Now

on fire. "Someone's really got something against my truck."

"Palmer…"

"It's all right. We'll be all right." He didn't know what the hell was going on, but he'd do everything in his power to make sure Louisa was all right.

"I know you're going to want to argue with me. But I need you to do what I say, exactly as I say."

"I'm not leaving you," she said firmly. Because she clearly saw where he was going with that.

It was the only way. "Lou." He swore inwardly at the stubborn lift of her chin but couldn't let it stop him. "I know how to handle this. We can't get help without some kind of cell service. I've got a gun. So you run toward where we came from. You should be able to get service not too far back."

"Would you leave me?"

He wanted to tear out his hair. "We do not have time for this. Someone shot at us and *someone* needs to be the one to get help. It's my gun. I know how to shoot it. So it doesn't matter what I'd do, this is what we have to do."

"Palmer—"

"Damn it all, Lou—"

"No, Palmer. Look." She was tugging on his arm and he finally looked over to where she was pointing. There was a man walking toward them. With a gun.

Luckily, Palmer had his own gun on him, had in fact been wearing it since he'd left the house this morning. He moved to remove it from his holster. He kept his eyes on the approaching man but reached for Louisa.

"Go. Now. I can handle this but only if you go get some backup."

He crouched behind the snowbank, making sure his body would be between Louisa and the gunman no matter what she decided to do. "You're going to run, staying low and zigzagging. Back toward where we came from. Find cover. Use your phone. Be smart. Someone starts shooting, you run harder. You hear me?"

"All right," she said. "But I'm coming right back. The minute I have service and get through to someone. I'm coming right back."

He didn't have time to argue with her. The gunman was somewhere behind the blaze that engulfed his truck. He held his gun at the ready, watching for him to come around either side. "Just go."

So she did. He heard her quiet footfalls but didn't dare look back at her. She was smart. She was capable. And he hoped to God whoever she got to come out and help them told her to stay put.

When the man with the gun still didn't appear from either side of the fire, long after the sound of Louisa's escape had faded, Palmer took a split second to glance over his shoulder.

He saw Louisa dart behind a tree then back out. Following instructions. *Thank God.* He wasn't sure how far she'd need to go to get service, but it didn't matter. There was something to deal with here.

He crouched as low as he could and still move, practically crawling behind the swell of snow that had been made by gusts of wind. He wanted to take the shooter off guard if he could.

But when he stilled, looked over the snow again, he could tell the shooter knew exactly what his new position was.

"Was it really necessary to ruin my truck?" he called out. He didn't expect an answer, but maybe there'd be some clue as to who or what he was dealing with.

Unfortunately, he couldn't think of a way this didn't connect to Louisa digging into her true parentage possibility. Janice Menard had sent them here— and the woman *had* been a nurse at the hospital. It wasn't just a strange coincidence.

Palmer started moving again, wondering if there was any way he caught this gunman off guard. He hated the idea of shooting first and asking questions later, but then again, this guy wasn't exactly asking questions.

So, Palmer decided to throw out a few more of his own. "I don't suppose we could clear this whole thing up with a conversation?" After he spoke, he quickly moved in the opposite direction he'd originally been moving.

Nothing but silence.

"Because I don't have a clue as to why you're beating up my truck." He thought about bringing up the fire at the orchard, but Louisa hadn't fully understood him when she'd accused him of playing dumb.

He did do what she said. Play down to expectations and act like he couldn't quite hack whatever was going on around him. He liked to, sometimes. Because it made people underestimate him.

When it came to investigating, sometimes that worked in his favor.

"I don't really want to shoot you," Palmer called out again. He knew the guy was creeping ever closer. In his mind, Palmer picked a spot that would be his last straw before he pulled his own trigger. "But I'm also planning to see Christmas, so it's going to be an inevitability if you don't stop where you are."

Palmer was surprised when the man actually stopped, though he still didn't say anything. He didn't move. He stood on one side of the snowbank and Palmer crouched on the other side. Seconds turned to minutes, and minutes stretched out. Until Palmer thought his toes, fingers and nose had gone completely numb.

He couldn't stand like this forever. He'd given Louisa enough time to get hold of someone—God, he hoped. He very carefully and quietly curled his finger around the trigger of his gun.

Before he could decide on his next step, the gunman's cell phone chimed. The man touched something in his ear. Listened and then touched it again.

Palmer heard something else...like a...scream? He scanned the surroundings, looking for Louisa, gunman forgotten until the man spoke.

"Bad news, bud. We don't need you," the man said, and then, before Palmer could fully dive out of the way or lift his own gun, pulled the trigger.

LOUISA WORKED IT out so that she zigzag ran for a count of thirty, then checked her phone. If she didn't have service, she ran for another thirty seconds. It killed her to have left Palmer, but he was smart and strong and... He could handle this. She had to believe he could handle this.

Because if he couldn't, it would be all her fault. Clearly, this all connected and, if she'd only kept it to herself, it wouldn't have gotten so out of hand. If she'd ignored that Facebook message, everything would be *fine*.

Her lungs were burning and there was a sharp pain in her side, but she didn't let up. When a bar of service finally popped up on her phone screen, she nearly wept with relief, but she didn't have time for that. She found a tree to huddle behind. It wasn't great cover, but it would have to do.

She wanted to call Anna or even Jack, but the smart thing to do was to call the emergency line at Bent County, where someone had to pick up no matter what. She squeezed her eyes shut as the phone rang.

"Bent County Emergency Line. What's your emergency?"

"We need help." Louisa didn't bother to explain what kind. She just rattled off the address. "Send someone quickly. There's a gunman and a fire and... just send somebody." Because she needed to get back to Palmer.

"Ma'am. Slow down. Give me more details."

"I don't have any. There's a man with a gun. He shot our truck. We need help. Now!" She didn't end the call. She couldn't stay on it either. Maybe it was foolish, but she left the phone there, resting on top of the snow. If someone needed to ping it, they could, here where she still had service. If she needed a phone later, Palmer had one.

Because this was the last time she was going to separate from him as long as someone was trying to hurt them. He would not take the brunt of this. She couldn't let him.

She ran back toward the house. She couldn't even begin to guess how far the distance was. She could see Palmer's truck smoking, though most of the flames had died out by now. She could tell Palmer was still huddled behind the snowbank, but she was still so far away.

She didn't zigzag this time. She needed to get to him as quickly as possible. So she could…? She didn't know. He was the one with the gun. Was she really expecting to run in and save him? She'd likely get herself, *and Palmer*, shot.

She slowed her pace. She couldn't make out the gunman's face from this far away, but she didn't think he was paying attention to her. Just yet. Maybe if she rerouted, she could come up behind him. Surprise him.

She couldn't hear anything other than her ragged breaths and the howling frigid wind. She needed to get hold of her breathing, carefully sneak around, and maybe the wind could help disguise her approach.

Louisa came to a full stop, planning to look around

to find the perfect route. Before she could, someone grabbed her from behind, pulled her back hard.

She tried to yell, but a hand slapped over her mouth so that it was just a muffled sound. She tried to fight off the strong arms that had banded around her, but the grip was tight. She was dragged backward a few steps as she fought to free herself.

She thought she was succeeding, or at least keeping the person from dragging her any farther, but then something was being put over her head.

She screamed this time, because there was no longer a hand over her mouth, but whatever was over her face muffled the sound as well. She couldn't see now. She could only fight her unknown attacker as she was hauled through the snow.

She kept fighting. Kicking out and jerking her arms as best she could. Whoever had her—however many of them there were—they were too strong. Whatever was on her head made it hard to breathe, impossible to know where anyone was.

She kept trying to scream, but inhaling a deep breath only pulled the material over her face into her mouth. Which caused terrible bolts of panic to beat through her. She had to fight them off—panic, the people. She had to get to Palmer.

Whoever had her was dragging her, so she decided to suddenly go limp. It seemed to take them off guard enough that someone lost their grip and she fell into the snow. She immediately tried to get to her feet, to roll away and throw out some punches, but the grapple in the snow only lasted a moment or two before she was lifted up.

Clearly, there were two people involved—someone carried her by her arms and someone by her legs, as she tried to jerk and bend her body in whatever ways she could to get them to drop her again.

Instead, she was given a kind of toss and shove, and she landed hard...*hard* against a ground. Not the snow this time. Were they inside? The house maybe? Or the barn?

Something exploded from not far off. A gunshot. Louisa stilled without thinking the thought through, listening hard for some kind of reaction to that shot. Was it Palmer shooting? The gunman shooting Palmer? Something else?

But there was only the sound of the howling wind, a thud, then an engine starting and something that sounded like...a van door rolling closed.

Her hands were pulled roughly back but she tried to wriggle away—to keep kicking and fighting and not choke out the sobs that had welled inside her. Had someone been shot? Was Palmer okay?

How was either of them going to get out of this?

Her hands and legs were quickly secured. She could only roll now, and she felt the rumble and acceleration of a vehicle. She was in a car of some kind, not a house or the barn. They were driving away with her tied up and some kind of hood fitted over her head.

Louisa tried not to panic. Desperately tried to keep her breathing even so she didn't suffocate in the material. She couldn't fight them off. She was in this vehicle now, so she stilled. She tried to count her breaths in and out.

And think. *Think*.

Surely Palmer was okay. Surely help was on its way. This was scary, but…it wouldn't end badly.

It couldn't.

Then she listened to what the voices were saying.

"Not dead yet, but he'll bleed out before anyone finds him," a man said.

Louisa made a shocked sound of pain, because there could only be one *he* in this scenario.

Palmer.

Chapter Fifteen

Palmer had never been shot before. For a moment, he could only sit there somewhere between realization and pain. He looked down at the sudden river of blood pouring out of his side and wondered how this had all come to be.

Focus, some inner voice warned him. He looked from the wound to the gunman. Even raised his own weapon to belatedly defend himself, but the man was running away. Toward the barn. Or something behind the barn. Palmer couldn't tell from his vantage point.

Well, at least the guy hadn't finished him off.

Palmer looked back down at the bullet hole in his side.

Probably hadn't finished him off anyway.

He realized dully he was in shock. And the fact that he wasn't screaming from pain just yet couldn't be good.

None of this was good.

But Louisa was out there. Getting help. She had to be. She'd probably do something ridiculous like come running back here and blame herself. She'd probably even cry over the whole thing. He sucked in a painful breath and forced his gaze away from the blood. He squinted into the snowy world around him.

He just had to wait it out. She'd be back and…it'd be okay.

Unless that strange noise had been her. Because the gunman had taken a phone call, so he wasn't acting alone. Had someone gotten to her? Hurt her? He didn't see her anywhere, and she should be visible, shouldn't she?

That thought pierced the weird fuzziness around him. They couldn't get their hands on Louisa. They couldn't hurt Louisa. He had to save her.

He tried to get up, but nearly passed out instead. *There* was the pain. He tried to tell himself that was a good thing as his vision blurred, threatened to go gray. It meant his body wasn't giving up just yet.

He'd been shot. He had to think. What was he supposed to do?

Save Louisa.

He shook that thought away. He would do that, yes, but first he had to make sure he didn't bleed out. He had to find a way to *get* to her without just crumpling.

He needed to put pressure on the wound. Stop the bleeding. It couldn't be good to lose this much blood, even if he was still breathing and mostly coherent.

How was he going to stop the bleeding out here in all this snow, his truck blown to hell? The only thing he could think to do was to pull off his gloves, ball them up and shove them against his torn, bloody shirt.

The sound that came out of him as he did this was

somewhere closer to animal than human, but he knew well enough that no matter how badly it hurt, he had to press harder to stop that tide of blood.

He breathed through that for a few seconds. Fought off the creeping blackness. He wouldn't give in to that. Not until he knew Louisa was okay.

Once he thought he could bear it, he tried to stand again, but he just couldn't move that way without such excruciating pain that his muscles wouldn't work. Everything gave out, and he was breathing so hard he thought he might throw up. He was lucky he didn't collapse in a heap.

Okay, so standing was out. But he had to move. He'd crawl, roll. Whatever he had to do to find Louisa.

He managed to get to his knees, one hand still pushing the gloves into his side and the other balancing himself upright on the ground. His vision swam and everything threatened to just give in and give out.

He had to find Louisa.

He sucked in a breath and let it out. He pushed in on the damn bloody wound and let himself make whatever terrible noises he needed to make to get through it.

Why had the gunman run off? Left him here to... Well, die.

No. He wasn't going out that easy. Not when Louisa might be in trouble. He couldn't leave her to the wolves. Something had to be done.

He wasn't able to stand. Not the way he was feeling. He wasn't steady enough, and a fall could send him over the edge. But he could move forward on his knees.

Or so he told himself. But moving was becoming increasingly difficult. His limbs felt heavy, and a numbness was spreading through every last inch of him. It was hard to focus. He just kept repeating Louisa's name—out loud, in his head. Whatever it took to focus on what was important rather than the pain. The fear. The fog trying to overtake his mind.

Eventually, he sensed movement. He was able to turn his head enough to see a car. With flashing lights. Followed by an ambulance. Both sped through the snowy street with more urgency than caution.

The cop car skidded to a stop and Jack was out of the driver's side before it had even fully stopped skidding. Deputy Brink got out of the passenger side, just a few steps behind Jack.

Who was shouting? Palmer tried to make sense of the words before he realized Jack was yelling at the guys in the ambulance.

Jack knelt next to him, reaching out to steady Palmer's wavering frame.

"What the hell happened?" he demanded, his hand coming over Palmer's and the wadded-up gloves trying to soak up the blood.

Jack pushed even harder, creating more pressure on the wound and more pain arcing through him. Palmer hissed out a breath.

There was so much to explain to Jack, but none of it mattered until they figured out where Louisa was. "I can't find Lou. She was with me then she called for help. But she hasn't come back. I don't know where she went. We've got to find her."

Jack and Deputy Brink exchanged a look. Deputy Brink immediately walked away, and Palmer could hear her ordering people around, though he couldn't make sense of what she said.

"Palmer. What *happened*?" Jack demanded, crouching just out of the way while the medics worked in tandem to examine his wound and get him on a stretcher.

Palmer did his best to explain it to Jack—all of it. From Janice Menard to this moment right here. He wanted to keep Louisa's secrets, but he needed her safe more than that.

He could tell from Jack's frustrated expression—and lack of more questions—that whatever he'd *thought* he'd been saying didn't make much sense.

"Tell Anna to go through my files," Palmer said, wincing as the medics started to move him. "She can hack into them no doubt. She'll figure out specifics. Janice Menard. Janice and… Jack, where is Louisa?"

Because if Louisa was okay, she would have come running once she saw the cops and the ambulance. She would be there. And she wasn't.

Jack said nothing. He looked over somewhere in the distance, but he did not answer Palmer's desperate question.

"Jack, where the hell is Louisa?" he yelled at his brother as the medics put him into the back of the ambulance.

We'll find her were Jack's terse words as the door closed, separating them.

Palmer was left with the medics and his own fading vision.

He had to stay awake. He had to help…but before he could even attempt to fight off the medics, his world went dark.

LOUISA HAD STOPPED putting up a fight. There was no point to it. Something tied her wrists and ankles together. If she got too worked up, she couldn't breathe well enough in this hood thing. She was clearly in a moving vehicle, so nothing could really be done in the moment.

She couldn't fight her way out—not yet—so she had to be smart. She had to listen and think and plan.

She could not dwell on the fact that the gunman thought Palmer would bleed out all by himself. She'd called for help. Someone would help him. He'd be okay and then he'd find her.

She knew he would.

So she had to stay alive. And get to the bottom of this the best she could so that when Palmer got her out of this, they'd have all the answers and be able to put all this…sheer insanity to rest.

Palmer couldn't die. It was just…impossible.

Well, Jack surely wouldn't allow it. She tried to convince herself of that. Jack Hudson was too rigid, too demanding, too perfect to ever let his brother die.

Tears came and went. She'd get a grip on them, then they'd threaten again, but if this hood got any damper, she'd struggle even more to breathe. She needed to keep it together from here on out.

It felt like they'd been driving forever. The people in the vehicle didn't talk. So far, only the man who'd spoken of bleeding out—the gunman she'd seen—had said anything. She tried to recall details of the man. He'd been average height and build. Nothing special about him, but he'd had a beard. Darker, maybe a little gray, so not a young man. She hadn't seen his eyes or anything distinguishing, but he'd been wearing tactical pants and a black heavy coat and hat.

She would get out of this and she would make sure everyone responsible was held accountable for their role in…whatever this was. So she would remember every last detail she could to repeat to police once she was saved.

Louisa held on to the belief she'd be saved.

She tried to determine how many people were involved right now. The man who'd shot Palmer. Someone driving the vehicle. There had to be at least one other person because two people had thrown her in. So, three people minimum.

They'd shot Palmer, left him to *bleed out* and taken her. Very much alive.

And that Janice woman had sent them here. She had to have known. It had to have been a setup. So, at least four people were involved.

How many others? Why?

It had to tie to Kyla Brown's message. There was no other logical explanation. Not that fires and shootings were *logical*. But she'd stumbled into something bigger than just…whatever she'd thought it was.

Louisa kept going over the information in her head,

trying to commit every detail to memory. Trying to keep herself from thinking about Palmer and bleeding out and how damn scared she was of where these people were taking her and why they were taking her alive.

There was no way of knowing how much time had passed when the vehicle finally began to slow. The people around her didn't speak. Not as it stopped. Not as doors opened.

Roughly jerked out, she was placed on her feet and her ties were cut. Someone held one elbow, while someone else held the other.

"Walk," the gunman's voice ordered.

She hesitated, because she wasn't ever keen on taking orders, even when she was scared to death, but that was the wrong move, apparently. The man squeezed her arm so hard, she yelped in pain.

"I said *walk*," he ordered.

Her feet began to move before she'd fully thought the motion through. She didn't want to follow his orders, but her arm screamed in pain. Walking made him stop hurting her, so she walked.

The hands on each arm led her in the direction she needed to go. The hood felt more and more suffocating until Louisa thought she was going to pass out. But she couldn't. She had to be alert for everything.

Because she *would* get out of this, and when she *did*, she would remember everything. And all of these people would pay.

They had to pay.

She was shoved and thought she would fall since

she couldn't see, but her butt landed on a hard surface, arms still holding her even as her body jolted with the impact. It was a hard chair she'd been pushed onto. Her arms—already tied behind her back—were suddenly wrenched and she realized they were now also tying her to the chair.

She didn't cry, though it was a hard-won thing. She breathed. Carefully. Focusing on her breaths over anything else. If she panicked, she wouldn't survive. So she couldn't panic.

She had to *think*.

With no warning, the hood was removed. The world around her wasn't bright, but Louisa still had to blink a few times going from fully dark to a dimly lit room.

Room might be generous. It was more like a... cellar. The ground was packed dirt, the walls were made of rocks. It was clearly some kind of old, deserted building that, at some point, a few people had converted into some kind of shelter.

She didn't see any supplies, just three people in this strange little space that smelled of earth and cold.

Louisa looked around. There was the gunman who'd presumably shot Palmer. She'd been right about the gray in the beard. His eyes were dark, and he had a scar across his chin. There was the hint of a tattoo peeking up from his collar.

She turned her attention to the two other people— both women, both young. One was dressed casually. Jeans, a hoodie, even average tennis shoes. Her hair was hidden in a knitted winter hat, but her eyes were blue. The only thing intimidating about the woman was the large and very dangerous-looking gun she held.

The other woman…looked familiar. Similar, even, to Louisa's own reflection. Dark hair, freckles over her nose. Her eyes were brown instead of green but…

And that's when Louisa realized. "Kyla?" The woman who'd messaged her. The woman who'd started this whole thing.

"Heya, sis." The woman smiled, as if they were meeting in a coffee shop, not with Louisa bound to a chair in a creepy old cellar. "Nice to meet you in the flesh."

Sis.

Louisa swallowed. "What…is happening?"

Kyla Brown stood by a small window. She was dressed in all black winter gear, and it looked vaguely tactical. Lots of pockets and hooks and things. Her hair was pulled back in a severe French braid. Her gaze was narrowed on that window that seemed to look out only into snow.

"That *is* an interesting question," Kyla said, as if mulling it over. As if this was a normal conversation and not kidnapping and attempted murder.

Attempted, because Palmer had to be okay. He *had* to be.

"These damn snowstorms have really messed with my timeline. If that wasn't bad enough, *you* and your boyfriend had to go poking around." Kyla sighed and shook her head as if despairing of them. "Oh, well, it'll be a nice Christmas gift."

Louisa wanted to believe this could be fixed. That everything could be okay, but there was something about the *casualness* in Kyla's tone with all these guns and bad things…that told Louisa this would not be okay. Very, *very* not okay. "What will be a nice gift?"

"You, of course." Kyla turned to face Louisa and her pleasant smile made Louisa's stomach sink and turn. Nothing about this should be pleasant. "It's time *everyone* pay," Kyla said. "And you're the key."

Chapter Sixteen

Palmer woke up in a hospital bed. He knew right away they'd pumped him full of something. He felt foggy and heavy. Thoughts wouldn't coalesce the way they needed to. Because he needed to do something. What was it?

He looked around the room, blinking away blurry vision. For a split second, he thought the woman sitting in the chair next to his bed was his mother. His heart leaped.

Then broke.

"Mary."

Her head shot up, like maybe she'd been nodding off sitting there. She hopped up and immediately her hand was on his face. "You are in *so* much trouble," she scolded, her voice a croak, like she was trying to hold back tears.

"I don't remember…" But he did. He'd been shot. He knew exactly where he'd been and what he'd been doing. He tried to sit up. "Lou?"

Mary's expression didn't change, but something in her eyes flickered as she pressed him back into the hospital bed. "You have to rest. You were *shot*. You lost a lot of blood. You've been in and out since they stitched you all up. They think you'll be able to go home tomorrow if you can walk around a bit, but you have to take it easy." She blew out a breath and studied him, clearly struggling with a lot of emotions she didn't want to let loose.

She hadn't answered the one thing he needed to know. "Mary." He fixed her with his sternest stare in his currently fuzzy state. "Where is Louisa?"

Mary inhaled. She tried to smile, but he knew his sister too well. It was only bad news.

"They're still looking for her," she said, clearly trying to sound chipper and failing spectacularly. "Everyone is looking. Jack, Grant, Cash, Anna. Everyone's out there. They'll bring her home."

"How long?"

"Palmer, the situation is being handled. Now, you were shot. Seriously. Just because they think you might be able to come home tomorrow doesn't mean it was a flesh wound. There will be a long period of recovery. So you need to rest. To take care of—"

"If you think I'm going to rest while you avoid all my questions, you're not as smart as everyone always gives you credit for. How long has Louisa been out there? How long have they been looking for her?" he demanded. He looked around for a clock but didn't see one.

He couldn't remember everything. His memory of the morning was kind of foggy, but he'd been with Louisa. He didn't know what time it had been, or what time it was now, but he remembered being shot and not being able to find her.

Now Mary was being far too quiet. "Damn it, Mary, how long?"

"It's been about twelve hours since you were shot." She sighed when he tried to sit again. "You are hooked up to an IV. You've been *shot*. Stop trying to be a superhero and think rationally."

"Think rationally? She's been missing for twelve hours. That means someone *took* her. She didn't wander off. She didn't get lost." He struggled to breathe past all the terrible possibilities. "She could be hurt. She could be—"

"We're not thinking about what she *could* be, Palmer," Mary said firmly. Not that *I'm-in-charge* kind of firm he was used to from her. There was something vulnerable about how forcefully she'd said those words.

She swallowed. Hard. "We're focusing on the facts. The facts are Jack and his department, along with us, and Bent County, and half the town are out looking for her. So we won't deal in abstracts. We will deal in facts."

Facts. The fact was Louisa was *missing*. She needed help. Because if she didn't, she would have made her way home. People wouldn't need to search for her. Louisa could handle herself, so if she hadn't come home on her own, she was...

Mary squeezed his hand. "If we think of all the possibilities, we fall apart. We can't fall apart. You need to rest. You need to get better. And you need to let everyone who's able to handle finding her. Okay?"

"How do you expect me to just lay here? *I* know what's going on. *I* was there."

"And you were shot in the process. You aren't any good to anyone if you're dead. If Louisa hadn't called emergency services, you would be. You *would* be." This time tears glistened in her eyes. "I don't know why you and Grant had to decide to be bullet magnets this year, but it's going to have to stop."

It was the tears that got him. Even though it felt like he couldn't breathe, even though Louisa was out there…with someone. Hurt or not, she was being held against her will. Still, he tried to smile reassuringly at his sister. "Thick skin. We're okay."

She shook her head. "But you could have not been."

He squeezed the hand she held. "I thought we weren't dealing in abstracts and coulds?"

She let out a little huff of irritation, and still she didn't cry. Because they'd been through too much. They'd learned how to carry too much on their shoulders.

But he couldn't bear this. "You gotta get me out, Mary. I can't just stay here. I have to find her."

"Do you think Jack or Anna or any of them are going to rest without finding her?" Mary demanded. Her voice faltered, but she didn't drop his gaze or his hand. "You have to do what's best for yourself and for Louisa. You charging out there and then passing out because you lost too much blood is not what's best for anyone. You will stay put. And you will rest."

Palmer opened his mouth to argue, but a tear slipped over and onto her cheek, so he shut it. She was upset, and he couldn't...push her. Mary didn't cry. Even when they'd been kids, she'd tried not to cry. When Anna threw tantrums or raged over a boy—complete with tears and swears and the occasional breaking of things—Mary had held it all together.

"Okay," he said to keep her from crying—not because he planned to do it. He'd just need to figure a way to outmaneuver her. "Why don't you go on home? Get some rest yourself."

Mary's eyes narrowed. "Do you really think I'm a fool?"

"What? You're going to spend the night here? In this cramped uncomfortable hospital room? I'm sure I can charm the nurse into taking care of me just fine."

"I'm sure you can charm the nurse into all manner of things I wouldn't approve of. So I'll be staying put." She reached over his bed and hit the button that would call the nurses' station.

Palmer wouldn't be deterred. One way or another, he was getting out of this hospital bed, and he was going to find Louisa and bring her home.

LOUISA COULDN'T REMEMBER ever being so cold. Her three captors had built a small campfire outside the structure's walls and took turns going to warm themselves by it. Inside the little cellar building, small battery-powered lanterns offered light to see by, but absolutely no warmth. Louisa shivered and struggled to move her fingers or her feet, or anything that might help warm them up.

No one spoke around her, so she still had no idea what was going on. Sometimes she could hear muffled voices outside when they were all out there, but nothing was ever clear enough to catch.

It was very careful and purposeful, which was both frustrating and terrifying. Whatever this was, it had been planned. That meant it would be harder to find the means to escape.

She had to escape. She just had to. Someone would come help her. She believed that too, but if she could get herself out of this, then there was less chance of anyone else getting hurt.

She swallowed at the lump in her throat because Palmer could be dead right now. All because of her.

Louisa looked at Kyla, who stood in her spot by the window. Even though it was pitch-black outside, she kept her gaze there. She would stand for what felt like hours, unmoving, just holding on to a gun and staring blankly out the window.

"Kyla?" Louisa ventured. When the woman looked over at her, Louisa tried to smile. "Can you tell me what happened to my friend? The one that guy shot?" She didn't want an answer, but... How could she not ask?

Kyla shrugged and looked back out the window. "It doesn't matter."

"Well, it does to me. I..." Why did she feel compelled to tell her kidnapper she loved Palmer? It hardly mattered in the here and now. But him being okay mattered. "I need to know."

Kyla shook her head. "You better be careful or you'll end up just like her."

"Like who?"

"Our mother." Kyla looked back at her and considered. "I hate to break it to you, but all she ever cared about was men. She was unfaithful to my dad, and that made you. That's why…" She narrowed her eyes at Louisa and took a few steps toward her. Louisa had to work hard not to instinctively pull away.

Kyla crouched in front of her. "I know you want the truth, and I want to give it to you. We're sisters." She smiled kindly. It died quickly. "But I also gotta be real careful. I have a plan. If I don't stick to the plan, things are going to go bad."

Louisa swallowed. "I just don't understand because I thought…I thought you wanted to be sisters. Family. I don't have siblings here. You don't have any back home, do you?"

Kyla shrugged and rocked back on her heels. "Depends on how you look at it. Like I said, our mother is a real problem."

Our mother. Louisa tried not to focus too much on that. Just because this woman said it was true didn't make it true.

But she saw herself in the woman. The *girl.* Louisa knew she was only nineteen. What was she doing with guns and plans that involved kidnapping?

"Maybe if you told me the plan, I could help."

Kyla stood to her full height, looking down at Louisa with a sneer. "Don't do that. You think I'm that gullible?"

"Of course not." Louisa tried to keep her expression neutral. "Kyla, I am freezing. This isn't good. None of this is good, but it could be okay. You can't keep me here. I'll die."

Kyla moved back over to the window. She didn't say anything.

"Kyla?"

Still no response.

Louisa sucked in a breath, held it for a few counts, then let it out. She had to think clearly. She couldn't cry. She couldn't panic.

She was alive, and that meant everything was within her reach. Palmer was okay because she'd called for help. She would just…believe it. There was no point in imagining he was dead. She might as well give up then.

And she wouldn't. She was going to figure a way out of this.

This woman was supposedly her sister, surely there was some way to appeal to that fact. She thought of how Mary or Anna would treat a sibling in this situation. Differently—Anna would yell, Mary would persuade, but they'd both be firm and clear.

"If I don't get food or water or warmth soon, I'm not going to make it," Louisa said firmly. "If that's the plan, fair enough. But if you want me alive, I need help. I'm *freezing*."

There was a moment where Louisa thought it wouldn't get through to Kyla. That she would keep standing there staring out the window with absolutely no response.

Louisa tried to think of a new approach, but Kyla moved. She said nothing, offered no explanation, but she left the cellar building.

When she returned, it was with a mug. Steam curled in wisps, indicating something hot was inside. Louisa nearly lost her battle with tears. She was so beyond hungry, she felt vaguely nauseous, but more than anything, she was so very cold. Something hot would… It would give her strength. Hope.

She was in desperate need of both.

"I'll untie you so you can eat this but understand that I'm going to shoot you if you try anything. Okay?"

Louisa nodded.

"I don't want to, but no one is messing up my plan."

Louisa nodded again. "I understand."

Kyla set the mug down on the floor and then moved behind Louisa. After a little bit of fiddling, Louisa's wrists were freed. This time tears did trip over and onto her cheeks, even though it made her even colder. But her arms ached—moving them was agonizing and yet the position she'd been in was painful too.

Kyla came back around to the front of her and looked at her disdainfully. "You're going to have to toughen up, sis. It's going to be a while yet. I've got a plan, but if your people track us down, I'm not afraid to start shooting."

She picked up the mug and handed it to Louisa. Louisa's ankles were still tied together and to the chair, so there wasn't really any chance of her escaping anyway. She one hundred percent believed Kyla would start shooting if she even *thought* Louisa was making a run for it.

She'd have to find a smart way to escape. Right now that meant eating the soup. It hurt to hold the mug, but Louisa wasn't about to drop the first touch of warmth she'd had in hours. For a few minutes, she simply cradled the mug.

Unfortunately, that gave her time to think. It looked like your typical canned soup, but what if it was something else? What if it was poisoned? What if *that* was the plan?

"I'm not standing here watching you forever. Once I'm ready to go outside, the mug goes with me. Eat or don't, but you better do it fast."

Louisa swallowed. Well, if it was poisoned... Maybe that was better than starving to death. Or being shot. She brought the mug to her lips and sipped the soup. If nothing else, it tasted as soup should taste.

And it was warm. Hot, even. It took every last ounce of strength not to start sobbing. She had to stay strong somehow though. So she slowly and methodically drank the soup. She didn't try to talk or move or anything. She kept her brain as blank as she could. All she focused on was the soup.

Once she was done, she tried to draw out the moment. Just holding on to the mug, taking a few fake sips from it. Because she knew the moment she stopped, Kyla would want to tie her back up again. The cold would return.

Kyla wasn't fooled for long. She moved forward

and tried to take the mug. Louisa knew it wasn't smart, but she held tighter to the mug. Desperate for this connection to something warm.

Kyla jerked it hard, so Louisa lost her grip. She would have toppled forward, chair and all, but Kyla used her body to keep Louisa upright. Then she set down the mug and went to work tying Louisa up.

Louisa didn't fight it. What was the point? She was certain Kyla would shoot her if she tried to run. For whatever nonsensical reason, she'd been taken and kept alive…but there had to be a *reason*.

"It's freezing in here when I can't move or do anything," Louisa said, trying to appeal to *some* humanity within the woman who now stood before her again. The woman who was supposed to be her sister.

Kyla studied her. Louisa couldn't read this stranger's expression. Clearly, everything was off about her. She wasn't behaving rationally, so there wasn't much point in trying to rationalize her behavior.

Then she simply walked out of the building, leaving Louisa alone again. Louisa squeezed her eyes shut, counting her breaths. If she was alone, she had time to consider her escape. If she was alone, she wasn't being hurt. Alone was good.

But it was so unbearably cold.

After a few moments of Louisa doing everything she could to keep her mind off the cold, Kyla returned, a folded blanket in her hands. Carefully, almost reverently, Kyla wrapped the blanket around Louisa's tied-up body. The girl's brown eyes studied Louisa. Then she shook her head, almost sadly.

"I'm sorry it can't be different," she said. "But it's all our mother's fault." Kyla shook her head again. "And she has to pay. You understand that, don't you?"

Louisa swallowed and held Kyla's gaze. Maybe she couldn't rationalize anyone's behavior, but she wanted to understand. She wanted to make sense of this in any way she could. So she worked on sounding agreeable. Understanding. "I want to, I do. But I'm not there yet."

Kyla reached over and patted Louisa's head. "Don't worry. Once they get here, you'll understand everything." She let out a long sigh. "It's just a shame that then you'll have to die."

Chapter Seventeen

Palmer hadn't been able to outsmart Mary, though he'd tried all through the night. He'd even once managed to take the IV tube out, capped off the needle in his arm and made it all the way to the end of the hall.

A nurse had stopped him, because somehow even all his charm couldn't get through to her. Because Mary had gotten to her first.

The nurse had threatened to call security. Palmer wasn't above fighting off security, but he'd been struggling to stay upright so he hadn't liked his chances.

The nurse escorted him back to his room and re-attached his IV. Mary had woken up in the time he'd been gone, and she looked furious. She had a phone to her ear, so she didn't start yelling at him while the nurse took his vitals for the five hundredth time.

"I believe I just proved I can walk around fine. Shouldn't that mean y'all can let me out?"

"That's up to the doctor, Mr. Hudson."

He smiled at the nurse even though he didn't feel like smiling. Or doing anything other than fighting someone. Not that he had the energy left in him to fight.

Once the nurse left, he turned to Mary. He already knew there was no new news or she would have immediately told him. Still, he had to ask. "Anything?"

Mary pursed her lips. She didn't meet his gaze. "They've got search parties. The police are on the lookout for Janice Menard. Cash has the search dogs out as much as possible."

"Not very helpful in the snow."

"No, it isn't, but he's trying. Everyone is trying."

He knew she was right. Rationally, he even knew him being out there looking wouldn't change anything, but just sitting here was like having needles shoved into every inch of him. It wasn't the pain from the gunshot. It was an emotional pain. A feeling of helplessness that he had worked so very hard to never have to feel again after his parents' disappearance.

And failed. When Grant went off to war. When Anna had insisted on rodeoing and getting herself hurt. When Louisa's house had burned down and he hadn't had any answers for her.

He couldn't just *sit* in these feelings. It was unbearable. "Couldn't you at least bring me my computer?"

"No. Because you are supposed to rest. You also need to stop refusing your medication."

"I'm not in that much pain." The physical pain had nothing on the twisting feeling inside his chest that Louisa might be hurt. Or worse.

Mary only gave him a look. Then she seemed to remember her phone in her hand and shoved it in her pocket. "Anna and I are going to switch off." Mary looked concerned about this. "Jack said the only way he could convince her to leave the search party was to put her on Palmer babysitting duty. She's running on fumes. So, I'll take her place, and that means you need to stay put so *she* stays put. Got it?"

As if on cue, the door opened and Anna stepped inside. She had dark circles under her eyes and a kind of grimness he remembered from those first days after their parents had gone missing. A grimness that hadn't belonged on an eight-year-old.

Still, there it was. All these years later. With more people they loved missing. Eight, twelve, twenty-four, twenty-eight, it didn't matter. It felt awful.

Mary looked from Anna to him and shook her head. "I don't trust either one of you."

"It's almost like you know us," Palmer offered, hoping to get a smile out of Anna.

Her expression didn't change. Palmer didn't know how to lie there and pretend it would all be okay if Anna didn't.

Mary rolled her eyes and crossed over to Anna. "Honey, I think you should go home for a few hours. Rest. I can stay here and—"

"If you're taking my place, you should go. We need all hands on deck." Anna swallowed. "It's already been too long. We can't let it go any longer." She didn't meet eyes with either Mary or Palmer.

Mary nodded then gave Anna a hug that Anna didn't return. "Be good, you two. *Please.*" Mary waited a beat, looking at Anna and then Palmer, then sighed and shook her head.

No doubt knowing that they would absolutely not

be *good*. How could they be? Louisa was out there and they were not sit-and-wait type people. Never had been.

Anna stared at him. "I got into your computer and Dahlia went through all your notes. She caught us all up as best she could. We still don't have any idea who took her, but the thought is it has to connect what you guys have been researching."

"Connect any dots?"

Anna shook her head. "Last I checked with Dahlia, not really. Probably need your computer expertise, though Dahlia is doing her best. They even brought Hawk up to speed, hoping something in the arson investigation connected, but they haven't found anything yet." She sucked in a breath. "Why didn't Louisa tell *me*? Ask for *my* help?" Anna asked, her voice rough from lack of sleep. "Why did she trust *you* with this?"

"We can go through all that," Palmer said, struggling to keep his voice even, "as soon as you help get me out of here. I've *got* to get out there."

Anna looked at him and the hospital bed. She was already shaking her head before she even spoke. "Palmer, you were shot. They said you could have died—"

"Yeah, Mary mentioned. Over and over again. That was yesterday. This is today. I'm fine. Or fine enough anyway. I cannot lay here while Louisa is missing, in trouble, possibly hurt. I can't. If you don't help me, I'll do it on my own. Eventually, I'll get past somebody and do it on my own."

"Why do you care so much?"

A sharp pain sliced right under his heart—again not physical. Nothing painkillers would help with. For so many different reasons, he couldn't meet Anna's sharp gaze. "You know why."

"Yeah, but I want to hear you say it."

"Fine." He glared at her, because leading with anger made more sense than feeling any of the terrible things rumbling around inside him. "You'll be the first. I'm in love with her, okay?"

Anna nodded, and she looked like she was about to cry. But she just blinked a few times and cleared her throat. "Yeah. Okay. I've got your computer in my truck. You can look up whatever you need to while we drive."

"Where are we driving to?"

Anna shook her head. "Hell if I know, but we're not going to stop until we find her."

Louisa woke with a start. She realized dimly her arms were no longer tied behind her back, though she didn't remember being unbound.

Had she been saved? Her eyes flew open and she looked around desperately. She was still in the cellar building, and it was daylight now. She was cold, but not as freezing as she'd been last night.

She was alone, and her wrists weren't bound together. She didn't want to get out from under the warm blanket, but maybe this was her chance. The door that had been open last night to the fire outside was now closed. Maybe it was locked or chained and that was why they'd untied her.

It didn't matter. She'd find a way to escape. She'd do whatever it took. She kept the blanket wrapped around her as best she could, sat up and began to try to untie the ropes around her ankles.

Everything hurt. Her vision swam. She was starving and cold and a million bad things. But the thought of escape fueled her. She *knew* people were looking for her. Maybe it had been an awful long time and no one had showed up, but she knew she couldn't just disappear into thin air.

Too many people loved her, and that was a bit overwhelming in the moment. Emotions battered her—likely from the lack of basic necessities that would have kept her mind sharper. She blinked the tears out of her eyes and focused on getting the ties off of her.

Everything hurt, but the pain all kind of melded together like a dull ache. She tried to jump to her feet and immediately regretted it—her legs nearly giving out. A quick and lucky wave of her arm found the wall and she was able to lean against it to fall with less impact than she might have without it to help her.

Louisa sucked in a breath and worked on sitting first, leaning against the wall, pulling the blanket back around her. There couldn't be any panicking. She had to be smart and careful.

This time when she got to her feet, she took it slow. She used the wall for balance and gave her legs the time they needed to have her blood circulating again.

She didn't think she was actually injured anywhere, just stiff and dehydrated.

If she could get outside, at the very least she could get some snow. She had no idea how long it had been since Kyla had brought her soup, but if her stomach was anything to go by, it had been a while.

Still using the wall as leverage, she made her way over to the window Kyla liked to stare out of. There was no actual glass in the window. It was just an opening. So much colder over here by the window. It was big enough, she could definitely crawl out of it if she had to, but the problem would be leveraging herself that high.

Louisa reached up, wincing at the twinge in her shoulder, but ignoring the pain as she tested whether there was any way to pull herself up or to jump up or—

"What did I tell you about trying to escape?"

Louisa whirled around to see Kyla standing in the doorway with her arms crossed over her chest. The gun was on a holster at her hip now, and Louisa felt slightly emboldened by the fact that Kyla didn't pull it out and point it.

"You told me I have to die," Louisa said. Maybe she should be soft and biddable, but she just…couldn't take it anymore. "You think I'm just going to sit here and *take it*?"

"You don't understand," Kyla said petulantly. "Our mother has to pay, and you're the only way I can make that happen. Better to be dead than like her, let me tell you."

"I can assure you, I don't agree. No matter what or who she is. I'd rather be alive. Wouldn't you?"

Kyla shook her head. "No. Never."

Louisa almost felt a twinge of pity for the girl. "Surely you don't mean that. I mean you get to choose. It's your life."

"My life?"

That was *clearly* the wrong thing to say.

Kyla's eyes practically blazed with fury. "*My* life? My whole life has been about *you*. About poor lost Colleen. Mom expected me to do everything because Colleen wasn't around to do it. No one could upset Mom because Colleen had been kidnapped! She was probably dead, but no one ever knew for sure. You got to be a picture on the news and all I ever was, was an *afterthought*. A problem."

"I'm…sorry, Kyla. I am sorry that that happened to you. I don't think it was my fault. Or your—our— mother's." It was impossible to think of a stranger from the news articles as her mother. Impossible even now to believe her mother had been part of some kidnapping scheme.

How could it be true? How could she believe this young woman with a gun and an unhinged plan was somehow telling more truth than Minnie O'Brien?

"You don't think. But you don't know, Colleen. You weren't there, so you don't know anything." She shook her head, like a dog shaking water of its fur. "Not the plan. This isn't the plan. Why aren't you tied up?"

"I'm cold and hurting and starving. You can't

just…keep me here and treat me like… This is worse than someone would treat an animal, Kyla. You have to at least give me some heat, some food and water, some—"

"Somehow I'm not surprised you've turned this around and made it all about you," Kyla returned.

If Kyla didn't have a gun, if even a second of this made sense, Louisa might laugh, because it wasn't all that different than how Anna and Mary had talked to each other when they'd been younger and arguing about something.

Louisa looked at Kyla. They looked so much alike. They had to be related in some way. There was just no way they weren't.

Could she really believe she was this woman's sister?

"Sit back down on that chair," Kyla ordered. She reached for her gun.

Louisa looked at the chair and then, probably ill-advisedly, shook her head. "I can't. I'm sorry. I am. But you can't tie me up again. I can't take it."

Kyla scowled but she didn't pull the gun fully out of the holster. "I clearly can't trust you to just stay put."

"No, fair enough. But maybe…maybe you could give me a reason to stay put. I know it's not the plan, but plans have to be flexible, right? If I understand why this is happening, or what you're trying to do, maybe I could agree to be tied up again."

"I could just shoot you."

Louisa swallowed and kept her gaze on Kyla's.

Imploring. Hopeful. "You could. But if we really are sisters, couldn't you just let me in instead?"

"We aren't full sisters, you know," Kyla replied, not as if she was imparting new information or even a secret, but as if that made her better somehow.

Louisa was having a hard time keeping up. "We aren't?"

"No. See, I thought if I could find out who took you, I could fix everything. Mom would be good to me. If I could get you back, then we could be a happy family. Dad would stop hitting everyone, and they could stay married. Then it wouldn't be about poor Colleen. About Mom. It could be about *me*."

"That's too much of a burden on one little girl," Louisa said, feeling some strange twisted compassion for her captor.

"It was," Kyla agreed, nodding emphatically. "But I was going to make it okay. Imagine my surprise when I found out that my mother was a lying *slut*. All those stories about a kidnapped sister were faked."

Fake. That didn't make any sense. "But I saw the stories. I... It was in the news. You said so yourself. Not fake."

"She *paid* someone to take you. So my dad wouldn't find out."

"That's absurd."

"You'd think, wouldn't you? But it isn't. It's true. I have all the proof. I found all the proof, and then I knew she needed to pay. She's on her way, and she's going to *pay*. She wanted to protect you, but she can't. She won't."

Louisa stood there and knew…no matter what parts of this story were true or fake, there was no getting out of this alive if she went along with Kyla's plan. Maybe someone would find them. Or maybe Palmer had died and no one had any clue where she was.

Maybe there was only her to save herself. It didn't matter either way because it was clear Kyla was not of sound mind. There was no reasoning with her, no getting to the bottom of things.

There was only escape.

Maybe it was the absolute wrong thing to do. Foolish and reckless and every rash thing. But she pulled back her arm and punched Kyla in the face as hard as she possibly could.

Kyla's head snapped back, but she didn't go down. She started to reach for her gun, so Louisa did too. If she could get control of the gun…

Anything was possible.

Chapter Eighteen

Anna drove—though Palmer wasn't convinced her sleep-deprived state was any better than his shot-yesterday state. At least *he* could keep his eyes open.

"Search warrant finally came through right before I got to the hospital," Anna said, catching him up to speed on everything that had happened that Mary either hadn't known or hadn't seen fit to tell him. "Jack sent Chloe and a team in to do the search. He's still out in the field with the search team, the O'Briens and some volunteer groups. They followed some vehicle tracks for a bit, but the snow and the dark made it hard to do much with it. Daylight should help, and as we hit twenty-four hours, the FBI will get involved soon."

Palmer typed away on his computer, trying not to think about *twenty-four hours*. It had taken more time than he'd like to set up his hotspot, and now he was combing through anything he had on Janice Menard and Birdie Williams. Addresses, prior residences, owned properties. Anything that might give him a clue into where someone might have taken Louisa.

"You should probably yank that," Anna said, jerking her chin toward the capped IV needle in his arm.

"Aren't you going to do it for me?"

She scowled at the road. If they had nothing else, they had this. They both knew the other didn't like needles. They could handle guns, being shot apparently, forcing their body beyond the limits of what it should do—both in the rodeo and as investigators—but the whole *needle* situation made them both a little squirmy.

If he thought about that—Anna's weaknesses, the needle—he wouldn't think about Louisa. About all those possibilities that could have happened in the past nearly twenty-four hours.

Because Mary had been right yesterday. They had to deal in facts, not in maybes. The fact was he didn't know where Louisa was. He could think of a million outcomes, but he didn't know which one was close to being correct. So. Present. Not future. Not past.

Just right here, finding the answers to get to her.

"It all begins with that Janice Menard. Someone set that fire at the O'Brien house, but it didn't hurt anyone. Louisa wasn't even home. Whatever that was, it wasn't the same as Janice sending Lou and me to that abandoned house. She sent us there knowing we'd be hurt."

Palmer typed and stared and tried not to get frustrated. Dahlia had compiled a tidy list of properties owned by Janice Menard and Birdie Williams. The address they'd been sent to had been owned by Birdie Williams but, according to Anna, the questioning of Birdie hadn't led anywhere helpful.

Also, according to Anna, police and search parties had already exhausted any and all other properties owned by either woman.

There was no sign of Louisa.

"If I take you to the original site, one of Jack's deputies is going to tell Jack. We have to be careful about where we go look if you're going to be in on it. I wouldn't put it past him to throw you in a cell if he thought it'd keep you staying put."

Palmer nodded. He'd known as much. "Just drive *toward* the Williamses' property. Maybe I'll come up with a new direction to take," he said, gesturing at his computer.

He was the computer expert. So there had to be something he could find. Some clue. Some possibility. Louisa couldn't disappear into thin air like his parents had. She just...couldn't.

He wouldn't survive it again.

Anna's phone rang and she answered it over the Bluetooth in her truck. "What do you have for us, Dahlia?" she asked.

"I found something," Dahlia was saying over the speaker. "It might be nothing, an odd coincidence, but it's worth noting. I've already told Jack, but I knew you two would want to know too. Janice Menard has a connection to the Brown family. The one that messaged Louisa over Facebook."

Palmer went very still. "What kind of connection?" he said, trying not to bark it out like an order. Dahlia might be dating his brother, but she wasn't a Hudson. He could hardly bark orders at the sweet librarian.

Even if he wanted to in the moment.

"It's very tenuous, but Janice's ex-husband, Pat Menard, is from Lakely, Ohio. Since that's where the Browns are from, I started digging. He's the cousin of the mother of the woman who sent that Facebook message to Louisa. It's kind of a roundabout tie, but I don't think we can overlook any kind of connection at the moment."

"No, we can't," Anna agreed. "Any other leads about where Louisa might actually be?"

"No, but I've started looking into property records for not just Janice's ex-husband but also *his* family in Lakely. If there's anything in Wyoming, I'll send it to everyone. I figured if you broke Palmer out of the hospital, you've got his computer and he can probably do it faster and more thoroughly than I can."

"How do you know I broke him out of the hospital and we're not just sitting here playing checkers?" Anna returned.

"Uh-huh," came Dahlia's reply.

Palmer was barely listening. He was tracking down Pat Menard and his family in Lakely. Finding anything he could. Because it had to connect.

It just had to.

"I'm going to have to stop for gas before we get any farther out of town," Anna said after she'd hung up with Dahlia. "Maybe you can find something by the time I'm finished."

Palmer grunted in assent. He focused all his attention on his computer. On finding anything about Janice's ex. Pat Menard and Janice had divorced some three years ago, and Pat had moved to Las Vegas.

Palmer found a previous marriage for Pat, which

included two adult children living in the Lakely area. Palmer had started doing some digging into both of them when he heard Anna talking.

Not to him.

He looked up from his computer and saw Anna standing there, driver's-side door open. She'd clearly already gotten gas, but she was glaring at a man.

Hawk Steele.

"What are you doing here?" she demanded.

"Likely the same thing you are," he replied. "They let me take a look around the property where Palmer was shot. I found some of the same accelerant in the barn that was used in the O'Brien fire. It all connects, so I'm investigating. I think I've got a lead."

"Does it have to do with Janice's ex-husband?" Palmer asked.

Palmer noted a small flicker of surprise on Hawk's face before it went back to being unreadable.

"Yeah, it does. Janice's stepson owns some property about fifteen miles away from the Williamses' residence. It's just property. Far as I can tell—"

Palmer was already typing away. He found it before Hawk got the sentence out. "Off Rural Route 7. No house. No buildings. Just property, and it doesn't look like he does anything with it."

Palmer looked up at Hawk, who was frowning. "No evidence of anything but a holding."

"Did you tell Jack?"

"Not yet. Just got the information myself. Was fueling up and figured I'd check it out myself rather than take the search party away from the area we know for sure she was in."

Anna looked over at him and Palmer considered. They needed all hands on deck, but his brother would likely cuff him and have a deputy send him back to the hospital.

But it couldn't just be the three of them, no matter how much he trusted Anna and himself. They needed everyone.

"Give him a call. Don't tell him you told us though. We'll have maybe a bit of a head start before he sends some people over, but it doesn't matter. All that matters is finding Louisa."

Hawk nodded, eyeing Anna and then Palmer. "Neither of you are in any shape to drive. Hop in the back, Blondie. I'll take it from here."

Palmer reached over the console hoping to stop his sister from her inevitably punching Hawk in the face. His hiss of pain as the move hurt his side distracted and kept Anna from her anger, he hoped.

Palmer wasn't sure if Hawk was that foolish or didn't give Anna enough credit for actually doing it, but neither mattered right now. "I'll get in the back," he said.

Because all that mattered was getting to Louisa.

Louisa didn't get a hold of the gun, but she did manage to knock it away from Kyla. She had two choices, and there was no time to decide which one was best. Instinct took over.

She ran.

The door had been left open and maybe she should have kept making a play for the gun but getting out and getting away just seemed far more important. Or maybe, if she were being honest with herself, she just knew she wouldn't be able to shoot Kyla, so escape was really her only option here.

She ran. Out into the cold morning. The snow made it hard to pick up speed, but as she looked around at her surroundings, she saw rocks and trees and far more possibilities for hiding places than there had been back at the original location.

There was still a campfire, but no one else seemed to be around. Or if they were, they were hidden. Louisa also didn't see any vehicles, though she did see vehicle tracks.

"Don't make me shoot you!" Kyla shouted from behind.

Louisa didn't even bother to look back. She just ran as fast as she could through the snow toward cover.

A gunshot went off, and an involuntary noise erupted from Louisa. A little gasp or scream of shock and fear. She didn't stop running. Because nothing hurt. It had sounded close, but no bullet had hit her.

She made it behind a boulder. She crouched so her head was hidden and didn't stop moving. Her eyes darted around her surroundings, constantly looking for shelter but knowing there was no stopping. As long as she was moving, she was less of a target and maybe she could find help.

She didn't really know if Kyla would kill her, and that was the problem. There was no way to predict how this was going to go. All she could do was run.

Which was also a gamble. In a Wyoming winter when she didn't know where she was. But someone would find her. Too many people would have to be looking for her not to find her.

So, she ran. She crouched behind boulders, darted behind trees, and though she occasionally heard Kyla yell something at her or scream in frustration, there was enough distance, enough natural elements, to hide behind so that she felt almost safe.

The sun was out in force, shining down on the snow making the world around her blinding. And showing her tracks all too well, but she didn't have time to cover them.

She didn't have *time*. She tried to fight off the panic, but she heard a man's voice in the distance. And not one that made her think she'd been rescued. She was almost certain it was the man who'd shot Palmer.

It wasn't just Kyla looking for her now.

She had to do something. She took a brief moment to stop, to look around. If she started climbing those rocks, she could get up off of the snow. Maybe hide her tracks a little better. If she could scramble high enough on that mountain, she could see farther. Get an idea of where she was. Maybe spot help.

It was risky, because she wasn't quite as steady on her feet as she usually was, thanks to lack of food and water, but she couldn't think of any better plan.

She started to climb. She didn't know where Kyla or the man were in relation to her position, so it was hard to maneuver herself in a way she thought would keep her hidden, but she did her best.

Her limbs were shaking. She wouldn't get much farther without risking a fall. She paused, trying to take in her surroundings. Trying to get an idea of what direction she needed to go in, or how she might signal to someone—someone who would help her, not shoot at her—where she was.

She wasn't high enough. All she saw was rock and a little bit of the place she'd come from. She also didn't spot any of her captors, which she supposed was good.

She had to climb higher, no matter how shaky she felt. She turned back to the rocks. They were getting bigger, so hard to get around and up. But it was her only choice. Her only shot at freedom.

So she reached and climbed, pushing her body way beyond its limits.

"Because I'm going to get out of this," she whispered to herself, a quiet motivation. "I am strong enough to endure this. I have to get home. For my parents. For my grandparents. For myself. For Anna. For...Palmer." She wanted to cry, thinking about the fact that Palmer might not be okay, but she didn't have *time*.

A gunshot went off again, and it startled Louisa enough that her foot slipped, her ankle gave out and she tumbled to the hard, rocky ground. Pain shot up her ankle. She barely swallowed a yelp and moan of pain. She breathed through it as her vision swam, as she tried to take stock.

It was twisted, yes, and she'd landed on a rock so now her side ached. She hadn't hit her head though or anything else, so that was good. Even better, there were very few tracks here since the snow only piled up in dips and crevices, so they'd have a harder time finding her.

That gunshot had been farther away, so she had

time. She just had to *think*. She tried to get to her feet, but the pain in her ankle was so excruciating, she nearly yelped and fell all over again.

Okay, running wasn't going to work, she thought, on her hands and knees, breathing heavily. She could still hide. On her own terms. She looked around. Where there were rocks and mountains, there had to be caves.

She saw an opening not too far off. It was *really* small, and she didn't *love* enclosed spaces, but it was better than sitting out in the open waiting to be found and shot.

She crawled, trying desperately not to sob in pain. Trying to ignore the hard ground, or the cold snow she had to crawl through, making her pants and sleeves wet.

Louisa didn't whisper anything to herself now. She just focused on that cave and did everything in her power to get there. To pretzel herself into the dark, enclosed space that made her want to scream in panic.

She huddled in on herself. Now cold and wet and hurt. It was better than being a prisoner. Anything was better than that.

She held on to that belief, and then tried to come up with a plan on how to get out of this.

Chapter Nineteen

Palmer didn't pay much attention to the drive. After he'd offered to get in the back, Anna had grumbled at him to stay put and she got in the back and let Hawk drive. Palmer focused on his computer, on this property.

He looked at the map, tried to memorize it. "There's no real road in, according to the map," he explained to Hawk as Hawk drove down the highway. "You'll get on the rural route and then we'll have to trust the GPS coordinates to get us to the right place to hike in."

Palmer hacked into some satellite imaging and considered. "It looks like there's some kind of structure on the southwest end. Not a house, but definitely a building of some kind. Or what was once a building."

"We'll get close to that spot then," Hawk said, turning off the highway and onto the rural route.

Palmer looked out his window for a minute. She had to be out there somewhere. This had to be the lead they needed it to be. It *had* to be.

"They would have wanted some shelter overnight,"

Hawk mused. "Especially with a captive. A building—even a structure of some kind that allowed shelter—wosuld be helpful."

"Unless they were prepared to camp and hide in the mountains. Or, you know, you're leading us on a wild-goose chase," Anna said from the back.

Palmer spared her a glance. She had her arms crossed and he wanted to say she was being petulant for the sake of it, but he saw in her eyes what he felt.

Bone-deep worry. And bone-deep exhaustion.

"It's a lead to follow," Palmer said gently. "Better to be wrong about it than not check it out."

"Your brother's sending a group out this way, but by no means everyone," Hawk said, his voice void of any inflection. It seemed to be something he *extra* put on for Anna. "No doubt when the FBI get here, they'll want to look into this lead too."

Anna let out a little growl of distaste, but she didn't argue any further.

Palmer focused on the satellite and GPS and instructed Hawk where to drive and then where to stop. It wasn't surprising the property wasn't used for anything. It was mostly rocks leading up into mountains. There was some tree cover around, but even the somewhat flat ground was mostly rocky.

"No fence," Hawk noted. "I could just keep driving. But it's going to bang up your truck."

"I don't care," Anna said. "Get us as close as you can."

Hawk nodded and turned the truck off the road. It was bumpy and Palmer had to grip the door handle and grind his teeth together to keep from making any noise of pain.

But *damn* that hurt.

"You see that?" Hawk asked, pointing in the distance out the windshield. Palmer leaned forward, trying not to grab his side in pain. But he did see it. It looked like rocks, but not like the mountains or boulders. More like a structure.

"Drive toward it."

Hawk nodded and moved forward, though he had to slow the pace given the rocky ground. Palmer could only be grateful. Much more jolts to his gunshot wound and he might just pass out.

"Better stop here," Hawk said. "There's still some cover in case we've got company."

Palmer and Anna nodded, and Palmer studied the structure from inside the truck. It was half in the earth, half out. A kind of cellar that wasn't fully underground. It had a door, but the windows were just holes in the stone, not glass.

More concerning than this creepy building was that there were remnants of a campfire, not lit but still smoldering right outside the open door.

As if on cue, Hawk and Anna pulled guns out. Anna handed Palmer one. They didn't even have to communicate getting out of the truck. They did it in unison, coming together and standing in kind of a back-to-back triangle while they each surveyed the world around them.

Palmer was breathing a little heavily from the pain in

his side. Sweat had even popped up along his forehead. But this was a lead and he had to follow it through.

"Maybe you should stay put," Hawk offered, no doubt concerned by Palmer's huffing and puffing.

"Maybe you should mind your own business," Palmer returned through gritted teeth.

"What do you think?" Hawk asked Anna.

She was quiet for a beat of silence, all three of them scanning the horizon for signs of people.

"We could leave him, but he won't stay put. So he might as well be with us."

"All right. Someone's clearly here or been here very recently. We don't know if it's who we're looking for, if it's dangerous or how many people we might be up against," Hawk said, clearly taking charge. Palmer was all right with it in the moment—he was busy trying to stay upright. The surprising thing was that Anna didn't seem to argue with him for the sake of it.

Because, for all of them, the important thing was finding Louisa.

"I think it'll be a good fifteen before Jack's people get over here, but I don't think we should wait," Anna said. "Every second counts."

"Agreed. We'll head out," Hawk said with a nod. "See what we can find, but we've got to stick together until we've got more information. We've got to work as a team. Understood?"

"Yeah," Anna said. "Understood."

Palmer nodded because he didn't trust his voice. The good news was that even if the pain wasn't subsiding exactly, he was closer to having a handle on it.

On not huffing and puffing and feeling like his whole body might give out.

"Let's search the building."

They moved forward as a unit. Hawk opened the door while Palmer and Anna held weapons to cover him. Then they entered in a line and quickly returned to their tactical positioning.

The building was empty. No rooms to hide in or things to hide behind. There was a chair in the middle of the room, and some ropes and a blanket on the floor.

Palmer's stomach tensed like a fist. Someone had been held here against their will. He didn't want to say that out loud, but he supposed he didn't have to. It was clear.

"She was held here," Anna said flatly. "Clearly."

"There's no evidence Miss O'Brien was here. There's no evidence that rope was used to tie someone to that chair," Hawk pointed out. "It could very well be unrelated."

"It's a reasonable leap," Palmer said, though his voice was rough—and not because of pain. At least, not physical pain. All too well, he could picture Louisa tied to that chair. All too easily, he could think of all the terrible reasons she wasn't anymore.

"You can't make leaps like that in an investigation."

"Maybe not in an arson investigation," Palmer replied. "But in a cold case, you've sometimes got to make the leaps that lead you to a new direction to go in."

"This isn't a cold case either," Hawk noted. "It's an active investigation."

"We've got lots of different teams working different angles to find Louisa," Anna countered. "So, we'll take this angle. We'll assume she was held here. By at least two people, maybe three. We follow all those prints outside and see what we can find. I'm an expert tracker."

She was already moving back out of the building, and Palmer watched as Hawk struggled with some inner argument before following her. Palmer then followed him, and Anna was already studying the prints.

"A struggle of some sort?" Palmer asked.

Anna crouched down and looked at the prints more closely. Most were just a mess of indents in the snow, but there were a few clearer ones. "There's one that I'd say is a man's boot," she said, pointing to one. "Much larger than the others. But…I can't really tell the others apart. There are an awful lot of prints, and they're all kind of the same size. There are some differences in tread, so I can tell we've got at least two others besides the man. I took some pictures at the original site."

She pulled out her phone and opened her photos. Then held it up against the largest one. "I think this might be the guy who shot you, Palmer." She held the phone so Hawk and Palmer could look and compare.

"I think you're right," Hawk said, "which means we're on the right track."

"These prints aren't frozen over either," Palmer said, crouching and making an *oof* sound in an effort to hide the groan of pain. He poked at the snow around the imprints. "But those are," he said, indicating the more uniform ones. "We can guess that those are from last night or even yesterday, and these less clear ones are from today." He squinted up at the sun. "Because they haven't had a chance to freeze over."

Though it grated, Anna took his arm and helped him to a standing position. Hawk looked at him speculatively.

"It doesn't matter if I'm up to this or not," Palmer said to him, though Hawk hadn't *expressed* any of his obvious concerns. "I'm not resting till she's found. It doesn't have to be me, but I can't sit around and wait."

Hawk didn't react to that in any way. He looked back down at the tracks. "I say we follow those. I assume that's what you want to do?"

"It's a miracle. You actually assume right," Anna said, keeping her arm linked with Palmer's like he needed the support. "Jack's guys can follow us. If we get into a scrape, they'll get us out."

Palmer figured she was speaking with more confidence than she felt—Lord knew it was more confidence than he had. But what else was there to do? They could hardly sit around and wait when it was clear Louisa had been held against her will.

With no discussion, Hawk took the lead, followed by Palmer, with Anna holding up the rear. They were careful to follow the tracks without disturbing them, so it was clear which ones were the search party's and which ones were the perpetrators'.

It was already pretty confusing because there were multiple people involved. Anna was an expert at tracking and even she couldn't tell some of the footprints apart.

They didn't move quickly. There were a lot of reasons, but they all annoyed Palmer. He didn't want to be careful. He didn't want to give a thought to the excruciating pain in his side.

He only wanted to find Louisa.

But he wanted her alive, so the tactical slowness would have to do, no matter how his impatience strained.

They started to climb rocks and Hawk and Anna switched places since Anna was better at tracking. But this was hard, because without the snow, she could only track places there *was* snow or different inconsistencies that she could only guess were tracks.

They stopped for what felt like the hundredth time as Anna crouched and studied a little area of snow. "Two people went this way." She poked at the snow, then looked up at the direction she must think the tracks went. "But at different times."

She straightened, did a little circle around a large rock. Then she pointed in the opposite direction. "Then two people—two different people, because the boot tracks are different—went this way. Together."

"Which one's Louisa?" Palmer demanded.

Anna inhaled, frowning. "It's hard to say. Three of the tracks are almost exactly the same size. Slightly different treads on one of them. If I'm making those big leaps I'm not supposed to make in an investigation, I'd say Louisa is the one with slightly different treads and there are two women, likely, with the same boots, working with the gunman." She pointed to the first direction. "Which makes me think maybe Louisa got away, ran off. Then someone followed. Hence, why they were hiking at different points in time. The other two people?" She shrugged. "I don't have a clue why they'd go in a different direction."

"We should split up," Palmer said.

Both Hawk and Anna looked at him dubiously. "Only if by 'splitting up,' you mean you go back to where we were and wait in the truck until the search party gets here, and Anna and I follow Louisa's tracks."

Palmer scowled. "Not on your life, bud."

"Then we stick together. Anna will…" He trailed off, frowning. He looked around, but all Palmer saw was blue sky. Then he heard…something. He glanced at Hawk, who nodded. He'd heard it too.

They all held completely still, listening to the sound. Almost like voices. Hawk made a hand motion to follow him, so Palmer fell into step behind him, Anna behind Palmer. They moved so slowly, it could hardly count as movement, but it kept them from making any noise and helped them continue to listen.

The voices had stopped, but there was still a sound. Like a rustle. Palmer followed Hawk, step by careful step, as they rounded a boulder.

Hunched over a bag in a little clearing between rocks was the man who'd shot him. He had a gun in one hand, his other hand in a canvas sack. His back was to them, and Palmer didn't think he'd heard them.

Hawk drew his weapon and stepped forward, so

Palmer and Anna did the same, flanking Hawk just in case.

"Drop it," Hawk ordered.

The man did not drop his weapon, but he looked over his shoulder at them. He eyed Palmer with some surprise. "Thought I'd killed you."

Palmer did his best to look like the gunshot was nothing. He stood on his own two feet, kept his grip on the gun firm but not tight, held the man's glare. "Thought wrong."

"You've got three guns on you," Hawk said, almost conversationally. "It's in your best interest to drop yours."

"Is it?" He jutted his chin above them. Palmer didn't look, afraid it was a trap, but he heard Hawk and Anna swear.

"Got a sniper up there," Hawk muttered.

The guy who'd shot him smirked, still crouched there next to a bag. "You shoot me, the girl here gets it," he said, pointing at Anna.

Since Anna and Hawk each had an eye on a gun, Palmer scoped out the area around them. So far, just this guy and their sniper—who wasn't that far up the mountain. From Palmer's vantage point, she looked young. Younger than Anna even. She wasn't quite dressed appropriately for the Wyoming winter, but she held the gun with clear comfort and adeptness. The scope was trained right at Anna's head.

Anna was still, but mostly appeared unfazed. She met his gaze and raised an eyebrow. An old sign. In any other circumstances, he might have laughed.

But this wasn't some bar after the rodeo where Anna wanted to start or finish a little trouble—with his help.

This was life and death.

He shook his head at her, but she rolled her eyes. A clear sign she wasn't going to listen. So he knew he had to wade in. Just like always.

Because, five seconds later, Anna leaped forward and tackled the guy on the rocky ground, the sniper fired and all hell broke loose.

Chapter Twenty

Something nudged Louisa out of the odd pseudo sleep she'd fallen into. Not a real sleep. There was nothing restful about it, but exhaustion and boredom had taken over, so she hadn't fully realized her eyes were closed.

And then jerked open because something… Something had happened. Something had changed.

She kept her body very still. It was hard to see since inside the cave was dark and outside was blindingly sunny. She willed her eyes to adjust to the contrast. She listened, or tried to listen, but her heart was echoing in her ears and it was hard to hear beyond that.

When she couldn't take it anymore, she took a deep, careful breath and then slowly and quietly let it out. When she moved, she did so slowly and carefully, but still she'd grown so stiff—not just in her ankle or side, but all over—it took a great effort not to let out any kind of noise of pain.

She closed her eyes in an effort to focus and just remember that she could survive any temporary pain if she could get out of this. She'd escaped that cellar, so survival was an option. She just had to be smart.

When she reopened her eyes and gave them time to adjust, she moved her body again, this time taking into account how much every muscle ached. She tried to account for her injured ankle in the small, cramped space.

When she finally managed to maneuver so that she could see outside the cave opening, she was sweating and her breaths were coming in short pants.

Temporary pain, she chanted silently to herself as she peered out the opening into the sunny afternoon.

She didn't see anyone or anything. The sky was still blue and the sun higher than it had been, but still not yet late afternoon. So she hadn't been here, half asleep, that long.

She listened for the sounds of anyone, or even an animal, but didn't hear anything. Until someone spoke. Loud and clear.

"You shouldn't have run, Colleen."

Louisa recognized Kyla's voice, but she didn't see her. Was Kyla talking *to* her or just to herself as she searched for Louisa somewhere nearby? There was no way to know since Louisa couldn't see her.

There was the faint sound of something small and light falling. Pebbles. They tipped over the cave opening and onto the ground at Louisa's feet.

Kyla was above her. Louisa tried to look up but the sun was too bright and the overhang of the cave too thick.

"Come out, Colleen. I know you're in there." More pebbles fell as Kyla shifted above her.

Louisa figured it was better to emerge while she

could, hiding her injured ankle as best she could, and giving herself more means of escape rather than be stuck in the cave. But Kyla definitely had the high ground. Still, Louisa turned to face off with her, even if she had to squint against the sun that seemed to shine down on Kyla standing on a boulder above the cave, gun in her hand.

"My name is Louisa," Louisa said firmly, hands curled into fists. Okay, she couldn't fight off a bullet, she couldn't even run at this point, but she could fight. "Louisa O'Brien."

"Your name is Colleen Brown," Kyla said, her finger curling around the trigger of the gun. "You're the reason my life has been hell. I was going to wait. I was going to make her pay. You ruined the plan. You ruined everything, just like always." She shook her head, and there were tears in her brown eyes. "I'll just kill you both. I'll just kill us all."

But she didn't point the gun at Louisa. Louisa used her peripheral vision to get an idea of where she could jump or hide if Kyla did. It would hurt, but there was a spot she could lunge for that would give her some cover.

For now, she looked at this woman and tried to figure a way out of this without any shooting. "Why, Kyla? Why should anyone die? I'm your sister. I thought you reached out because you wanted family. I could be your family."

Kyla stared at her. She shook her head sadly. She was crying now, and Louisa honestly didn't know how to play this situation. "I had a plan," Kyla repeated. "You always ruin the plan."

"Okay." Louisa nodded even though she knew the plan was her being *murdered*. Kyla looked more disheveled than she had last night. Like she was unraveling along with all her plans. "You had a plan. It didn't work out quite the way you wanted it to. That's okay. That's life."

"What do *you* know about life? You got everything. I was left with *nothing*," Kyla snapped. Whatever grasp she seemed to have on control was slipping. The girl was crying harder now, and again Louisa felt a sliver of sympathy for her. Even as Kyla's grip on the gun tightened.

"You don't have nothing," Louisa said, though her throat was tight with both fear and sadness. "Because we're sisters. That could mean something if you let it. But not if you kill me. Then you really do have nothing. It'll all be over. And you'll end up paying the price. It doesn't have to end this way."

"If I showed her… If I proved to her that I was the better daughter. That she was wrong about me. About my dad. Then it would all be okay." She wiped her tears and running nose on her sleeve. "But it was never okay because of *you*. He was only hard on everyone because of *you*. She only left everyone because of *you*."

Louisa felt torn because this was just sad, heartbreaking really. She wanted to reach out for the girl, help her. But without a plan, with all this emotion, Kyla was even more unpredictable. Even more dangerous. "Kyla," she said, trying to sound calm, trying to hold Kyla's off-and-on stare. "Killing me doesn't change anything."

"She'd pay. She'd finally pay."

"But if our mother... She set up the whole kidnapping thing like you said, because I wasn't your dad's—" Louisa didn't know if she believed Kyla's story, but she knew it best to act as though she did "—but she didn't kill me. She didn't try to find me. She...gave me up, I guess? I don't matter to her. She threw me away."

"Don't you see?" Kyla demanded. "You matter the most. She got you out. She knew. She knew what he was. What he'd do. But I had to stay. I had to make it all work. She saved you. She sentenced me."

"I'm sorry," Louisa said, and she felt her own tears threatening. "I am so sorry for whatever you've had to go through, Kyla. I *am*. But it didn't have to do with me. You have to see that."

"Why do I have to see that?" Kyla replied, lifting the gun a little, not fully pointed at Louisa, but close enough to be a problem. "If you hadn't been born, if you hadn't been given up, everything would be different."

"Different isn't always better."

Louisa moved a little to the left, trying very hard not to make her limp noticeable. Kyla's finger was still on the trigger and the gun hadn't moved from that too-close-for-comfort position. If Louisa had enough of an idea of when she'd shoot, she could jump out of the way.

Oh, it would hurt. She'd likely break something,

but it would be better than being shot, wouldn't it? Of course, Kyla would probably just follow, shooting again. So it was a temporary solution to a long-range problem. What other choices were there?

Before she could decide—or Kyla could decide anything, for that matter—there was a shout from not too far off. Followed by a gunshot. It all distracted Kyla enough that Louisa could limp behind a boulder.

Maybe someone had come to help. Maybe she was free.

Either way, she had to do what she could to make sure Kyla couldn't kill her. She hobbled over the rocks, ducking behind them to create as much of a shield as she could. Before, she'd climbed up the mountain thinking that would be escape, now she went down. If someone was out there, someone had come to find her, she could get to them.

She could get to safety.

She skidded down one flat rock and had to take a little leap. She focused on landing on her good foot, but the force of it nearly injured that one too.

Somehow she managed to stay upright. There was pain, but not the same kind of pain that was in her other ankle. She moved to the next boulder, kept working her way down. It was the only chance to survive.

She didn't know if Kyla followed or was heading toward the shouts and gunshot. It didn't matter. All that mattered was getting down. Finding someone who could help.

Louisa's entire body was shaking, and she lost her

balance once, enough to kind of roll down a boulder. She tried to fall at least somewhat strategically, but in attempting to keep from hurting her ankle any more, she left the rest of her body unprotected and her temple slammed far too hard into the edge of the boulder as she came to a skidding stop.

She didn't shout or scream in pain. She was already in too much agony for that to really penetrate. But she felt something kind of sticky run down her forehead and lifted her hand to try to wipe it away before it got into her eyes.

It was blood, of course. Hell. She could not afford this on top of everything else. She wiped as much from her forehead as she could so it wouldn't impact her eyesight. But of course it was a head wound, so it just kept bleeding.

She looked around. She'd fallen into a spot between rocks, and as long as Kyla didn't come from straight up, Louisa might be able to hide here out of sight if she stayed low.

At least for a little while. At least until help came. Help had to be coming.

That's when she heard something. Footsteps, grunts. The sound of flesh and bone hitting flesh and bone. Gunshots. She rolled onto her stomach and peeked through the opening between two rocks to see if she could find the source of the sounds of a fight.

Because a fight had to mean help.

Down below was a clearing, and she immediately saw Anna's blond head. Anna was crouched behind her own rock, while the girl who'd been working with

Kyla shot from a higher position across the clearing from Louisa. Hawk was fighting off the man who'd shot Palmer with punches and kicks. Two guns were on the ground around them and they both seemed to be fighting to keep the other from reaching them.

Then she saw Palmer. Alive. God, he was *alive*. She nearly wept right there. He held a gun, was pointing it at the girl on the rise. He was alive and here and…maybe it could all be all right.

She heard footsteps behind her and knew she had to brace herself for Kyla before any of them could be considered safe.

PALMER CURSED HIS shaky hands. He didn't want to take a bad shot, but the sniper just kept firing off rounds at the rock Anna was huddling behind and, from his position, he couldn't get a good angle on the shooter— even if his hands were steady.

Anna had lost her gun in the skirmish. After she'd launched herself at the guy, and the sniper had missed a few shots, Hawk had waded in and taken over, while Palmer had shoved Anna behind the rock she was currently behind.

There'd been a near miss from the sniper and he'd had to dive behind his own rock rather than help Hawk disarm the man on the ground. Not that Palmer had much of his usual fight in him, he knew. Hawk was holding his own, and as long as the fight went on, the sniper couldn't risk taking a shot at Hawk without shooting her own guy.

They needed to take that sniper out, but Palmer could not find the angle he needed.

"Would you hurry?" Anna shouted at him.

"Can't. Need a better angle." He surveyed his surroundings one more time. He needed higher ground but getting there would put him out in the open, not to mention be more of a struggle than he'd like with his injury. Maybe—

He saw the flash of movement up above, out of the corner of his eye. He immediately whirled, thinking it was a threat, before he realized he recognized that coat, that black hair. He almost shouted, but at the last moment, he understood she was alone. Hidden.

She had to stay that way, but he needed Anna to know she was there.

Because Louisa was alive. Right *here*. Safe in her little alcove of rocks. The relief was so potent, his legs nearly went to jelly.

"I can take her out," Anna yelled at him, bringing his attention back to the problems at hand. "Toss me the gun," Anna said, gesturing at him.

Tossing the gun was a terrible idea, but Anna had a better angle and, if she took out the sniper, Palmer could get up to Louisa. He looked at the sniper's location one more time, then Anna's, and fired in the general direction so the sniper would duck.

He used that break to run like hell across the way to Anna. He skidded to a stop just as another gunshot exploded around them. He pressed the gun into Anna's palm, ignoring the stabbing pain in his side that was thankfully yesterday's pain, not a new gunshot wound.

"Take her out if you can, but no matter what, keep covering me. Louisa is up there. I'm going after her."

Anna looked up at the rocks above them. Then swore. "She's not alone."

Palmer didn't think, not about the sniper or the guy Hawk was fighting. He just took off, doing his best to scale the rocks even as his body screamed at him to stop. Even as gunshots and shouts sounded around him.

He reached Louisa almost at the same time the other woman did. Looking so much like Louisa, Palmer finally realized what this was.

"You're Kyla Brown," he said, firmly placing his body between Kyla and Louisa. Because Kyla had a gun and Louisa was already bleeding. So much blood on her in fact, he couldn't focus on anything but the attacker or he'd fall apart.

"And you're the interfering boyfriend." Kyla pointed her gun at him. "Weren't you already shot once? I don't need you. I'd happily shoot you again. Step out of the way."

Palmer only spread his arms, as if that alone could shield Louisa. He'd do anything. Play human shield. *Anything*. "I can't let you kill her."

Kyla shrugged. "Then I'll just kill you both."

Louisa tried to push around him, but Palmer only grabbed her and held her back, still hidden behind his body. She looked up at him, the blood smudged all over her forehead causing his stomach to cramp.

"Let me go," she said. Her eyes full of tears. Her

face bruised and scratched and pale. She was favoring one leg and her clothes were torn.

"Like hell," he replied.

She huffed out a breath and pulled far enough away from him that she could look at the woman and speak.

"Kyla. It's over. If you put down the gun, no one has to die. And you can… We can get you the help you need. It'll be okay. I promise you. I will do everything I can to make this okay."

Kyla shook her head. She had her finger around the trigger, the gun pointed in their vague direction, though she didn't seem to be aiming. The girl seemed more desperate and devastated than determined to gun them down. She wasn't as beat up as Louisa, but she'd undoubtedly been crying. She was clearly lost.

"It'll never be okay," she said. "You ruined everything."

Palmer saw the moment when Kyla just gave it up. He knew what was coming. He jerked Louisa to him, hoping he could get them both out of the path of the bullet, but using his body to shield Louisa regardless.

The shot rang out, loud and far too close. It echoed in his ears, but there was something…odd about how it sounded around them. How he didn't feel that slice of pain. Was it shock? Had she missed?

He looked down at Louisa, running his hands along her body. Surely the bullet hadn't gotten to her. "You're okay?"

"Yes, I… Palmer." She pointed behind him.

Kyla was on the ground. Behind her crumpled form was Jack. He was already moving forward for

Kyla's gun, which had clattered to the ground. He had his radio pulled to his mouth and was shouting out orders.

Louisa pushed around Palmer and rushed forward to Kyla.

Palmer noticed her limp and followed with some errant thought that he would carry her away. He would do anything to get her away from all this.

But she knelt next to Kyla, who lay on the ground. Kyla wasn't dead, because she was kind of crying and making an odd whining sound, but not writhing around exactly, which was a concern.

Jack knelt on her other side and pulled something out of his pocket. Ironically, Kyla seemed to have been shot in almost the exact place Palmer had been.

"Will she be okay?" Louisa asked Jack.

Palmer didn't know how she could be worried about this woman when Kyla had literally just been about to kill her, but he rubbed Louisa's back and didn't say anything while Jack answered.

"We've got medics on-site. It'll be rough getting all the way up here, but everyone's doing their best. They found Hillary Brown, Kyla's mother, tied up in the truck of a car not far from here. She also needs medical attention. As does the sniper Anna took out and the man Hawk beat up."

"She deserves to die," Kyla said between gritted teeth. "Mom. Colleen. They all deserve to die."

"Who's Colleen?" Jack asked, looking up at them.

"Me," Louisa said, her voice just a croak. "I'm apparently Colleen Brown."

Jack sent Palmer a quizzical look but didn't question any further. There'd be time for that yet. The medics crawled up the rock face and took over. Palmer pulled Louisa away from Kyla. He wanted to carry her down to the ambulance himself, but he wouldn't be able to hack it.

"Louisa needs a hospital too," Palmer said to Jack once Kyla had been taken away.

"Yeah, so do you," Jack replied. "You would have been dead if I hadn't shot her."

That was probably true. Maybe the first gunshot wound hadn't killed him, but likely the second would have. If it would have saved Louisa… He'd choose it a million times over, but…

He had Jack. "I guess it's a good thing I've got a big brother looking out for me."

Jack heaved out a breath. "What kind of recklessness would ever make you think it's a good idea to run an escape mission twenty-four hours after being shot?" he muttered. He didn't wait for an answer though. He moved away and began shouting orders at people below.

Meanwhile, Palmer held on to Louisa while they waited for the more pressing injuries to be looked at.

"I knew you had to be okay," she said into his chest. "I knew you all would come. I knew it."

He pressed his mouth to her temple. "Always, Lou."

Chapter Twenty-One

Louisa was taken to the hospital with Palmer. Hawk and Anna were given on-site treatment but hadn't needed to be transported. All of Kyla's crew, including her kidnapped mother, had.

Louisa supposed in some strange way, Hillary Brown was her mother, but she just couldn't…grasp that. The problem was, she didn't know how in touch with reality Kyla had been. Had anything she said been true?

At the hospital, Louisa had been checked out and patched up. She had a brace for her sprained ankle, a few stitches in her forehead and some concussion protocol. She sat in a room, waiting for the all clear to go home, which was supposed to be coming.

Police came in and out. At the point she was just about ready to yell at her next visitor, Mary ushered her family into the room.

They were all crying. Even Grandpa. That made her cry too. They huddled around her, and Louisa realized that, no matter the truth, she was so lucky. Because this was her family.

"We don't understand this story, Louisa," Dad said. He looked so tired. He'd been through too much. The house fire, now this.

"Let me go get Jack for you," Mary said, offering a smile. "He should be able to explain some things better."

While they waited, Mom fussed with Louisa's hospital bed. Grandpa and Dad paced and Grandma settled herself in the chair and pulled her knitting out of her purse.

Louisa was certain, no matter what the actual truth was, they hadn't *kidnapped* her. They weren't those people.

After a few more minutes, Jack came in. He was in his uniform, and no doubt had been up for over twenty-four hours straight. She'd heard from various people how many people had gotten together to look for her—not just the police departments, but townspeople and her own family. She'd heard how Anna had busted Palmer out of the hospital before he was supposed to go, how even Hawk Steele had worked to help find her.

She had this whole community that cared about her, which made it just…really hard to hold on to any anger toward poor Kyla Brown.

"We tracked down Janice Menard," Jack explained after greeting her family. "She didn't talk, but Birdie Williams did when we explained that a lot of this went down on her property. She claims she wasn't involved, and so far the evidence backs that up, but Janice was, and Birdie shared what she remembered."

He told the story in quick, concise facts, making sure to meet the gazes of her parents and grandparents. Louisa knew Anna and Palmer both complained about Jack, even while they hero-worshipped him in some respects, and she fully understood that in a way she hadn't before.

For all the times he could be rigid and interfering and overbearing, he excelled at this. Giving people in trouble and trauma what they needed.

"Along with the nurses we've talked to, Hillary Brown has confirmed a lot of this story," Jack continued. "She faked a kidnapping of her infant child because she was afraid of her husband finding out the baby wasn't his. She worked with a nurse, Janice, who she knew through her brother, to create a kind of baby-swap situation. Her baby would go to someone who'd just had a baby, and that infant would be left with family services."

Mom gripped Louisa's hand so tightly it hurt. Louisa didn't say anything. She just gripped her mother's hand right back.

"Are you saying my baby…?"

Jack crossed over to Mom and put his hand on her shoulder. "Birdie explained that, unfortunately, your biological baby was stillborn. Instead of telling you that, Janice simply put Louisa in her place."

Mom let out a shaky breath.

"It seems Kyla Brown has been planning this for some time. Some initial investigation, and some of Kyla's own statement, indicates she had found proof of this and was blackmailing Janice to help her get to you, Louisa. Hawk is leaning toward Janice being the prime suspect for the fire, at Kyla's directive." Jack looked around the room. "This is a lot to take in," Jack said. "We're still collecting details. While we are, I'd encourage you all to take care of yourselves. Answer law enforcement's questions as best you can, and trust us to clean up this mess. We'll be coordinating our efforts with all agencies involved to make sure all the culprits are brought to justice."

Mom nodded dully, still clutching Louisa's hand.

"I know you're waiting on the doctor to let you out, Louisa, but if your family doesn't mind, I'd like to take you over to Palmer's room." He gestured to the wheelchair in the corner. "If I don't take you to see him, he's only going to bust out again, and he needs to stay put."

Louisa looked up at her mother. Not so much because she needed permission, but she needed to know her mom was going to be okay.

Mom smiled, though it wavered. "You go on. We'll get everything ready so we can take you back to Grandma and Grandpa's as soon as you're released."

Everyone worked together to help her out of the bed and, even though she insisted she could walk with some help, everyone insisted harder that she use the wheelchair.

Eventually, she gave in. Jack wheeled her from the room and over to the wing Palmer was in.

"Can you tell me if she's okay?" Louisa asked once she'd braced herself for whatever answer there might be. "Kyla."

"She'll make it. There will be a psych eval. An investigation into her mother. The man who shot Palmer?"

Louisa nodded.

"That was her father. We already knew he had some priors, but it looks like he's got some aliases too, that might have even more warrants. The young woman who was working with them is connected to him in some way we're still untangling. So, everyone's going to survive, be investigated and checked out, and we'll work to make sure all the outcomes are the best for everyone."

"Thanks, Jack. I…" She sucked in a breath. "You…" He'd saved her life. Oh, it had been a joint effort, she knew, but he'd been the one on that rise. Because the Hudsons were just…built that way. To run in and save.

"I'm sorry this all happened," Jack said gravely, stopping in front of a door she figured was Palmer's. He crouched down so they were eye to eye. "And we didn't get to you sooner."

She knew he meant that, and that no doubt it brought up some memories of his parents' disappearance, for both him and Palmer. That made her feel a guilt she knew probably didn't belong on her shoulders. But if she hadn't asked for Palmer's help… "I'm sorry I dragged Palmer into it."

"I imagine he dragged himself just fine," Jack replied. He studied Louisa for a long minute. "I know he seems to think I see him only as a screwup…"

"That's because you treat him like a screwup."

"Fair enough."

"You could change that, you know."

Jack stood, clearly done with *that* line of discussion. "I'll see what I can do."

PALMER EYED THE IV in his arm and the door. There'd been enough hubbub that he'd finally found himself alone in this dang hospital bed.

So he'd needed a few stitches redone, and to be pumped full of antibiotics, and blah, blah, blah. He hadn't lost consciousness again, so wasn't that something? He was just fine.

And he needed to see Louisa.

She was here somewhere, so he didn't have to sneak out of the hospital. He could even take the IV tower with him. He just had to time it right. In between nurse visits and his family descending on him like a plague of locusts.

He was staring at the clock, trying to determine that perfect timing, when his door opened. He didn't see anything at first, except Louisa.

She was in a wheelchair, a bright white bandage on her forehead, but her green eyes were clear and direct. Because she was okay. They were both okay.

Something that had been bound around his chest for the past two days finally lifted.

Then he realized Jack was the one pushing her wheelchair, still in his uniform, and he came to a stop so Louisa was pointed right at Palmer in his bed.

"Visitor. Can't stay forever because she's getting sprung before you," Jack said. "If you don't stay put, I'm going to make sure you never have a visitor again."

Palmer managed to look away from Louisa and up at his brother. The man who'd saved his life and then, with everything he had going on as the sheriff, had thought to bring Louisa to him. "Thanks, Jack."

Jack nodded. "I'll just go check on some things." He left without so much as a lecture. That truly *was* a gift.

Then Louisa was stepping from her wheelchair. He reached out in some dumb attempt to stop her. "Hey, you shouldn't be getting up."

She didn't stand long. She scooted into the bed with him. "I'm fine. They just don't want me putting weight on my ankle for a while. Nothing broken, just a sprain. So this will work." She wiggled in next to his good side and he slid his arm under her neck as she rested her head on his shoulder.

She let out a contended sigh. Then turned her forehead into his shoulder. "I was so afraid you were dead."

"Same goes, sweetheart." He pressed a kiss to the top of her head and held her close. "But we both made it out okay, so I guess we're stuck with each other."

She huffed a little laugh and he was glad he could lift her spirits, even if it was temporary.

"They're saying that what Kyla said was true."

"Yeah," Palmer said, stroking his hand down her hair. "Jack filled me in. You okay?"

"I don't know. I guess I feel more sorry for my mom than anyone."

"She's a strong lady. You all will get through it. They love you no matter what, Lou. You'll all find a way to deal."

She inhaled deeply. "Yeah. I think so. I just... I guess I feel sorry for Kyla too."

"She was going to kill you," he said flatly. Because Kyla almost had. So easily. In those twenty-four hours they couldn't find Louisa, Kyla could have done anything. So many bad outcomes could have happened, and he wouldn't have been there to stop it.

"She wasn't well, and I don't think anyone ever gave her a chance to be. I just hope she can get the help she needs."

"Well, I'll hope for that too then." Because he wanted Louisa to have whatever she wanted, however she wanted it. All he wanted was for Louisa to be happy, and she had a lot of complicated stuff to wade through. So if this would ease some of that pain, he wanted that for her.

It was a lot to come to terms with, even if they'd uncovered a lot of it before Kyla had taken her. But he still had a question. "There's just one thing I don't understand. What was your grandpa doing skulking around when we were investigating? You were suspicious of him, but he didn't have anything to do with this."

"He said he was trying to hide Grandma's Christmas present and was mad because he thought I was stealing his hiding place."

Palmer chuckled then winced, because he'd refused the heavy-duty pain meds so his side *hurt* now that the local anesthetic was wearing off from the redone stitches.

Louisa snuggled closer. "You're in pain."

"Those painkillers just make me fuzzy."

"They help you rest and heal." She lifted her head and glared down at him. "Next time the nurse comes, you're taking something."

He didn't know why it struck him then, when she was glaring at him, with that terrible bandage on her head and her hair a mess and him in pain a thousand times over, but he just...was so glad she was there. In his life. In his bed...even if it was a hospital bed.

He reached up and tried to smooth some of her tangled hair down.

"Okay." And maybe that *okay* should have been an *I love you.* But he didn't want to say that under the harsh hospital lights. With her head bandaged up and him in a hospital bed. He wanted something...better.

For her.

For both of them.

Epilogue

Christmas dawned snowy and cold. In some ways, it was a bit like the Christmases of Louisa's childhood. She was in a house with her parents and grandparents. They ate breakfast, opened presents.

No one spoke of what had happened, but there was a different weight to the day. A gratefulness that might not have been there otherwise. Because, despite all that had happened, they were so incredibly lucky to all be all right and all have each other.

In the afternoon, Dad and Grandpa drove over to the orchard to check on things while Grandma and Mom discussed and bickered a bit about dinner preparation plans. As she always had, Louisa retreated to her gifts and appreciated the normalness of it all.

It was all she wanted from here on out. *Normal.*

Until she saw through the living room picture window Anna's truck pull up. And Palmer get out. Then she didn't want *all* the old normal things.

Louisa grabbed her crutches and, against Mom's and Grandma's admonitions, snatched her coat and went outside.

"Do not go down those stairs, young lady. You let him come to you," Grandma called out the door.

She would have listened, but she didn't even get the chance because Palmer was already jogging over and up the stairs.

"Whoa, whoa, whoa. Too snowy for those crutches, Lou."

"Are you supposed to be driving?" she demanded.

"Doctor gave me the all clear."

She studied him, looking for a sign of a lie, but he seemed to be telling the truth. "Did you bring me a Christmas present?"

He grinned down at her. "I'm your present."

"That's ridiculous. Even for you." But she wrapped an arm around his neck, her other arm holding on to the crutches. He was on the mend and here and…

It wasn't like all the pain of the past had magically been cured, but she was okay. Her parents and grandparents were okay. There was pain. There was confusion, but at the end of the day, what held them all together was love.

Because it didn't matter that someone else had given birth to her. It only mattered that her parents had raised her and loved her.

She'd met with Hillary Brown a few days ago. There'd been no real connection there. Louisa couldn't say she wanted one, and the woman was even less interested.

Whatever issues Kyla had, they'd at least partially come from a very troubled family life that, in a strange way, had very little to do with Louisa at all. It wasn't easy to let that go, but she was working on it.

And there was Palmer. Every day. Just…there for her, in all the ways she needed him to be.

"Come on. I'll take you for a drive if you let me help you to the truck. I already cleared it with your mom."

"Did you?"

He offered his arm and she went ahead and left her crutches behind. Because wherever they drove, he'd be there to help her. It was very hard to feel sorry for herself with all this upheaval when she had so many people in her life who rallied around and helped.

He got her into the truck and then drove out toward the Hudson Ranch. He didn't say much. Asked what she'd gotten for Christmas and the like, but he was otherwise uncharacteristically quiet. Even as he pulled onto what she knew was Hudson land, but more on the west side, farther away from the main house.

She didn't ask where they were going. He seemed to have some kind of plan. He took the truck off road, then pulled to a stop in a pretty little clearing. It was a Christmas postcard. Untouched snow and pine trees, the mountains in the far distance.

He didn't move to get out, just stared through the front windshield. "I was thinking about building a place out here. This is my share. Nice place to have a house, don't you think?"

She studied his profile. He was being very…odd. She figured that's how she knew it was important. So, she looked out at the spot. It was pretty. It'd be a nice quiet place to have a little spot. Private enough to feel like your own place, but close enough to the main house it would be his.

"It's perfect," she agreed.

"Probably take a while but, you know, eventually." He finally looked over at her.

He was just so handsome. So…hers. "Eventually," she echoed.

He smiled, shook his head and let out a gusty sigh. "Lou, I love you."

She let it sink in. Really sink. Into all those places so convinced he never would or could. Palmer Hudson loved her. Yeah, she was a lucky woman.

"Well?" he demanded when she didn't say anything.

She just smiled up at him, really enjoying the look of confusion on his face, even if it was a little mean of her. "Well what?" she replied.

"Aren't you going to say it back?"

She pretended to think about it, because he looked so out of his element and it wasn't every day someone could make Palmer out of his element. Might as well enjoy it. "I might just let it sit awhile."

He stared at her, completely and utterly speechless, for a good full minute. Until she couldn't hold her laughter back any longer. Palmer Hudson loved her and was talking houses and eventually. With *her*.

"I love you, Palmer." And she had, for a very long time, but this was more than that. Not just a feeling, kept deep inside. But something shared, that they'd work on together.

She leaned across the middle console and pressed

her mouth to his. "And I like the sound of eventually," she added when she finally pulled back.

He grinned at her. "I should hope so. I did take a bullet for you."

She rolled her eyes, but she liked him back to himself. "I was wondering how long you'd wait to pull that card."

"I'm not really sure I've gotten an adequate thank-you," he continued. "I'm basically your personal hero," he added.

"Yeah, you are," she said, far more serious than he was being. Even as she reached over and kissed him again.

Because he was her hero, and he always would be.

* * * * *

Helicopter Rescue
Danica Winters

MILLS & BOON

Danica Winters is a multiple-award-winning, bestselling author who writes books that grip readers with their ability to drive emotion through suspense and occasionally a touch of magic. When she's not working, she can be found in the wilds of Montana, testing her patience while she tries to hone her skills at various crafts—quilting, pottery and painting are not her areas of expertise. She believes the cup is neither half-full nor half-empty, but it better be filled with wine. Visit her website at danicawinters.net.

Visit the Author Profile page
at millsandboon.com.au.

DEDICATION

To my readers, I appreciate your support more than you could ever know.

CAST OF CHARACTERS

Kristin Loren—When someone needs help, she is the first one everyone calls. Dependable, strong and never one to pull punches, Kristin is the woman any man would be lucky to have at his side when the world comes crashing down.

Casper Keller—Casper is a former military spec ops helicopter pilot, and the name of his game is knowing when to take orders and when to give them—but his world is turned upside down when he is faced with Kristin Loren.

Hugh Keller—Casper and William's father, who is suffering from advanced Alzheimer's and goes missing in the rimrocks outside Billings, Montana.

Greg Holmes—Kristin's ex-boyfriend who is nothing more than a hotheaded jerk with an ego the size of Texas.

Michelle Keller—William's estranged wife, who sells life insurance. She loves to work, run and be outdoors. If she isn't careful, her passions may be her downfall.

William Keller—Casper's brother, who becomes a hermit after Michelle decides to leave him in charge of Hugh and his nursing duties. With everything on his shoulders, his reclusive ways nearly cost him his sanity and his life.

Chapter One

The man stepped out of the ditch, a stuffed lobster dragging on the ground behind him. The orange bailing twine was looped around the animal's neck, and the lobster bounced like it was hoping for the sweet release of a figurative death—if only it could have been so lucky. Instead, it was the perpetual stuffed clown of a man who seemed to have as much apathy toward the thing as he did self-awareness.

Kristin Loren glanced down at the man's Bermuda shorts, one leg markedly longer than the other and tattered and torn, with a strip of hibiscus-printed cloth flapping against his leg as he teetered toward them.

From what she had been told about the man, he was in his eighties, was a former dean of the physics department at CalTech and suffered from Alzheimer's. Seeing him now, his ripped and dirty clothes, and stumbling gait, she had a hard time seeing him as the powerful authority on astrophysics that, according to the internet, he had once been. He was proof of the ravaging effects of the disease, and how it could even bring an intellectual juggernaut to his knees.

Perhaps one day in the not-so-distant future, due to her own family's history of Alzheimer's, she would be found like this man had been, confused and disoriented and smelling of sweat and urine. She hoped not, but it made the ache in her chest for the man intensify.

"Wh-where am I?" the man stammered, a look of uncertainty in his eyes. "Who're you?"

"I'm Kristin. What's your name?" she asked, hoping the man was capable of answering.

"I'm Hugh." He pointed at the flight crew as the nurse approached. "Who are they?"

"We were sent out here to help you get back home. That is Greg," she said, motioning toward the pilot, "and he will be helping to make sure you make it home safely. This lady here—" she indicated the thirtysomething brunette woman at her side "—is a sweet nurse who wants to get you medical assistance. Okay?"

The nurse smiled up at Hugh. "Is it okay with you if I check your vitals really quick?"

The man frowned but nodded, then pulled the lobster into his arms like he was not an eighty-seven-year-old man and was instead a seven-year-old boy. The nurse set to work, slipping on her stethoscope.

"How are you feeling this afternoon, sir?" the nurse asked.

"I'm fine," the man said, shrugging. The man seemed not to realize they had spent nearly a day looking for him, or that the nurse appeared to be slightly alarmed by his condition.

According to his son, the man had managed to

escape the confines of their home and disappeared into the night. They had only noticed he was missing when they woke up and found the man wasn't in his recliner watching reruns of *The Price is Right*.

She could almost imagine Bob Barker yelling "Come on down…" as this man with a stuffed lobster rocked away, engrossed. Then again, at the thought, she could understand why the man would have wanted to get up, slip out and disappear into the scrubby landscape of the rimrocks.

"You look nice," the man said to Kristin, seeming to forget about the nurse as she worked. A droopy, sad smile adorned his lips like forgotten party streamers left to the rain.

"Well, thank you. You look nice yourself." She sent him the closest thing to a real smile as she could muster. He deserved some respite from the chaos in his mind, if even just for a moment, thanks to her fleeting grin.

Kristin had been on so many of these types of calls for search-and-rescue that most didn't really faze her anymore, but there was something about this old-timer that pulled at her. Perhaps it was his utter lack of understanding, or the way he had seemed to look into her soul when he spoke. He reminded her of her grandfather in the last years of his life, when she was small enough to pull on his beard and whisper Popsicle-stick jokes into his failing ears.

She missed him.

"Do you remember your full name, Hugh?" she

asked, glancing over her shoulder at the double-bladed helo that rested in the pasture behind her.

The man's gaze slipped toward the helicopter. "I used to fly in the war," he said, not bothering to acknowledge, or not knowing the answer to, her question.

She'd long ago learned that the best way to get answers from someone who was aggressive or confused was to take a round-about approach. The wrong style of communication in fragile situations only led to undesirable results. For now, it was imperative that she handle him gently so that they could get him into the helicopter and transport him to the hospital in Billings, and hopefully then get back into the hands of his family.

"Which war were you involved in?" Kristin asked.

He stumbled as he took a step and she put his arm around her shoulder, helping him to walk. "Vietnam. Did two tours." He glanced up at the sky, then covered his eyes as if he was staring into the midday sun. "I should have never made it out."

She wasn't sure if that was a statement or a wish; either way, the agony of his tone set against the precariousness of his situation made her want to sob, but she couldn't pay heed to her emotions when there was a life to be saved.

"His BP is pretty low. We need to get him some fluids and get him stabilized so the doctors can sort him out," the nurse said as she moved to the other side and helped to walk him toward the helicopter as Kristin tried to keep chatting with the somewhat listless man.

By keeping him talking about the details of his war years, it didn't take long to get him loaded. They spent the next forty-five minutes pushing IV fluids while she and Hugh chatted about her job at FLIR Tech and their forward-looking infrared equipment that they had used to locate him in the field near the edge of a sage-lined cliff. Every time she tried to get him to answer more questions about his identity or where he lived, he avoided them and turned the conversation back to his younger years.

She watched as the nurse on the flight took the man's blood pressure as they neared the helo pad outside the hospital. The nurse's face pinched, and she took it again.

"Everything okay?"

The nurse seemed not to hear her, and instead glanced over at the EKG monitor. The green lines on the screen were jagged and irregular, like the thrusting peaks and valleys of freshly shorn mountains. Kristin didn't know a great deal about the line on the screen, but she knew enough to realize that with a heart rate at 43 bpm and a read like what she was seeing, it didn't point at anything good.

The nurse took out a syringe, then glanced down at her watch and turned to the pilot. "How much longer until we touch down?"

The pilot pointed down at the ground, where Kristin could just make out the red circle with an *H* in its center. As they got closer, she saw a group of personnel waiting near the doors of the hospital with a gurney.

Reaching down, Kristin took Hugh's hand. He looked up at her, his actions slow and deliberate, as though he was struggling to control his body. "It's going to be okay, Hugh," she said, positioning the lobster deeper into the nook of his arm. "We're at the hospital. They're going to take you from here and get you the help you need."

He answered her with a broken nod and an almost imperceptible squeeze of her fingers. The chill of his skin made her wonder if this simple exchange would be one of his last.

"Tell my son…" He took in a gasping breath as the nurse plunged the needle into his arm. "Tell him, I'm sorry."

The man closed his eyes just as the helicopter touched down. Before the blades even stopped rotating, there was a rush of nurses and hospital staff, and Kristin was pushed out of the way. Hugh was pulled onto the pad and put on the gurney, then he was whisked out of sight, into the belly of the industrial building.

She wanted to follow him, to make sure that he would be okay and that she had been wrong in her thoughts. The man hadn't been hurt, only left in the elements for too long. He couldn't be dying…not on her watch. If anything, she had just let her fears get the better of her. There had been dozens of other rescues she had taken part in where the persons they had rescued were in far more precarious medical states and had pulled through.

Hugh would be fine.

Yet, she couldn't help but step out of the helo and make her way inside the hospital in hopes of hearing good news. The staff had disappeared into the triage area, so Kristin made her way to the waiting area. It was empty, aside from a couple holding a small, ruddy-cheeked baby who was pulling at his ear and starting to cry. The poor mother had dark circles under her eyes and the father was pacing, as if each step would bring them closer to relief for their child.

She wasn't a parent, but there was no amount of pacing that could quell another's pain—she was well-acquainted with that concept.

After ten minutes or so, she was unable to watch any more of the parents' struggle and she made her way to the check-in area. "I'm part of the flight crew that came in with Hugh Keller. I was wondering if you have an update on his status?"

The secretary behind the desk nodded, the action stoic. "Hold on for just a moment and let me check for you."

As the secretary headed for the glass doors leading to the ER, the automatic doors at the entranceway slid open and a man came rushing in from outside. He was wearing blue-tinted Costa sunglasses and a tight-fitting, gray V-necked shirt that accentuated all the muscular curves and bumps of his body. Though she couldn't explain why, she caught herself catching her breath as she stared at him. He definitely wasn't bad-looking; in fact, she could safely say he was the hottest man she had seen in person in a long time. But standing here and waiting on a man's medical status seemed like the last moment that she should have found herself stunned by a handsome brunette.

The man walked up beside her and she caught a whiff of expensive cologne, made stronger by his body heat. If she had to guess, it was Yves Saint Laurent or some other haute scent, but as quickly as she tried to name it, she noted how out of place it was in the industrial austerity of where they were standing.

"Is there anyone working here?" he grumbled, tapping on the counter.

"She just ran to check on something for me. I'm sure she will be back in a sec," she said, her initial attraction somewhat dampened by the man's annoyance.

The man grumbled something unintelligible under his breath, but she was sure it was a string of masked expletives and she frowned.

"Sorry," the guy said, finally seeming to notice that she was a real live person and not just a source of information. "I'm not trying to be an ass… It's just…" He ran his hands over his face and bumped against his sunglasses, realizing he still had them on. He gave a dry chuckle as he took them off, then looked up at her with eyes that were even more blue than the lenses on his glasses. She thought he was handsome before, but now he was absolutely stunning and she found herself unable to look away. "It's been a long day."

"Uh-huh. I get it." She glanced at the little line

next to his mouth, a crease that came from a life of smiling—which seemed at odds with his current mood.

"My father. Yeah…" He paused. "They recently brought him in."

Just like that, she was whipped back to reality. She couldn't just ask who he was because of privacy laws, but even without knowing his father's name, she could tell from the shape of his eyes and the curve of his nose that he was Hugh's son. She wasn't sure how she could have missed it until now. There was no denying that the man before her was a younger version of the man whom she had found deep in the middle of nowhere.

"I'm sure your father is going to be okay."

His face darkened, but she wasn't sure if it was because he feared that it was an empty platitude, or if he was actually angry at her for her attempt to mollify him—either way, she wanted to make that look disappear.

The glass door through which the secretary had disappeared reopened and she walked out. She glanced over at the man at Kristin's side, then back to her. The woman raised her eyebrows, a silent question. Kristin gave her a furtive nod.

"The man you accompanied, Hugh, is currently with the doctor."

"Hugh? Hugh Keller?" the man asked.

The secretary nodded.

The man gripped the edge of the counter. "That's my father. I'm Casper Keller. I'm going to need more information. What's the doctor saying? Is he going to be all right?"

The secretary's mouth opened and closed, as if she was hoping the right words would just magically appear on her lips in this challenging situation. "I... I'm afraid I can't speak to—"

"But you have an answer. Please, if this was your father..." Casper pleaded, making Kristin's chest ache. "Please."

The secretary wrung her hands and looked down at the desk. "I'm sorry, Mr. Keller." There was an agonizing pause before the woman finally looked up. There were tears in her eyes. "I heard the doctor say he didn't think your father will survive. I'll try and get you back to see him." The secretary turned and slipped back through the door.

Kristin didn't know what to do to comfort the man when her heart was breaking for both Casper and the man who had reminded her so much of her grandfather. Something about this situation made it feel like she was losing the patriarch of her family again.

"I'm so sorry, Casper."

He looked at her, but there was no recognition in his eyes, and the look was so much like his father's that she was thrown off balance. "Yeah."

In that single, breathless word, she felt every ounce of his loss...and it tore her to pieces.

Chapter Two

The incident command trailer was parked to the left of the pad as Casper set down the helicopter beside an AgustaWestland AW101 helo that was geared up to the hilt—it even had a large ball-shaped camera unit on the nose. He couldn't wait to get back to work after losing his father a couple of weeks ago. He would never understand how his father had gone missing so far from his brother's place, but there was no going back and righting wrongs—there was only accepting that their father was dead.

The second his phone picked up reception, thanks to the myriad of communication networks the tech gurus had set up at their base camp, he was flooded with a wave of notifications.

Speak of the devil. Of course, his brother, William, had texted.

He opened up the three messages his brother had sent. The first was a long and rambling diatribe of what could best be described as him seeking absolution. From the time stamp, it appeared as though William had sent that one in the middle of the night, probably between glasses three and four of whiskey.

Casper didn't want to admit to himself that he found a certain amount of comfort in his brother's downward spiral of guilt—William had it coming. Yet, in the same thought, he didn't wish it for him. William and his wife, Michelle, had stepped up to the plate in a way he never could have…and, truthfully, he wasn't sure that he could have emotionally handled. Before this mishap, he had been singing their praises, so to go in direct opposition and criticize their generosity now only made him feel like the worst kind of person.

Regardless, his brother could wait for him to text back.

Work. I just need to work.

Casper unstrapped himself and got out of the bird, making his way onto the pad. It felt good to stand up and walk, after flying for the last hour in near darkness and questionable winds. Truth be told, though, he loved flying in the kinds of conditions that would make lesser men's asses pucker. It was as if each time, he proved his merit not only as a good pilot, but also as a better man.

Many could fly like he could, but what he prided himself upon—and what he hoped put him above many others in his line of work—was his integrity and honor. These qualities had been hammered into him during his time as a pilot in the army, and they would be his core values until the day he died.

It was just too bad he couldn't say the same of his

brother, setting aside his caretaking…though even that could now be called into question.

Damn it. I can't go there. It doesn't do a damn bit of good.

He unzipped his flight jacket, taking in the cool summer morning as he gave one more look at the horizon. The sun was finally starting to climb over the tops of the mountains, reminding him of the scale of the things going on in his life. The pain he was feeling, and the anger, wouldn't last forever—nothing did.

The flaps at the front of the canvas-wall tent were tied back and he made his way into the base camp's incident command center. It was abuzz with people talking. At first glance, there had to be about fifteen people standing around, mostly men. The SAR team leader, Cindy, spotted him and gave a quick wave, and he made his way over to her and the group of people she was standing with.

He recognized most of the people in the room as fellow SAR members, but there was also a smattering of new faces. They had just done a recruitment and this was the first training event with the new people. He couldn't say he was overly thrilled, but it was nice to get some fresh blood. They needed a shake-up to bring in updated ideas and methods, even if it was a bit like teaching old dogs new tricks.

Cindy gave him her trademark strained-lip smile, the one that made him wonder if it actually hurt. "Glad to see you made it. You ready for this fun?"

"About as ready as a dog is to go to the vet." He smirked.

Cindy chuckled. "Why do I get the sense that you'd be far more at home in a vet's office than a doctor's?"

"Hey, now, you calling me a dog?" His grin widened.

"If the shoe fits," she said with a laugh. "You know I heard about you and your pack of girlfriends."

He laughed and it felt out of place—he was riddled with guilt. At a time like this, having just lost his dad, what right did he have to joke around?

She must have sensed that her comment had struck a nerve. "By the way, Casper, I'm real sorry to hear about your old man. It's always tough losing a parent."

"I appreciate that," he said in a clipped tone. "How many newbies do we have on our hands this round?" he asked, moving his chin in the direction of four new faces.

"We have six coming in—we're going to break them in or break them down." Cindy put her hand on his shoulder, letting their real conversation pass by with as much sentiment as either could muster. "By the way, I have you training with a FLIR Tech employee today. She's supposed to be the best of the best in this new and burgeoning technology. Be warned, I was told she has a bit of a chip on her shoulder."

"Great. Can't wait to see what that means."

"Oh, I can tell you exactly what it means—she is going to be a pain in your ass." Cindy paused, looking in the direction of the tent's entrance. "Actually, it looks like she is ready to start chapping you right about now."

He turned in the direction of Cindy's gaze and

walking in was none other than the stunning, yet beguiling, blond woman he had first talked to at the hospital ER in Billings. The woman stopped and stared at him, as though she was just as surprised to see him. She stumbled as she recognized him, but then regained her composure, drew back her shoulders and moved toward them. However, from the pace of her tentative steps, he could sense she was hesitant to speak to him.

As she neared, Cindy began, "This is Kristin Loren, your newest—"

"Oh, we've met before," he said, cutting off Cindy. "What're you doing here?" He hadn't meant to come off as brusque, but there was no taking back his near growl.

She took a step back from him as if she was moving away from a punch square to the gut. "I'm here as an instructor—teaching one of the tracks on using tech in rescue situations…like your father's."

He flashed back to the first time he had seen her. She had been wearing jeans and a sweatshirt, nothing that would have given away her identity as the woman who had likely held a pivotal role in getting his dad to the hospital in time for him to receive care.

Just like that, he found himself the heel.

If it wasn't for Kristin, his father would have likely never been found…or rather, found alive. His father had died in comfort and peace, instead of lost in the woods, confused and wandering. He owed her his thanks, not his derision.

"Kristin, I'm—"

She gave him a warm smile that told him he was forgiven, but it didn't assuage his guilt.

"I'm truly sorry for your loss," she said.

"Thank you and I apologize for being…less than welcoming." He offered her his hand and she graciously accepted the meager apology. "It's why Cindy, here—" he let go and motioned toward the SAR leader "—doesn't usually let me be the public face of the organization. Smart move on her part, really. I do best in the sky."

"You're the eyes in the sky for the whole crew. I would say that you are a critical part of our group," Cindy said, giving him a quick blow to the shoulder. "You're not going to be getting any other compliments, so you better write that one down."

Casper rubbed where she had struck him, feigning pain as he laughed. "I'm surprised you even assume I can write, the way you talk about me most of the time," he teased.

"You're not wrong," Cindy countered, smiling. "Which brings me back to why we are here—I am hoping you and Kristin can get along. Nonetheless, she has graciously agreed to put up with you for the next few days."

"Great. What're we going to be working on?" he asked, smiling at Kristin.

"FLIR. And *speaking of* you being the hapless face of our organization, unwitting or not, we need you to get us some good press about the FLIR program so we can get public funding to get our own equipment." Cindy gave him a serious expression.

He hated playing politics, but in the world of search-and-rescue, it was critical. The community held the figurative purse strings and it was make-or-break that they kept a positive reputation in the court of public opinion. Nothing was better than making timely rescues, rather than recovering remains. It was also critical for their team's morale that they saved lives. Bringing loved ones home to their families was what kept many of them going in their intense and brutal calling.

"That your bird out there on the pad?"

Kristin nodded. "My team's pilot is over there," she said, motioning to a thin-shouldered guy with a receding hairline.

"Oh…" he said, the sting to his ego echoing in his voice. He glanced at Cindy. "I guess I'll be riding shotgun."

Cindy laughed. "Only if you're not up to flying the beast."

Kristin gave a slight nod. "You know how to fly her?"

He couldn't control the smile that overtook his face. "I can fly anything with a rotor."

Cindy nodded her approval, but there was concern in her eyes. "Just make sure that you grab your information packet, get yourself up to speed on the training scenario and then bring her back in one piece—we can't afford to replace it and we certainly can't afford to have you doing something stupid."

"You can trust me. I'd never let you or the team

down." As he spoke, he could feel the weight of his words press down on him.

"I have no doubts," Cindy said, turning to Kristin. "You need to make sure you keep an eye on him, though. Casper is a top-notch pilot, but a lot is riding on this flight."

"As long as he listens to my instruction, we should be all good." Kristin smiled, and as he looked into her green eyes, he wondered if his role with SAR wasn't the only thing on the line.

Chapter Three

Casper opened up the throttle and he went light on the skids. The red-and-yellow SAR trailer parked near the pad pitched from the pressure of the rotor wash. Casper neutralized the helicopter's movements and readied to lift. He loved that feeling—the moment of calm right before the storm.

He was excited to show her what he could do on the sticks, while also getting the job done and learning about her work. He glanced over at Kristin for one last preflight check. Her blond braid was poking out over the collar of her coat, beneath her flight helmet. Her expression was tense, as if their flight relied on the strength of her concentration and willpower, and not his flying abilities. As if she could feel his gaze upon her, she sent him a sidelong glance, but he wasn't sure if the look in her eyes was one of excitement or concern. If anything, the slight squint of her eyes only made her more interesting—a mystery that was waiting to be solved.

"My team has set up a small, smokeless fire for us to find a hypothetical missing hiker. The current search radius is based on the hiker having a two-day head start from the PLS. Often, as I'm sure you know, when people go missing, they are told to build a fire and stay put. This way, we can train in typical conditions. Okay?" She sounded a bit nervous.

"Two days from point last seen. Roger."

According to Cindy, Kristin had spent thousands of hours working with FLIR cameras, sensors and the accompanying tech, which had to have meant she had nearly as many hours as him in the belly of a helo. Yet, in watching her, he wasn't sure his assumptions had been on point.

"Ready to rock and roll?" Casper gave her a thin smile and a thumbs-up.

She answered with a nod almost as stiff as her back. "You going to lift off or stare at me all day?" she said, sending him a mischievous grin.

Maybe there really was hope for a working friendship between them.

"I wasn't staring at you. Don't get ahead of yourself there, dude." He smirked, loving the way her eyes squinted with the hard jab to the friend zone.

She laughed, but there was a touch of mirth in the sound. "You know, between the two of us, you are the more replaceable on this assignment. Watch yourself."

There was a certain sting in her words that made him wonder if he had taken his teasing a step too far. He was probably just imagining things and she was merely fighting fire with fire. Regardless, it made him like her incrementally more, and at the same time, want to pull pitch and press her back in her seat so hard that she would question the nature of life.

He lifted the skids off the ground and they took to the sky. According to Kristin's training module, the fake missing hikers were within a fifteen-mile radius of their PLS, a pin on a map sent to them by Cindy.

In real rescues, one of their major battles was against the weather—both for their teams and for the people they were tasked with locating. In the winter, the wind chill and the snowpack could greatly hamper any rescue attempts. Often, the victims would attempt to build a fire, but the fires tended to be small because of the lack of dry wood. In those cases, FLIR would definitely give them an edge in spotting the minuscule heat source and getting their teams to the exact location of missing persons instead of spending valuable limited time in trying to locate.

Seconds in a search often became the thin line between life and death. There were none to waste.

He always liked training missions where he got to show his true colors. It was a nice break from the civil flight crew he had joined after leaving the army. In his former line of work, before he'd retired as a chief warrant officer and Black Hawk pilot for the 160th SOAR, he'd had the chance to do this kind of thing about as often as he wanted to, and was always honing his skills. Since then, he could feel himself rusting. He hated the eroding sensation.

He looked out at the pitted, shadowy summits of Lone Mountain and Wilson Peak, which protected Big Sky. They reminded him of his last active mission, when he had attempted to rescue two SEALs who had found themselves stranded at the top of a mountain in Northern Colorado. There were several reasons the 160th's motto was Death Waits in the Dark, but in the case of the SEALs, it had been the brutal, piercing blades of cold that had ushered them to the grave.

As they moved steadily through the sky, Kristin turned to her computer screen. The images that filled it were black-and-white, but were as crisp as if they were looking at their launch pad at the height of the day. When he'd began flying, almost twenty years ago, he'd started with little more than a tiny screen with grainy imagery. Now they could identify the heat signature of a rat denned ten feet down. It was crazy to think where the technology would be in another twenty years.

Ten minutes into the flight, he glanced over and noticed a herd of elk standing at the edge of a timberline in the FLIR images. The herd was all cows, not surprising, given the time of the year and the pressing calving season. If they hadn't been working, he would have been tempted to get closer to the herd to get a better look, but then he wasn't sure it would have made a difference given the limited light.

"How many head?" he asked.

"There has to be thirty or so, more bunched in the tree line. Hard to count."

He glanced back at the screen one more time before turning back to his duties. "Any sign of our fire?"

"Negative. We close to the PLS?"

"Five miles out, but we will be there in a few minutes." The rest of the SAR team was lined up to hike in to the same target for training, but they wouldn't be there for at least a few hours.

"Does our fake victim have any known medical conditions?"

They had gone over all the information before they had taken to the air, but Kristin mustn't have been paying attention. It annoyed him slightly, but he reminded himself that she was probably feeling about as awkward with him as he was with her.

Kristin looked over at him, but there was a tightness to her features that made him wonder if she was thinking about her last mission as well—the rescue of his father.

"No known issues."

She nodded, like her question hadn't really been to gain information, but had been to test him. If she thought she was going to catch him ill-prepared, or not up to the task, she would have another think coming.

He had been volunteering for SAR for the last few years and always focused on the task at hand—even now, with this incredibly beautiful woman by his side. Sure, he would have liked to stare at her and showboat in this borrowed bird, just to show her that she was flying with a man who had spent his life perfecting his skills...until lately.

His elbow popped as he moved the control stick, reminding him that even his body was eroding. His clock was ticking for being a good pilot and if this flight didn't go right, his position with SAR could be in jeopardy.

Even if his body and his reputation held, sometimes he worried about his soul. His last call for SAR had been an especially brutal one. A fly fisherman from Massachusetts had gotten his raft trapped in a strainer—or logjam—on the river and found himself trapped under the vessel, and deeply entrenched between a variety of snags.

He had been underwater for three days before his remains could be safely recovered. When they picked him out of the debris, he was cut up and his skin had started sloughing from his exposed hands. Fast water played havoc on remains.

He would also never forget the call when he had arrived first on scene at a small airline crash. The little commuter plane had taken a nosedive straight into the ground so hard that the pilot's body had been severed by the restraints meant to hold the man in place. The lines where the straps had moved through the body were cut with surgeon-like precision and blood had been everywhere. That one, that scene, still haunted him at night.

As if merely thinking about an airline crash could bring down their helo, he felt a sudden surge coming from the engine. He glanced at the gauges, but there was nothing that looked abnormal. Perhaps he had merely had some kind of psychosomatic response to the memory of the horribly disfigured pilot.

"You okay over there?" Kristin asked. "You look a little pale."

"Fine... Everything's fine," he said, not sure if he was being entirely honest with her.

"I wasn't asking if everything was fine," she said, leery. Her gaze moved to the instrument panel, which made him wonder if she, too, had felt the disturbance. He wasn't about to ask her if she wasn't volunteering the information.

"I'm okay," he said, faking a smile.

"Good, we are just coming over the PLS."

He looked down through the glass floor of the nose. There were no light sources from fires, flashlights or glow sticks. "You see a heat signature?"

She shook her head.

The helicopter shuddered and there was a high-pitched moaning sound. *Hydraulics.*

The damn hydraulics had failed.

He stopped moving for a moment, feeling the helicopter's power start to fade in his hands. From here on out, he would have to control this beast on straight muscle.

Goddamn it. The engines are going.

He had been through one autorotation scenario in a helicopter before, and no matter how anyone looked at it, it was nothing more than a controlled crash. If he screwed this up, they were going to die.

"Engine failed," he said, trying to sound calm and collected, though his mind was going over how their bodies would be found—usually there was a fire and very little was left. "We're going down."

He was met with dead silence from Kristin.

They were at 500 feet AGL, nose into the wind.

He looked out—ahead of them was a small opening in the timber. It wasn't big, but it would have to do if there would be any chance of them making it out of this engine failure alive.

He adjusted the pitch of the blade to neutral as the rotor decayed. The upward flow of air continued to turn the disc. He lowered the collective. They started to descend as he watched his air speed and altitude, making sure everything was clear for the glide to the ground.

Arresting the descent, he pitched up and he flared. He leveled off the flight path, attempting to become parallel to the ground in an effort to reduce the forward air speed and be at the lowest rate of descent as possible. He didn't want the bird to roll when they hit.

He'd done his fair share of flying in the bush, but there was a big difference between landing in a predetermined location and being forced to land in an autorotation situation. As they lowered, the pines enveloped them. The sweat beaded on his lip.

One limb or one downed log in the wrong spot and the bird would roll and they would both be dead.

He took a look at the ground, praying that the area was clear beneath. Near the center of the landing area was a scattering of downed timber that looked like some kind of giant game of pick-up sticks. They were going down, and damn it if they weren't screwed.

Chapter Four

On a handful of her search-and-rescue calls, Kristin had had individuals tell her they knew they were going to die. After some research, she had come to learn that moment of awareness was called terminal lucidity. According to what she'd read, it could happen moments to weeks ahead of a person's actual death. It was one hell of a phenomenon and now that she was staring at the grim reaper's scythe, she wondered when that moment would come for her.

They were falling.

At the nose of the helo, she could make out an opening in the timber—it was the only area where they had any chance of bringing down the bird without crashing directly into the huge lodgepole and ponderosa pines.

The acrid scent of hydraulic fluid permeated the air.

It had crossed her mind on more than a few of her flights that going down was a real possibility, but she had found comfort in the human condition of "it won't happen to me." Oh, how the Fates were laughing at her right now.

This isn't it. This isn't the way I'm meant to die.

She grabbed her flight harness as the bird started to descend rapidly.

As long as they could land flat and manage not to roll, they would be okay.

She thought of the helicopter crash she had been called out to three years ago. From the follow-up NTSB accident report, they had gone into an auto-rotation just like what she was experiencing now; except, when that crew had hit the ground, the nose had dipped and the front of the skid had struck hard and thrown them, rotor first, into the dirt. The blades had sheered and the shrapnel and the ensuing fire had taken the pilot's and passenger's lives.

A ball of fire...

Her entire body tightened.

The opening widened as they lowered. Below them was a smattering of logs. To the right, in front of them was a tiny opening; if they landed there, they had a chance of survival. Yet, at the speed and angle of their descent, there was no way they were going to make it that far. If they hit the downed timber, they were going to be just like the pilot and passenger whose bodies she had been sent in to recover.

Death happens to us all.

She watched as the timber below her grew larger.

"It's okay. You've got this," she said, glancing over at Casper.

His expression was stone-cold and deadly serious as he held the sticks and stared ahead. She wasn't sure whether or not he had heard her, but it didn't matter, as she was trying to comfort herself just as much as she was trying to comfort him.

Casper. Hell, it was like he was even named after a ghost, like even his name was an omen of the death that awaited her. Why hadn't she thought about that before?

Even if she had seen his name as some kind of macabre sign, she couldn't say that she wouldn't have gotten in this bird. Maybe it was that attitude and failure to acknowledge and respect her intuition that had gotten her here in her life. Though, if she had been frightened off of everything and anything that made her slightly uncomfortable, she would never have lived the life she had; she had done some great things—loved and lost, achieved and failed, and hoped. Above all, it had always been hoping that had gotten her through every downfall.

She looked over at Casper. There was a bead of sweat moving down his temple, like his body was preemptively crying for their loss. Casper glanced over at her, finally breaking away from his steady concentration. He gave a stiff nod, like he had finally registered what she had said and agreed they were going to be okay... Or maybe the nod was to say he was sorry, that he knew they were going down and he was to blame.

His blue eyes were dark and stormy as he turned away.

If she was going to die, at least she was going down with the most handsome man she had ever met. For these few seconds, she could be comforted by the knowledge that she might share some infinite and eternal moment with this man. It was odd, but she loved the thought and her hands loosened slightly on her harness.

Yes, relax. She exhaled as she found a tiny respite from her terror.

It was always the ones who were asleep or drunk who survived accidents—those whose bodies were completely at ease.

She had to trust Casper. He would land this. They would be safe.

Letting out a long exhale, she closed her eyes and tried to calm her body.

The bird hit hard.

The impact ran up her legs and through her spine, rattling her like she had just rear-ended a car at thirty-five. She braced herself for the pitch forward, for the impact of the roll. Yet, nothing came. No pitch. No roll.

The chopping sound of the blades overhead slowed and quieted, and the alarm pierced the air. Until now, she had barely registered the blaring sound. Now, together with those wails and the timpani drumming of her heart, her world sounded like an out-of-tune marching band.

"Are you okay?" Casper reached over and touched her arm.

His sudden touch drew open her eyes. There, feet from the glass nose of the helo, was a copse of timber. They were so close to the trees that she wasn't even sure how their blades weren't weed-whacking them down.

"Holy…" She said the word on an exhale, making it sound like a whispering wind rather than a reprieve from terror. It was as if all of her emotions filled the air of her lungs and escaped from her in one single sound.

It was strange how a whisper could hold far more power and pain than a scream.

Chapter Five

Given their situation, Kristin had taken this disaster as well as he could have hoped. She was sitting on a downed log about fifty yards from the flightless bird and tapping away on her satellite phone. By now, everyone in the training unit had to have known what had happened, and how he had not only let her down, but also his entire team.

Cindy was going to be pissed.

Casper walked around to the front of the skids. Everything looked as it should, without any bending or warping, which, given the fact they had come down hard, was impressive. The components of the bird were manufactured to take hits like that on occasion, but by the same token, hydraulic lines weren't supposed to fail in midflight, either.

The worst part of all was that he had no one to blame but himself. Though others may have pointed the finger at the last PIC, his role as the new pilot was to do a full-system check before ever leaving the ground. He had failed more than his machine had. He should have known of a potential problem.

There was a long, jagged tear in the red body of the helo where a branch from the downed log to his left had penetrated the aircraft's skin. It was incredible that the skeletal grasp of the dead tree hadn't pulled them sideways. They were damn lucky.

His gaze moved toward Kristin, who was holding the phone in her hands but was staring out at the timber around them. A gust of wind whipped up her hair, lifted it and pressed it against her wet lips. She didn't seem to notice.

It was hardly an imperfection—her hair being stuck—but the violation of her tender skin made him want to come close to her and pull it away. How could he have been jealous of a wayward lock?

He shook his head, trying to clear his mind, but found himself drawn back to the woman who had nearly been killed. The color had returned to her features and he couldn't help but see exactly how beautiful she was. Perhaps it was that she seemed at home out here in the woods, even considering what had happened.

Maybe she was like him, could find comfort in the middle of chaos more than in any moment of peace and tranquility. Even as a kid, when he had been living the latchkey lifestyle with his brother, William, the times when things seemed to be "normal" were when everything was falling apart. They had always been moving around thanks to his father's position in the army.

It had been a wonder that their mother hadn't left him outside a firehouse. She'd often talked about how, as a baby, he had never slept and had preferred to cry anytime the house was quiet. That was one reason he was a little weak in the knees whenever he thought about having a family—karma would definitely come around to bite him given half an opportunity.

"What are you looking at?" Kristin asked, breaking his stream of consciousness and pulling him back to the fact that she had probably just caught him staring.

"Sorry—" he motioned toward her mouth as he moved to her side "—you have something on your lip."

She frowned and picked the hair away.

Before she had a chance to ask him why such an inconsequential thing had managed to draw his attention, and he'd have to admit that he thought she was, hands down, the most beautiful woman he had ever seen in real life, he spoke up. "Did you manage to get ahold of your team back at the base?"

Her gaze flickered to the phone in her hands before returning to him. "This thing is slower than your reaction up there."

He stopped moving, unsure if she was condemning him for his failings or teasing him. He yearned for it to be the latter, but if he was right and she was gunning for him, he wasn't sure if he was ready to face the firing squad.

"You don't know how sorry I am." He looked down at his hands. His fingers were caked with hydraulic fluid and dust, and his fingernails were dirty.

She was an adventurous woman, or so he could assume by the fact she was a SAR volunteer, just like him, but that didn't mean she would want a man like him—a grubby failure.

"I have no doubt you are sorry," she said. Her voice had taken on a soft edge that seemed to go against the directness of her statement—or was it an accusation? "Are you actively trying to kill me? If you are, tell me now and I will leave you alone."

"I wouldn't have taken her up…or you…" He reached out to touch her shoulder, but stopped, as if grazing her skin would be only further reminder of how much he could have just cost them both.

"Just don't try to kill me again. I like breathing," she said, taking his hand and pressing it gently to her shoulder as she looked up at him. Her hand rested on his—her skin was icy and it worried him.

"I'd never want to have anyone in my care get hurt. I wouldn't—"

She waved him off. "Don't worry, I'm kidding." She squeezed his hand and then let go. "I guess I'm just really bad in these kinds of situations."

"You mean knowing how to react after you nearly lost your life?"

"Now who is the one being over-the-top?" She smiled up at him and the giant knot he hadn't known was in his chest finally loosened. "You landed that thing like you had crashed a thousand times… You *haven't*, though, have you?" She eyed him playfully.

The rest of the knot disappeared. "Yeah, that's me… The number-one crash dummy in the air today."

He grunted and moved around in his best imitation of a great ape.

She giggled, covering her mouth, and the phone antenna jabbed her hard in the cheek, just below the eye. "Oh, my God," she said, dropping the phone in her lap and touching the spot beneath her eye that was already turning into a welt.

He laughed, hard. "I thought I was the accident-prone one today."

"Have you ever had one of those days—*heck*, one of those *years*—that you just wanted to start over? Like, pretend it never happened, erase it, or whatever?"

He loved that she had actually said *whatever*. He was definitely with *his people*—not that he'd ever accidentally poked himself in the eye.

"I've had decades that I wish had never happened, but even as crappy as today has gone... I can't say that I'd want to take it back." He smiled at her.

She let go of his hand and moved slightly, and he let his fingers fall away from her jacket.

"Are you okay?" he asked.

She gave him a sidelong look, as though she wasn't sure if he was asking about her in the moment or overall.

"I mean—" he nudged his chin in the direction of the helo "—you didn't get hurt or anything, did you?" He wasn't sure he could face himself in the mirror if she was.

"I'm fine."

"That is the female equivalent of saying that you may have an arm coming out at the socket. Do I need to give you a look to assess you for damages?" He laughed, sending her a smirk that had worked on a few women in the past.

"Don't you dare look at me like that," she said, but there was a distinct ruddiness to her cheeks as she looked away from him.

There was a warmth to his cheeks as he realized how his comment had come off, and how, though she had been coquettish, he may have taken things a bit too far. "Did you hear back from base?"

She shook her head. "They haven't texted back yet—not anyone. I think my messages are sending, but these damned GPS messengers aren't known for their speed in sending and receiving texts."

That was a concept—Montana backcountry being at the hind end of the technological bandwidth—he knew all too well. There were a number of meetings he had been forced to take in the Super 1 grocery-store parking lot because it was the only place with enough speed to conduct a proper group video chat. Any more than a couple of people on Zoom and he was just about better off sending smoke signals.

Yet, that lack of tech had rarely bothered him. It was a quaint reminder he was residing in a place that put more of an emphasis on living in the moment instead of focusing on the virtual menagerie of staged social-media poses and fraudulent family photos. Montana living was gritty and ugly, a visceral reminder of nature's unforgiving bite. At the same time, the challenge and exacting manner was what made this lifestyle beautiful. The Montana wilderness was his home, through and through, and it was a place he would never leave.

"Well, there is good news and bad news here."

"Don't tell me… The good news is that I get to spend an extra few hours with you? Though, if you ask me… I'd say it could also be considered bad news as well." She looked him square in the eye, like she was measuring his response.

"I was going to say that the good and bad news is that we were going to have to start hiking out of here or stay put and wait for the team to come in and get us. If we stay put, it would be dangerous, as night temps are supposed to be brutally cold. Yet, if we hike out, any number of things could go wrong. I don't want to put you in harm's way again, but I don't think it's avoidable."

The rosy color returned to her cheeks. She rubbed at her neck and set the sat phone on the log. She chipped off a piece of wayward bark and crumbled it between her fingertips. "I've never been the kind of girl who sat around and waited to be rescued."

He'd always found that it was the women who didn't need saving who were the ones he fell for the hardest…and hurt him the most when they left him in the wind. He couldn't fall for another of that type again…no matter how sexy she was, or how hard he found himself once again staring at her lips. Why did he have to be like this? Why couldn't he be more of a *normal* dude, who could hit it and quit it when it came to the women in his life?

Then again, dudes who hit it and quit it weren't the

kinds of guys he found himself hanging out with. In fact, his best friend, Leo—also a SAR member—was a hopeless romantic. So much so that he hadn't given up on the self-proclaimed love of his life, who had left him shortly after they had graduated from college. That guy was a lost cause when it came to love. At least he, Casper, wasn't that pathetic. He could get over loss… Well, at least he could *eventually*.

His last girlfriend had left him for a woman she had met on an online dating app—one swipe and everything he had built his world upon had been erased and replaced. If only his heart could have been repaired as quickly as it had been broken; and yet, he still found himself occasionally thinking about her and hoping she was doing well. Who did that after having been broken up with like he had been?

In every other respect, besides women, he would have considered himself an alpha, but damn it if the right woman couldn't do a number on him.

Yep, he definitely couldn't find himself falling again. Not until he stopped thinking about his ex, Felicia, once and for all. Wait… What was her last name?

A smile overtook his features as he realized, for just a moment, that he had started to forget.

"You okay over there?" Kristin asked, pulling him back to reality and the choices he actually needed to make instead of the hypothetical fantasy he had rolling through his mind right now.

"Just thinking that in any rescue situation, we instruct everyone to stay where they are, so they can be found. Yet, that is assuming we need *rescue*." His smirk returned as he played on her statement. "So, we got this."

Oh, those famous last words. Even as he spoke, he could hear the doom that could come.

He brushed off the feeling, though. If anyone could get themselves out of the woods, they were definitely the ones. There was nothing to worry about. Yes, there were bears and mountain lions, freak blizzards and freezing rain, and criminals and jaded mountain men with a hatred of outsiders. Oddly enough, none of those things scared him half as much as spending more time with a woman whom he felt undeniably attracted to and was totally off-limits. Fangs, hypothermia and bullets weren't half as painful as heartbreak.

Chapter Six

The man was a walking red flag. Kristin had no business noticing the way his eyes crinkled just so when he smiled over at her, or the way when he really laughed, he tipped back his head ever so slightly. *No business.*

Even if she wanted to think about how sexy he was, she had a job to do. Not to mention the fact that they were, in effect, stranded in the woods. It struck her as a little funny that she was more worried about being so close to this man when she should have been focused on their life-and-death situation.

She spent the first mile walking in front of him and as she stepped over the fallen timber and through the thickets of willows in creek bottoms, she was more than certain she could feel the weight of his gaze on her ass. Or maybe it was her simply hoping that he was busy staring at her.

She wasn't the kind of woman to seek validation and value based on the attention and attraction levels of a man, but she yearned for his interest nonetheless. What was wrong with her?

Pausing, she pulled up the map of the area on her phone. She had a pretty good idea where they were and how they needed to get out—it was another ten miles west through some rough terrain.

"So we are here," she said, pointing haphazardly at her phone.

He took her phone and zoomed in on the map. "I think if we follow some of the game trails, those will be our best bet. We need to avoid this area here." He pointed at an area of steep topography, which indicated a sharp drop-off. "Yet, even if we go around, it's going to be some tough going. Are you sure you don't want to wait?"

"Absolutely not. It's dangerous going, but this is the best option." The thought of sitting and waiting was torturous. It may have been partly ego and partly the fear of inadequacy, but she couldn't be idle. Besides, if they waited, she would be forced to talk to him more and that would only lead to a deeper bond.

"The best option would have been to have a working helo, but I hear what you're saying," he teased.

"Do you want to lead the pack?" she asked.

He nodded and brushed against her. As he did, she noticed a long cut on his arm. A gasp escaped her.

"Why didn't you tell me you were hurt?" She shrugged off her backpack and pulled out her medical kit before he even spoke.

"What?" He looked down his body, assessing himself.

"Your arm," she said, pointing at the bloody gash on the back of his left arm.

He lifted his arm, gazed at his wound. "Well, hell..."

"Where else are you hurt?" she asked, realizing now that while he had checked on her, she had failed to do the same to him.

Maybe she was more selfish than she had ever realized—not that her exes hadn't accused her of it before. Her last boyfriend and the SAR pilot, Greg, had been more than happy to point out every one of her seeming faults. His constant critique of everything that made her who she was—even down to how she always wore white socks instead of socks that matched her clothing—had directly led to their breakup.

Devaluing in a relationship was a real thing. Her therapist had talked to her about it, at length. Men and women who started to fall out of love, or who wanted to fall out of love, often tore down the person they were with in order to emotionally distance themselves. It was Psychology 101, but it hadn't made it any easier to live through or endure.

Though she couldn't have proven it, she had always felt Greg had been stepping out from their relationship. He would hide his phone and take late-night calls that he would give her vague answers about when she questioned his actions. She could have sworn that he had even flirted with her best friend, but he had brushed her off, claiming he was just being friendly.

Just thinking about having a boyfriend made her want to call her therapist and have her remind her of all the reasons she needed to get out of the woods and away from the man she was finding herself wholly attracted to, gash and all.

She grabbed the saline wash and cleaned the wound on his arm. He didn't flinch as she dabbed at his skin and then pitched the stained rag into a Ziploc bag and back into her pack. "What did you catch your arm on?" She took out a bottle of hydrogen peroxide as she spoke. "Did you cut it on the bird?"

He shook his head. "I have no idea." He glanced back over his shoulder at the stand of timber they had just come through. "I have a feeling I may have torn it up coming through there. I gotta admit that I may not have been totally paying attention to where I was walking when I was following you." There was an edge of joy in his tone.

She was more than aware of the next steps in this dance. If she asked him why he wasn't paying attention, it would open up their friendship to something *more*; and if she two-stepped around that, it would likely be the end of any further flirtation… *maybe*. That is, if she was reading it all right. As adept at relationships and flirting as she was, she could have been completely off base in how she was seeing this—it had been a while since she'd danced, figuratively or otherwise.

As quickly as she could, she dressed the wound. He would be fine, but there were a couple of spots that looked as though they would benefit from a stitch. She zipped her bag and tossed it back over her shoulder. "If we're going to make it out of the woods further unscathed, we both probably need to be extra vigilant."

As if he was oblivious to her warning, he walked up beside her, his uninjured arm brushing against her and making her skin spark to life.

Why did he have to go and do that? He wasn't making it any easier to push him away, when he literally wouldn't even stay at arm's length.

"How long have you been doing FLIR?" he asked.

Their footfalls crunched on the dirt path that was just wide enough for two people. "I dunno, a few years."

"How did you get started in it?" he asked.

She appreciated his attempt at small talk since it kept her from thinking so much about how he smelled of hydraulic fluid and sweat—a heady combination if ever there was one… If danger and sexiness had a trademark aroma, it would have definitely been this.

"I have always really been a tech girl, and imaging technology specifically. I was the girl who was studying radar signatures as a kid." She chuckled. "My parents never really understood what I found so fascinating, but they were super supportive. I can't tell you the number of times I made them watch the show *Radar Men from the Moon* from the 1950s. It was *awful*, but my grandfather got me started. We would sneak away to his den and watch the show."

"So you'd say that your entire life has been built on a kitschy show?"

"Not just that one," she said with a laugh, though

she tried to watch her footing as they started to move into denser forest. "Basically, anything with talk of going to outer space and Martians…and I was all in. It was silly."

"That's not silly. It's pretty cool, actually. Plus, it sounds like you have a really great grandfather."

"I did," she said, smiling at the memory of the man who had helped bring her up. "I went to his house every Sunday to help him with his yard in the summer and then his housework in the winter. Basically, though, we'd just have milk and cookies while we watched movies and talked football."

"So you're a football fan as well?"

"I loved the movies more, but I did learn enough about football to know that Joe Montana is the best football player who ever lived. Most people would disagree and say it's Tom Brady, thanks to his million and one Super Bowl wins, but Montana played in a time with less rules and when the game was far more physical."

He started to laugh. "That is one hell of a contentious opinion. Your grandfather sounds like he did a good job with you."

"Oh, my grandfather's more of a Namath fan. I'm a Montana girl, through and through." She chuckled.

"You're definitely that. Even if I don't agree with your taste in football players."

"Oh, you don't agree?" She grinned. "Don't tell me you are a Brady fan."

"I never said anything of the sort," he said, looking affronted.

"Don't start hedging your bets and laying up just because…" She paused, questioning whether or not she should say what she was thinking.

"Because why?" Casper asked, giving her a cheeky grin. "Why do you think I'd hold up?"

She readjusted the straps of her backpack on her shoulders, like they were the source of the additional weight she was feeling. "I think it's because you want me to like you."

He slowed down slightly, but she kept the same pace, leaving him behind her. A knot formed in her stomach. What if she had gotten her assumption wrong?

If she was in for a penny, at this point, she was in for a pound.

"Am I wrong?" She looked over her shoulder at him.

He was opening and closing his mouth like he was trying to get the right words out, but was failing.

"In all honesty, I didn't think that having a friendship with you was something that was really on the table."

She looked away, forced to pay attention to her footfalls on the trail as they started to ascend the mountain in front of them. She hated that she couldn't look at him while he was talking to her, but at the same time felt like it was silly she even had that thought.

"Why would you think friendship with me was off the table?"

"I'm sure you don't really want me to remind you,

but…" he said, and jabbed his thumb in the direction they had come from.

"Unless you did that on purpose, which I'm fairly certain you didn't, then I'm going to say accidents happen and will leave it at that. No hard feelings." She paused as she thought about their first meeting and all the reasons he could have hated her. From his lack of response, she wondered if he was thinking about it as well. "If anything, I'm the one who should really feel bad. It was my inability to find your father sooner that may have resulted in his death."

"Don't even say that." He moved to her side and touched her shoulder, motioning for her to stop.

She turned to face him, but tried to look away. "Yes?"

He lifted her chin with his finger, forcing her to gaze up at him. "My father being out there and missing was no fault of yours. I hope you haven't been holding on to that all this time. If I am to blame anyone, I blame my brother and his wife." He looked her deep in the eyes, like he was trying to gauge her reaction and decide whether or not she believed him.

It didn't matter what he said—she would always feel like she hadn't acted quickly enough. It would be one of the incidents in this job that would haunt her for the rest of her career…if not her life.

"Do you know how far my father walked before you found him?"

She chewed on the inside of her cheek as she thought of the incident management plan her team had created before they had gone to search for the man. "He had last been seen by a hiker. They were the ones who called us and helped us to isolate his last known location."

"Who called to tell you he was missing?"

"I think it was the hiker, at least that's what I remember them saying in the briefing before the mission." She started to breathe harder as her body pushed to stay in pace with him as they worked their way up the mountain and toward the next ridgeline.

Casper simply nodded.

Her legs were burning and she let him move ahead of her as the trail narrowed and they gained elevation. Roots were sticking up out of the ground, forcing her to pick her steps carefully as she moved steadily up the mountain.

They had to have gone at least a mile, crawling over half-down logs and pushing through the bushes, which clung to her like they wanted her to stay in the woods forever. She could make out the sounds of Casper's heavy breaths in front of her. Her mind wandered as she tried to focus on something other than the tightness that was moving up from her calves and starting to twist through her thighs.

If she was already this tired so early in their hike, she would have to be careful not to hurt herself. Weariness led to accidents, and accidents to death.

Her GPS messenger pinged with a text.

"Casper," she called out, and he stopped. She took out the phone and clicked on the screen. He walked back and stepped beside her. "Cindy wants to know if she needs to send a team to intercept. She is concerned for our safety."

"At least she didn't tell me I'm fired." He gave her a weak smile, one that made her wonder exactly what all was on his mind.

"Can she fire a volunteer?"

He chuckled, but the sound was hard and dry. "If I was still in my old job, my ass would be gone. I'd be sitting at my commanding officer's desk and waiting for my formal investigation and write-up."

"You're a veteran?" She had always thought he was hot, but seeing him from this aspect made him seem just that much sexier—not only was he a pilot, but he was also a military man. For some reason, she ached to see him in uniform. A uniform that she could promptly rip off.

"Army. I was a member of the 160th. SOAR."

Yep. Just like that he went from a ten to an impossible eleven on the hotness scale.

"So you were a Night Stalker?"

He sent her a devilish grin. "You've heard of us?"

It could have been the stress of the hike, but her heart fluttered in her chest as his gaze seemed to penetrate straight to the center of her. "Uh-huh." She swallowed hard as she tried to gain control over her body. "Who in our world hasn't? You are the best of the best."

"Clearly, that can't be true. I just dropped us out of the sky, but I appreciate your belief in me." He laughed. "I have a feeling that when we get out of the woods, Cindy will be waiting and I will be the first chief warrant officer to be let go from a volunteer piloting position." He ran his hand over his face. "I can't wait to hear what my buddies will have to say."

"You don't think she will really let you go, do you?"

He scowled. "I potentially just lost my team hundreds of thousands of dollars…not to mention your crew as well. Your bird is laid up. What if someone needs you? I may have just cost someone like my father their life."

She reached out and touched his arm. He was sweating from their hike and his muscles were pressing against his shirt. She shouldn't have touched him—it only made her attraction for him grow. "What happened out here, it wasn't your fault. If someone needs us, there are options…" Yet, even as she spoke, she couldn't deny he was right—this accident could very well end up costing more than either of them could imagine.

Chapter Seven

It was a crazy-ass feeling to come out of a life-and-death situation and wish that he could return to the uncertainty. Though Casper hoped Cindy would be understanding that what had happened was outside of his control, he wasn't sure the same could be said for the rest of the SAR unit. If he was turned away from his role in search-and-rescue, he would have nothing left. His entire identity would be stripped away and he would be left as an empty shell of the man he had once been.

He'd be nothing. He'd have *nothing*.

Though he wasn't the kind to give up at the first sign of adversity, he didn't have a backup plan for his life if everything fell through any more than it already had. Retiring from the military early had not done him any favors.

Kristin paused as he stopped to take a breath. The night was falling upon them and there was a bite to the air that promised frost.

"You going to be okay?" she asked, almost as if she could read his mind, or perhaps his body language.

"Am I that obvious?" He sighed.

She reached over and took his hand, lacing her fingers between his. "You saved my life. You know I'm going to have your back, no matter what happens down there."

At the edge of the timberline below them, in the valley bottom, there were the sounds of vehicles coming and going from their incident command center. Voices were carrying, but he couldn't make out words, only the manic tone of chaos.

He and Kristin had thrown the entire team on their ear.

Though he was grateful she had faith that he would make it through the investigation and ensuing debriefing without getting laid out, he wasn't about to point out the fact that she was probably wrong. And he *really* didn't want to talk about his feelings, or why he felt as he did and was so afraid.

So what if they had nearly died together? That certainly didn't mean he was ready to be *vulnerable*.

"Casper, we don't have to go down there and face the world until you are ready," Kristin continued, her voice soft.

He both liked and hated that she could be so understanding. They hardly knew each other, but it was like she could see right through him, and damn if it didn't jar him even more than the crash.

She leaned into him and put her head against his shoulder.

"You are a great woman," he said, leaning his head on top of hers.

Her hair smelled of sweat, fresh air and sunshine, and the effect was intoxicating. It struck him how something, some little action like this—one of kindness and understanding—could calm the storm within him. Whatever was to come would come, but at least in these few moments before he would have to face the crushing waves of questions and possible accusations, he had found a safe harbor.

Without thinking, he turned slightly and kissed the top of her head, pulling the scent of her deep into his lungs, as if this moment was the last peace he would find before his life fell apart. She gently moved back and looked up at him.

Their eyes met and he stared into the calming green he found. He had noticed her eyes before, but now it was like he was seeing them for the first time. Or, perhaps, it was that they were truly finally seeing one another. Until this moment, they had been forced to be together. As soon as they stepped back into the real world, they might not ever have to be this close again.

He had to take his chance. Yet, before he could move, Kristin lifted to her tiptoes and her lips met his. This time, she was the one who breathed him in, and the whisper of her breath matched perfectly with the soft, yearning tempo of her kiss.

Until now, he hadn't realized that he was the one who needed to be saved...but mostly from himself and the battles within his mind.

The kiss was gentle and as full of grace and tenderness as Kristin. She let her lips linger against his and then touched her forehead to his, the simple act as sexy and sweet as the kiss. What he would give to be with a woman like her.

"I'm your ally. No matter what happens down there, I won't let you take the fall." She brushed the back of his hand with hers as she moved away from him. "When you are ready..." She waved in the direction of the camp.

"In case I don't get to say this later, thank you." He smiled at her, but even he could feel the tiredness in his eyes.

It was matched in hers. "Save your thanks until we are through this."

He touched her shoulder as he moved by her. "Let's go rip this Band-Aid off."

BY THE TIME they reached the camp, the light had faded from the sky and everyone in the camp had heard about their mishap. He and Kristin walked by the helo pad where his bird rested. There was a cacophony of voices coming from inside the different tents, but no one seemed to be outside. He was relieved no one had the chance to stop them as they made their way inside the wall tent that stood at the heart of the camp. Cindy was sitting in a folding chair at the main table sipping a cup of coffee and staring down at a topographic map like it held all the answers they needed.

"The party has arrived!" Casper called, slapping the guy nearest to him on the back as he made his way inside.

Kristin didn't recognize the man, but her friend,

and the regular pilot of the helo, was sitting two seats down in another folding chair. He turned toward her and his face was tight. He quickly looked away, though she couldn't imagine why. Perhaps he was upset with the crash, or he felt as if he was somehow culpable in what had transpired. She would definitely need to deal with him later—she could hardly wait.

"Get your asses up here." Cindy pointed at the open seats at the table, and while her action was authoritarian and ordering, there was undeniably relief in her tone.

Forcing herself to ignore the urge to slink toward the woman in charge, Kristin straightened her back and readied herself to go to the gallows at Casper's side. He couldn't be blamed for what had happened.

Cindy said something behind her hand to the man to her left before turning to the rest of the people who had gathered around. "Hey, guys," she called loudly, "we appreciate all your efforts in making sure that Kristin and Casper arrived safely back at the camp as well as taking care of the teams. However, we will need anyone who isn't one of the board members to leave the area for a bit…until we have gone over what transpired."

There was a collective grumble and a few choice words that Kristin could hear whispered under breaths. If all these folks had been a part of their return, she could understand their reticence in being sent from the room at such a pivotal moment.

"Yeah, yeah… Keep your griping to yourselves." Cindy pointed toward the door. "There is a food truck outside with some damned good barbeque. Eat and we will meet back up in an hour."

The pilot bumped against her shoulder, almost knocking her off balance. "Greg?" Kristin asked.

He didn't look at her and instead barreled outside and into the night.

"Damn, he is charming," Casper said, nudging his chin toward the guy. "Should I be jealous?" He smiled.

"Greg isn't like that, *usually*." She looked back over her shoulder in the direction in which her ex-boyfriend had disappeared.

"Casper. Kristin. We're waiting." Cindy lost any softness that had been in her voice earlier, when she had first seen them.

Casper let out a long exhale before making his way to the table with her at his heels.

She wanted to speak up. To intercede and tell Cindy and the other three lieutenants sitting at the table that this had merely been an accident… Really, they had made it out of the woods almost unscathed.

"First things first," Cindy began. "I can't tell you how relieved I am. We *all* are—" she motioned to the camp "—that you have made it back. We had a pool going whether or not we would have to come in with a stretcher."

Casper chuckled. "I'm glad to hear that you guys didn't let an opportunity to gamble on our welfare pass you by."

"Are you saying you wouldn't have done the same thing if you knew I was accounted for and healthy,

but needing to self-rescue my ass from the woods?"
Cindy laughed.

"When you put it like that, I think I would have
doubled down," Casper said, the aluminum folding
chair scraping on the gravel on the ground of the tent
and making a pinging sound. "Which side of the bet
were you on?"

She waved him off with a laugh. "You know that I
have the utmost faith in you… Even if you did crash
a helicopter that didn't belong to our team and ruined
our chances at funding."

The words coming out of her mouth and the tone
of her voice were inconsistent. It sounded almost as if
Cindy was empathetic and understanding about what
had happened. Kristin had prepared herself for almost every possible scenario with Casper's team and
what would happen in this moment, but she hadn't
accounted for this possibility.

She glanced over at Casper and he looked as utterly confused as she was feeling.

"Kristin," Cindy said, turning to her, "I must offer
my sincere apologies. I'm sure that we will get to the
bottom of what happened and why. In the meantime,
we will make sure that you and your pilot will be
taken care of and have anything you need to make
it back to Billings safely."

"Thank you," she said, sounding almost breathless.
"I… I'm going to need to get our mechanics out here."

"Greg, your pilot, said he would take care of things."

At least someone knew what was going on.

"Good. Glad to hear he is on top of things."

"As for what happened, you have stated in your texts that you believe none of what happened was due to negligence on Casper's part. Am I correct in this?"

She had the sickening feeling that she had suddenly found herself in the court of Judge Cindy and she was front and center on the witness stand. Though she wasn't exactly sure of what she should say that would keep her lawyers happy, but she had made a vow to Casper and she intended on keeping it.

"From what I witnessed, there was a critical hydraulic leak. Your pilot, Mr. Keller, did a commendable job in bringing us down in a safe and effective way even though the environment around us didn't lend itself toward success. I would go so far as to say that Casper saved our lives."

Cindy sent her a wide smile.

"Now, if you don't mind, I need to talk to my pilot and make sure we have everything in order to get our helo back and in working order. We have lives to save."

Casper ran his hand over her lower back and the simple action made a warmth roll through her body.

Apparently, she had passed the questioning with flying colors. Better—in doing so, she had also fulfilled her promise…at least for now. As it stood, the future was in their hands.

Chapter Eight

Greg had no real excuse to act as he had, at least not as far as Kristin was concerned. The man had known the risks that always went with flying. No pilot was immune to the inevitability that at some point or another, they would go down. If anything, he should have been glad that the helo would probably come through this event to fly another day and he hadn't been the one on the stick.

She, on the other hand, couldn't say she was raring to jump back into a bird.

Regardless, she needed to get to the bottom of what, exactly, was getting to him the most about the accident. If everything went her way, maybe she could talk him down off the ledge and perhaps even turn this melee into a positive. She definitely wasn't sure how she would go about that, even though she had been trying to come up with something the entire hike back. Every time she tried to focus on the political game, which would have to be played once they returned, all she could focus on was Casper and the way his voice made her body clench.

He was not good for her attention span or capacity for critical thinking. Damn him. Or, maybe, damn her for being so at mercy to her baser needs. She was a professional woman, and as soon as she got back to her desk at FLIR Tech, she would have plenty of time to think about Casper's round, bounce-a-quarter-off-it ass.

At the mere thought of what she had just said to herself, she ran a hand over her face.

Here, she had been thinking that the hardest part of the wreck was already over—they had landed it and self-rescued. Never had she thought the assuaging of feelings and tiptoeing through confusing politics would be the hardest part.

Casper was still in the tent with Cindy, and she was grateful, as it would give her the chance to come back to her senses and ground herself in reality.

She made her way toward the food truck, where she hoped to find Greg. He couldn't have gone far, as they didn't have any private area or tent that she was aware of; though, she doubted from the look on his face when she'd last seen him that eating was at the forefront of his mind, but if he wasn't there, she could expand her search as need required.

She chuckled at the thought of how all day she had been searching for something, and even at camp, she was on the hook. Truth be told, though, she kinda loved every second of it. It was a hell of a thing to be needed—more, required.

When she and Greg had been dating, most of the

time he could have been best described as indifferent. Maybe that was what was bothering him. He was jealous of her spending time in the air with Casper, or maybe he was just mad that she was finally moving on.

Nah. That couldn't have been it. They had been broken up for more than three months.

Thinking back, it might have been even longer than that. It was Greg who had informed her that he was going to start seeing other people. She'd agreed and he had left her with the old cliché—"Don't worry, we can still be friends." It was in that moment she had been more sure than ever that he had already been sleeping with other women. It sucked knowing she hadn't been enough for him.

As if Greg could sense that she was replaying their relationship of convenience in her mind, he stepped out from behind the tent nearest the food truck. He was holding a white foam container, and even from here, she could smell the Cholula hot sauce and barbecue sauce. She liked both things, but couldn't wrap her head around why he would want to ruin two great condiments by mixing them together.

Yeah…there was no denying her feelings for him were solidly dead if she could dislike everything about him down to the way he ate.

"Greg, you have a minute to chat?" she called to him.

He looked up from picking at his food and popped a piece of what looked like pulled pork into his mouth. "Whadya want?" he said, a tendril of pork sticking out of his mouth as he spoke.

Yep, he was gross. How had she ever been attracted to this guy?

"What just happened in there?" she asked, pointing vaguely in the direction of the main tent.

"Are you kidding me?" he asked, wiping at his mouth with the back of his hand as he finally remembered to swallow his bite.

"No. I thought we were fine. I thought we were getting along…and now you are throwing shoulders? What in the hell?" Her jaw hardened as she tried to control her bubbling anger at the man. She had gone to bat and called him a friend, and now he was treating her like this… *How dare he.*

He crushed the container in his hand. "You have, and will always be, one of the most self-centered people I've ever met." He walked toward the garbage can and threw away the box so hard it made the steel can ring.

His words made her take a quick inventory of her life. There were a number of incidents where she hadn't done her best, but she had always thought she had gone out of her way to not only care for her self-interest, but also for other's wishes, especially when it came to Greg. She had even gone so far as to take his mother to and from pretty much all of her doctor's appointments for six months because he was "too busy." That should have been a red flag, but apparently her dumb ass thought those flags were opportunities for a man to experience personal growth—growth she had once believed she was capable of inspiring.

What a fool she had been.

"I—I get that you think you have a right to be mad because your bird went down." She tried to stop the quaver that had somehow stupidly made its way into her voice. This wasn't the time to be weak. "However, you have no right to start attacking me—personally or professionally. You work *for* me."

His eyes grew wide, but his surprise rapidly turned into an angry scowl. "First, we both know you don't have the authority to fire me. Even if you did, don't think for a second that I can't blink and get another job."

"Don't think for a second that you're not replaceable."

The sound of his stupid laugh made the hair stand on her arms. "You are the one who is replaceable—not the other way around. What I do takes skill. Few are as good as me. As if I have to remind you that it was your new *buddy* who nearly killed you." He blew out a dismissive snort. "I bet FLIR already has applicants lined up for your easy gig."

It took everything in her power not to punch the smug look off his face. Even if it took every ounce of her willpower, as soon as they got back to Billings she would work on getting him relieved of duty. Good or not, he was not the best man for the job. Until then, however, if he wasn't going to quit on his own, they were going to have to get along.

"Look, we got off on the wrong foot here. Let's restart this whole thing. All I wanted to really know was whether or not you called in the mechanics. We need to get the bird out of the woods."

"If you hadn't signed us up for this stupid training session, then *my bird* wouldn't be stranded out there in the first place. I hope you know that I'm holding you personally responsible."

She turned on her heel and did a quick about-face as she tried to hold in her rage in front of this shark.

There was being stupid and there was opening a vein in the water. This was her fault. She had foolishly thought that exes could be friends…or, at the very least, civil to each other.

Drawing in a breath, she turned back to him when she was just far enough away that her face could be masked by the darkness. "Greg, I hope you know you've become a man I wouldn't wish upon my worst enemies."

"It's funny," he said, his features hard, "I could almost say the same of you. In fact, you are dumber than a box of crayons and just about as useful. No one needs someone like you in their life—any woman is better than you."

Hot, angry tears filled her eyes. Fuming, she headed toward the main tent. Rounding a corner, someone grabbed her. Instinctively, she threw up her hands and felt her palm connect with a man's nose.

"Damn it!" Casper exclaimed, cupping his nose in his hands. "Why did you do that?"

"Oh… Oh, I'm so-o-o sorry. I…" She stumbled

to find the right words. "I didn't know it was you. I just reacted."

"I heard you and Greg fighting and I was trying to come out to help." He tilted his head back in an attempt to staunch the stream of blood that was dripping down his chin.

Patting her pockets, she came to the one on her thigh and withdrew a black bandana. "Here," she said, gently swabbing at the blood on his chin before motioning for him to use it for his nose.

"Thanks." He took the cloth and dabbed at his nose before holding it still.

"So you heard all that, huh?" She nibbled at her lower lip.

He nodded.

"I'm guessing that everyone else did as well?"

"Without a doubt."

She ran her hands over her face and gave a long exhale. "Well, so much for coming off as professional."

"I think professional left the building when you punched me in the nose," he said with a laugh, but the sound was cut off as he winced in pain.

"Yeah, about that…" She cringed.

"If you were going to punch someone, you really should have made it Greg."

"Trust me, I wanted to punch him."

"So did I." He motioned in the dude's direction. "Want me to go do it now?"

"If I can kick your ass, I don't think you have a chance. Sorry." She laughed. "Seriously, though, thanks for trying to come to my defense, but all I'm going to really need is a drive back to Billings."

He motioned toward the helicopter on the pad. "I can do better…"

Chapter Nine

"I'm going to need to be talked into going back in the air," Kristin challenged, but there was a cute smirk on her face that said it wouldn't take too much convincing for her to come back up with him.

"Lucky for me, I have an ace in the hole." Casper lifted the cloth to reveal his blood. "You did just hit me in the nose."

She frowned, but the tremble in her lips gave away the fact she was trying to stop from smiling. "I don't think that really compares to you crashing us into the ground."

"*Crash* is such a strong word." He laughed, but stopped as the pain from his nose pinged through him. *Thinking about pain...* "So I'm assuming Greg is your ex?"

Now she was the one who looked like she was hurting, and he wished he hadn't brought up the obvious.

"I can't say that I want to talk about it, but, yeah. Though, I would never have considered us to be in a real relationship."

"Was it you or him that didn't *define* what you

had?" He was genuinely curious as to who she was in a partnership, the giver or the taker.

She quirked an eyebrow at him. "I never pushed and he never offered."

Kristin was definitely the giver.

He was a giver in relationships, too. Maybe that was another reason they couldn't really be anything besides a quick kiss in the woods and maybe a night or two in Billings before he returned to Big Sky. Yeah, they might see each other at a work function here or there, but the eight hours drive time between her home and his definitely put yet another damper on things between them.

Kristin sighed, signaling an end to any more questions about her ex. He didn't mind, though. There was nothing worse than talking about the past. At least, the painful moments. He had no desire to open up, give her the dirty details and talk about the times in life when he had been brought to his knees. They had already been through enough just in the last twenty-four hours, so going through another wave of emotions sounded like the next ascension in their levels of this hellish day.

"I bet you are exhausted. You camping here tonight?" he asked, motioning toward the tents.

She looked over her shoulder in the direction of where she had been talking to Greg outside the food truck. "We were going to grab a hotel."

Did that mean that she and Greg had planned on spending the night together? The thought made him surprisingly jealous. Now he was aching to ask her how long Greg had been her ex and what had happened to bring their *thing* together to an end, but it was conversation non grata.

Really, though, he reminded himself, *what does it matter?*

"If you want, I have a house with three bedrooms. You could help yourself to the spare."

"That would be great. I have my stuff in the helo…" She pointed in the direction of the helicopter pad, but then her arm fell. "Strike that—beyond what is in my backpack in the tent, I may need to stop and get a few things. Would you mind?"

"Not at all," he said. "If it's basic stuff, though, I have extras."

"In the event your girlfriend stays over or something?" she asked, but he could tell from her tone that it was more than just an attempt to be playful and she was really questioning him about his personal life.

"No girlfriend."

"Then why do you have a three-bedroom house with only one spare bedroom?"

He smirked. "You promise not to laugh at me?"

"Do you have a sex dungeon or something?" she teased. "If you do, you have to tell me now. I think that is legally required." She giggled.

How did one little sound make him want to pull her into his arms and kiss her again?

"I don't know what kind of guy you think I am, but if I'm single, I feel like a sex dungeon might be a bit of a waste of space."

"If being an adult has taught me anything, it is that regardless of relationship statuses, sex happens."

She had clearly been broken by men in her past. Maybe being broken by exes was something they could have in common.

He paused for a moment. Was all this sex talk implying that she would be interested in spending the night with him in more than a spare-bedroom kind of way? Though he wanted to clarify things between them to a certain extent, asking her what she wanted from him tonight seemed like he would be taking things too close to *real* for his liking.

The thought made him laugh. Here they were, talking about relationships, but asking her about what she wanted from him was *too real*.

"Sorry," she continued, seemingly uncomfortable with his silence. "I didn't mean to take things that far. I…" She swayed from foot to foot nervously. "That was all out of line."

"Kristin," he said, realizing that it was the first time he had spoken her name aloud and, secretly, he loved the way it felt rolling over his tongue. "You never have to apologize for talking to me. You're hilarious."

She turned her face slightly, hiding it from him as though she was blushing.

"I won't judge you as long as you don't judge me about my bedroom situation."

"Oh," she said, sounding relieved of her embarrassment, "are you going to tell me your deep, dark secret?"

He laughed. "It's not deep or dark, but I do have the most pampered dog on the entire planet." He glanced down at his watch. "Actually, I probably need to pick him up from the dog-sitter."

She gave a jovial laugh, but it was a light and loving sound. "Oh, my goodness. That may be the cutest thing you've said to me since we met." She paused. "What kind of dog is this prince or princess?"

"Prince. His name is Grover and he is a goldendoodle. He's four and needs a lot of exercise."

"I can't wait to meet him. I *love* dogs." She put her hands to her mouth in excitement in a way that made him almost as excited as her. "I warn you now, though—you may not get him back. Dogs tend to adopt me as their people." They walked into the tent and she grabbed her bag as they spoke.

"I'm sure he is waiting impatiently to meet you," he said as they walked toward the parking lot and his waiting pickup.

She smiled at him as he opened up the door for her and she climbed inside. Before he got in, he took a long breath, trying to control the strange nervousness that was building within him. It was one thing to talk about her staying at his place overnight, but it was another thing entirely to actually make it happen.

He attempted to remind himself that he had no reason to feel like this—it wasn't as if they hadn't been alone all day. Yet, he kept circling back to the fact that this was *different*. Things between them had shifted with their kiss, and there was no going back and putting his attraction back on the shelf.

He glanced in the truck, and saw that she had pulled down the visor and was rubbing something beneath her eye. It made him wonder if she, too, was feeling the same kind of push and pull that he was. If anything, though, she seemed generally at ease with going home with him.

She had made it clear that she wasn't comfortable taking things between them toward sharing a bed.

He climbed into the truck as she closed the visor mirror and it slapped back into place.

"Yeah, I definitely look like I fell out of the sky today. It's a good thing you aren't taking me on a date."

He inadvertently jerked the wheel as they started down the road. Did she want to go on a date? Was that like a midwestern hint that she wanted him to take her out? Or was that a subtle strike into the friend zone? He wasn't sure he wanted to know, and he didn't want to have to play any more games.

"I have to say, I'm glad you know you can trust me." He smiled over at her, but what he really wanted to do was reach across the console and take her hand. He wanted to touch her so bad.

"What do you mean?"

"I just mean that in all reality we just met."

"Technically, we met a few weeks ago, but I know where you are going with this," she said, correcting him.

"True," he said with a little nod. "Yet, we really only talked for the first time today. I don't know many women who would feel comfortable going home with a guy the same day."

"You must not have ever gone drinking at a college-aged bar, then," she said with a laugh.

"Damn, you know what…? Now that I hear myself saying that out loud, I…" He laughed with her. "Seriously, though, I'm taking it as a compliment that you know you are safe with me."

"You're always a damned hero, aren't you?" she teased, her smile not wavering on her lips as she spoke.

He moved like he was going to grab something out of the back seat. "Ah, man…"

"What?" she asked, looking behind them. "Do you need me to grab something?"

He chuckled. "Nah, it just looks like I forgot to throw my superhero cape in the back seat again."

She gave him a playful nudge. "You are ridiculous. You know that, right?"

"I may be ridiculous, but I have a feeling that you may like it." He couldn't help himself—he extended his hand in the hope that she would slip her fingers between his.

He wasn't left disappointed when her warm hand slipped in his and they interlaced their fingers. He could get used to having this beautiful woman at his side.

Chapter Ten

Grover was even cuter in person than Casper had described the dog. He jiggled and wiggled as his tail whipped back and forth and he pranced in excitement as she petted him. He looked so much like an apricot teddy bear, that if he had round ears he would have almost been a dead ringer for a stuffed animal... Well, one that whined to get scratches right at the base of his tail.

This combo of Casper and Grover proved that there was such a thing as immediately feeling at home.

"He is a charmer." Casper gave the dog a pat on the head as he led her down the hall and toward what she assumed were the bedrooms.

The house was nicer than she had thought it would be, not that she had really *expected* anything. Everything was in order, all the way down to the blanket that had been folded neatly over the leather couch in the living room when she had walked by.

"Do you have a housekeeper in addition to a dog-sitter?"

"Nah," he said, shaking his head. "I'm not really

busy enough to need one. Plus, I enjoy taking care of things myself. I find that if I keep my boots on the ground, I have a better idea of what awaits me."

She wasn't sure she knew what exactly he was referring to when it came to *awaiting* things, but she assumed it probably had something to do with his time in the military. "Do you work in addition to volunteering for SAR?"

"I'm a trained mechanical engineer. I got my PhD in engineering while I was in the army. Lately, I've been doing some freelance stuff from home in my downtime. Mostly, I play with Grover and then SAR stuff. It doesn't sound like much, but I'm generally pretty busy."

She unintentionally scrunched her face at his words.

"You don't like that I have my PhD?" he teased.

Kristin touched the back of her hair, smoothing it as she glanced over at him. "No, that's not it at all."

"So I read you right—something is bothering you."

"It's just that," she continued, taking a breath as she weighed whether or not she truly wanted to say what she was thinking, "it sounds like you are really busy."

He put his hand on her lower back and the simple action soothed the compression in her chest. "Kristin…" He said her name like it was a prayer. "I am busy because it keeps me from thinking about the things that I don't have in my life."

She glanced down the hallway at several oil paintings of mountains and one of a moose that were hanging at the end of the long corridor. "Don't take this the wrong way, but it actually looks like you have everything you could want."

He gave her a sidelong glance. "That may be true when it comes to materialistic things, but over the last few years, after having retired from the army, I've just come to realize that what is important in life isn't the *stuff*." He started to walk down the hallway.

"Then what is important to you?" she asked, following him and ever so nonchalantly trying to catch a glimpse of his ass. It really was a thing of beauty, and she could definitely see it becoming something important to her.

Grover wagged his tail as he meandered up beside her and leaned against her leg, then glanced at her like he had caught her checking him out and was now hoping for pets, as if they were some sort of blackmail for his not telling. The word *cheeky* came to mind as she scratched the dog's head.

"You may think I'm trying to blow smoke up your dress, but I've got to say that the most important things in life are the relationships which you build and devote yourself to."

"So, family?"

He huffed. "I would like to agree with that, but my family is a bit of a mess. I'd hate for others to define me or judge me based on their behavior. Though…" He paused as Grover pranced over to him and looked at his master with his tongue lolling out of his mouth. "I would make an exception when it came to my mom and dad. They were good people."

"You mentioned you had a brother. Is it just the two of you?"

He nodded. "William and his wife, Michelle. They don't have any kids yet, but I know they have been trying."

"Are you close with them?"

There was something about the way his eye twitched when she asked that told her there was a lot of unpacking that would have to be done when it came to the subject of his brother and his wife.

"It's *tenuous*."

From his clipped response, he wasn't ready to talk about them. She hoped it was because he was having fun with her that made him reticent to open up and not that he wasn't willing to be himself with her.

He stopped beside the first bedroom door on his left. Inside was a beautiful queen-size bed with an antique-looking white bedspread. It was the heavy kind with lace tatting on the edges. In the corner of the room was a treadle Singer sewing machine. If she had been given a lifetime to guess what was in his guest room, the last thing she would have guessed would have been a shabby-chic throwback that she might have expected to see in a bed-and-breakfast.

Stepping into the room, she was actually impressed. There was a bookshelf against the wall filled with everything from Austen and Brontë, to Stoker and Poe. "You have all of my favorites covered," she said, motioning toward the shelves. "I've always believed you can safely judge a person by what they enjoy reading."

He gave her a guilty look. "While I have read some of those," he began, "I have to own up to the fact that this house used to belong to my parents. This was my mother's stuff."

She paused, trying to reconcile herself to the fact that this handsome man had not only kept his mother's things on display, but had also welcomed her into this place filled with mementos that clearly must have meant something to him. Some of her friends may have hated this kind of thing, but it had been a rarity in her life to meet a man with an emotional range larger than a toothpick.

"This is make-or-break," she said, smiling at him as she kidded around. "Austen or Brontë?"

He walked over to the bookshelf and pulled out *Jane Eyre* and *Emma*, but left *Pride and Prejudice* sitting lonely in the corner. It pulled at her, as if he had done something profane, and she moved to pick it up.

"Hey, now," he said, stopping her gently with an outstretched hand. "What do you think you are doing?"

She pointed at her favorite book and gave him doe eyes. "No one leaves Elizabeth Bennet in the corner."

He laughed at her. "I should have known you were a romance fan."

"What is that supposed to mean?" she asked, slightly worried about her fantasy world, where he was the one straight man on the planet who not only understood the Elizabeth Bennet reference, but also appreciated the works for the glorious keystones of romance that they were.

"I just mean that all the best women have a thing about romance novels." He smiled. "Hear me out, but I have always found that all my exes who enjoyed reading romances were the most open-minded and sexually free lovers I've ever had."

"Oh, you've had a lot of lovers, have you?" Jealousy flashed through her.

"Not where I was going with that at all. And, no." He slipped his hand in hers, but as he did, Grover nudged them to pet him and she was forced to oblige.

"Grover is jealous." She scratched behind his ear as he gazed up at her.

"I don't think he is the only one," Casper said. "Seriously, I hope you know that there is nothing to worry about when it comes to that kind of thing. I'm a one-woman man when I'm in a relationship, or even a *situationship*."

She wanted to ask him if that was what he could see them becoming, but at the same time, she didn't want to press the issue. They could have this night and maybe a few more days together, but their time this close to one another was preciously limited. She didn't want a long-distance thing or even a situationship. If she was going to give her heart to another, she wanted to give it all, without reservation.

"I will set things out in the bathroom in the hall for you," he continued, as though he could pick up on the fact that their conversation had pulled out feelings within her that she couldn't reconcile. "If you need anything, I'm down at the end of the hall. It's the door on the left. Grover's door is on the right.

Just so you know, you got the larger bedroom." He smiled, but there was something in his eyes that spoke of his holding something back.

"Thank you, Casper," she said.

"It's my pleasure. And I hope you know, I won't try and put you in danger again," he said, giving her a look so sweet and kind that she yearned to touch him, but if she touched him, she wasn't sure she could stop her hands from slipping down to his round ass.

Grover definitely wouldn't approve.

"I appreciate that." She couldn't help but feel like his keeping her out of danger was one thing he couldn't promise.

Casper looked nervous as he moved toward the door. "Again, if you need anything…" He gestured vaguely in the direction of his bedroom. "Night." He paused for a second and his hand started to move toward her, but he stopped himself and instead turned on his heel, like he had thought better of reaching out for her. The door gently clicked shut behind him.

Disappointment swelled within her, but in its wake was a strange sense of gratitude. There was something inexplicably sweet about this man who didn't encroach on her boundaries or make her uncomfortable. She appreciated it, but in other circumstances, she would have wished he'd have pressed her up against the wall and taken what they both wanted.

It didn't take long for her to take a shower. Luckily, she always packed a change of clothes in her go bag, but they had been packed away inside it for so long that they had a strange, musty aroma, like they had been sweaty and dried several times thanks to her many adventures trudging them around. She shrugged off the odor—it didn't really matter what she smelled like. It wasn't like anyone was going to be close enough to her to notice. Yet, she thought better of wearing them as they were.

After wrapping the towel from her shower tightly around her, she put her phone in her pocket and picked up the clothes she'd been wearing and walked them down to the laundry. It felt weird using his house like it was her own, but if they were going to be together again all day tomorrow, she needed to get cleaned up so she wouldn't be putting herself in a situation where she would be even more uncomfortable or ill-at-ease than she already was. She needed to bring her A game.

After putting her clothes in the washer, she was met with the *click-click-click* sound of Grover's nails on the tile outside the door in the hall. He came around the corner, stuck his head in and gave her what she could have best described as a dog smile.

"Hey-a, buddy," she said, pouring the soap into the machine and then reaching over to pet the dog.

His tail thumped against the doorjamb as he moved closer to her. She started the wash and then knelt down to give Grover some proper attention. Her towel shifted slightly, opening at the bottom, and she tried to move it closed, but it didn't really matter if the dog saw her thigh, so she conceded the battle.

"He really is the world's worst guard dog," Casper said, stepping into view at the door to the laundry room.

She jerked slightly, reaching to close her towel as she stood up, but in doing so she loosened the knot at the top and it slipped, almost exposing her nipples. Thankfully, she grabbed it just in time, but she wasn't sure exactly how much Casper had gotten to see of her naked body.

She flushed with embarrassment. "I—I..." she stammered. "He is." She sounded breathless. "I hope it's okay that I'm using your washer, I just needed..." Feeling stupid for explaining the working of a washing machine, she stopped herself.

Casper's gaze was steadfast on her face, like he had maybe seen more than she had hoped, and was now concentrating as hard as he could on not trying to make her feel embarrassed about the slip.

"You... You can do whatever you like," Casper said, his stare even more pronounced than it had been, like he was afraid to blink. "I mean...my house is your house."

He may have been even more embarrassed than her, and she found it to be endearing. She moved closer to him as the washing machine started to fill with water and the sound echoed through the small room. Grover moved out of her way, disappearing into the hallway.

Lightening her tight hold on her towel, she let it sink a little lower on her sides, exposing her pale skin. Casper's gaze shifted downward, but then shot back up. Moving even closer, she could hear his erratic breathing. She kept inching nearer, ever so slowly, almost timid. She waited for his consent, but was steady in her progression toward him.

"Casper," she said softly, as she hoped he saw the want for him in her eyes. "I know we haven't really talked about what we want...*from each other*. We have, but...well, you know."

He didn't say a word and stood as though he was afraid if he moved, she would dart away.

"I know it's not possible for us to be in a real relationship, but what if we treat this night as a one-time thing. We can go back to working together in the morning." Even as she spoke, she knew her idea was far-fetched and idealistic at best, but they had already taken one step into the realm of awkwardness. What were another few leaps?

She extended her fingers, brushing the backs of them against his in a silent question. He answered by wrapping his fingers through hers and bringing them to his mouth, softly kissing their embracing hands. His lips were hot against her skin, but his breath was even hotter. Something about the cadence of his kisses and the lust-filled look in his eyes made it obvious that he wanted her as much, if not more, than she wanted him.

He took her other hand and pulled it gently away from where it held her towel in place. The white cotton cloth fell to a heap on the floor, but Casper didn't look down at her nakedness. Instead, he wrapped his arms behind her back and pressed her body against his. Melding her lips with his, he kissed her like she had never been kissed before. His body grew hard against her.

His kiss deepened as he pulled her hands tighter behind her, her shoulders constricted and her body grew wet in anticipation of his touch.

Leaning back, she lifted her chin and his kiss moved down the skin of her neck. "Casper," she moaned.

"Mmm-hmm," he said, moving his kisses lower until he found her nipple and he drew it into his mouth and gently sucked.

"That feels... So... Good."

He let go of her hands and took hold of each side of her hips. He gripped her as if he wanted to kiss every inch of her until there was no part of her left untouched. She clenched and ached with want. His lips glided over her as he moved lower and lower between her legs, taking his time in the descent, and into the madness that came with making love.

Now on his knees, he stopped kissing and looked up at her. Their gazes met and she sent him a dazed smile. She would be happy if this could be her forever, but for now, she would merely be euphorically satisfied.

There was a buzz as her phone rang. She tried to ignore it, holding Casper's head gently as to keep him from moving away from her, but it was of no use. "You should answer that," Casper said, stopping and looking up at her.

She gave an audible groan. "I'm sorry. There're not very many people that I have on bypass. Usually, my phone never rings. When it does, it has to be some-thing important."

"You know I understand," Casper said, kissing her stomach gently as he rose to his feet.

The phone buzzed again and she begrudgingly turned away and picked up the offending device.

Greg.

She could only imagine what he wanted, but just seeing his name pissed her off. She couldn't believe she had forgotten to demote his call-bypass status when they had broken up.

"What?" she answered angrily.

"What the hell do you think you are doing?" he yelled into the phone, making her pull it away from her ear.

"What are you talking about?" she asked, her eyes darting to Casper.

"I can't believe you went home with the pilot. What are you thinking? You have no right leaving me here at camp while you go out and are—"

She lowered the phone, aware that only a line of expletives would be following in his tirade.

From the wide-eyed look on Casper's face, he could hear Greg. She mouthed *I'm sorry*. Casper, waving her off, grabbed her towel and handed it to her, then motioned that he would wait outside.

She tried to indicate that he should stay, but he was insistent and he quickly made his way out of the room while she ignored the berating coming from the other end of the line.

As the door clicked shut, she turned her attention back to the abusive jerk who was still yelling.

"Listen, Greg, I don't need to hear from you right now. This isn't an emergency and I'm not accountable to you. I'm not your subordinate or your girlfriend." Ire rose within her. "Regardless of what role you think you play in my life, you have no right to treat me like this. We will discuss this tomorrow, when I'm back at work."

She hung up the phone.

She clicked on his name, then blocked him.

Wrapping the towel back around her, she walked out of the room, but Casper had disappeared. She paused as she looked up and down the hallway, waiting to hear the click of the dog's nails, or Casper calling her name, but she was only met with silence.

Though she wanted things to continue as they had been with Casper, Greg had killed the mood. If she went to Casper now, things would be weird and she would have to explain more about her former relationship with Greg.

As the flush from Casper's kisses started to fade, logical thought flowed back into her. Maybe Greg-the-ass had really done her a favor. His ill-timed and kiss-blocking call may have just saved her from a future heartbreak.

Chapter Eleven

Grover wagged his tail hard against the seat as Casper pulled into the house with fresh coffee and croissants. He had a few things in his house, but he assumed Kristin needed a little bit of privacy to get ready for the day and he could probably earn a few bonus points by bringing her the best coffee in town.

As he put the truck in Park, Kristin came rolling outside. Grover stood up, his tail moving faster, and he started whining as he waited for her to walk over to them.

"Where have you been?" she asked, her voice a mix of annoyance and what he guessed was fear.

"Don't worry, we didn't leave you. Just wanted to get some breakfast."

She opened up the truck door and Grover assaulted her with licks.

"Grover, no. Get in the back," he ordered the dog, who gave him an annoyed look before jumping over the console and into the back seat. "Sorry about that, he was missing you this morning. It took everything in my power to get him not to scratch at your door until you woke up. He has no manners."

"Are we dropping him off at the sitter's?" Kristin asked, jumping in the truck.

In all actuality, he hadn't planned on leaving as soon as he got back with coffee. If he had his way, they would have picked up where they had left off last night, right before her ex had decided to butt back into her life. They way Greg had sounded on the phone had kept him awake for hours last night, wondering if they were as over as she had said they were. From the guy's annoyance, it seemed like he thought he still had a chance of getting back into Kristin's private life.

Casper wasn't perfect by any means, and he had said any number of stupid things when talking to women he cared for, but he'd never broken down or disrespected a woman he had loved, even after a breakup. He always believed that just because a relationship hadn't worked, it didn't mean the woman he'd been attracted to wasn't a good person... She just wasn't the person for him. This *vaya-con-Dios* attitude had left him with most of his exes still considering him as a friend.

Kristin had said she considered Greg a friend, but if those were the kinds of friends she had...well, she could do better.

She clicked her seat belt and Casper handed her the breakfast he had brought. "I was thinking we could bring him along. What do you think? I have a buddy in Billings who offered to watch him if we needed."

"You can take him in the air?" Kristin looked surprised.

"Oh, he loves it," Casper said, reaching back and giving the dog a good scratch. Grover wagged his tail wildly, as if he knew he had just been selected for the flight. "He's been going with me since he was just a few months old. He even has a special set of goggles and ear protection. I had to rig it up for him, but he knows when he is wearing his gear it's work time."

"He sounds like a great copilot," she said as he pulled onto the road and started back toward the helo pad at the training area.

She loved on Grover, cooing into the pup's ears, and Grover ate it up as they made their way into the mountains. She was so focused on the dog that Casper wondered if she was doing her best to ignore him and what had happened.

If she didn't want to talk about it, he didn't, either. He'd just have to accept she had allowed her ex to come between them, so much so that she didn't even come to his room after she had gotten off the phone. In the end, regardless of Greg's call, she had overtly shown Casper that she didn't want him.

He had been hoping all morning that as soon as she saw him, she'd have an outpouring of apologies and explanations, but he hadn't expected this pointed avoidance. It made the sting he'd endured last night burn with a renewed pain. She had shut him down, and as much as it hurt his ego, he had to admit it probably hadn't been a bad thing.

"I talked to Cindy this morning," he said, pre-empting the mess they were heading into. "She said the mechanics were dropped onto the location of the helo."

Kristin perked up. "That's great. Maybe we can get the bird up and working today." Then, as if a cloud had moved overhead, her face darkened and she chanced a look at him. "Then again, that would mean I would be missing out on our adventure."

Her words made him question himself.

"So you are looking forward to our flight to Bill-ings?" He tried to control the little sensation of gid-diness that threatened to take over the logical part of his brain and make him hope for things to grow between them.

"Of course. Though," she said, smiling at him, "I've got to admit that I hope this flight goes a lit-tle bit better. Maybe less dramatic." She stuck her tongue out him as she giggled.

The little ribbing was endearing. Especially that damn giggle.

Her phone lit up and she clicked it open, sighing.

"Good news?" he said, shifting the truck as they hit the highway.

"Oh, Greg is at it again." She clicked off the phone and dumped it into her purse.

This was his opening—it would be the perfect time to bring up his feelings about her and the guy, but based on her reaction to him simply texting, he could infer some things. Yet, assuming had never done anyone any real favors when it came to potential romances.

He had to do it—he had to get some answers. "So you said you were broken up. Yes?"

Her face grew impossibly darker. "Yes."

"If you don't want to talk about your relationship with him, I respect that," he offered, slightly relieved that they could slip that subject to the back burner as she relaxed slightly. "That being said, I do need to ask you one thing."

"What is that?" she asked, but there was an edge of a growl to her tone.

"Was he ever physically abusive toward you?"

She drew deeper into her seat. "What?" She looked out the window, making him wonder if she was thinking about the truth of their relationship. She had to still have had feelings for Greg. Moreover, she definitely didn't have feelings for him. If she did, she would be trying to fix things between them.

Rage filled him as he thought of the man. As soon as he saw the bastard, he would be missing some teeth. "So he was?"

She shook her head. "He never hit me." She paused. "Again, though, I don't even know if what we had was a *relationship*."

Even if Greg hadn't touched her, it didn't mean that he hadn't used her and left her hurting—or worse.

He loathed the bastard.

She sighed. "I hate talking about this. I know this has to be as uncomfortable for you as it is for me."

He tapped his fingers on the gearshift as he tried to control himself.

He didn't care that they had slept together—that wasn't what bothered him, not really. He'd had relationships in the past. What bothered him was the fact this asshat had not appreciated what a wonderful woman Kristin was… Here he was, struggling to find a place in her life, but fighting against the nature of reality, while Greg had had every opportunity and hadn't seized his chance.

"Just know that I am done with him. I promise," she said, reaching out for him.

He took her hand in his. "No more feelings?"

Her phone buzzed from within her purse—she took it out and looked at the screen before pitching it back.

"Him again?" he asked.

She nodded.

"So he still has some feelings for you."

She squeezed his fingers. "I don't think so. He treats me like crap—calls me names and demeans me. If he wanted me back he's going about it in all the wrong ways."

"Well, he is definitely having a meltdown, so I guess that leads me to my next question…" He paused, trying to find exactly the right words to ask the question that needed to be asked. "Would he have set us up for failure? You know…cut that hydraulic line or anything?"

"What? No. Never." She spoke the words with conviction, but the look on her face spoke to the fact that she was considering the possibility. "There's no way he would have wanted me dead."

"Are you sure? The way he's acting isn't in line with him not being a little emotionally compromised."

She put her free hand to her neck, instinctively covering her weak point. It struck him how such a simple action could speak volumes. Though she was trying to convince him Greg wasn't their enemy, that he wasn't dangerous, her body was saying something else entirely.

"We left my bird at camp. Do you think he would have messed with anything?"

The color drained from her face. "No. There's no way." She rubbed at her neck. "I really don't think he would have done anything to put me or you in danger. He isn't a great person, but just because a dude is a jerk doesn't mean he's a criminal."

He squeezed her hand, trying to reassure her and let her know that he was listening to what she was saying, and trying to believe as she did. If nothing else, but for Kristin's sake. She didn't need a that sort of person in her life.

"He has had a lot of bad things happen to him in the past," Kristin continued. "I cut him a lot of slack in our relationship, but I would hate to think he was capable of murder."

"Anyone is capable of killing if they are given the right motivations."

She shot him a questioning glance and he could tell their conversation was making her uncomfortable.

"I just mean that Greg doesn't have a lot of great qualities, is all." He tried to deflect some of the tension, which was rising between them. "I'm not saying your taste in men is questionable, but I think you like me, so…"

"I happen to think my taste is on point." She smiled, but the action was strained. "All I'm saying, though, is that he isn't a villain."

There was dust on the road in front of them, like someone else was making their way up to the camp as well. He tried to tell himself that Kristin was right. She knew the guy way better than he did; and, if anything, his perspective of the guy would be warped because of his feelings for Kristin. He was never going to like any guy whom she had been with—it was against human nature. Though, that wasn't to say he wouldn't try.

Her phone buzzed again, but this time she didn't reach into her purse and she just let it ring.

"He will need to prove to me exactly what kind of guy he is, but right now on my list, he is enemy number one."

Chapter Twelve

Even when it came to fiction, she hated love triangles, and yet Kristin had somehow found herself right at the center of the weirdest dynamic ever. All she really wanted to do was get back to Billings and her everyday life, maybe with Casper at her side, and yet, she couldn't stop thinking about Greg and what he might have done.

If she or the team of mechanics found any indication Greg may have ambushed the helo, Casper would have been correct and she would never be able to apologize enough to overcome her failure to see the truth.

Cindy was already up and running around camp, readying for the next day of training and the next track with the rest of the team. When they parked, she was digging around in the back of her state-issued pickup, going through a large black tub of gear.

"How's it going?" Casper asked as they approached the commander, Grover at their heels.

Cindy looked up at them with a semi-annoyed expression on her face. "No matter how organized I think I am, I'm always looking for something. It's starting to really piss me off." Cindy withdrew a roll of duct tape. "There." She slammed the lid back on the tub and stood up with a look of triumph on her face.

"If you needed tape," Casper said, pointing back at his pickup, "please tell me you aren't about to go out there and try to fix the bird with it."

"Real funny." Cindy waved him off. She jumped out of the back of the pickup and gave Grover some scratches. "By the way, we dropped the mechanics at your helo earlier this morning. They haven't gotten out any word, but from what your buddy was saying, it will be at least a week to get the full go-ahead to fly it all the way back to Billings."

"Greg isn't what I would call a *buddy*." He nearly snarled.

Cindy looked surprised, but just as quickly she nodded in acknowledgement, like she understood the strained relationship the two had. "I bet you want to get back to Billings soon. I'm sure you have work waiting for you, Kristin?"

Kristin looked a little surprised, but nodded. "There's always something waiting."

"I know the feeling," Cindy said, still staring down at Grover. "If you guys want to split, I can let Greg know you headed out."

"I think that would be great," Casper said. "But, let me know if you see Greg slithering around. I was hoping to ask him about something before we left."

"You got it," Cindy said, finally looking up from the pup and sending them both a smile. "I'm sure you aren't even at the point of thinking about wanting to come back over to try and redo your training, Kristin, but we really would appreciate another chance to get the public on our side."

"I will have to take it to our team, but I can probably sell the idea." She slid a look to Casper, who was smiling. "In fact, I will try to bring it up to them as soon as I get back to Billings. I can make some calls in the meantime."

"When do you think you two are going to hit the skids?" Cindy asked.

"Actually," Casper said, "we were going to go as soon as I did a once-over on the bird."

Cindy nodded, seemingly pleased that their course for public funding could self-correct so quickly. "That's great. We can schedule your return as soon as we get word on the helo."

Casper touched her shoulder, driving excitement through her.

"If you want, I will talk to the team in Billings as well. Let's get some press on the joint efforts in the meantime. Cool?"

"I'll make the call." Cindy gave them an excited smile.

Kristin couldn't help but revel in the fact that for once, they were all getting something they wanted.

The red helo was waiting for them, and Casper lifted Grover up and in—complete with doggy goggles—and then he helped her inside, her hand in his, the effect making her even more nervous than she already was for getting back into a bird. She would have liked to have been able to talk herself into thinking everything was going to be fine and that they would have no problems in the flight or otherwise, but her thoughts kept moving to Greg and his potential sabotage.

No. He isn't like that.

Casper clicked the door closed. He walked around the helo, doing his preflight check, then climbed in next to her.

"Everything okay?" she asked, her stomach clenching.

"Looks like we are a go." He gave her a thumbs-up.

She nodded, slipping on her flight helmet and readying herself to hit the air.

Everything will be okay. A knot formed in her gut at the thought of taking to the sky again. *The odds are in our favor. This flight will be fine.*

She took a deep breath and tried to control her nerves.

It will be, as long as Greg didn't sabotage this bird, too.

She had to have been right—Greg wasn't behind them going down. If he was, their lives could once again be on the line.

The blades began to spin, picking up speed.

As they took to the air, some of her nerves stayed on the ground. Once they leveled out and moved steadily east in the sky, Casper reached over and took her hand. They were both quiet, like each was waiting for the jerk and hiss of a broken hydraulic line. Yet, time passed and nothing happened.

They twisted between the mountains, watching the lush green timber turn to the budding grasses and then river bottoms complete with the white-barked birch and stoic blue herons. Moving into the rolling plains, they crossed over a herd of antelope, their tawny bodies and white bellies flashing in the sun as they streaked away from the hum of the chopper.

There was just nothing better than being safely tucked in the air with a snoozing dog in the back. After their last flight, this was exactly what she needed—a flight to remember just how incredible her lifestyle was.

It was almost wild to think about, after their mishap, but up here in the sky she felt more in control than she did in many of her past relationships. This was her world, her happy place.

Casper squeezed her hand just a little tighter, making her wonder if he was thinking something similar.

She was glad to be here with him. Even if they couldn't have the world together years from now, at least they could have today.

The flight didn't seem like it took any time at all and the rimrocks of Billings sprung up in the distance. Part of her wanted to tell him to keep flying, to keep them up in this reprieve from reality for as long as possible, but she also had a job to do.

They touched down on the helo pad, and he let go of her hand as she unfastened her belts. Stepping out of the helo, the euphoria she felt while they were in the air drifted from her like it too wished to be back in the sky.

Casper walked around and smiled at her as he stuck his flight helmet under his arm, Grover prancing at his side. He looked like some hero out of a Hollywood blockbuster—how had she gotten so lucky not only to befriend this man, but also to get the opportunity to kiss him? If given the chance, there was no way she could not make love to him…at least for the sake of memories.

"That went a hell of a lot better than I anticipated." Casper stretched, his T-shirt pulling tight over the curved muscles of his pecs.

How hadn't she noticed how muscular he was before? Or how he had almost a perfect six-pack that was just a little bit hidden by that low patch of hair pressing against his shirt?

If she wouldn't have felt like it was out of place here at the aviation center, she would have moved to him and made him want her just as badly as she wanted him. What she would have given to take him into a dark corner and show him what kind of an effect he had on her body.

"You okay?" Casper asked. "You look upset."

She nodded awkwardly. "Yeah… I'm fine. Just fine."

After taking care of the helo, they made their way to the parking lot with the excited Grover in tow. She texted away, working to set up a meeting with the SAR chief and coordinators in her county. As it stood, they probably wanted to meet with her to talk about the events of the weekend as well. While she wasn't in a hurry to explain the problems, and where and how things may have possibly gone wrong, she wanted to get ahead of things as much as possible. It was always better to head off problems rather than let them fester and grow.

Her phone pinged. "We have a meeting tomorrow with my team to go over the accident. I'm going to sell them on the idea of further training. No worries."

Casper nodded, but was surprisingly quiet.

"Is everything okay with you?" she asked. Oddly, an old saying came to mind—"when someone points their finger at you, three fingers point at the speaker."

He shrugged as they made their way out into the parking lot, toward her Durango.

"You know that response is going to keep me asking questions." She bumped into him playfully.

He sent her a tired smile and gave Grover a scratch. "You are going to think I'm a wimp if I admit it."

Her empathy spiked and she wanted to take him in her arms like she was his protector. "There's nothing you can't tell me."

As they stopped by her SUV, he helped Grover climb in the back seat and then stared at her. "Why do I feel like I could actually tell you anything and you wouldn't judge me?"

Touching his arm, she met his gaze. "It's because you can. We are two parts of a single soul." She smiled. "No matter what, I'm a safe place for you. You can say anything you want and it won't leave my lips. You can cry and wail and cuss, and I won't think you less of a man."

He shook his head like he didn't believe her. "That... *Why?* Why would you do something so genuinely kind for me?"

"It may sound naive, but I feel like I could do the same with you. I think it is rare in this world when two souls like ours meet. If we can't trust each other, then there is no one in this world we can."

He reached his arm around her, pulled her into him and kissed her. The motion was hungry and full of want, echoing the yearning she felt. He took hold of her face with both hands, gently stroking the soft hairs near her cheek, until she felt a heady mix of comfort and lust. When he broke from their kiss, she moved forward for more, but found him looking upon her like she was the most beautiful woman in the world.

"Let's go back to my place," she said, breathless from the power of his desire.

"Yes. Let's." He opened her door for her, grabbing her butt as she stepped up into the driver's seat.

As he moved away, she wondered if he could feel the heat of her core as his hand had played with her ass. He had to have.

He got in, and as he did, her phone pinged with a message. Then another and another, as it buzzed and rang.

"Uh-oh," he said, motioning for her to answer the angry beast. "You better take care of that."

She cringed, picking up her phone to answer the myriad of messages hitting it. "Oh, I can't wait."

Poring through the texts and dispatches, her heart sank.

Why, when everything was finally starting to come together and go right, did everything have to go to complete chaos?

"What happened?"

Another advisory came in. "It looks like there is a missing female, thirty-one. Was last seen by her husband at their place of residence near the Rocky Mountain College."

Casper gave a long sigh. "We have to go."

The last thing she wanted to do was give up an opportunity to finally get to see Casper naked. Every part of her wanted him. *Right. Now.*

"We can continue what we have started later. I'm not going anywhere for a while."

For a while. There were the key words, and the reason it probably was a good idea for them to go to this call.

She nodded as her phone pinged again. The county's entire search-and-rescue team was gearing up and getting ready to be sent out.

"Text them back. Tell them they have air support if they need it. We may not have FLIR on my ride, but we can still get up there and look."

She tapped out a message to her team. "I let them know we are available. At the very least, I think we could be some more boots on the ground until they are ready to call in the big guns."

Her phone pinged several more times.

"As much as I wanted to take you back to your place, I have to tell you I love the call to arms. There is something about it—the adrenaline hit that comes with knowing we are about to go out and make a difference."

"Yeah, I know that feeling. I don't ever want to lose it. The day I do, I know that my time doing this is over." She started the car, checking her phone one more time.

"Where are we meeting the team?"

"At the bottom of a trail where a man reported she had been hiking. It's not one that many people frequent. It's steep and rocky terrain. It's very possible that she had a medical emergency, so we will need to prepare for that possibility, I'm sure." She pulled out of the parking lot and got onto the main road.

"Do you have an ID?"

She looked at her phone again, quickly pulling up the woman's photo and identifying information, and handed it over. "Take a look."

Taking the phone, he let out an odd, strangled sound. "Oh, holy…" An expletive followed.

"What is it?" she asked, slowing down.

"That's—that's my brother's wife."

Chapter Thirteen

This couldn't be a coincidence. First, his father had gone missing in this city and now his sister-in-law? What in the hell was going on?

His brother picked up on the first ring. "Hello?"

"Why didn't you call me?"

"What?" William sounded totally confused. "Casper? Why would I call you?"

He huffed in a bitter laugh. "Your wife goes missing and you don't think that I should be on your list of people to inform? Are you kidding me?"

There was a long pause on the other end of the line.

Kristin had a surprised look on her face, but then gave him a little nod, as if encouraging him to continue down the road of the tongue-lashing.

Casper paused as a thousand thoughts and questions poured through him. "You were the one who made the report, right?"

William cleared his throat. "No. Are you done jumping down my throat? If you think I didn't want you to know about Michelle going missing, you are stupid. Yet, if you think that just because you are my brother that you would be the first person I'd call when Michelle went missing, you are a complete narcissist. You don't even live here... Which begs, how did you find out?"

Just like that, he was furious. How dare his brother come at him like that? As he opened his mouth to start unleashing his fury on William, Kristin reached over and touched his arm. Her touch had an instant calming effect, like a shot of Ativan. His brother wasn't exactly wrong—he could see where he was coming from in his argument—but he didn't need to be such a jerk about it. Then again, neither did Casper. He needed to be patient with his brother. His wife had gone missing and there was no doubt he had to be lashing out due to sheer panic and desperation.

"I'm sorry," Casper said, attempting to self-correct before things took a turn that they didn't need to take. His brother already had enough on his plate. "Do you want to tell me what happened with Michelle? I'm here in Billings, going to go out with the SAR team. I want to help."

Kristin gave him an approving pat on his arm. He let out a long sigh as he gained control over all the feelings that he was trying to work through.

There were the sounds of voices, authoritative, strong and sounding of law enforcement, coming from somewhere in the background at William's location.

"Where are you right now? Do you want me to come get you? Do you want and to try to get out there and volunteer with the unit?" Casper's questions came out in a long string, since he wanted to get everything asked as he could hear how busy his brother must have been.

"Actually, I just got done at work and now I'm talking with my lawyer. I had an appointment I couldn't get out of. I have to go. Thanks for calling and I appreciate your help."

The line went dead.

Had his brother really just hung up on him…and for a *lawyer*?

All his warning bells went off.

Why would his brother be at a lawyer's office at this very moment? Was he trying to hide something by way of his lawyers?

He threw his phone on the dashboard and sat back in his seat as he watched the city of Billings pass by his window. They were on top of one set of the rimrocks, looking down onto the belly of the beast. There was a long stretch of pull-outs, where people could park and watch the city lights from above.

Ideally, the place would have been perfect for a 1950s-style date night, but unfortunately there were a number of rusted-out and taped-together cars that had been abandoned. On the ground, as they passed, was trash, and even as they cruised by, he could make out an assortment of drug paraphernalia.

"Do you want to talk about it?" Kristin asked, sounding unsure as to whether or not she should have said anything or just let the subject of the unusual phone call rest.

"My brother is a jerk. He's always been a jerk and he will always be a jerk."

"I could hear most of it, but did he say anything about his wife—Michelle?"

He shook his head, looking back and checking on the dog, who was sitting down nicely and staring out the windows as he made himself comfortable with another adventure.

"When we get to our location, I'm going to need to get Grover set up. He's not really a trained rescue dog, but given the circumstances, I'm not leaving him in the car and I don't want to waste time handing him off. Who knows, he may surprise us."

She smiled. "I'm sure he will be an asset. I have to tell you, he really is a good boy. I can't believe how well he did on the flight."

He was glad that he wasn't having to talk about his brother. If he did, he wasn't sure that he would have anything nice to say—even though his brother did have some almost redeemable qualities when he wasn't being a total jackass.

"Grover is my dude." At the sound of his name, Grover moved toward them, close enough that Casper could reach back and give him a good ear rub. He was lucky to have a buddy like him. He wasn't sure how he could make it through this life without his companion. It would have been unbearably lonely without him.

"Do you get along with Michelle?"

He sighed, hating to accept the fact he was going to have to face the whirlwind that was pressing down upon him and his family. "Yes, she is a nice woman. She was great about taking my dad into their home and getting caregivers for him."

"Do they have a big place?"

He motioned toward the east. "Yeah, they live on one of the bluffs on that side of town. My brother is a car salesman. Used to own a dealership, but it shuttered during the pandemic. Now, he has gone to work for a friend of his…so far as I know. Michelle was selling insurance, but I don't know much about her work."

"Did she hike a lot, do you know?"

He shrugged. "She was fit. I'm thinking she was active."

"That's a positive. If she is out there and hurt on the trail, if she is prepared for an emergency, then there is a good possibility that we can get to her and get her out pretty quickly."

"Has your team pinned her phone's location?"

"Its last location pinged at her residence."

He frowned. "That doesn't sound like her. She wouldn't go anywhere without her phone. She lives on that thing, just like the rest of the planet."

Kristin coyly slipped her phone back into the cup holder as she drove. "Maybe she wanted a break from the thing. Let's not jump to any conclusions."

"I'm not jumping to anything. All I'm thinking is that this is all just too close to what happened to my father. I mean, what are the odds that my father and now Michelle must have search-and-rescue called to find them? If she's hurt, my brother's going to have to answer to me."

"I'm sure Michelle will be fine. She is probably just out on a walk and got lost because she didn't have her phone. Time got away from her...you know the norm." Kristin tried to make him feel better. "I won't deny it's odd that your brother is on the edge of two SAR calls, but it doesn't mean that he has done anything wrong. It just means that maybe your family, and your brother specifically, are having a run of bad luck and even worse timing."

"You know I want to believe you. I want to think you are right. I just know my brother and I know he tends to do things that I wouldn't."

"Does that mean you think your brother would kill your father? Or somehow be involved in his wife's going missing?"

When she put it in those words, so simply and yet so incredibly stark, he couldn't say that he thought his brother was capable of being *evil*.

"You're right. Sometimes, and maybe this is all my years dealing with the worst of the worst, I make assumptions. Right or wrong, they have gotten me out of some tough situations." He picked up his phone again. "It's just that action is better than inaction. I guess I just want to blame what happened to my father on someone. I should have been there to take care of him more."

"You know that I can understand that. It always hurts to lose someone you love and it hurts a thousand times more when you feel like you were somehow responsible."

Her words made him think of his brother's refusal to come in and volunteer in helping to search for Michelle—though, in all reality, he wasn't really supposed to be on scene in the event she was found deceased. Normally, family members were kept at bay.

When they arrived on scene it was much like his own unit. The Billings team was setting up the command trailer at the base of the trail and there was a flurry of activity. For a while, he and Grover followed behind Kristin, tagging along as she made introductions within the small group of people. It was fun watching the activity from the perspective of an outsider, if nothing else than to see where he and his team could learn by their examples of what to do. Most people he met were friendly and nice, welcoming him in and shaking his hand. Of course, everyone loved Grover, and it made it easier to ingratiate himself to this other team.

A black Suburban pulled up to the area, and as it did, there was a slight shift in the mood. Smiles disappeared and a seriousness took over as a middle-aged man stepped out. His face had the deep wrinkles and dark eyes of a guy who had seen more death and pain than any single person should have to endure—Casper knew that look all too well. Sometimes he worried he would become like this man—marred by the trauma of his life.

"Hey, guys," the man said, his voice as rough as the man it belonged to. He made his way toward them and the nine other people in the group moved together into a circle around him.

Kristin leaned over to him and whispered, "That's our director, Roger Bell."

Even if she hadn't told him that he was the one in control of the scene, he wouldn't have questioned it. Maybe one day, if he carried on for a search-and-rescue team, he could behave like this man—in command and carrying an air of authority. It was something to see a person who was so well-respected that without even saying a word, he could be in power.

In his days in the army, he had seen people with more stars than this man, and they hadn't garnered such a response.

"First of all, let me start off by saying that I'm glad you could all make it today," Roger said, standing at the center of the group. "I know you have a lot going on in your personal lives and jobs, but we appreciate you being out here. It's my goal that we find Michelle swiftly and with as little fanfare as possible. I have been informed that media outlets are monitoring the situation, and as such, I want to remind everyone not to post or share anything on social media or with family and friends."

Already, he liked the man.

Roger looked over at him and gave him an acknowledging dip of the head. "I'm sure most of you have met our guest here today, but in case you haven't I want to introduce Casper to the group. He's a pilot out of Big Sky, near Yellowstone Park. As I'm sure most of you have heard by now, he was in an incident involving our bird."

Casper's stomach dropped. He hadn't expected the man would know who he was, let alone out him as the pilot who'd cost them their helo.

"I want to extend my thanks to you, Casper. Without your superior flying skills and knowledge, one of the greatest members of our team would have likely lost her life."

"As much as I appreciate the acknowledgement, sir," Casper said, "I feel as if I need to clear the record. All I did was my job."

The man nodded in appreciation. "And he's humble." He offered his hand and Casper took it, giving it a shake.

The group around him muttered their thanks and as he stepped back, the man closest to him slapped him on the shoulder. The woman next to Kristin leaned in and whispered something he couldn't make out, but a smile erupted on Kristin's features.

"Cute dog, by the way," Roger said, putting out his hand. Grover walked over and sniffed the man before coming back to Casper. "Kristin let me know that this case is involving your sister-in-law, and as such, I'm concerned for your welfare in this search."

Before the man could continue, Casper put up his hand and waved him to stop. "Sir, while I appreciate your concern for my well-being, I can assure you that and I am practiced in search-and-rescue and all that it may imply. Though Michelle is my sister-in-law, my relationship with her will not impact my ability to do my job."

As soon as he finished speaking, Casper ques-

tioned himself. While he had done a great deal of re-
coveries and lifesaving operations, it was an entirely
new thing to promise that he could keep his cool if
Michelle was injured.

Chapter Fourteen

Their boots crunched on the gravel as they took to the trail looking for Michelle. Casper walked in front of her, talking to Roger. As he walked, his pants pulled tight against his ass. Watching him move was making it hard to remember what task was at hand, when all she wanted to do was reach out and squeeze.

If things went well, they would have Michelle safely returned to the city before the sun disappeared from the sky. Unfortunately, ever since she had met Casper, not much had been going their way. That didn't mean things couldn't take a turn for the better, but she hated to hold out hope.

Roger turned to face her, slowly walking backward. "I wasn't aware the guy you'd been training had such an interesting résumé," he said, motioning toward Casper.

Though she couldn't really identify why, she found herself a bit proud. Casper was her friend, but she was also grateful he was making such a good impression on Roger. It would make selling the idea of going back and redoing the training that much easier.

"He's a good dude," she said. Grover came over to her and brushed against her leg as she walked, pushing his head into her hand and forcing her to love on him. There was something about the dog nosing his way into her life that reminded her a little of Casper, but in all the right ways.

They were both painfully cute, though Grover may have had the edge.

She smiled at her thought.

"I'm going to head back to the incident command center. If you need anything, and I mean anything, let me know," Roger said, looking back at Casper as he spoke.

"We got this." Kristin took a dog treat out of her pocket and handed it to Grover. "We have the best additional team member we could hope for, so it won't be long before Michelle is back with her family." Which included Casper, and once she was back, Casper could get on his way back to Big Sky and out of her life.

Maybe she didn't want to rush this search too much, after all.

"Good luck," Roger said, letting her move by him.

Though the landscape was different, scrubby and dry compared to the timbered mountainsides of the western side of the state, as they walked, she found herself thinking about how much time she had already spent hiking through the wilderness with the man in front of her. Even in the face of chaos and mayhem, she found comfort in his presence. It was strange.

They went for about a mile before she realized that the only sounds were of them walking and nothing more. "Hey, Casper?"

He stopped. "What's up?"

"Have you seen Grover lately?" she asked, looking around them, but not seeing the tan, curly-haired dog anywhere.

"I'm sure he couldn't have gone far. He normally sticks around pretty well." Casper gave a long, shrill whistle. "Grover!" he called.

They listened, and though she expected to hear the clicking of nails on rocks and the breaking of brush as the dog came running back to them, she heard nothing.

"He never runs away." Casper whistled again.

She didn't want to point out that, right now, that didn't appear to be true. "He couldn't have gone that far. I mean, how long has it been since we saw him?"

Casper cringed. "I don't know. Ten, fifteen minutes?"

"Do you think he followed Roger back to the camp?" She took out her phone and sent Roger a quick text, asking him about the dog. "I asked. I'm sure he will get back to me soon."

"Hopefully that's all that happened. Grover can get a little preoccupied and lose track of what he is supposed to be doing sometimes."

Her phone pinged and her heart sank as she read the message. "Roger hasn't seen him. We could turn around and go back?"

"He was out in front of us. Unless he got a little

lost, I'm thinking we just need to keep pressing forward. Like you said, he couldn't have gotten that far." He called the dog again, but this time she could hear the panic in his voice.

"We will find him." No man or beast who had spent any real time with Casper would want to be away from him for very long. Or maybe that was just her.

She took hold of Casper's hand, trying to console him in the only way possible. "You know, maybe he got on Michelle's scent."

He nodded, looking at the trail in front of them, but there was a terror in his eyes that she hadn't seen since they had gone down. "Yeah." He whistled loudly.

Her phone pinged again with another message from Roger. "The boss wants us to stick to the plan. He will send out a crew-wide text for everyone to keep an eye out for the dog. He will be picked up by someone from our team in no time."

She had thought losing Michelle was bad enough, but she hadn't really considered losing the dog and the impact it would have on Casper.

He started to hike faster and she struggled to keep up with his pace as they both yelled for the dog. After ten minutes, her voice had started to grow hoarse from the yelling and they paused again.

"Can you text Roger, see if anyone has a ping on Grover?" Casper asked. "I shouldn't have taken him along with us, but I swear he hasn't done this before. He's never disappeared like this. I'm getting worried that something happened to him."

She patted their entwined hands. "I'm sure that nothing happened. He probably just got on the scent of something."

"Yeah, but we haven't been here before. He's not going to know how to get himself out. If someone doesn't catch him…"

"Is he chipped?" she asked.

He nodded. "That's great if someone else finds him, but what if he fell? I've heard of dogs making mistakes and going down embankments and getting hurt. What if he has a broken leg somewhere?"

She tried to comfort him, rubbing the back of his hand with hers. "Don't freak out. Any number of things could have happened to him, but I highly doubt that he is hurt. We will find him."

She pulled out her phone, but there was nothing from anyone on her team about the dog. There were only a series of pinned locations, where people had last moved during their search for Michelle.

"It looks like there are two teams to the east and four to the west. We have lots of boots on the ground," she continued.

"No one needed this," Casper said, running his hand over his face in aggravation. "I should have left Grover with my friend."

She shook her head. "You didn't know that he was going to take off—no one did. These things happen, though, and you can't blame anyone."

"Hell, yes, I can. I can blame this completely on myself. I should have leashed him."

She couldn't argue that fact with him, and it did

nothing to make her—and undoubtedly him—feel any better.

They kept calling, sometimes for Grover and other times for Michelle. According to the team's plan and the time limit that the current members were on, they were only supposed to search for another mile and then they were all to head back and trade out with the next team of volunteers. The new volunteers would be searching in the dark. If no one had found the pup by the time night fell, she had the sinking feeling Grover truly would be gone.

First, Casper had lost his father, then his sister-in-law and now even his dog. As strong as he was, she wasn't sure if he could keep himself together if things didn't start turning around for him.

Her phone pinged again. There were a series of coordinates of her teammates and another message from Roger—no dog, no Michelle.

With each second and meter that passed by, Kristin's desperation intensified and her calling grew louder. Her throat was aching now, the back feeling like with each yell she was stripping away a layer of skin, like a sacrifice to the rescue gods.

As they neared their waypoint, where they were supposed to turn around and come back, Casper's hand got sweatier in hers. Though neither spoke of the reality of their situation, he knew it as well as she did. Her phone pinged as they hit their boundary point.

She stopped, pulling him to a halt beside her. He strained against her hand as he moved to keep going, but she shook her head. "We have to follow orders, Casper."

"But...they're out there somewhere."

She nodded. "And we will find them both, but we can't put ourselves in danger."

He looked out into the scrub. "They could be anywhere."

"Exactly," she said, touching his arm. "Let's go home and come back tomorrow, when we have better equipment. Let's get the drones out here."

"Yeah, drones."

His voice was choked. "Grover! Come on, buddy! Grover!"

Her heart ached from the sound of desperation in his tone. "He will come back. Our team will find him. Until then, I won't leave your side—I promise."

Chapter Fifteen

Nothing was going his way and no matter how hard he seemed to try to keep things in line, his life seemed to unravel twice as fast. Back at the base camp, they switched out with another set of volunteers to work a new set of coordinates. Roger was busy talking to the new teams and setting them up for the next track of looking, including the search for Grover.

Casper had been upset about Michelle going missing so soon after his father's death, but with his dog nowhere to be found on top of it all, it was making him lose his damn mind. In the four years he'd owned him, Grover had never done this before. In fact, he had rarely ever even left his sight. The thought that his dog was truly gone tore at him. It just wasn't possible.

Why hadn't he just put him on a leash?

He ran his hands over his face as he tried to reconcile the reality with his self-loathing.

All they could do now was keep searching.

He turned to Kristin. "I'm going back out there. I know you need to get some rest and it's getting dark, but I can't leave. I can't stop looking."

Kristin looked exhausted, but she didn't argue. "Did you hear from your brother?"

He shook his head. "You should give him a call and let him know how the search is going. In the meantime, I'm going to make some calls to my team at FLIR and see if we can get some other equipment out here."

He nodded grimly, feeling as though they were grasping at straws.

It was strange, he had been on so many of these search missions and yet this was the first time he had ever felt so helpless…and hopeless. Maybe it was because it was his dog and it wasn't like searching for a person who could possibly call out if and when they got close, even if they were hurt. Grover, if hurt, was at the mercy of the team.

He went to his bag and withdrew a leash he had stuffed in the bottom of his gear without any real intention of using. If he got Grover back, he would be on this thing anytime they even thought about getting out of a vehicle. In perpetuity, the dog was grounded.

Taking out his phone and walking to the edge of the camp for a little privacy, he called William. Just when he thought his brother wasn't going to pick up, he answered. "Did you find her?"

"So I'm taking it that you haven't heard from her, either?" Casper asked.

William huffed.

"Don't give me that," Casper said, his patience almost nonexistent. "Are you on your way or are you still too busy with your lawyers to come out and actually look for your wife?"

"What are you talking about? Some guy, Bell… I've been talking to him, and he told me that you all had it under control. 'Our teams are on it'…and 'we won't stop until we find her'. That's what he said. Are you telling me that you guys are incompetent? That you think sending me out there is the best course of action?"

Everything his brother was saying was making sense, but he couldn't come to terms with it. "If it was my wife out there, I would be the first person working the grid and trying to find her. She needs you and you are sitting who knows where and twiddling your thumbs."

"Is this really about me, Casper? Or are you angry that I'm making you look bad, or something? I don't get why you are so upset when it's not your wife who is gone."

He stopped for a moment. What was he really mad at?

"I'm not responsible for who or what you are, and I don't care what I look like to people I don't know,"

"Then what in the hell is your problem, Casper?"

"You are not going to make this my fault."

"You're crazy," William said, huffing from the other end of the line.

"William, once and for all…" He paused, knowing what he was about to ask would piss him off and possibly draw a close to any relationship they had, but he needed to know. "Did you have anything to do with Michelle's disappearance?"

His brother made a strangled noise and the phone cut off.

Just like that, his relationship with his brother was unquestionably over.

He wanted to throw his phone and yell at the sky, but he wasn't sure if it was because of his brother, or the hundred other things he was feeling right now. Maybe he had been out of line for asking his brother if he'd had anything to do with Michelle being missing. For all he knew, she would come rolling back home any minute. Maybe she was just running late or maybe she was out with girlfriends and was pissed off and playing some kind of trick on his brother. She hadn't even been missing for thirty hours yet.

He didn't know where she came from or how long she had been there, but Kristin stepped out from behind him. "So that sounds like it maybe didn't go quite as well as you were hoping."

"You can say that again." He didn't want to ask how much she'd overheard.

She cleared her throat and lifted the black plastic case she was carrying so he could get a better look. "I got my drone. We can start there. It has a small FLIR system and it's not as good as the helo unit, but it may get us on to something. I figured it's worth a try. We can run it until we can't see anything, we run out of batteries, or we find them. No matter what, though, we aren't stopping."

He pulled her into his arms and gave her a kiss

on the top of her head. "Where have you been all my life?" He spoke the words into her hair. She smelled like sweat and fresh air, and it made him appreciate her that much more.

"I've been out here, searching for you…and, lately, your family," she teased, trying to make light of the darkness in which they had found themselves.

He laughed, appreciating that she wanted to make him feel better…and was succeeding. "You think you're real funny, don't you?"

"Not funny, but I'm glad I made you smile." She ran her free hand over his lower back. "I'm here now."

Now. The word was like a razor blade, but he tried to ignore the sharpness that only he must have felt.

"By the way," she said, stepping out of his arms after a long moment, "the team working a half mile from where we were said they heard a dog barking. They can't say for sure whether or not it was Grover, but at least we have a place where we can really start looking."

It was the first glimmer of hope he'd felt since losing his furry friend.

"Let's pop smoke," he said, and she gave him a quizzical look. "You know…let's hit the trail."

"Wait, I know we talked about going from here, but let's change up," she said, stopping him in his tracks. "Let's take my truck to the lower road. From there we can work that line. It's closer to where they think they heard him and we can run the drone from the car."

"Perfect." He kissed her hands. "You really are an incredible woman."

"Do you have your bag?"

He nodded. "It's in the rig."

She pointed at the leash that was looped around his shoulder as they walked back toward her car. "You know you don't need that to drag me around. I'll happily go with you."

It caught him by surprise that she could turn his entire mood around so rapidly and he was smiling as he got into her car.

As she started to drive, her face turned serious. "Do you think your brother would hurt his wife? Really?"

He shrugged. "I don't know. I'd like to think he wouldn't, but he isn't acting like a man who is innocent. Apathy isn't the right response from a man who lost his dad. You don't see me acting like him."

"Your father's death was an accident."

"Was it?" he countered.

She frowned. "Your father got out, got lost and succumbed to his illness. There was no evidence of foul play or neglect."

"I agree," he said, putting his hands up and instinctively distancing himself from murder. "All I'm saying is that it's strange that you found him so far from where he should have been. My brother said he snuck out, but he had gone too far for him to have walked there. Someone had to have picked him up or given him a ride."

"Do you think someone picked him up on the road? That he hitchhiked?" She was playing devil's advocate, but he didn't blame her for wanting to know more.

"Someone would have seen him if he had been hitchhiking. Billings isn't a small town. No one would have picked him up, not when he was clearly having a mental-health crisis. Passersby would have likely called something like that in."

Kristin chewed on her lip like she was struggling to hold back her thoughts. "Unless they thought he was a transient."

"Was that how he looked when you found him?" he asked, an ache forming in his gut as he thought about how far his father had fallen from the powerful, loving and professional man he had once known.

"He was carrying a stuffed lobster with bailing twine around his neck. I wouldn't say that he looked like he was well-centered."

"So he did look like a transient. That only makes me suspect my brother more."

"I'm not saying that your feelings about your brother aren't valid. You know I've got your back— especially when it comes to your intuition—but to accuse someone of events that could be best described as negligent homicide…that's pretty damned serious."

"You're telling me." He sighed, trying to staunch the ache. "I'm not about to let anyone else know what I'm thinking, though. I'm not going to jump to anything until I have definitive proof one way or another."

She pulled to a stop a few miles from incident

command center and put the car in Park. "I'm sure your brother wouldn't want anyone in your family to be harmed. I mean…on top of him being your brother, you haven't given me any reason or motive behind his wanting to hurt your loved ones."

He nodded, tapping his fingers against his thigh. "You're right."

"Now, let's work on finding them." She stepped out and grabbed the drone, then set it into flight.

There was a small screen in front of her, showing the thermal readings of the environment as it flew. He tried not to delve into his fears, but they gnawed at him. He wasn't wrong about his father being too far away to easily explain his location. Someone had to have taken him to the rims. If they had, it was feasible that they wanted him to simply disappear…or jump.

The Billings rimrocks were notorious for their use as a launching pad for those who wanted to end their lives. Yet, his father hadn't seemed suicidal at all. Maybe he had escaped from the grip of whoever had taken him out there to die. Or maybe they had experienced a change of heart and decided to leave him to the mercy of the elements.

Overhead, the drone hummed as she moved it methodically over the area. Nothing unusual appeared on the screen, but he knew she wouldn't give up. She had made Casper a promise—she wouldn't be stop searching until they found Michelle and Grover.

Yet, as she flew the UAV, Casper had a sinking feeling that they weren't any closer to finding either.

He tried to control all the feelings that swelled within him. There had been so much death, then the accident and now this… He was living under a dark cloud.

He was staring at the thermal images. "What is that?" he asked, pointing at something that was far too small to be anything of interest.

"Probably a rabbit, maybe a skunk." She smiled, but the action seemed forced.

He nodded, crestfallen.

There was barking in the distance. With the flick of the stick, she sent the drone screaming off in the direction of the noise as she looked hopefully to Casper. "Do you think that was him?" There was a light in her eyes he hadn't seen there before, and a smile blessed her lips.

"That had to have been him. It just had to." He started to move in the direction of the barking. "Grover! Is that you, buddy? Grover!" He yelled the name, his sound deep and filled with hope.

The barking changed pitch, almost matching his voice, but the sound didn't grow closer.

"That's him!" Casper exclaimed, picking up his pace and hiking faster, almost at a jog.

Hopefully, Grover wasn't hurt. If he wasn't moving toward them, there had to be a reason.

They twisted through the sagebrush that littered the hillside, careful to avoid the prickly pear and step around the yucca. For a desert landscape, it was beautiful.

"Grover!" Casper called again after a few minutes.

Once again, they heard barking, but there was no sign of the dog approaching.

She flew the drone ahead of them. "There," she said, pointing at her screen. "About a quarter mile ahead. I think we found him."

Casper stopped just long enough to glance at the picture. "Does it look like he's okay?"

"I can't say. He doesn't seem to be going anywhere. Do we have a way to get him out if he is hurt? I don't want to have to waste time coming back to the car to get a blanket or something if we need to carry him out."

She lowered the drone on the dog, pulling his thermal image in closer, but as she did, Casper noticed there was something else…something cooler.

"Casper…" she whispered his name as she looked up at him with wide eyes. "We need to call the rest of the team."

He stared at her in the waning light. "Why?"

"Casper… I think he may be lying with a body."

Chapter Sixteen

He had known the second he heard Kristin whisper his name. He couldn't explain how or why, but he just knew Grover had found Michelle.

Grover jumped up, almost skipping as Casper approached his dog. He came running over in the beam of the flashlight, his tongue lolling out of his mouth in true Grover style.

"Where have you been, buddy? You need to listen," he said, trying to sound mad, but even he could only hear the relief in his voice.

Grover licked his hand and then turn and sped back to the woman on the ground. Her dark brown hair was whipped around her face, obscuring her features. She was wearing a long black set of leggings and a sweatshirt. Over top was a light gray down vest.

"Michelle?" he called her name in hopes that she might possibly still have been alive.

However, the thermal scan had already made the possibility of her being alive slim to none—unless she was extremely hypothermic.

There was no response.

He was surprised, but a hollow sensation filled him as he moved toward her.

Her head was turned and she was lying on the ground, a pool of blood around her... It was Michelle.

There was the glow of red and blue lights coming toward them in the distance.

They didn't need to rush.

Grover came back to him and sat in front of his feet as though he was blocking him from going any farther, like he didn't want him to have to witness the gruesome scene before them.

Kristin stopped beside them. "Why don't you just stay here? I can take care of this."

There was no way he was ever going to let her fall on this sword. "No, let's do it together."

He took the lead and moved closer to the body. Michelle was lying on her stomach between a large yucca plant and two round sage brushes. Her head was turned at a strange angle. Not far from where she was lying was a large overhang. There was no rise and fall as she tried to breathe. There was only...*stillness* and the damn emergency vehicle lights.

Knowing what he would find, he kneeled down and pressed his fingers against the cold flesh of the woman's neck. There was no pulse.

Though he knew he shouldn't disturb the body, he pushed back a bit of the hair that had stuck in the blood near the corner of her lips so he could make out the woman's face. What little hope he had been carrying that this may have been someone else drifted away. Without a doubt, this was the woman they had been hoping to find alive and well.

Kristin grazed the top of his shoulder in question.

"Nothing. She's gone." He stood up, rubbing his fingers against the legs of his pants, like he could somehow wipe the death from them, but what he had felt he could not unfeel.

"Are you okay?" she whispered, as if speaking loudly would somehow disturb the woman lying before them.

"Yeah," he said, his voice cracking, so he cleared his throat. "Yeah, I'm fine."

He moved the flashlight from the top of her head down to her feet. She was wearing running shoes, with dirt on the toes. Her left arm was wrenched behind her body and the ring on her finger flashed in the harsh beam of light.

He hadn't asked his brother if he and Michelle had been fighting or if anything had been off between the two of them. It was possible that Michelle had been running in the early morning hours and not seen the steep overhang.

He flashed the light in the direction of the cliff near them. It was high up, but he wondered if it was a far enough fall to actually result in her presenting as she was. Then again, someone could fall a matter of inches, and if they hit their head just right it could result in death. The human body could be so fragile, but on the other side of the coin, could withstand so much—and that was to say nothing of a person's heart.

"Did you see any indication as to the cause of death?"

"There's blood in and around her mouth." He closed his eyes for a second and he thought about the way her lifeless eyes had been staring into the nothingness. "That could indicate a possible trauma event to the lungs. Or she could have bit her tongue. Who knows. Without moving her, it's hard to even guess."

He moved the light over her back again, looking but not seeing any obvious bullet holes or bludgeoning marks.

"If I had to guess," he said, motioning in the direction of the little cliff, "she fell. Maybe she broke some ribs and she laid there, unconscious until she died."

"I hope she went quickly."

"That's all anyone can hope for," he said, moving Kristin away from the body.

There were the sounds of voices as people moved up the hillside toward them. Even though he had yet to see them, he could make out the crackle and static of handsets of the law-enforcement officers who must have been leading the charge.

Grover came over to him and sat down, so Casper clipped the leash firmly in place, giving it a gentle tug and ensuring it wouldn't go anywhere. The dog leaned against his leg and looked up at him, giving him the biggest eyes in what he assumed was an apology.

"How do you think Grover found her?"

"Doodles have an incredible sense of smell and

they have even more incredible hearts. All this dude does is love."

"And find people." She smiled, but it weighed on her.

"Yeah, and well, that. That is new talent, though." He scratched the pup. "I guess his food can be a write-off if he is an active member of the SAR team. Right?"

"I think they may start asking questions when you feed 'him'—" she did finger quotes as she teased "—filet mignon every night."

"Oh, and I'm... I mean *he's* a burger fan, too." He laughed and the sound hit a sour note as his flashlight's beam moved over the body lying near them.

Kristin reached over and started to love on Grover. "It's okay to seek a little levity in situations like these."

"Michelle was married to William—she had to have a sense of humor." He smiled. "I mean any poor woman who had to see him in the buff would have to be able to laugh."

Kristin giggled, but she clapped her hands over her mouth like she felt as off about their joking as he did.

Normally, he didn't have these kinds of issues when he was dealing with the dead. In fact, he had grown more accustomed to it than he would have liked. Before his father's death, he was known for being able to go from a body retrieval to his buddy's baby shower. The baby hadn't liked him, crying when his buddy's wife had put the little one into his arms—he'd blamed the smell, but he couldn't really blame the baby for not liking him. He'd never been much of a baby person.

Michelle and his brother had been talking about having a family for a long time. From what his brother had alluded to, they'd been having fertility issues. IVF had been outside their budget, and adoption was something Michelle hadn't wanted.

"I need to call my brother."

Kristin met his gaze in the dark. "Do you think that is the best idea?"

"Why? Don't you?"

"You are already at odds with him. If you are the one to tell him his wife has been found deceased, whatever chances you have of rekindling your relationship with him would be gone."

"You think he would rather hear the news from a stranger?"

"Sometimes a stranger is the best person when it comes to delivering bad news."

He sighed. There was a lot riding on this decision. If his brother was somehow involved with anything to do with Michelle's death, it would be best if the police were the ones to speak to him first. He didn't want to give him a chance to be a step ahead of the investigators if he was guilty. If he was innocent of any misdeeds, as Casper hoped, he would forever think about him as the one to drive the stake of loss.

If nothing else, he needed to be careful about any legal ramifications.

"She and your brother were getting along? I know

how rifts happen in relationships." Kristin shifted her weight, like the conversation was striking a little too close to home for her comfort.

"My brother doesn't open up to me."

Grover whined.

A light flashed over them as one of the officers in the front of the group of hikers came over the top of the hill and into view. He was wearing a fleece cap with a search-and-rescue patch sewn to the front. He was big and carried himself like he lifted weights more than the average guy.

"Hello, Officer," Casper said, giving the guy approaching them an awkward wave. "The body is here."

"Did you identify her as the woman we have been searching for?"

"Yes. It's my sister-in-law, Michelle Keller."

The guy gave him a wary side-eye. "Your sister-in-law? Really. Interesting."

"I'm a helo pilot from the Big Sky SAR team, I was here with—"

"Me," Kristin said, speaking up, "I'm the FLIR tech. You and I have met before, Sergeant Miller."

He moved his flashlight so he could better see her face. "Hey, Ms. Loren, sorry I didn't recognize you."

She waved him off. "It's dark. We're just glad you're here."

"You guys didn't touch anything, did you?"

Kristin shook her head.

"I moved Michelle's hair slightly so I could see if she had a pulse."

"And you both arrived on scene together?"

Casper lifted the leash slightly. "Yes, but my dog was actually the one to find her. I didn't see any evidence that my dog bothered her, but with it being as dark as it is… I can't say for sure."

Sergeant Miller nodded. "I'm glad your dog found her. This the dog we were supposed to be keeping an eye out for?"

"He self-volunteered for the search." Kristin chuckled. "Turns out he was better at finding Michelle than the rest of us. He actually barked, if he hadn't, I don't know that we would have found the body until tomorrow. Everyone was still working the primary location."

Miller walked up and patted Grover on the head. The dog gave him a lick and the guy actually smiled. The action was so fleeting and awkward that he could tell it was something the man rarely did. He felt for the guy.

The rest of the group made their way over the hill. One of the men was huffing like he had jogged to catch up. Officer Miller turned to face the three people who had followed him up. "All right, everyone, we have a death on our hands. This area is now under an active investigation. As such, please do not touch any items, or disturb the area." He turned toward the body and, as if he had to reaffirm Casper's findings, kneeled down and reached to check Michelle's pulse.

Finding none, he wiped his hands on his pants. The action was so strangely the same as his, that Casper found himself wondering if it was something that everyone inadvertently did—as if this aversion to death was part of the human condition.

Miller stood up, slipped out his phone and proceeded to take a variety of pictures around the body. The camera flashed, making orbs dance in Casper's vision as he stared out into the night. Seemingly satisfied with the photos, he tapped away on his phone. He was probably reaching out to the rest of his people so they could come out and help him investigate the scene.

If things went well and they determined Michelle's death had been nothing more than a tragic accident, they would have her off to the medical examiner by dawn. If not, it would take longer, as they would have to get the on-call detective out here to go over the scene and pull together all the information for a more thorough investigation. If that was the case, he and his brother would be in trouble.

It would look strange to the detectives when he told them about the phone call with his brother and his meeting with the attorney. And, while it was explainable, Casper's being here was a little strange. This was all to say nothing about the fact of his father's recent death and search to find him.

There was such a thing as a string of bad luck, but in cases like these, nefarious deeds and family drama were far more common.

Kristin had moved toward the group of on-lookers and he recognized the man she was speaking to as Roger Bell. He looked exhausted, but maybe the thin light of the flashlights was doing him no favors.

Roger caught him looking and waved him over toward them, and he obliged.

"So sorry to see things go this way, Keller."

Casper gave him an acknowledging tip of the head. "'Preciate that. I was hoping we would find her, unharmed."

"As we all were." Roger gave him a bump to the shoulder. "You know—" Roger looked to Kristin "—you both went against orders in coming out here, to this area. You were supposed to be having your legally required break. That's not our policy or procedure and, you know, if lawyers get a hold of it…it could affect the ruling if there is any kind of criminal case."

Kristin frowned. "I'm aware, sir, but given the circumstances—this being a member of his family and his dog that were missing—there was no way we could walk away."

"I understand that, but you shouldn't have gone out here without letting your superiors know." He turned to him. "Aren't you one of the more important members of your team in Big Sky?"

"Just a regular member," Casper said, not wanting to add the fact that his role after the crash was tenuous. The only thing, or person, keeping him safely in his job was Cindy.

"Regardless, you both knew better. I am grateful that you all found Michelle and we can let the family know the search is over, but we are going to have to revisit both of your blatant disregard for procedures."

Casper wasn't worried about Roger calling Cindy

and voicing a complaint. There were always standard time limits for SAR members to work, but as far as Casper knew, there were no policies in place in his unit that talked about a private citizen working an area outside the immediate search area. If there was one, he doubted he could be let go from the unit Though, if anyone else besides Cindy got the call, there might be slightly more fireworks.

The same couldn't be said of Kristin.

"You shouldn't be condemning her for her actions. She wasn't the one on point here. I was the one who made her come along so I wouldn't be searching alone. You should commend her for wanting to keep an outsider safe."

"Keeping you safe wasn't her job. Her job was to listen to orders. In fact, as a FLIR tech, she is lucky that I even allowed her to be out here on scene—especially given the latest drama with her and her aviation team. She's already given me enough headaches. I didn't need this one on top of them all."

Though the man was officially following protocol, he was annoyed. There was enough gray area in their line of work that the man could have turned a blind eye.

"Look, Roger..." Casper said, trying to remain calm though he wanted to tell the man to take his reprimand and stick it where the sun didn't shine. "You have every right to be upset with all the events of the week, but none of the events, and I mean *none* of them, were her fault."

"Casper, need I remind you that you are here by invitation only?" Roger said, fire in his eyes. "As such, you and your friend here are relieved of duty."

Chapter Seventeen

Just like that, Kristin was sent home. When she went back to FLIR Tech, she would have a lot of explaining to do. She'd already had enough without being handed her hat for one of the tech business's best partnerships.

They made the drive back to her place in silence, which she appreciated. She didn't bother to ask him if he wanted to stay with her and he didn't bring it up. Him sleeping alone in some hotel wasn't an option. They both needed company tonight.

She wasn't anticipating sex, no. What she really wanted, and needed, was to know that there was another soul in this world who desired her, who wanted to be close. That's it. If she wasn't needed and living for others, she was without purpose. Though it wasn't healthy to see life like this, she didn't care right now—self-pity needed to happen. Or, was it self-care in taking as long as it took to look into herself and accept attention, and perhaps affection, from someone who cared for her?

If he left in the morning and went back to Big Sky,

it called into question whether bringing him to her home was really the best idea. If they ended up in bed together, it was arguably self-sabotage. Yes, it would feel great to have him for the night, but it would only leave her more broken in the morning.

Before pulling down her street, she considered turning left and running back toward the city center and the DoubleTree.

She tapped her hands on the steering wheel like some attempt at Morse code to the universe, begging for it to answer. Instead of the universe, Casper reached over and took her hand, lacing their fingers together in solidarity.

"It's been a long day. Don't overthink this." He smiled and his eyes looked as tired as her heart. "You are safe with me."

In those simple words, she felt the truth, and it was freeing.

He truly was an incredible man.

"You don't know how much I needed to hear you say that." She pressed their hands to her face and he gently stroked her cheek before they dropped their hands down to the console and let the silence take over once again.

She parked in her garage, and the place was nearly empty except for a few plastic bins, some normal maintenance tools and an unplugged extra fridge the former owner had left behind. It was strange, but she'd never really paid attention to how devoid her garage was of her personality—or maybe it personified it.

She released an audible groan.

"What's wrong?" he asked, looking almost afraid that she was going to say something that would hurt him, making her realize he was feeling just as vulnerable.

"Oh, don't worry. I was just thinking about how pathetic my place is. It's pretty minimalist."

"All I need is a blanket and a spot for the pup, and even the blanket is negotiable."

"Isn't everything?" she teased.

"Truth," he said with a little smile.

"I can do better than a blanket. If Grover needs his own bedroom, like your place, we can figure something out, but it may include you and I sleeping together." Her statement made her blush. She hadn't intended to make it sound so *dirty* and yet, she didn't regret saying something.

"If the offer is on the table," he said with a huge grin.

"Well, it's not on the table, but I guess it could be there, too, if you wanted."

"Oh, Kris, I like you talking like that."

"What did you think? I was just some plain Jane? I'm a goddess when it comes to pleasing and being pleased."

He leaned over and kissed her, the action so powerful and hungry that her entire body throbbed with want. Reaching over, he took her face in his hands and pulled back slightly, just so he could look her in the eyes. "I know you are playing," he said, his voice raspy with lust, "and if you don't want to take things any further than this, I promise it'll end here. I told you that you were safe with me, and I meant it. I'm not going to push you for something you are not ready to give."

Right now, he could have asked her to give anything and she probably would have done it just to have him in her bed. However, she appreciated that one of them was still using their right brain. They didn't need to bring sex into their relationship. If they didn't, they could keep on holding hands and being safely attracted to one another without the additional complications that came with spending a night in the other's arms.

"Let's just go and get Grover settled. I'd say we could have a glass of wine or a beer or something, but as things are, I think it would be best if we both came to our decisions with a clear head. If we take things further, I don't want you to regret anything, and neither do I."

He let go of her hand, but he looked lighter. "I have to say it is nice being with a real adult. You know… someone who thinks things through instead of just jumping into bad decisions."

"So you think that taking things further would be a bad decision?" She frowned.

He put his hand to the car's door handle like he was looking for a quick escape. "That's not what I was saying. I didn't mean for it to come out like that. I guess what I should have said was that it's nice to have someone who is self-aware and wants to make choices that are the best for everyone involved."

She wasn't sure that his second attempt in reassuring her their sleeping together wasn't a bad idea was any better than the first, but she didn't want any more clarification. He was on the fence about the idea of being intimate just as much as she was—and that was enough to take it off the metaphorical table.

Grover led the way into the house, and the smell of trapped air and vanilla candles filled the space. It was strange how one open door could make something go from stale to refreshed in just a few moments. Maybe she was like this place—used to her safety and her routines and comfortable with her doors closed, but needing to push that one part of her life open so she could refresh her soul.

Ugh. She hated self-reflections. It was just so much easier to constantly work, to face the needs of the day instead of the needs of her being.

Grover led her straight to the kitchen.

"Are you hungry, buddy?" She went to the fridge, knowing before she even opened it that it was about as barren as her garage. "Are you hungry, Casper?"

It had been several hours since they had eaten last and as she stood with the dog, she couldn't ignore the growling deep in her belly.

Casper walked up behind her and put his hand gently on her back as she leaned down and stared at the lonely block of cheese, eggs and some bacon still in its wrapper.

She looked over her shoulder at him. "I have enough to whip together a little breakfast for supper."

"Did you just say *supper*?" He chuckled. "My grandmother used to say that all the time."

"Are you saying I remind you of your grandmother?"

He really hadn't been earning any points in the last few minutes.

A faint redness moved into his cheeks. "Damn it. No, that's not what I meant, at all. I was just… *Gah*." He ran his hands over his face like he could rub away his embarrassment. "It was a compliment, I swear."

"Uh-huh," she said, reaching into the fridge and taking out the ingredients she needed.

"Seriously, why am I suddenly acting like such an idiot?"

"I must be making you uncomfortable, but you don't need to be." She touched his arm as she moved by him, trying to put him at ease.

He tensed under her touch as though she was what was making him uncomfortable, not the situation. She could understand the situation, but he had been the one to make the move in the car…and pretty much every move before so it made no sense to her that he would be ill-at-ease with her fingers.

Nothing was going as she had hoped…not that she'd had any expectations.

She moved by him. "Here, open up the bacon. There is a pan by the stove there," she said, pointing toward the white shaker-style cupboard beside the range. "You good in the kitchen?"

Even though there had been nothing provocative about what she said, she couldn't help but hear it in her words. What was wrong with her?

Lust. Lust was what was wrong with her.

She was losing her ever-loving mind.

The world always said men weren't that compli-cated. This was a lie and whoever had made that universal assumption was an ass. Men were just as complicated as women, even if no one wanted to admit or talk about the reality that no one was dif-ferent when it came to navigating emotional and relationship minefields—only the naive ventured, unafraid.

Grover lay down at the mouth of the kitchen, watching them work and do the dance of cooking. They moved almost in tandem, like they had done this kind of thing a thousand times before. She found a beauty in the dance, a familiarity that came with him even when few words were spoken.

She couldn't remember the last time she had felt something like that, and she was met with a blade of sadness that he didn't feel this same level of comfort in her home—and yet, as they worked some of the awkwardness seemed to slip away from him.

The bacon started to sizzle and they stood there, watching the meat shrink in the pan as it gave off its delicious aroma. Her mouth watered.

He moved behind her and wrapped his arms around her waist. His mouth moved against the back of her head and she could feel some of her hairs stick to the moisture on his lips. He reached up and flipped away the offending hair.

"I'm sorry for being weird." He pulled her gently against him and she let her body relax into his.

"It's okay. Ours is a strange world and there isn't a road map for where we've been or where we might want to go."

"Where is it that you want to go?" He asked the question into her hair.

She was glad she wasn't facing him so he couldn't see the tug-of-war of emotions playing out on her features. "Casper, to be honest… I don't know."

It felt strange speaking her truth, but at the same time she was proud of herself. In so many relationships of her past, she had been afraid to be direct with her needs.

"What do you mean?"

"We both know that the elephant in the room, aside from Grover," she said, trying to joke a bit to try and alleviate some of the tension, "is that there is a big distance between you and me. If we are going to try and have a relationship there are going to be a lot of windshield hours. We are both old enough and experienced enough to know how that kind of thing usually works out. I've had relationships fail even when we were in the same city because there was a lack of time."

Her mind wandered to asking him if he was interested in moving, if they were together. He had mentioned that he was a freelancer and retired from the military, but he owned a home and was settled in his life in Big Sky. Besides, they had just met. She wasn't completely sold he wanted to spend the night with her in the same bed, let alone move hours away from his home just so they could go out on regular dates.

He slowly chewed a piece of bacon he had popped in his mouth and was staring down at the pan like it held all the answers. "I think if you wanted to try, I'd be game to seeing if we could give it a go for a bit." He looked over at her and his eyes were wide with what she could best describe as insecurity and fear.

Did he really think she would turn an offer to date him—*really* date him—down?

She hated to think of Greg at a time like this, but what Casper had just offered was more than nearly any promises Greg had made. In fact, she couldn't remember the last time a guy had wanted anything from her besides a meal and a night in the sack.

Wait...that's what we're doing now. She smirked at her thought. *This is different.*

"You want to try?" He stood up and pulled her into his arms, and looped his hands around her hips. His hands fell to her ass, but all she really noticed was the way he was looking at her.

He wanted her. Not just for tonight.

"You know I want to, Casper."

It wasn't love. It wasn't promises. It wasn't forever. However, it gave her something she hadn't felt in a long time—hope for a better life.

She turned off the stove, then moved the pans onto the back burners and covered them up so the food wouldn't dry.

"I know I promised to feed you, but I want something else right now."

"Oh?" He gave her a knowing but sly grin. "What is it that you want?"

She pressed her body harder against him. "If you have to ask that question, maybe I shouldn't—"

He cut off her words with a kiss. It was deep, hungry with want. He tasted like bacon and salt, and she savored the flavor of his lips, licking and nibbling as they gave in to their desire for each other.

Oh, to be kissed like this.

She wrapped her arms around him, reached up and pressed her fingers into his hair, pulling him harder against her lips until their tongues met. He kissed her, slowly but wild and free, pressing and holding, tracing her lips and moving deep. If his kiss was any indication of what he would be like in bed, she was a lucky woman.

Hell, she was already a lucky woman for finding herself standing here in her kitchen with the most handsome man she had ever laid eyes upon and a man who wanted something more than a one-night stand.

"Kristin…" He spoke her name into her open mouth, like he wanted her to swallow the sweet sound. "I want you."

She took him by the hand and led him a few steps into the open living room and the large couch at its center. After letting go of him, she grabbed the remote for the TV and turned on a 90s hits channel.

"Sit," she ordered, pointing at the chaise lounge section.

"Yes, ma'am." He had a huge grin on his face and his eyes were bright. "What is happening here?"

She reached up and slowly unbuttoned her shirt,

moving her body with the rhythm of Def Leppard's "Pour Some Sugar on Me." This song had been around longer than her, but anytime she heard it, she had always imagined a moment like this, stripping for a man who waited to ravish her body.

Her fingers trembled with excitement as she undid her last button and slipped the cotton shirt from her shoulders, exposing her black lace bra. She would have been lying if she didn't admit that she had been imagining the day would lead here when she'd dressed. Better, she had even shaved and had an everything-gets-exfoliated-and-buffed shower.

She unzipped her jeans and pushed them down her thighs, trying in vain to keep with the music, but realizing that she was not equipped or lithe enough to make stripping her career. Thankfully, he didn't laugh at her or seem to be anything but intoxicated by her best attempt to be sexy.

She stood up and moved closer to him and he ran his fingers over the smooth skin of her lower belly, just above her panty line. She sucked in her breath as he reached around and took her ass into his hands and pulled her against his mouth. He kissed her over her panties like he had kissed her mouth, his tongue flicking against her.

A moan escaped her lips as he let go of her with one hand and moved her panties to the side so he could slip his fingers into her wet center.

"Casper…" She exhaled his name as he found the spot at her core… "Yes. Right there."

He worked her harder, faster, running the tips of his fingers over the sweet spot and licking her through the lace. As good as her fantasies about him had been, the reality of feeling him inside and on her were so much sweeter.

Her legs started to quiver and shake as he worked with the pace of her breathing. She edged to the moment, so close. Her release was right there, but she stopped, wanting the pain and ache of the climax to prolong. "I want you inside me."

Though she wasn't sure he'd heard her, she pulled down her panties and he unzipped his pants. He moved them just far enough down his thighs to not be painful, but no more than necessary as she moved on top of him. He was larger than she had expected, and she groaned as he pressed into her.

Moving her hips to the cadence of his body, it didn't take long for her to know this man was everything she had been hoping to find. He filled her to the point of nearing glorious, blissful pain, the kind that made her want to tip back her head and howl like a primal animal in the deepest recesses of pleasure.

He was hers.

She was his.

And, damn it, did he know how to pleasure her.

Every inch of him fit her as if he'd been made especially for her body. His tip pressed upward, hitting parts of her that she didn't even know existed. He rubbed against her, harder and faster, until she could feel the pressing need to release.

"You… I'm going to…" she panted as he moved faster.

She couldn't hold back. A howl escaped her… and she was free.

Chapter Eighteen

There were a handful of nights in his life that he would have given anything to go back and relive, and last night had been one of them. When Kristin had fallen asleep in his arms, he had tried not to stare at her perfect, round-tipped nose, or the way her eyebrows arched like bows over her long black eyelashes. She'd hummed lightly in her sleep, like she was singing to the night and to him, and it had made him fall for her that much more.

After letting Grover out and getting him comfortable in her place, they had taken off to work for the day. As she drove toward his brother's house, he watched as the morning sun danced on her hair and caressed her face in the places where his fingers and touched her skin last night. Oh, he would need to make love to her again and again…and again.

There was no way he could ever grow weary in making love to her. Everything was the best—maybe it was the passion that burned between them and the lust for each other, or maybe it was that they were both just *in*, but whatever it was no one had ever made him feel as she had.

The future was written on everything about her.

She looked at him and caught him staring at her. "You okay over there? Nervous about seeing your brother?"

He shook his head. If she hadn't spoken up, he would have probably stayed in his happy place, looking at her until he had completely lost track of what they were intending on doing today.

"Did you text him to let him know we are on the way?"

"I'm not sure if I told him we were coming that he would open the door." He wished he was kidding.

"Roger said that he had been notified about Michelle's death. I think the officer may have asked him a few questions, but I don't know if they are going to look at him as a suspect in her death, or not."

"Did Roger say if they had any more idea as to the cause of death?"

She tapped her fingers on the wheel. "Nothing conclusive, but they found some interesting evidence this morning. He didn't tell me what, but I think they are leaning toward her death being a homicide."

The ache in his gut, the one that had been there since he'd found out about her being missing but had forgotten about in the night, returned, tighter than ever. He couldn't say why, other than his brother being at the lawyer's yesterday, but he had a feeling William was somehow involved and he hated it.

He hoped that he was wrong and his brother was

an innocent man, but until he looked into his eyes and asked him to tell him the truth, he couldn't be sure.

"I'm impressed that you have been talking to Roger, at all." He hadn't wanted to bring it up, but since she was talking about him, he had to say something.

"He was upset last night. I'm hoping that with a little buttering up he will come to his senses and see that, if we did somehow step out of line and not follow a policy, it is the policy that is wrong and not us."

He wished he could agree with her, but he could understand why her commander would be upset with them not listening to orders and skirting his authority. In the military, nothing like that—no matter how well-intentioned—would have been considered acceptable. A person was to do as ordered.

When he'd been active, he'd been the kind who followed orders well. Toward the end of his career, though, he'd been the one giving them—and maybe that was why he had been okay in coloring outside the lines a bit last night.

His brother was outside, watering freshly planted flowers in the small garden in front of his and Michelle's house. The last time he had been there was Thanksgiving, and at the time the house had been warm and inviting. His father had been alive then, living in their basement apartment, and all in all, the holiday had been tense, but nice.

Michelle had been very inviting.

Damn. That was the last time I saw her alive.

He blinked and the image of her dead body flashed to the front of his mind. He could clearly make out the hair covering her face. He hadn't noticed it yesterday, but as he thought about the scene, he could recall the strong smell of sagebrush and something else…something chemical.

His mind must have been playing tricks on him. Maybe he was planting false memories or something just because Roger had mentioned they'd found some *interesting* things on the scene. Maybe now Casper was trying to remember all the things he might have missed.

He couldn't go there. No doubt there were high-caliber detectives on the case who were paid to go down the what-if and whodunit rabbit hole. His job was to support his family and be there for his brother in his time of need—no more, no less.

If someone had murdered Michelle, he couldn't help but wonder if they had also played some kind of role in his father's death as well. Although the official cause of death was a heart attack, it had been brought on by exposure to the elements. If someone had dumped him, he was sure that a good attorney would at least go for a charge of negligent homicide.

His brother looked up as they approached and pulled to a stop in front of the house. When William spotted them, Casper saw the passive look of a man tending to his garden was quickly replaced by one of surprise.

He half expected his brother to turn and head into the house, locking the door, and them, out of his life.

Instead, William walked out toward the Durango and waited for them to step out of the car.

"I'm glad you're here. I didn't think you'd come."

His brother's warmth was in direct opposition to the coldness he felt after yesterday's conversation.

"Are you doing okay?"

William opened his mouth to speak, but looked as though he'd choked up and swallowed his feelings down.

Giving him a moment to regain his composure, he motioned toward Kristin, who was standing at the front of the car, her hands folded in front of her like she was deeply uncomfortable being here. Maybe he had made a mistake in having her come along. "This is Kristin. She was one of the volunteers who helped find Michelle...and Dad."

William reached out, took her hand in his and looked her in the eyes. "I can't tell you how grateful I am for your help. I'm sorry I couldn't be there when you found Michelle." As he spoke, there was a crack of emotions.

As genuine as his brother seemed to be, it came off to Casper as cloying at best. His brother had never really been the emotional type. Maybe it was just his brotherly animosity that was pulling him in so many directions and kept him wanting to be mad at his brother, or maybe his intuition was trying to pull him in the right direction.

As much as he told people that they had to trust their gut, his feelings for his brother were so in flux that he couldn't rightly condemn him for a crime or crimes he may not have committed, no matter how badly he wanted to continue to point the finger.

He had to quell his annoyance. Emotions were good. In fact, in this situation, they should have been expected—if it had been anyone else, he would have. It probably didn't help that his brother was touching Kristin.

Stomp the anger down, he reminded himself.

"It was a good thing you weren't there." Casper pointed to the door. "Why don't we go inside and we can talk without your entire neighborhood being in the know."

His brother nodded, letting go of Kristin's hand, much to Casper's relief. "Yeah, I think I have a beer in the fridge or something."

Casper looked at his watch. "Bro, it's nine in the morning." Kristin shot him a look of admonishment. "But, hey, if you need to tie one on to get through the day, I get it."

Kristin gave him an almost imperceptible nod.

"Yeah. I don't really know what I need right now." His brother turned and went to the front door. As he walked, Casper noticed that his shorts were torn up and dirty in the back, and they reminded him of the state his father had been in when they found him on the rimrocks. The majority of his feelings of annoyance slipped from him.

His brother was hurting.

In all reality, so was Casper. And seeing his brother in such a state made everything that was happening so...*permanent*. Up until now, he'd been in what he could have best described as a stunned trance. He had liked Michelle, he had been sad when they found her, he had thoughts and memories of her and their family, but he hadn't been forced to see the hole she had left behind. Losing her was compounding his brother's grief in ways he hadn't imagined.

When they walked into his brother's house, the smell of rotting garbage filled his nostrils. There were open food containers sitting on the living room table, stacked and buzzing with flies—a far cry from the last time he'd been here. Every other time he had ever been to the house, it had been picture perfect to the point it could have been in a magazine or something.

"How long was Michelle gone?" he asked, walking past his brother toward the kitchen.

"She—she left right after Dad." William threw himself down on the couch, not seeming to notice the chaos or the group of flies that took flight as he flopped.

"Two weeks?" Kristin asked, looking around like she could tell just as Casper could have easily been months and not simply weeks based on the disarray.

"Well, we have been working on things ever since Christmas. She didn't officially move out until Dad passed, but she really hadn't been living here for months."

"Did you think she may have had the intention to return home at some point?"

"I wanted her to come back. I've been calling her all the time, trying to get her to see reason. She knows

I needed her. Dad's death was really hard on me."
William dropped his head into his hands.

"Do you know where she had been staying?"

"I am not sure, but I think she was staying with
another guy. It would take her hours to drive back—
so maybe on the other side of the state. Who knows,
though. She wasn't telling me anything."

Casper opened up the kitchen pantry, grabbed a
large black garbage bag and started to pick up the
empty beer and wine bottles that were littered all
over the kitchen counter, some tipped over and having spilled their contents onto the surface, where they
had been left so long that there were only purple and
tan sticky globs.

Even in college, his brother hadn't been this bad
off. If anything, he'd been a meticulous neat freak.
He'd even made a point, regardless of his girlfriend
status, to change out his bedsheets every four days.
Clothes never sat in the washer and dryer—he'd even
folded Casper's and put them on the bed when he'd
been too busy to get to them before William had
needed the washer. Casper may have depended on
his brother cleaning up behind him on more than
one occasion, and, of course, William had done so
without much complaint.

On the corner of the counter, next to the empty
coffee maker, was a huge stack of orange-and-white
pill bottles with his father's name on them. There
must have been at least forty different bottles. He
recognized a few as normal heart meds and the like,

but others he couldn't have named if he had a gun to his head. They looked rather untouched in comparison to the rest of the house and he found a strange comfort in the thought.

He filled the first bag and grabbed another, handing it to William. "I know you probably don't want to hear this, but the best thing we can do is to get you moving. Looking at the state of this place, well…you should have called me and told me what was happening with you."

"You were already pissed off," William countered, correctly. "I've been working from home and everything would have been fine, but then…" He choked up and rubbed the back of his hand hard under his nose.

Kristin was shaking her head at him, like she didn't agree with his method for helping. He didn't know if it was the right thing, either, but he couldn't just let his brother sink further into self-pity and pain.

"Come on. Get up," Casper said, wishing he had been more patient with his brother. He had just never seen him behave like this. It was so out of character, but so was losing most of the people a person loved in a short span of time.

He held out his hand, pulling his brother to standing. Kristin walked to the kitchen and started unloading the dishwasher. Casper had William hold the garbage bag and he threw more refuse into the thing.

It didn't take them long to have the place back to a livable standard. Kristin had started to vacuum, and the sounds of crumbs and detritus whipping through the tube filled the air.

After throwing six bags of trash out into the dumpster, he made William follow him upstairs to the bedroom. It was almost as bad as the living room, but instead of food boxes, there were layers upon layers of dirty clothing. The closet had just a smattering of empty hangers, except one, which had a suit jacket hanging precariously from it.

He couldn't leave his brother like this, in this state. Even if they got it all cleaned up and looking okay, his brother was not in a place where Casper could trust him to be alone. Especially after last night. Though he still couldn't say with one-hundred-percent certainty that his brother had a role in Michelle's death, he could at least say that he doubted his brother could have, or would have, left his house to commit the crime.

He started to pull the sheets from the bed after grabbing handfuls of clothing and throwing them into the center of the bed, making a makeshift laundry roll. "Didn't you say you had a meeting with your lawyer yesterday?"

William nodded.

"Did you go to their office?"

"It was online. Talked to the mediator, mostly."

"What were you talking to the lawyer about?"

"Michelle gave me the divorce papers yesterday. It was the first time we'd *actually* talked in a while—about right."

His stomach sank. As soon as the detective found out that little piece of information, his brother would be suspect number one. He already would have been number one on the list, but now they would be unlikely to look at anyone else until they could solidly prove that he wasn't responsible—which, in all honesty, Casper wasn't sure they would be able to do.

"Why didn't you tell me?" he asked, already knowing his brother's answer—because Casper had been acting like a jerk and a terrible brother. All he had done was concentrate on his own grief and anger.

How could he have been so self-righteous?

He continued to beat himself up as he carried the bedding roll downstairs to the laundry and got it started while William kept clearing things up in his bedroom.

Kristin turned off the vacuum and made her way over to him as he poured a lid full of laundry detergent into the washer.

"I'm sorry," she said, touching him gently.

"Are you leaving?" he asked, suddenly afraid by the tone of her voice.

She shook her head. "I will stay to help as long as I can. Roger just texted me, though, and I have to go into his office to discuss the disciplinary plan."

"That's nothing to be sorry for," he said, somewhat relieved that she hadn't said she couldn't deal with all the upheaval and chaos in his family and she had made a terrible mistake in opening up her body and her heart to him last night.

He wouldn't have blamed her, if she had told him

to pound sand. His life had hit a new disaster level, one lower than ever before. After the way she had seen him treat William, she probably didn't think he was a man she needed in her life.

Chapter Nineteen

She had made a terrible mistake. They should have waited to share Kristin's bed until she'd had a chance to know Casper better. The man he had appeared to be was a stark contrast to the man who was standing in his brother's house.

He'd made William out to be such a jerk since she had known him, saying that they'd not had a close relationship, and he'd even implied his brother had played a role in his father's death, but looking at his brother now, she couldn't begin to imagine how Casper could have jumped to those kind of conclusions. If anything, his brother was nothing more than a broken man.

She was being unfair, though. So many things happened between brothers, wedges that couldn't be easily explained and that she wouldn't understand. She had to trust her gut in the fact Casper was a great man.

She was so confused. Her heart and her mind were being pulled in different directions and she hated every second of it.

"Did you come check on your brother after I saw

you in the hospital?" she asked, standing with him in the laundry room as he worked to help with his brother's bedding and dirty clothes.

"I didn't." He shoved the soap drawer closed and pushed the buttons to start the machine. "Turns out, I should have."

"Didn't you say your brother and his wife had a nurse coming into their place to help care for your father?"

He nodded.

"Wouldn't they have been helping to keep the place clean and well-kept?"

He sighed. "That was the impression I was under. The last time I was at the house was Thanksgiving. It had been in good shape—*perfect*, actually."

"Caring for a loved one can take a toll on a relationship. Do you think that was what happened between he and Michelle, or do you think it was something else?"

He shrugged. "I can't tell you. All I know is that I didn't really know my brother like I thought I did. I've made a lot of assumptions—wrong assumptions. Assumptions that will haunt me for years to come."

Her heart wanted her to take him in her arms and comfort him, but there was a wave of anger coming off him that seemed to radiate with *don't touch*.

She really had made a mistake. "You did the best you could, with the information you were given."

"Something like that."

She hated the way he sounded. Part of her wanted to shake him out of this funk in hopes she could have back the man she had fallen for.

"I'm going to go."

He nodded, not looking at her as he opened up the dryer and started to fold a load of clothes that were almost hard from sitting in there for so long. "Yeah. I get it."

"If you need anything, call me. A ride, whatever. Let me know when you plan on going back to Big Sky."

"Sure," he said in a clipped tone, but there was a strangled noise in his voice that made her want to turn him around so she could see his face.

If she did that, though, it was possible that she would get sucked back into this in a way she wasn't sure she wanted to be.

They both just needed a moment to think. She had a lot going on in her life and as much as she wanted to help him, after this week, she was already going to be doing a lot of cleanup. To be hit with this level of family drama on top of it all... Well, maybe this relationship wasn't something she wanted. Sure, she wanted to be there for Casper, but it would come at one hell of a cost to herself. It already had.

Turning away, she made her way out of the house and it wasn't until she was outside that she found she could breathe. There was so much going on in there, so many feelings, so many questions, that it was suffocating. After getting into her car, she picked up her phone and texted Roger that she was on her way.

As she drove, she couldn't help but feel like she had let Casper down, but he hadn't argued when she told him she was going to go.

When she arrived at the SAR building, Roger was already there. His truck was parked outside, along with a number of other cars she recognized as belonging to the chief and the rest of the board. This was going to be a long afternoon. Hopefully, though, she could learn more about Michelle's death.

When she made her way inside, Roger was sitting with the board in the meeting room. It was a glass room in the center of the building with drop-down blinds for privacy that no one ever seemed to use. If they did, someone was getting fired. If anything, it was a good sign that they weren't already drawn.

Her stomach ached.

She tapped on the wooden door and Roger waved her inside.

"Hey, guys," she said, sounding less confident than she would have liked, but unable to summon anything more than she was feeling.

The three other members of the board gave her a curt welcome.

She sat down next to Roger, unsure if she wanted to be so close to the man wielding the axe.

Roger gave her a tip of the head, but his face was impassive.

"Any word on the cause of death?" she asked, trying to quell the ache in her gut.

Roger looked at the others sitting at the table, but no one seemed to want to meet his gaze. The head of the board and the woman to his left, Mayor Marcy Davis, looked over at Kristin and smiled. "Actually," she began, "we were hoping to ask you a few questions about her and your actions that led to locating her body."

"Absolutely, I'm happy to answer." She tried to smile, but it didn't take.

Roger started to say something but Marcy cut him off with a sharp look.

"Roger, here," Marcy continued, "said that you blatantly ignored his orders in going outside the search perimeter after you had conducted your initial search track and had been asked to rest. Is that accurate?"

She squirmed slightly in her seat, but she hoped they didn't notice. "I wouldn't say we *blatantly* did anything. My teammate's dog had gone missing. It would have been unethical and morally questionable to stop searching at that time."

Marcy smiled, but Kristin couldn't make heads or tails if the action was friendly or malicious, and that only amplified her anxiety.

"You didn't listen to my orders. You could have put more people at risk by acting on your own accord." Roger looked furious.

"For that, I do apologize. I can see your concern, sir," Kristin said in earnest. "I wasn't aware that we were going to cause a problem for you. If we'd known, I can promise that we wouldn't have taken a risk. As it was, we are both well-trained in self-rescue and in search techniques and we felt comfortable in continuing our search not only for the missing woman, but also the dog."

"I consider you a friend as well as a colleague,"

Roger continued, not really seeming to listen to her apology. "As such, I think you just assumed that you could do as you wished without fear of reprisal."

"Sir, I wouldn't wish to compromise our work or our friendship in any way."

"Both of you," Marcy interjected, "let's talk about why we are really here. Roger informed us that he put you on a leave as a result of your actions. That being said and after further review, the board and myself have decided not to enforce the punishment and reinstate you fully."

She smiled widely. "Thank you. I appreciate—"

Marcy put her finger up, silencing her. "That being said, we do not condone your cavalier actions. In this case, we see validity in your argument and in the fact that you and your teammate found the missing woman."

Suddenly, the truth of the situation hit her. *This could have been easily resolved in a phone call. They wanted me face-to-face for another reason.*

"As of late, you have been involved with a number of *interesting* events."

She gripped her hands together tightly in her lap, under the conference table. "Yes, but—"

"We know that you are not the cause of any of these events," Marcy said, cutting her off, "but it is odd that you are at the center of so much."

She looked down at the table.

Roger tapped his pencil against a pad of paper that she hadn't noticed he had been writing on.

"We are concerned for your well-being." Marcy

reached over like she wanted to touch her, but then retracted her hand.

She jerked as she looked up at Marcy. "Why? What do you mean?"

Marcy opened up a yellow file resting in front of her. "We received the mechanic's report on the helo after it went down in Big Sky." She flipped to a picture of a mess of black hydraulic lines and turned it so she could see. "If you look here," she said, pointing toward an opening in a black line, "they found clear evidence of not breakage, but what appeared to be an intentional cut mark."

Holy crap.

"What?" Kristin choked on the question.

"There were marks on a couple of the other hydraulic lines as well. As if, whoever was responsible had been making sure that at least one of the lines would fail midflight."

"That doesn't make sense." Kristin shook her head. "No one at that location or in Billings would have wanted to compromise our bird."

"We think that it may have had something to do with you. Maybe Casper?"

The blood drained from her face. Casper. Someone was targeting *Casper.*

Of course, they were. Why didn't I put it together?

"Did you see anything? Anyone who seemed to have a problem with your teammate?" Roger asked, his tone taking on a new softness.

Her first thought went to Greg, but he hadn't really had a problem with Casper—aside from the fact he had taken his bird. That was a pretty big thing, but at the same time Greg had signed up for the training with the knowledge that he may not be the only person operating the helo. It would have been against his own self-interest to make a move like this.

She stared at the picture.

"How long do you think the cuts would have held before breaking?" she asked, though she wasn't sure that they would really have an answer.

"It's tough to say," Marcy said. "According to the mechanic's findings, it would have been dependent on the pressure the aircraft was under and the stress of the flights."

A terror filled her. "Okay, but do you think it happened here in Billings…before we ever went their direction for training? On our last rescue mission, we were only flying for about an hour and then it was about an hour to Big Sky. Neither flight was in harsh weather or with much altitudinal changes."

"It sounds like you are thinking it happened in advance?" Marcy countered.

She shrugged, letting out a long sigh as she tried to order her thoughts. "There is no way I could know anything for sure, but I don't think I have anyone who would really wish me harm. Casper, on the other hand, like you said, he's had a lot going on his life recently. The last mission we went on before travel and training was the one in which we were looking for his father. My hang-up is that Casper wasn't on that flight."

"Who was on the flight with you?" Marcy asked.

The other board members at the table looked anxious. The man to her left was scratching at the back of his neck and the other was chewing at his lip. Apparently, no one at the table was very pleased with the conversation they were having.

"On the flight to locate Hugh Keller we had three on board—myself, a nurse and our pilot, Greg." She winced at the sound of his name. "As some of you may know, I'm aware that Roger does at the very least, Greg and I had been dating until a few months ago. Things were amicable between us and I don't think he would wish me any harm."

"Wow." Marcy sat back in her chair as she studied her. "You were quick to explain the situation between you and Greg. Is there a reason for that?" Her question came off as more of an accusation than a query.

"I just don't want anything to come out later that would give our organization a black eye."

"And we do appreciate that." Roger nodded.

The other two men at the table mumbled in agreement.

Marcy shuffled the papers in the folder on the table. "So…this Casper. What is the nature of your relationship with him?"

No… Why did she have to ask? Was it even any of their business?

"We are friends," she said, trying not to let the truth flare on her cheeks. She and Casper's relationship didn't need to be on trial here.

"Did you know the deceased?" Marcy asked.

She shook her head.

"What about Michelle's husband, Casper's brother…" She fluttered through the file as if it held the man's name.

"William. Yes, I met him today." Her entire body stiffened at the mention of him, but she didn't really know why.

"How did you meet him?" Roger asked.

Again, she wasn't sure why they would be asking all these questions.

"We went over to check on his welfare. After I texted you and you told me he had been notified by law enforcement of her death, Casper wanted to see him."

"And you were with Casper this morning?" Marcy asked, like she could see right through her and to the reality that Kristin had spent the last night in his embrace.

Thankfully, Roger didn't wait for her to answer. "In what state did you find him… William, that is?"

"His place was a dumpster fire. We ended up helping him to clean it up a bit."

Roger's jaw dropped. "You did what, now?"

She frowned, wondering why he'd had such a strong reaction to an innocuous thing. "We helped him throw out some trash. You know, picked up his place."

"I heard you the first time." Roger ran his hands over his face in exasperation. "You do realize that he is under investigation for his wife's murder?"

"What?" She was genuinely confused.

"So…in helping to clean up what very well may be a crime scene," Roger stated, "you may have just become an accessory, after the fact."

Chapter Twenty

He was petting Grover and William was in the shower when Casper's phone rang. Kristin was in a panic when he answered. "Someone cut the hydraulic lines. You were right, someone out there wants one or both of us dead," she said, her words becoming almost one as she spoke.

"What is going on? Are you okay?" He tried to remain calm, though his anxiety immediately spiked and Grover hopped down from the couch, going on alert.

"I'm fine, but you have to stop whatever you are doing at William's."

He looked around the living room. "What do you mean?"

"Your brother is being investigated. They think he may have done something to Michelle and…"

"Are you kidding me?" The ache in his gut returned.

"You called it with him." There was the slam of a car door in the background of the call. "I'm on my way back to you. You need to get out of there."

"I didn't call anything." He sank deeper into his

brother's couch, listening for a moment until he could once again make out the sounds of his brother's shower going overhead. "My brother didn't have anything to do with Michelle's death. You saw him. He was destroyed."

"Destroyed or not. In helping him with his place, we have just made ourselves possible accessories after the fact in a homicide."

He shook his head, disbelieving. "No. No way." The knot in his stomach grew as he thought about what she had just told him and the huge mistake they had made in his attempt to help his brother.

"Does your brother have a criminal defense attorney?"

"I have no idea." He stared at the coffee table, still covered in crumbs, as Grover came over to him and nudged his hand.

"Well, if he does, *we* may need their number."

She was overreacting. They hadn't done anything wrong. "We will be fine. My brother is innocent."

"Are you sure? I'm not, Casper." She paused, but he said nothing. "I'll be there in twenty minutes." She ended the call.

He had known it was possible that William would be questioned about Michelle's passing, but he hadn't really thought he would be heavily investigated. From everything he had seen at his brother's house when they'd arrived, he hadn't walked out of that house in weeks. He would be happy to testify to the fact, if push came to shove. He got up and let Grover into the backyard.

William was in his bedroom with the door closed when he charged toward it. He knocked so hard that he heard a picture drop from the wall, its glass breaking as it hit the floor. Normally, he would have felt bad, but right now, he felt no guilt about destroying pieces of his brother's world.

"William? Can I come in? We need to talk." He couldn't wait to really talk to him and get the answers that they all needed…and to learn what had been going on between his brother and Michelle. If he could just give Casper some insight into their relationship, beyond the fact that it had been rocky, maybe he could help William get out of this pinch.

There was no answer.

Maybe William was still in the bathroom, shaving or something.

He knocked again.

No answer.

His heart started to race. His brother had been upset, clearly. He hadn't appeared suicidal when they'd arrived or anytime since—depressed, yes, but he hadn't expressed guilt or a desire to die. William wouldn't have done anything stupid.

He tried to open the door, but found it locked. It didn't budge as he pressed his weight against it, and there was no noise coming from inside.

His heart was thrashing in his chest. His brother was inside. Something was wrong. He pulled out his phone, dialed 911 and then dropped it onto the ground. He backed up as he heard the dispatcher answer, but he didn't care what they had to say—all he needed was for them to send help.

He kicked the door as hard as he could, next to the latch. It took all of his strength, but it busted open, the force breaking the doorjamb and sending cracked wood in a variety of directions as the door flew open.

"William! Where are you?" he called, searching frantically for his brother.

The shower was off in the bathroom, but once again, the door was closed and locked. It didn't take as much force to bust the door open this time. On the floor, in front of the shower, was his brother. He had a towel wrapped around his body and vomit was slipping down his face.

"What did you do, William?" He fell to the floor by his brother, pulling him into his lap and doing a sweep of his mouth to clear it of anything that could possibly choke him. He tried to find a pulse, but failed. His was racing so much, though, that he worried he wouldn't have been able to feel it even if it had been as fast and erratic as his own.

His brother was limp as he moved him to the floor.

"Send medical help!" he screamed, hoping the dispatcher would hear him and know to send an ambulance.

Maybe his brother wasn't as innocent as he had hoped, or as guilty as he had once assumed.

PULLING AROUND THE corner and onto the block, Kristin was met with the distinctive red and blue lights of law enforcement and panic washed through her. The house was surrounded by an ambulance and several police cars as Kristin pulled up to William's place. Grover was peeking through the fence, panting, as he watched all the people come and go from the house.

She hadn't been gone for her meeting that long. What could possibly have happened?

Picking up her phone, she tried to dial Casper, but her call went straight to voice mail.

He wasn't dead. He couldn't be.

No one wanted to hurt the brothers, no matter what her bosses had said, no matter what the evidence said… They were just experiencing a wave of bad luck—that was it, nothing more. Or, at least she would have tried to continue to convince herself, but there was no denying there was something going on—something that could very well cause them all to lose their lives, even her.

Regardless, she couldn't leave Casper. She had to protect him even if it cost her life. She didn't care. He wasn't perfect, he had a lot happening in his world, but that didn't mean he was the cause of it or that she could hold it against him. If anything, he needed her to protect him, to help him get through this gauntlet in his life.

And right now, that meant getting into that house and making sure that he was okay. If he wasn't… well, she would cross that bridge when she got there, but needless to say there would be hell to pay to whomever had done him harm.

She parked her car down the street, her tennis shoes grinding in the dirt on the sidewalk as she ran toward the house. There was an officer standing guard and securing the scene, and he put up his hand in a feeble attempt to stop her.

"Excuse me, ma'am," he called toward her as she approached the house. "You need to stop right there."

She said nothing and sprinted toward the front door of the house.

"Ma'am. Stop. Right. There. Get down!" the officer ordered.

She should have responded, but she couldn't. Her body wouldn't let her stop her advance toward Casper. He needed her. Before she reached the doorknob, the cop grabbed her from behind, throwing his shoulder into her and tackling her to the ground. Grover barked from the backyard, like he was trying to help.

Her face cracked hard against the ground, and grass and dirt filled her mouth as she tried to explain in muffled garbles that she had to get inside. She was sure the officer couldn't understand her, and as he pressed his body weight into the middle of her back, pain shot through her.

"I'm sorry," she said in a breathless wheeze.

The officer eased his pressure on her spine. "What's your name?"

"I'm Kristin Loren. I'm a member of the Yellowstone County SAR team. I was just here with another member of my team and I am concerned for his welfare." She tried to sound as professional as possible.

"As a first responder in this county, what in the hell were you thinking?" The officer stood up and dusted off his knees as she stared up from the ground at him.

"I..." The truth was that she wasn't thinking, she was acting. Acting in a moment of pressure was what she had been trained to do. "I was relying on instincts. I apologize. I just..."

"You lost your damned mind." The cop extended his hand and helped her to standing. "You know, thanks to how you acted, I'm going to need to see some ID." He held out his hand as if he expected her to have her driver's license in her back pocket.

"I don't have it on me," she said, motioning toward her SUV. "It's back there in my purse. If you want to walk with me, I'd be happy to show you."

He sighed. "What exactly were you trying to accomplish by getting into the house?"

"I need to know that Casper and his dog are okay."

"Casper?" the officer said, frowning. "Give me a sec. You stay right here, got it?" he asked, pointing at the spot where she stood.

"I got it. I just need to know he is safe."

He clicked on his handset and started to talk as he walked away. His voice was muffled, but she could tell that he was asking about Casper's status.

There was static from the headset and she could hear something about EMS, but beyond that it was too garbled.

Finally, the officer turned around and walked back to talk to her. "So according to the officers inside the house, Casper is unhurt. He is giving a statement about what transpired here today."

"Which was?" she asked, some of the panic she was feeling starting to twist away.

"We are just bringing William Keller out to transport him to the medical-care facility, but it appears that he was either drugged or tried to commit suicide."

Drugged or suicide?

William hadn't been doing well, but she hadn't gotten anything from him that would have made her worry about him self-harming. If anything, he had seemed to perk up and be grateful that she and Casper had arrived to help him.

The thought made her think of Roger and Marcy… Maybe she hadn't helped in the way she had intended—instead, she may well have helped him destroy evidence and get herself wrapped up in a murder investigation that would end with her going to jail.

She had to be reasonable. Though she hadn't approached the scene with as much grace and aplomb as she would have wished, she needed to pull it together now…especially if she was going to come under some kind of investigation in response to all of this.

"Like I said, Officer, I'm incredibly sorry. I'm just extremely tired." She tried to force a stretch and a yawn, but she was sure that he saw right through it. "I was out all night helping with that lost woman. You know, the one we found dead."

He nodded. "Oh, yeah, I heard about that one. Sounds like she might have gotten clipped."

She motioned toward the house. "This is her estranged husband's place."

The officer opened his mouth in surprise. "Oh, damn. I had no idea. You think that's why he tried to possibly off himself?"

She was glad that they had a professional camaraderie going, but she didn't really want to play this game. Yet, there were limited options if she wanted to get her hands on Casper and see that he was, in fact, okay.

"There have been a lot of odd things happening in connection to this family."

"And you want to go in there?" The officer scowled at her.

"Only to make sure that my flight partner is still alive. I have a feeling that with enough time, he could be the one getting clipped next." She wasn't sure where her admission had come from, but she felt the truth of her words in her bones. It seemed as though someone wanted every member of this family dead, but she couldn't understand why, no matter how hard she tried to piece it all together.

The front door to the house opened and the EMS team brought out William, strapped down, on the gurney. His eyes were closed and she couldn't tell if they been able to bring him back to consciousness, or if was still at risk of death. Depending on what he had taken, or was given to him, there could be any number of effects and only a few outcomes— she hoped this time he would come out of it on the full-recovery side.

Following William, Casper walked out. His face was colorless and his shoulders sagged. He helped the EMS workers move his brother down the steps and watched them as they wheeled him to the ambulance and loaded him up. He looked over at her and then stared back at the ambulance like he wasn't sure if he should come to her, or get in the vehicle with his brother.

She walked toward him, noticing what looked like vomit on the legs of his pants. She could only imagine what he had been forced to deal with while he had waited for everyone to arrive.

"Casper..." She said his name softly and just loud enough to break him from his stupor. "If you want to go with your brother, I can grab Grover and follow you guys there."

"My buddy is going to come get Grover. He'll watch him for a few days while I take care of things." He shook his head. "I need to at least keep him safe."

"You didn't have anything to do with that, did you?" she asked, motioning her chin in the direction of William's house.

"Are you kidding me? Are you really asking me if I tried to kill my brother?"

She hadn't meant it like that—*accusatorial*. "No. Casper. I'm sorry. I didn't."

He turned from her, walking until he disappeared into the belly of the ambulance and out of her life.

Chapter Twenty-One

After she had handed off Grover to Casper's friend, she sat outside the emergency room. Every thirty minutes for the first three hours, she sent a text off to Casper, trying to let him know that she was in her car and waiting for him, and to text back if he needed anything from her. After the sixth text with no response, Kristin couldn't stand it any longer and made her way inside.

As she approached the secretary's desk, it struck her that the last time she had stepped foot in a hospital had been the day she had met Casper—the day his father had died. She silently prayed that history wouldn't, once again, repeat itself.

The college-aged woman behind the desk looked up at her, a tired look on her face, as if she was just a few hours from getting to go home and wishing that she was anywhere but behind the plated glass leading to the triage area. Or maybe she was projecting her own feelings onto the poor woman.

"Hi," she said, "I'm Kristin..." She paused, trying to decide if she should give her real name to the woman, knowing that if she did that, she would likely be turned away without ever getting a chance to see Casper and check on William because of privacy laws. "I'm Kristin Keller," she lied, but somehow saying the name made a warm and cozy feeling spread through her. "I'm here to see my brother-in-law, William Keller. I think he was brought in a few hours ago."

The woman nodded, not seeming to notice Kristin's best attempt at a lie. Instead, she started clicking on her keyboard. She handed back Kristin her ID and relief filled her as she slipped the card back in her wallet. "Yep, we have admitted him. It looks like they are just about to transfer him up to the floors."

"Which floor?" Kristin held her breath. If the woman said ICU, then it meant that William was still struggling for his life, but if it was a step-down or medical/surgical unit, then there was a chance they were just keeping him for observation and IV fluids.

The woman clicked on her keyboard and tapped downward a few more times, and as she did so, each tap was like a slice of a blade on Kristin's soft skin. "It looks like he just made it up to room 331. It's on the third floor—take a left and it will be a way down on your left."

"Thank you," she said, waving as she hurried toward the stairs.

She took the steps two at a time, her legs burning as she ascended the last flight of stairs. She was winded as she hit the door to the third floor and burst out in the ICU.

The place was abuzz with the sound of dry IV pumps and the shrill alarms of cardiac and respiratory monitors. She wondered if anyone ever really got used to the cacophony of sounds and they just became white noise.

She made her way down the hallway until she came to 331. The room was surrounded by glass, but the shades were pulled, obscuring everything inside. She tapped on the door, but before anyone answered, a nurse came down the hallway and cut her off.

"Hi, how can I help you?"

"I'm here to see my brother-in-law, William Keller," she lied again, this time the lie coming out with greater ease.

The nurse frowned as he looked at the door and then back to her. "We only allow one guest in the room at a time, due to safety concerns. Right now, I believe he already has a visitor."

She nodded, but she didn't really care what the hospital's arbitrary policies entailed.

"Can you please tell Casper I'm here?" she said quickly, as if every second she stood in the hallway was a second they grew closer to trouble and further loss.

"Sure," the nurse said, holding up his hand. "Wait here."

The man disappeared into the room. It seemed to take forever, even though she could hear the murmur of men's voices coming from inside. Finally, the nurse stepped out, Casper in tow.

"Thank you," Casper said to the nurse. He waited

for the man to walk away before he finally turned to her.

"Do you have your phone with you?" she asked, hoping that his lack of the device was why he had hadn't answered.

He patted his chest pockets and then the back pockets of his jeans, finally pulling out his phone and clicking it on. "Yeah." He clicked the buttons. "Sorry, I didn't look at it," he said flatly.

"I'm sorry about the thing I said at the house earlier," she said, trying to right her major wrong.

He looked away from her and toward the door leading to William. "He hasn't regained consciousness. They Narcaned him and got him breathing. They pumped his stomach when he got here, but they aren't sure what he took. There were so many pills in the bathroom and the house that it could have been any combination of things."

She grimaced, wanting to ask if they thought he would make it, but also not wanting to know the answer if it hurt Casper any more than he was already hurting. "Are you going to stay the night with him?"

He looked down at his watch, seeming to realize most of the day had passed in the chaos. "I don't know yet. I'm hoping that he regains consciousness, and I want to be here for him when he does. I need to talk to him."

She remained silent, though she wanted to ask him so many questions.

"The paramedics said they couldn't be certain from the scene whether or not he had intentionally ingested the pills or if he had accidently overdosed. There were no spilled pills or suicide notes. I found him down in the bathroom after his shower. I didn't see any open bottles or anything."

"Then what made them decide it was an overdose instead of another kind of medical emergency?"

"They weren't one-hundred-percent sure until they gave him Narcan. He came around a little bit and his blood pressure started to climb. I thought he was going to come out of it, but he plateaued at one-ten over seventy-two, and his oxygen saturation leveled around ninety-eight percent, and everything has stayed there since he was brought here. They said Narcan only works on opioids, so it's possible that the overdose was on multiple medications."

"How long do they think it will take him to come around completely?"

"If he didn't poison himself, he may come around in a couple days. However, they are probably going to want to get a psych eval. The doc warned me that most people leave AMA, against medical advice, before they can be treated for mental-health problems. And, I fear that if he leaves, he will be arrested as soon as he steps out the doors."

"Wouldn't they have to charge him with something in order to arrest him?"

"His trying to commit suicide is circumstantial. I don't think they have any physical evidence that he actually tried to kill anyone or had any role in Michelle's or Dad's deaths. However, I think his attempt would be enough to book him on suspicion.

It would give them time to dig without fear that he would run or follow through on his suicide attempt."

"If it helps, I talked to one of the officers outside the house. They didn't even know he was in any way involved with Michelle. I don't think he was even on their radar as a suspect."

He tipped his head in acknowledgment, but his face pinched. "He may not have been, but he definitely is now. If I was the detective on this case, I would be on him after this incident."

"I know you said you thought he did have something to do with her death, until you saw his place. Then you did an about-face. What made you change your mind...or did you?"

He leaned his body against the wall and looked down the hallway. The nurses had all retreated to other patients' rooms or the nurses' station, far enough away to be out of earshot. "I can't say he didn't do it with complete certainty, but I can say that I've never seen him so screwed up. I've lived with him off and on throughout the years—college, breakups and our mother's death—and he's never just *given up*."

"Do you think that this odd behavior is indicative of wrongdoing?"

"If you mean that he murdered someone, I don't think so. She had served him with divorce papers around the time our father died. I think it was the combination of factors that did him in."

She sucked in a breath. "She did *what*?"

"Oh, yeah, she served him with papers the day she went missing."

She couldn't take the way his face fell as he spoke. "Casper, I'm so sorry," she said, moving closer, silently begging for his reassuring touch.

He took the little step toward her. "I'm just glad you're here," he said, pulling her into his arms and against him until she could feel him breathe into her hair. "I'm surprised they let you in."

There was just something about that action that she loved. It was like he was breathing her in and she was a part of him, and in that moment, even though it wasn't the physical entwining of bodies, they were still one—two halves of a greater whole. "I may have fibbed a little and said you and I were married." She looked up at him and smiled.

"Oh," he said, sounding surprised. There was a pause. "What happened with your board meeting?"

She let him hold her as she stared into his eyes. "We discussed the cut hydraulic lines."

He nodded stoically. "Do they know who was responsible?"

She shook her head, but her thoughts went straight to Greg. "My board is worried that there may be someone targeting your family."

"Anything is possible," Casper said, sounding resigned.

There was a shrill beep from William's hospital room. "Do you think it would be better if I stepped back? You know…so I could keep my drama out of your life? You have enough on your plate without my garbage."

He held her tighter. "I need you. I need your insights. You can do what you want, and you can go if you want, but know that there is no question in my mind about you and how important you are to me. You've been there for me through this, a time when I needed so much support. You're the only person standing strong and staying by my side."

He acted like she really had a choice...but didn't he understand that her heart wouldn't have allowed her to make any other decision? She had been inextricably linked to him since the moment she had first seen him in the hospital. Ever since then, the world and their lives had only strengthened the signs that they were meant to be exactly where they were, exactly right now.

"I need you, too," she said, taking his face in her hands and giving him a kiss.

He kissed her like he was a man starving, searching in a desert of abandonment and pain, and finally finding her and the fullness of her promises.

A nurse walked by and cleared his throat, and she pulled out of Casper's embrace, once again remembering where they were and what was going on around them. Now wasn't the time or the place.

"Casper?" she said, her voice slightly raspy.

"Hmm?" He closed his eyes as he tipped his head back, moving his face so it was out of her view and making her wonder what all he was feeling, yet not wanting to cause him pain by poking at a sensitive spot.

Yet, there was no avoiding certain things. "I think we need to get ahead of the investigation."

"Is this because of the meeting with the board? Did they say something I need to know?"

She let the silence speak for itself.

He dropped his chin and she watched as the storm came back into his eyes. "What is it that you think we should do?"

She shook her head. "I don't really know, but I'm thinking that the best thing we can do is try and find out what happened to Michelle. Depending on how that goes, we can pivot from there. But, if there's any truth to what people are saying, and she was murdered and William is the primary suspect, then we need to either clear his name or clear our own."

He sucked in a long breath, holding it in as he paused to think. "What if we dug into my dad's death?"

"When it comes to his passing, the only person who could really answer any questions…well, he is unconscious." She took his hand.

He nodded, but there was pain on his face like she had lanced him with her words.

"I'm sorry, Casper… I didn't mean to be callous—"

"That's not it. You're right. I know you're right. I just hate it—*all* of it." He gripped her. "I wish you could have met my family a few years ago, before my mother passed and everything went to hell."

"When a family goes through a shake-up, it rocks everyone to their foundation. Everyone has to rebuild, we all hope for something strong and better, but the truth is that many families collapse." She took his other hand and looked him in the eyes. "It is in those moments you have to dig deep. You have to find your own way, and do the best you can for yourself and for those who are still part of your life."

"You...are the one still in my life." He stared into her eyes. "I want to do the best we can, together. We will figure this all out."

She smiled, but her heart was breaking. "First, focus on *you*. You need to come back stronger and better for *you*. Then, we can be the strongest *we* that we can be." Tears started to form in her eyes, but she feared letting them fall in front of him. He needed a place of respite, not a continuing disaster.

Chapter Twenty-Two

Casper wasn't sure how he had found himself standing inside the local sheriff's department. Yet, as they
walked to Detective's Terrell's office, there was no
turning back now. Kristin had wanted this, and he
had to agree that she was being smart—they needed
to get in front of the investigation and keep any fall-
out from coming back on them.

Detective Terrell motioned for them to take a
seat. "So you are Michelle Keller's brother-in-law?
And you, Kristin, had a hand in finding his father
while working with our SAR team?" He looked from
Casper to Kristin.

She nodded.

"Does your team's law-enforcement coordinator
know that you have decided to show up in my office?"
he asked, frowning.

"She's not the person who needs to worry about
being in the wrong here, or at least I'm here to tell
you that she is free of any guilt. I'm here to clear
our names and see if there is anything we can do
to actively help in your investigation of Michelle's

death." He wanted to say "investigation into his father's death" as well, but he needed to know where this man stood before he opened himself up.

"Why do you think you'd need to clear your names?" The detective worked on his computer, probably pulling up the report from Michelle's disappearance.

By now there had to be several reports filed, and maybe they would even have the date and time of the autopsy.

"We—*I*—made a mistake." Casper rubbed the back of his neck.

"Oh?" Detective Terrell looked up at him.

He didn't know how much detail the man needed and he didn't want to throw his brother under the bus if they weren't already looking in his direction. Maybe they had made a huge mistake in coming here.

"What he is trying to say is that he is interested in learning more about the findings as to the cause of Michelle's death. Was it homicide or accidental?" Kristin leaned forward like she was putting her body between Casper and the firing squad.

There were some bullets that she didn't need to take.

"Is there some reason you believe it would have been a suicide?"

Casper looked at the man's badge. "Detective, I know that you are doing your job… I get it. I would, however, appreciate if you would let me know what you have, so I know where to start."

Terrell smiled, the action not threatening but not

entirely friendly. "As I'm sure you know, her death is under active investigation."

"When we found her," Casper began, more anxious now that when they had arrived at the sheriff's office, "she had blood around her mouth. Do you know what caused it?"

"From our initial findings, she had a series of broken ribs. One of which punctured her lung."

"Was that the cause of death?" Kristin asked.

Terrell shrugged. "I can't give you any answers to that right now, until we get through her autopsy."

"Is it scheduled?" Casper asked.

"Tomorrow," Terrell said.

"She smelled of chemicals," Casper added. "Do you know what could have caused it?"

Terrell shook his head. "Again, I won't know until tomorrow, but I included the scent in my report." Terrell's phone pinged and he looked at it and frowned, making Casper wonder if they were keeping him from doing other, more important things.

"We can just get out of your hair," Casper said, moving toward the door of the man's office. The place wasn't very big, and when he turned, the chair behind him slammed against the wall and made the pictures beside the man's desk rattle against the wall.

Terrell stood up and touched his framed picture of George Washington, then straightened it slightly, like it was a part of him that Casper had unwittingly disturbed.

He definitely wasn't ingratiating himself with the guy. "Sorry. I just bumped the—"

Terrell stopped him with a raise of his hand. "No matter. And, no, you don't need to go anywhere, so please sit back down. I'm here to help your sister-in-law by getting answers about her death. If you think you can help me, and bring peace to those who loved her, then I would be glad to hear what you have to say."

Kristin grimaced as Casper folded back down into the hot seat.

"Let me start by saying I think my brother, Michelle's husband, is innocent of any crime. He is in a dark mental place, but I think it is because of her and not because of what happened to her."

"What makes you say that about your brother?" Terrell tented his fingers in front of him on the desk, giving them his full attention.

"I'm not here to get my brother in trouble, but it's important that we be as transparent as possible." As quickly as he could, he explained the divorce papers and how they had cleaned his brother's house.

Terrell sat back slightly, taking in all the information. "Did you see anything while either of you were cleaning up that would lead you to believe that William wished Michelle harm?"

They both shook their heads.

"It was mostly food garbage, but I helped him throw a few loads of laundry into the machine... and some sheets."

Terrell's eyebrows rose, but then his normal, unflappable expression returned. "Did you see anything that looked like blood or any other form of bodily fluids on the sheets or mattress?"

Casper shook his head. "Like I said, I didn't see anything. My brother's place was just a disaster. It looked like he had been living on his own for at least a month."

"Wait—" Terrell turned back to his computer and clicked on a few buttons "—didn't I see somewhere that your father had been staying with your brother and his wife until he slipped from the home? He, your father, died of a heart attack? Yes?"

He wasn't ready to open up a whole can of worms, but there was no going back now. "I hate to say it, but I'm worried that my father may have been out of the house for a longer time than my brother reported. If you look at the report about my father's disappearance and rescue by SAR, he was quite a distance from the home and he was wearing ripped and tattered clothing."

"What is it that you are saying, Mr. Keller?" The man stared at him like he was reading every twitch on his face and trying to see if he was telling the truth or something else.

"I'm saying that my brother was clearly suffering from some mental-health issues. I think that it is very possible that my father walked away from the house. I don't think my brother would intentionally have neglected my father, but it appears that Michelle had left the home some time before my father went missing."

Kristin reached over and put her hand on his back and he leaned into her reassuring touch. It was amazing how a simple touch could calm his nerves.

They were doing the right thing. His brother could get the help he needed and they could all get the answers to hopefully clear his name.

Terrell opened up another file on his computer. "I'm sure I can get in touch with her lawyer and see when she had first started talking to them about filing for divorce. They may not tell us anything, but as this is now a death investigation, they may be willing to help in at least providing us with dates. We can go from there, and get your brother cleared as quickly as possible."

Casper nodded in agreement. "I think that would be great."

Kristin's face tightened, like she wanted to say something, but was holding back.

"What are you thinking, Ms. Loren?" Terrell asked, obviously noticing the same thing Casper did.

She pulled her hands into a tight ball in her lap. "Are there any other leads as to who may have played a role in Michelle's death?"

Terrell shook his head. "Not at this time, but we have been in contact with Michelle's boyfriend."

Casper tried not to give away his shock. *She had a boyfriend?*

That changed a few things.

"What was her boyfriend's name? How long had they been together?" Casper asked, questions flooding through him. "It's important that we know if this guy is behind things… If he is coming after us."

Terrell shook his head. "At this time, I'm not at liberty to share that kind of information."

"So this is becoming a criminal investigation?" she asked.

Terrell set his jaw. "I think it would be best if you guys laid low for a bit, until things calm down. We don't know for sure that these events are related."

"They are." Casper could feel it in his bones. "If you care at all about our safety, you need to bring him in."

Terrell tapped his finger on his desk in annoyance. "Look, I want you both to know that I appreciate you coming forward with all of this information."

"Are we allowed to go back into my brother's house?" Casper countered.

"I recommend you don't do anything rash, but yes. As of right now, until we get the autopsy reports and do some legwork, we aren't pursuing any criminal charges. You are free to do as you please, as it isn't officially a crime scene."

Chapter Twenty-Three

Kristin couldn't believe how much better she felt after having left the detective's office, but she wasn't sure she could say the same of Casper. He had a torn expression, one that hadn't changed since they'd left over an hour ago. She had asked him several times if he wanted to talk, but he'd simply shook his head. At dinner, she was hoping he'd open up a bit more, but he'd still refused to talk about things with his brother.

After quickly stopping by his house to let Grover out and checking on his brother, who was still unconscious, he finally spoke up. "Would you mind dropping me off at my brother's place?"

She hit the brakes instinctively. "Are you kidding me?"

He looked at her. "I need to make sure everything is taken care of there. Now that we know we aren't under investigation, I don't see the harm."

"You don't see the harm?" she repeated disbelievingly. The relief she had been experiencing evaporated. "Just because we aren't under investigation *yet* doesn't mean that we won't be. Do I need to remind you that we were only ever planning to get out in front of the thing in hopes to remediate any future issues?"

"I agree, but since we left I've been thinking about our helo. *If* it's related to all of these things that are happening—which, truthfully, I don't know—if it *is*, William wouldn't and couldn't have cut those lines. He doesn't have the knowledge or a reason to want to kill us. He doesn't know you or Greg, and I don't get the impression that he would want me dead."

"Who, other than you, would have the knowledge to down our helo?" As soon as she asked the question, she already knew the answer. "Greg wouldn't want me dead, either," she answered, before he even had time to ask the question she could feel coming.

"Are you sure?" He eyed her.

She didn't want to defend Greg, and she didn't think he was a great man, but the thought of him trying to kill her seemed completely crazy. "Just because two people had a relationship and it ended, it doesn't mean that they hate each other or wish each other harm."

"He was angry, though. You can't deny it."

She thought about bringing up the fact that his brother had a better motive for wanting everyone around him dead—if he was the only person left standing in the family, any and all of their father's death benefits or other inheritance would likely automatically revert to him. If he knew Casper was on the helo, or going to be on a helo, it was easy enough—with a little bit of internet searching—to figure out exactly how to go about sabotaging them. Yet, bringing up his brother right now didn't seem like the right move—not only was it juvenile, but it would also only push them apart.

"I won't deny that there is animosity between us," she admitted. "However, before we start trying to fill in the blanks on what has happened over the last few weeks, let's get solid evidence to support any assumptions."

"Now you understand another reason why I want to go to my brother's house," he said, smiling roguishly. "Last time, I just wanted to help him, but now I want to help all of us. Maybe I can find something he or Michelle left behind…or something that will point us and law enforcement in the right direction."

She didn't have any other ideas, at least any that wouldn't require a search warrant, so she nodded. "If I go along with this, we don't move or change anything. In fact, we should take pictures when we go into the house in case things go sideways."

"Fair," he countered. "I was actually thinking the same thing. I agree that I don't want to make things worse for us. Which brings me to my next point…"

She glanced over at him as she started to drive toward his brother's house. "Which is?"

"In order to protect you from falling under any further scrutiny, especially when it comes to things with Roger and your law enforcement coordinators, maybe it would be best if you didn't go in with me."

She shook her head vehemently. "No."

He paused, waiting for her to elaborate, but she didn't feel like it was necessary to validate her refusal.

"That's it?"

"Yep. You're not going in alone." She shrugged. "If you do that, it's very possible that you could get accused of tampering with evidence in the event we do find something. At least if I'm there, you have some kind of witness."

He sighed, probably because he knew she was right.

The door was unlocked when they got back to William's place. Even if for nothing else, she was glad they could lock things up for him.

It felt strange going in the empty, deathly quiet house. Even though it was cleaned up, it still had an air of unwelcomeness.

"Where should we start?" she asked, hoping they would sift through for clues as quickly as possible.

"I'm thinking I'll go into his bedroom and poke around in his closet to see if he has a lockbox or anything. Why don't you start in his office? I'll meet you in there," he said, pointing down the first-floor hall to where a spare bedroom and the office sat.

"On it." She started to walk away, but he stopped her, spun her around and planted a kiss on her lips.

"Thank you," he said, a softness in his eyes that she had only seen once before—when they were making love.

"You're welcome." There wasn't anything she could think of that she wouldn't do for him. She hated to name what emotion was the motive for her feeling this way.

He let her go, but gave her one more peck as she turned. With that simple action, she felt lighter and less torn about what they were doing. Casper was right—they needed to find the answers.

She hadn't been in the office when they'd been here before and she opened the door to an aroma of rancid food. Holding her breath, she walked to the window and opened it, then did the same in the spare bedroom to help create a cross draft. Making her way back, she started by looking on the chair by his desk. It had a stack of unopened mail, including magazines, bills and political ads. She fanned through the mail, but nothing jumped out at her as important other than the fact that he was probably behind on his mortgage.

Moving to his desk, there was a medley of Chinese food containers and discarded sushi trays. She picked up the trash can and moved to start cleaning up, but as she picked up the first container, she looked in the bin. Inside, on top of used tissues and covered in what looked like coffee grinds, she could make out the top of legal paperwork.

Fishing it out and wiping away some of the coffee grounds that were stuck to the paper, she found that it was a certified copy of Michelle's petition for divorce. Montana was a no-fault state, but it still cited irreconcilable differences.

She flipped through it. There was a list of assets, and as she started to scan it, she immediately started to notice a trend. Before continuing, she put down the bin and made her way out of the office. "Casper!"

She heard the sound of footsteps as he moved overhead in the main bedroom. "Yeah?" he responded, his sound muffled.

She made her way to the living room so he could hear her better. "I found the divorce filings."

His footsteps sounded loudly as he left the bedroom and made his way down the stairs. "Nice find," he said, making his way to her in the living room.

She handed it over to him, pointing at the assets, where it showed a combined debt of nearly five hundred thousand dollars. "It looks like your brother and his wife were in severe financial distress."

"And right there, we have a motive for my father's murder."

"What? How is that?"

He sighed. "My father had a trust. He had set aside a great deal of cash while he'd been alive and invested it wisely. My brother was the administrator on the trust."

"Is that why he chose to keep your father in his home and under his care…so they didn't have to spend your father's assets on a care facility?"

"Trusts keep a family from losing a loved one's assets or home because of long-term care, but only after five years. It had only been three years since my father had begun the trust. As such, his home and his investments would have had to have been used for nursing care, or they would have been beholden to the government for the cost of his nursing."

"So, yes?"

"Exactly. I told my brother it was better to have my father in a trusted and well-rated care facility, where he could get everything he needed. Sure, he hadn't wanted the money to go to his care and had wished for it to go to those listed in his will and trust, but I didn't want my father to get put in a place where he would be forgotten."

Kristin's chest tightened. "And I'm sure you trusted your brother and his wife to treat your father with the love and care he deserved."

"You know I did," he said, his voice heavy with emotion. "I checked on them all at Thanksgiving and everything was looking good. My father had lost weight and was declining cognitively, but I thought that all had to do with his aging process."

Kristin noticed that the divorce paperwork was shaking in his hands. "It may have been. You don't know. Again, we have to prove anything we are thinking before we erroneously make conclusions."

He gripped the paperwork tightly and slapped it down on the living room table.

"We need to find your father's financials—the ones your brother controlled. If he was spending anything he shouldn't have been spending...then perhaps you are right. We'd still need more proof that he was mistreating your dad or being negligent in his care."

"It may have nothing to do with that, too. We just need to keep digging." Casper stuffed the divorce filing into his back pocket.

"Did you find a safe or anything upstairs?"

He shook his head. "I'm thinking that whatever paperwork my brother has about my father or anything else has to be in his office." He pointed down the hallway.

She made her way back to the office. If nothing else, they were on the right track. Casper followed her inside and started on the bottom left drawer of the desk. The thing was stuffed with files and he started by pulling out the first and sifting through before moving to the next. Going over the stacks of papers on the desk, she set aside anything that could be potentially interesting on further inspection and anything inconsequential on the chair.

When the stack on the chair started to shift and she feared it tipping, she lifted the pile and dropped it to the floor. It wasn't her intention to disrupt William's life any more than it already was, but there was really no system to his paperwork that she could discern—at least not in the last six months.

She glanced over at Casper, who was about halfway through the drawer. He looked so incredibly focused and drool-worthy. She really was an incredibly lucky woman to have found him.

As he moved, she wanted to take him in her arms, kiss him and tell him they would come through this, and that his brother wasn't the monster that all the signs seemed to be making him out to be.

"Did William ever say anything about his and Michelle's relationship to you?"

"He told me he was in love." Casper set down the

file in his hand and moved to the next. "Legitimately, he seemed happy."

"What about Michelle?"

He furrowed his brow as if he was struggling to remember. "She was…not super talkative with me. She was working a lot and not around."

"What did you say she did for work?"

He sat down on the floor as he sifted through another stack of papers. "She was an insurance salesperson."

"Okay…" She tried to pull her thoughts together. "Would an insurance person be working on a holiday?"

He shrugged, not seeming to give it a great deal of thought. "William said she had a party to go to. You know…normal stuff."

"But he didn't go with her?"

"No. I was staying here. He said he wanted to hang out with Dad and me."

She leaned against the desk. "Michelle didn't tell him to go with her since you were here to care for your father? Doesn't that strike you as odd?"

He stopped what he was doing. "I see where you are going with this. It is possible that she was already dating this other dude, her current—or the guy who *was* her current—boyfriend. Maybe that is why she didn't care about William going."

She nodded. "That's kind of what I'm leaning toward. I have to tell you, when my mom and dad had anyone else to watch me—especially when there was a holiday party involved—they took the opportunity."

"At the time, though, I thought William wanted to hang out with his younger brother. I don't spend a lot of time with them. You know?"

She gave a stiff nod. "You guys definitely have a complicated relationship."

"It has been, but when push comes to shove, we've always been there for one another."

"Is that why you changed your opinion of him when we got here?"

He nodded. "That's a huge part of it. Like I said, what you saw isn't the man I know." He sighed. "And I'd still like to think that my brother isn't the kind of guy who would hurt his wife. I know this is terrible, but I'm hoping that she fell and her death was just an unfortunate accident at a crappy time."

"I've heard of stranger things happening," she said, trying to give his hopes a boost.

He pulled out the entire desk drawer and put it on the floor between his legs. As he moved, something beige caught her eye. It looked like a large envelope and she leaned down to get a better look. "Casper," she said, pointing. "What's that?"

Looking up, he spotted the envelope. Its edges were taped to the wooden paneling under the desk and, unless someone had done exactly what Casper had, it would have gone completely unnoticed and undetected.

He pulled it out and ripped off the tape. After unfolding the clasp on the manila envelope, he opened it and pulled out a stack of paperwork. "Oh, holy… crap." He looked up at her with wide eyes. "You need to call Detective Terrell—he needs to know my brother isn't our killer."

Chapter Twenty-Four

The two younger deputies had arrived first and Kristin had led them inside and into the office where they had found the paperwork. They had taken a series of pictures and had left them to do their work, and were now on the front porch, waiting. Detective Terrell had been running a few minutes late, but had been beyond grateful when they had reached out. As they stood to wait for him, Casper couldn't help the nerves that were rising within him.

He needed to make sure that William's name was cleared. Better, before he was even awake. It would be one hell of a gift if they could go to him, before he was transferred to the mental health unit, and tell him that he was cleared of any wrongdoing. Maybe it would help with his recovery.

A part of Casper wondered if that would actually be true. No matter what had happened to Michelle, William would undoubtedly feel as though he played a role.

Perhaps his proving that William wasn't behind her death was more for himself than his brother.

Casper needed to know his brother was innocent and still the person whom he had played baseball with in the backyard, the kid whose laugh would wake Mom and Dad in the middle of the night when they were supposed to be sleeping and were instead up playing video games. He couldn't be the man who could willfully end a life.

Detective Terrell pulled up in his black pickup and turned off the engine. After what seemed like an eternity, he stepped out and walked to them on the front step. "Hey, guys, thanks for calling. I'm sorry about my late arrival. I had to take report and it took a little longer than expected."

Casper shrugged off the apology. "No matter. We are just glad you are here now." He reached into his back pocket and pulled out the folded and dirty divorce paperwork, and Kristin handed him the envelope she was holding against her chest.

The detective took the paperwork and flipped through the divorce order first. "That seems pretty normal."

"Yeah," Casper said, "except the part about the debt. My brother was frugal. I have a hard time imagining how they were that far in credit-card and loan debt. I mean, look…" He pointed at the page where the debts were listed. "The amount owed on the house was only a hundred and four thousand. Everything else is credit cards and personal loans."

"Many people are in debt in this day and age," the detective said. "Don't get me wrong, that is hefty debt, but that doesn't indicate any sort of wrongdoing or illegal activity."

"No," Kristin said, "but it would give someone motive to kill. At least for the right amount of money..." She pointed at the envelope beneath the divorce paperwork.

The detective looked around and pointed inside. "Why don't we make our way into the house. It looks like we are starting to draw a little extra notice." He motioned in the direction of a man and woman across the street who were peering out their window.

Casper followed behind Kristin and the detective. "I'm not sure if it's enough to arrest anyone, but... it's a place to start your investigation."

The detective closed the front door behind them. They heard the sound of the two other officers coming from the office. "Like I said, we haven't made this a criminal investigation until we get the official results back from the medical examiner. I am going to need to step in on the autopsy in another hour."

"You have to have some kind of idea as to what happened to Michelle." Kristin sounded annoyed, but he could tell it was just that she was concerned.

The detective stared at her for a long moment. "Why did you guys come back to the house?"

"You said we were good." Casper rubbed the back of his neck nervously. "Plus, we wanted to make sure the place was locked up. As I'm sure you know, there is more robbery in this area than anyone wants to admit. If people saw William being wheeled out, they would know the place was empty."

"You made it clear that we weren't under investigation. As such, we wanted to help his brother," Kristin argued.

Casper reached over and put his hand on her arm, trying to help keep her calm. "We aren't trying to make waves, Detective. We saw an opportunity not only to help my brother, but your team as well. As it turned out, it was a positive." He motioned toward the envelope. "Take a look."

The detective opened the envelope and pulled out the insurance policy. He scanned it, flipping through the pages.

"If you look, there are three separate policies there," Casper said, waiting for the detective to read.

"Hmm," the detective began, "it states here that there is one for Hugh Keller, Casper Keller and William Keller. That isn't odd."

"No, it's not." Casper sighed. "However, I didn't even know there was a life-insurance policy out in my name, except that which I pay for through the military."

"Again, and I mean this as nicely as possible, there is nothing illegal here." The detective sent him a pitying look.

"Look at who the beneficiary is on the policies," Kristin said, shifting her weight in anticipation.

The detective flipped farther into the first policy. "Michelle Keller." He read the name like it was nothing. "Again, no evidence of a crime. You guys told me that you found something I had to see. This is it?" He lifted the papers accusatorially.

"Did you see the second beneficiary?" Kristin reached up like she wanted to take the papers from the detective's hand, but she stopped herself and let her arm fall back to her side.

The detective went back to the paper. "Greg Holmes."

Kristin made a slight choking sound as the man spoke her ex's name. "That's the pilot of the helo… our helo that went down in Big Sky. A helo that had the hydraulic lines scored so they would break…"

"Oh," the detective said, sucking in a breath. "Are you aware—" he looked up at them "—that this is Michelle's boyfriend?"

Casper couldn't help the smile that broke out on his face. "I wasn't, but when I saw his name…we had a feeling."

"Explain," the detective said, looking back down at the papers. "Why would you have a feeling?"

"Well, respectfully, I'm no detective here," Casper began, "but it finally all clicked into place. All the crap we have been dealing with, all the things that have been happening to my family. At least now, I think I know why."

The detective peered up at him. "Which is?"

Casper tried to control the flux of emotions that had been roiling within him ever since they had found the paperwork. "This is just a guess, but I bet that Greg and Michelle had been seeing each other for at least the last few months. During this time, they accrued a great deal of debt." He motioned toward the divorce paperwork.

"We haven't found anything in this house that

would point toward the debt, or what they spent the money on, but we did find William's personal credit-card statements. He hadn't spent any more than he could pay off with his salary each month," Kristin added.

The detective started to nod. "Okay, I'm tracking what you guys are surmising, but... If Michelle was the primary beneficiary on the life insurance policies..."

"I can't prove it, but I think Greg was going for the money the entire time," Kristin said.

"And you dated this man?" the detective countered.

"It wasn't a great relationship."

"When did you break up?"

She shrugged. "About three months ago. It really wasn't a breakup, though, it was more of going our separate ways. We just kind of stopped talking about anything that wasn't focused on work."

"Did he ever give you any indication he wanted you dead, or do you think he was just gunning for Casper?"

Kristin shrugged, but there were tears forming in her eyes. "I wasn't a great girlfriend... I mean it was just a relationship of convenience. There were no hurt feelings, but—"

"He was verbally abusive toward her," Casper said, interjecting. "I don't mean to talk over you, but he treated you like garbage back there at the camp." He looked at the detective. "He isn't a good man. I'm telling you, everything in my entire being is telling me he is the one behind all these deaths."

"Even your father's?"

"I think that my brother has been in such a low place that he may not have noticed if Michelle came and took my father from the home…or if anyone else did. I know he, my father, was supposed to have a nurse who came and went from my brother's. From the way we found the place, they weren't helping with any sort of upkeep."

The detective tapped the paperwork on his fingers. "So you saying you think Greg came in and took your father out of the home?"

Casper shrugged. "I have no idea how my father got to the area in which he was found. I don't. I also can't believe that he got there himself. Even lost, due to his Alzheimer's…"

"Stop," the detective ordered, putting his hand up. "Your brother was the one to report your father missing…according to the 911 dispatcher."

Casper's stomach sank. Maybe their ideas were wrong. If they were, Greg would get the money from the life insurance policies and there was nothing he could do to stop him from benefiting from his father's death.

"Can we listen to the call?" Kristin asked.

"That's always my first action item," Detective Terrell said, pulling out his phone. "I didn't pull anything outside of what we already knew from the call, but maybe you can hear something I missed."

She shrugged. "It's worth a shot."

The detective clicked on his screen and an audio

recording started to play. He skipped past the dispatcher and went straight to the man speaking.

"My father, Hugh Keller, escaped from my home this morning," a man said.

"Escaped?" the dispatcher countered.

"He has dementia and somehow made it outside. I tried to look for him, but haven't found him. I'm worried for his safety."

"Dude," Casper said, sucking in a breath.

"What?" the detective asked, stopping the recording.

"That's not my brother's voice." Casper pointed at the phone like it was some kind of fake.

"No, it's not." The color had drained from Kristin's face. "It's not William's... That voice—that's Greg."

The detective opened his mouth and closed it as the news sank in. "Are you one-hundred-percent sure that is Greg Holmes?"

"He sounds like he was just waking up, but yes," Kristin said, rubbing the front of her throat. "That was him."

The detective slipped the phone back into his pocket. "You guys...you need to get somewhere this man wouldn't know about—get a hotel room. In the meantime, I'm going to run down this lead." He began to walk away, but turned back. "If you need anything, call me directly. Until I see you again, stay safe."

Chapter Twenty-Five

Kristin stared out of the hotel's window and into the distance, where the rimrocks stood like dark reminders that they were hiding out. Grover was sleeping on the room's couch, his snores filling the air. Her entire body hurt, but she wasn't sure why, entirely. It could have been because of the crash, but it struck her as odd that it was just now noticeable. It also could have been from the hike, but they hadn't covered that many miles while looking for Michelle's body.

Michelle's body… Greg's message… She felt as though she was living someone else's life—this couldn't have possibly been her own. Everything had been so normal, even her relationship with Greg— as short-lived and apparently nonmonogamous as it had been.

Based on the way he had treated her, she should have known that she had not been the only woman in his life. He had never spoken to her about the future. He hadn't even wanted to define their relationship or make definite plans. Everything had always been tentative…and now, it all made sense. She had been nothing but a booty call.

It shouldn't have hurt her; a part of her had known from the very beginning with Greg that they weren't anything but bedroom buddies. Yet, he could have just been honest.

She chuffed. He'd also gone on to possibly kill people for money, so maybe the fact he had just used her was better than the alternative.

"Are you okay?" Casper, who was lying on the bed, asked as he looked up from his phone.

She nodded, but the anger and hate roiled within her. "I—I just feel like an idiot."

"Welcome to the club," Casper said, patting the bed next to him. "I had been working under the falsehood that everything was under control in this city. Little did I know how out of control things had become. If I had just been more involved…"

"And if I had just been more observant…" She walked over to the bed and sat down on the edge, touching his stomach over the soft cotton of his shirt. "I owe you an apology—if I had just been more…" She struggled to find the right word. There were a thousand things she should have been better at in the past, but she had never thought that one of them would have been her poor ability to identify a potential killer.

"You are not to blame. From day one, this has been my circus. Your clown and my clown just decided to join forces."

She giggled, the sound unchecked. "He was definitely a clown. Rather, he *is*." She looked over at Casper and some of the pain she had been feeling dissipated. "Have your people said they have seen him?"

"I have been talking with Cindy." He lifted his phone for her to see. "She said that they tried to take him into custody, but by the time they arrived at the camp, he must have caught wind that they were on their way and disappeared."

She dropped her head into her hands. "You have to be kidding me. How would he know that they were coming for him?"

He shrugged. "It's not that big of a camp, privacy is lacking—need I cite your conversation with Greg? All it takes is one person running their mouth and he could have heard everything. Or maybe he had a feeling. Who knows?"

She lied down on the bed and moved into his nook, putting her head on his chest and looping her arm over him. "You don't really think he would be coming for you, do you?"

"I don't think he would be coming for either of us. At this point, if it is proven he had anything to do with Michelle's death or my father's, he won't be getting any of the insurance money."

"When were the policies purchased?" she asked, stroking the smooth cotton that was stretched tight over the muscles of his chest.

"They were all less than a month old. It looks like Greg had purchased them from Michelle's company—they must have had this all planned out well in advance. From everything I've managed to pull together, they had to have been having an affair for at least the last year. Really, it was pretty clever, but I'm sure he didn't think Michelle would hide those policies in her house."

Casper's phone buzzed and she moved aside so he could sit up and answer the call. "Hello?"

There was the sound of a woman's voice coming from the other end of the line and Kristin could make out about every other word, enough to piece together that William had awakened.

"Is he up to seeing a visitor?"

There was more talking, but Casper smiled excitedly. Not waiting, Kristin moved to the side of the bed, then put on her shoes.

Casper hung up, jumped out of the bed and threw on his shoes. "You ready?"

She was glad he was finally starting to smile again. She couldn't handle any more hurting. They needed things to start going right—especially now that they had the answers they needed.

As they walked out the door, he slapped her playfully on the butt. "You do know that I'm going to need to see you naked again…as soon as possible?" he said, half whispering.

"Oh, do you think that I should let you?" She giggled.

He smirked and the simple action made her knees threaten to give way.

"If it wasn't for my brother, you know we wouldn't be leaving this hotel room right now." He reached forward and gave her ass a squeeze as they made their way down the hall.

"If you're lucky, maybe later I'll let you show me what you are thinking about doing to me. You better be on your best behavior—until then, I'm watching," she teased, swaying her hips as they made their way out to her car.

She loved the way he was looking at her, like she was something he wanted to lick off his lips. Though she didn't know what the future would bring for them, at least she had the guarantee that there would be more.

WHEN THEY ARRIVED at the hospital, they had to park in the underground garage. The lot was about half-full, and there was a couple making their way into the elevator bay. Stepping out of the Durango, her footfalls echoed on the concrete. Though she couldn't quite put her finger on the cause, a sense of dread filled her.

She'd never loved going into hospitals as a guest, but there was something more in the air beyond her normal apprehension. Maybe it was that Greg was somewhere out there, unchecked and dangerous.

As she reached for Casper's hand, there was a strange but unmistakable sound of a gun's slide as someone racked a round into the chamber. The world around her slowed down.

She had to be wrong.

That couldn't have been a gun.

The garage was empty as the elevator closed ahead

of them and the couple disappeared. Maybe it had simply been the slide of the metal doors shutting.

Then the heat hit, and the boom. That bang echoed against the concrete until it was a deafening maw of inescapable terror.

Casper pushed her down to the ground and dropped beside her. She belly-crawled behind the nearest car until she was behind a tire. Casper moved beside her, by the opposite tire.

"Are you okay?" he asked, fear in his voice.

She nodded, putting her hands to her belly. Her shirt was hot and *sticky*.

Lifting her hand, she stared at the dark red blood on her fingers.

I've. Been. Hit.

Her hands started to shake as the pain cascaded through her. Someone had shot her, but why? She hadn't done anything wrong. She didn't even have a gun on her.

She had to fight back.

"I'm fine," she whispered to Casper, lying, as she put her hands down so he couldn't see the blood. As she spoke, a fresh wave of pain coursed through her. He couldn't know she was hurt—it would only make her a burden.

"Do you have a gun on you?" she asked, hoping he was carrying.

He shook his head.

It was too late now, but in the future she would never be without a gun again. Why hadn't she thought to bring one with her, knowing Greg was out there?

She closed her eyes, wishing she could go back and do so many things over again. The pain pulled her down into the darkness of her mind.

Though she had thought about how she would die, bleeding out in a concrete garage beneath a hospital had never hit the list of imagined possibilities.

"If you come out, Casper. I will let her live," a man yelled, his voice echoing like the shot, and though it wasn't as loud, it was almost as terrifying.

Casper moved like he was going to step out into the open.

"No!" she ordered. "You're going to be a target for this guy to kill you. I won't allow that." She scanned the ground around them, looking for anything that could be used as a weapon. Her cell phone and her keys were still in her hand. "Here—" she slid her phone on the ground to Casper "—call 911."

He grabbed the phone and dialed the number and hit send before dropping the phone on the ground. The dispatcher's voice filled the air and she found a tiny amount of comfort in the knowledge the police would be on their way.

"Casper is down!" she yelled into the garage, hoping the man would believe her.

There was the sound of laughter. "You know, your taste in men is ridiculous. First, you banged me... Which let's both just say was *subpar*," Greg said, mirth in his chortle. "Then you decide to screw this piece of garbage."

Casper leaned over toward her. "We need to move.

He is using our sound to track us. If he finds us, we are dead. I'll take point, and you follow me."

She nodded, ignoring the fire radiating from the round in her abdomen. Trying to hide her wound from Casper, she gingerly stood up. On the concrete pillar next to her was a large, red fire extinguisher. She pried it loose, the metal making a clinking sound, and she ducked down.

Casper rushed behind the car next to them, a red sedan, and disappeared. She moved through the pain as she tried to follow him. Two vehicles over, she still hadn't caught up with Casper, but she could see him through the window of the truck that was between them. Glancing in the truck's window, she spotted an aluminum baseball bat in the back seat.

"Casper," she whispered, trying to be just loud enough that only he could hear.

He turned and she pointed at the bat. A smile erupted on his face. On his side, the window was cracked just enough, and he slipped his arm inside and pulled the weapon out. She lifted the canister in her hands. Pain shot through her again, but as he nodded, his smile widened and it helped to control the ache in her side. All she had to do was concentrate on how to make it out of here and then she could think about the pain.

"Greg!" she yelled, pulling the pin from the fire extinguisher. "The only piece of garbage I ever allowed in my life was you."

Greg's evil laughter rang out through the garage—he sounded as though he was moving closer.

"I'm glad you didn't try to argue your skills in the bedroom. I've had socks that were more adventurous than you."

Under normal circumstances, what the man was saying might have bothered her, but a condemnation coming from a mad man didn't really have the same amount of sting as if it had come from someone she actually cared about.

Casper twisted the bat in his hand, wringing it like he was envisioning it as Greg's neck.

Here, boy... she thought, wishing she could lure Greg closer like the dog he was. Though, a dog would have probably been more loyal. To call him one was a disservice to animals.

"If I was so bad in bed, why did you keep coming back for more?" She tried to laugh, but the sound was strained, and all she could really think about was her shaking hands. Hopefully, she could do what needed to be done.

"I'm not going to turn down free and easy."

She hated him. If she got the chance, killing him would be something she wouldn't regret. Casper moved toward the front of the truck, readying himself to pounce. It would be a race to see who could get to the jerk first.

"Is that what you told Michelle about me? Or did you even admit you were cheating on her, too?"

"She didn't need to know about you." Greg was so close now that she could make out the sounds of his footfalls.

Just a few more feet.

Her hands were violently shaking.

"Had the stupid woman just not lost her nerve... That family can all go to hell." He was so close she could hear his labored breathing. There was the grinding of dirt under his shoes as he moved next to the car beside her.

She couldn't wait—any closer and he would have a shot at her.

He couldn't get a chance to raise his weapon.

After lifting the black hose over the top of the car, she hit the release and opened up the fire extinguisher. The white foam flew out in the direction of her attacker.

The diversion worked and she stood up and rushed toward the man, but Casper was already ahead of her. Watching in relief and shock, Casper drew back the baseball bat and swung with all of his power, striking Greg square in the side. Greg started to lift his arm and Casper struck him again, in the arm. Greg released the gun in his hand and it fell to the concrete floor.

Still pressing the trigger, she rushed toward the weapon, kicking it out and sending it skittering and under a car.

Greg fell to his knees, holding his arm and side. He was wailing in pain and anger, a string of expletives pouring from his mouth—none more colorful than what he was saying about her.

Casper moved to swing again, but she put up her hand, stopping him. "No more. The police can deal with him. They are on their way. He will be arrested."

"Don't you hear him? What he's saying about you?" Casper pointed at him, angry and full of rage.

"Yes, but you are better than he can ever hope to be. You are my future. He is my past. If you beat him to death, then we will have become the monsters."

Chapter Twenty-Six

She had known her future was bright, but Kristin had never expected to be flying the brand-new Madison County SAR, FLIR-equipped helo with Casper at her side. After months of waiting for the trial and sitting on the witness stand, Greg had been found guilty of murder in the first degree in the case of both Michelle and Hugh. He was still awaiting sentencing, but from what the prosecutor said, he would likely get life without the chance of parole.

Casper was on the phone with William, who had fully recovered and was spending some time in Maui in an effort to help him to move forward. He'd found a new girlfriend who'd agreed to go with him, and things seemed to be going well for him after his suicide attempt.

She smiled over at Casper and he made a silly, tongue-out face and she giggled. The action pulled at her scar from her bullet wound. It had taken longer than she would have liked to recover from being shot, but she had made use of every moment of downtime from work over the last eight months and had finally gotten her pilot's license. Really, it had all been thanks to Casper. Last month, she'd even transferred to his SAR team as a FLIR tech for their new bird—her bosses had been great in allowing her to work from home.

Everything was finally on the upswing and even things between her and Casper had been better than ever.

"You're doing great, babe," he said, hanging up the phone. He pointed toward a flat spot in a mountain meadow. "Why don't you put her down right there? I'm ready for lunch."

She dropped the bird, landing gently before powering down. "I can't believe you never told me how fun this was before."

"It is so freeing, flying," he said, smiling as he unclipped his belt and stepped down from the bird after the blades stopped spinning. "After everything we've been through, I'm proud of you." He grabbed his backpack.

She truly, deeply loved this man. Seeing him looking at her the way he was, with admiration, pride and familiarity, she found that the true freedom came with having him at her side.

Getting out, she followed Grover and him to the heart of the clearing and helped Casper spread out the blanket they had brought for their mountain picnic. Grover charged off into the distance, staying close enough to be seen, but far enough to sniff away.

In all of her dreams of the future, she had never imagined herself being a pilot, but after Greg's attack…she needed to become someone new, someone Greg hadn't known or damaged.

In spite of Greg and with the help of Casper, she had become even more independent and stronger than before.

Casper set out the food—a tray of meats, fruit and cheese and a bottle of red wine. In the middle of the tray was a little black box. Her heart moved into her throat. That box… It couldn't have been what she thought—or, rather *hoped*—it was.

"Casper?" She said his name like it was a question.

"Yes?" He sent her the knowing grin that she had come to love so much over the last few months.

"What is that? Some sort of dip?" she teased, pointing at the ring box.

"Oh, if you want it to be, but it was slightly more expensive than your traditional mustard." He dropped to one knee and picked up the box, then opened it.

Inside, tucked into the folds of velvet, was a simple gold band with inset channel diamonds.

She sucked in her breath, realizing how silly she must have sounded in teasing him, but realizing that this simple exchange, this *authenticity*, was who they were as a couple. They would never be perfect, they would say and do dumb things, but when it came down to what was important—each other—they would never give up.

"Kristin, I have loved you since the first moment I met you… In a moment of pain and sorrow, you lifted my grief and carried it until I could heal. Then I helped you in your time of healing. Together, we have been through so much, and as hard as it has been, and though we have already suffered, I wouldn't wish for anything but to spend my life with you."

She smiled widely, tears filling her eyes.

"Would you do me the honor of becoming my wife?"

Looking into his eyes, she saw only one thing—their future. It was incredibly bright.

"I know it's not mustard, but…" He paused, a faint blush rising in his cheeks that made her realize that he must have been thinking she was about to refuse.

"Oh, no."

"No?" he choked, sounding crestfallen.

"No, I mean *yes*. I will marry you." She put her hands over her mouth as she skipped from one foot to the other in excitement. "I love you, Casper Keller. I want to be your Mrs. Keller, from this day and to the rest of time—with or without mustard."

He laughed and there was a look of relief on his face as he reached into the box and took out the ring. Gently, he slipped it onto her finger. "I love you, too, Mrs. Keller. You are my queen."

She leaned down and put her forehead to his, pulling his scent deeply into her lungs. "And you—you are my king."

"We will be side by side forever," he said, taking her hands in his.

She moved to kiss him. "Yes, my love, *forever*."

* * * * *

Don't miss the stories in this mini series!

BIG SKY
SEARCH AND RESCUE

Helicopter Rescue
DANICA WINTERS
January 2023

Swiftwater Enemies
DANICA WINTERS
February 2023

MILLS & BOON

INTRIGUE

Seek thrills. Solve crimes. Justice served.

Available Next Month

A Place To Hide Debra Webb
Swiftwater Enemies Danica Winters

....

K-9 Detection Nichole Severn
The Perfect Witness Katie Mettner

....

Wetlands Investigation Carla Cassidy
Murder In The Blue Ridge Mountains R. Barri Flowers

Larger Print

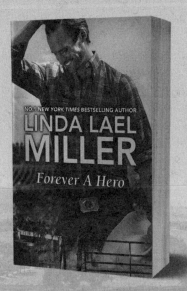

MILLS & BOON

Want to know more about your favourite series or discover a new one?

Experience the variety of romance that Mills & Boon has to offer at our website:

millsandboon.com.au

Shop all of our categories and discover the one that's right for you.

MODERN

DESIRE

MEDICAL

INTRIGUE

ROMANTIC SUSPENSE

WESTERN

HISTORICAL

FOREVER
EBOOK ONLY

HEART
EBOOK ONLY

Subscribe and fall in love with a Mills & Boon series today!

You'll be among the first to read stories delivered to your door monthly and enjoy great savings.

WE SIMPLY LOVE ROMANCE